100
YEARS
SIMON &
SCHUSTER

JADED

ELA LEE

Simon & Schuster
NEW YORK LONDON TORONTO
SYDNEY NEW DELHI

1230 Avenue of the Americas
New York, NY 10020

This book is a work of fiction. Any references to historical events, real people, or real places are used fictitiously. Other names, characters, places, and events are products of the author's imagination, and any resemblance to actual events or places or persons, living or dead, is entirely coincidental.

First Simon & Schuster hardcover edition March 2024

Simon & Schuster: Celebrating 100 Years of Publishing in 2024

For information about special discounts for bulk purchases, please contact Simon & Schuster Special Sales at 1-866-506-1949 or business@simonandschuster.com.

The Simon & Schuster Speakers Bureau can bring authors to your live event. For more information or to book an event, contact the Simon & Schuster Speakers Bureau at 1-866-248-3049 or visit our website at www.simonspeakers.com.

Manufactured in the United States of America

1 3 5 7 9 10 8 6 4 2

Library of Congress Cataloging-in-Publication Data is available.

ISBN 978-1-6680-1099-0
ISBN 978-1-6680-1101-0 (ebook)

A truth was being revealed to me: that I had always tried to attach myself to the light of other people, that I had never had any light of my own. I experienced myself as a kind of shadow.

—Zadie Smith, *Swing Time*

Prologue

I considered myself an honest person. At the job interview, he asked *what three words would your friends use to describe you?* I paused, then replied *they'd say I'm honest, hardworking, and loyal.* I said it with a curt nod and slightly pursed my lips, upon which the interviewer's eyes lingered. The "luminous lip tint" I'd applied was effective. I knew I ought to be found attractive in these situations.

Having to appraise yourself like that, in three solid words, is strange. What adjectives could adequately capture a person's idiosyncrasies? Doing so is like looking at a Monet landscape with a telescope. What attribute could describe the fact that I think bread is sacred because my father breaks a loaf across our table to cure any problem? That my pockets are constantly gummed together with Blu Tack because it helps to knead something when I get anxious. That supermarkets are relaxing because family time was going to ASDA. That I'm too impatient to suck on mints, so I grind them with my molars. That I only use Maldon salt flakes because Kit told me it's uncouth to season food with anything else. That I order an oat flat white in the same breath as a grilled cheese.

That I wear my backpack on my chest in crowds because my mother gave me a flogging when I "let" myself get pick-pocketed. That showers are never long enough, because of him. That Jade isn't even my real name. That Jade began as my Starbucks name, because all children of immigrants have a Starbucks name. That I was an honest person until I realized how easy it was to just say *I'm really good, thanks, and you?*

It might be self-indulgent to want someone to see all these peculiarities of mine. But at one point, I didn't have a single word to describe myself.

PART ONE

1

The Lincoln Room was at full capacity. Dotted about were expansive round tables, with bushy bouquets at their centers, each named after a prominent female politician: "I'm on Maggie Thatcher! Where are you sitting?" Guests arrived plucking a champagne flute from the white-gloved servers' trays. The reception was at a pleasant hum; we'd timed our arrival to perfection. Knowing British people, there were at least five concurrent conversations about "this mental weather we've been having!"

"You ready?" I asked, pausing under the unconscionably lavish flower arch. The ground floor of the Savoy had been monopolized tonight to celebrate thirty years of the Firm. I spotted in the corner a Willy Wonka–style cart offering cupcakes iced with "1988" and "2018" in the Firm's colors.

"If I can get through this evening," Adele said, lips stretched into a ventriloquist's smile, "without cracking into my cyanide tooth, I'll consider it a success."

It seemed the women of Reuben, Fleisher & Wishall LLP had sold out Van Cleef's Alhambra collection. Men signaled their earning capacity with discreetly indiscreet watches.

When we first met a year ago, I read Adele's insistence on wearing black Dr. Martens and mismatched Celtic earrings as a tiresome display of rebellion; a statement that *I may be another cog in this machine, but I'm an individual and, crucially, I am not a sellout.* When she got her forearm tattoo—an outline of a nude woman with flowers sprouting out of her nipples—she essentially plastered *vive la résistance!* over the door to our shared office. I knew now that nothing Adele did was performative.

I had yet to reach such dizzying heights of emancipation. I'd spent the last ninety minutes assembling myself. Neutral-but-smoky eye makeup, legs smoother than dolphins. I got a manicure earlier today, returning to a Post-it on my desk in my boss's scrawl: *Jade, this isn't play school. An hour for lunch?* I wore a fir-green dress that cinched my waist and had a wraparound bodice. Despite its low cut, the dress remained professional, given my lack of breasts. I felt some feminist guilt over the hours I've spent researching boob jobs, but enough aunties at enough weddings have lamented that my "childbearing" hips are disproportionate to my flat chest. The last straw was Auntie Ebru's exclamation that *Jade has the face to launch a thousand ships, and the backside for them to harbor under!*

"There you are! I've been looking for you forever!" Eve grabbed me in a hug as Adele was pulled into another huddle. "Jeez, love this dress, and it has pockets?"

"Hey Evie." I grinned.

"Come, let's mingle." She tugged on my wrist toward a group of colleagues. I looked over my shoulder and flashed Adele an apologetic smile, reciprocated with a minimal wave as she dissolved into the crowd.

"It's always about the oil," Will Janson—of Post-it fame, and also the partner who headed my team—cried. There were more partners at the Firm called William (nine in total), than female partners. "That's all the US involvement in the Middle East has ever been about."

"Now, we're not talking politics, are we?" Eve stepped into the conversation, sidling up against Will, one hand perched on his shoulder.

"We were just talking about the Pentagon's planned withdrawal of troops from Syria," Will said.

"I'd know nothing about that," Eve said, doe-eyed. "Could you walk me through it?"

The thing is, Eve has a first-class politics degree. Her thesis charted how the unassuming Bashar al-Assad went from reserved ophthalmologist to dangerous dictator. On an August day, in a muggy lecture hall that smelled of feet, I crept in late to the first session of postgraduate law school. Eve was in the back row, messaging someone under the desk. Her proud chin and severe cheekbones were incongruous with the battered dungarees slung over her shoulders and the carton of apple juice she reached for. She smiled at my dithering by the door and shuffled to make room for me.

"What'sa girl gotta do to get a pint around here?" she whispered as we filed out of a seminar on insolvency that had made time stop still. "Paid a fiver for a cider the other day, gave me a fucking heart attack."

Eve's over-familiarity, and the confidence it displayed, made me shy.

"That's London for you," I said.

"It was always gonna be spenny here, but no one signed up to starve."

"I know a place around the corner," I offered, "a student bar, if you fancy it?"

Frolicking down the back streets of Bloomsbury, we peeked into the cream Edwardian houses saying we were putting ourselves through this grind to get ceilings that high. Eve ended up pulling pints for the rest of law school at that student bar. At the time, she had an older boyfriend who paid her rent and understood she didn't love him, but she still needed extra cash to maintain the lifestyle she emulated. We went on to submit our applications to Reuben together. We both got in, secured contracts together, trained together, qualified together into different departments. We ran on parallel tracks and, luckily, have never collided. After our shared blueprints, Eve didn't hide the fact that my rapid free fall into best friendship with Adele was a thorn in her side.

Eve was the most uniquely intelligent person I'd ever met. She understood the person her audience wanted her to be. For Will, she knew to play the role of the gorgeous junior who hung on his alpha word with wonderment. As she requested, he "walked her through" the news story while she innocuously grazed her hip against his leg, to indulge his belief that he could have her if he wanted. It reminded me of the scripted flirtation between a father and his son's girlfriend (*I can see where your son gets his good looks from!*). By the same token, Eve knew to mention her desire for motherhood when speaking to a colleague who had just returned from maternity leave, or to play up her Northern accent when the Geordie head of IT came to fix a computer bug. She once referred to herself as *the right Spotify playlist*.

"Jade, tell us," Will said, turning to me, "given your background, what are your thoughts on potential British involvement in Syria? History repeating itself?" Being mistaken for Downing Street's foreign policy advisor was an occupational hazard for people who looked like me. I didn't get the chance to bluff my way through a response stolen from the *Guardian*, as just then, we were called to take our seats.

"Have you seen the seating plan?" Will asked.

"No, I haven't," I mumbled, looking around for it.

"You're on Hillary Clinton." Will nodded toward the table. "In the *place d'honneur*, I should add."

"What do you mean?"

"To the right of David."

"Oh."

"That bastard," Will chuckled. "Every year he helps himself."

He winked as he walked toward his table, Angela Merkel.

"Miss Kaya," David Reuben said, approaching me with an outstretched hand.

"Mr. Reuben, please, call me Jade." I felt an overwhelming urge to curtsy.

"I've heard a lot about you." *What has he heard about me?* "Very pleased to finally meet you in person."

We actually had met before, three years ago. I'd scurried into his office to procure his all-powerful signature for a contract. He hadn't looked up at me.

He pulled out my chair and I perched in the most ginger fashion I could muster.

"So, tell me about yourself," he began. "What are you working on?"

"Project Arrow." The Firm had been brought onto the case four months ago to defend the ethical investment fund Arrow against the first whispers alleging fraud. After settlement discussions failed, a claim was filed with the High Court, bringing to the public's salivating attention what had previously been terse talks in conference rooms over glasses of sparkling water.

"Jade, listen." David beckoned me with a curl of his index finger. As I leaned in, his breath purred against my cheek. "Genevieve and her team at Arrow are top tier and are to be treated as such, do you understand?" His left eyebrow jerked like it had a life of its own.

"Absolutely." Genevieve was Arrow's devoutly French founder who'd hurricaned into my life. I admired everything about her. Her meeting etiquette was artful. She referred to herself as a "market leader" and never uttered the word "just." I felt chic merely as the recipient of her texts that read *RDV a 9h*. In our first rendezvous, she asked me which university I went to. When I answered, she said *pfft, why do you sound so sheepish? Say it again, this time like it's yours to say.*

"The standard is perfection." David turned a beady eye to me. "Got it?"

I nodded. The political machinations of client networking were usually withheld from us more lowly associates, so now the pressure was on.

"Good." David nodded back. "Enough business. Tell me, where are you from?"

"Born and bred London."

"You said that with pride, but I meant where are you originally from?"

The magical realm of Narnia. I sneak out the back of the wardrobe whenever I fancy going home.

"David!" I turned to see Josh, a senior associate, striding toward us with open arms. "To what do I owe the pleasure of sitting at high table with you?" They hugged, slapping each other on the shoulder with the familiarity of two friends living on different continents reconnecting by chance. I quickly looked engrossed by the menu, attempting to channel indifference to Josh. We had worked together over the summer. Long, sleep-deprived nights, alone in meeting rooms with him. The way he murmured his agreement with me. How when he took off his cuff links to roll up his sleeves, the errant undressing made me prickle. The way he suddenly stretched next to me, and it made me exhale slowly to refocus. How his Adam's apple vibrated when he laughed at my jokes. How we shared a lukewarm beer when he turned thirty-two in the office. He had said *you weren't who I expected to spend my birthday with*, but it sounded like a compliment. I'd remained distant and standoffish since the case settled. That was the best way to keep it professional.

Tonight's starter was salmon tartare and a radish garnish, with a side of *you're mixed race? Your mother came to the UK as a tourist and married your father? For visa purposes, I assume?* As he asked, David refilled my glass with a delicious Austrian Riesling. I guzzled the wine to avoid answering his question and immediately felt woozier.

"Miss Jadey, what fun plans do you have on for the weekend?" David asked, while he ceremoniously swirled, sniffed, and sipped the cabernet taster that was paired with our minute-steak main. *Miss Jadey? Delighted to announce my debut as one of the Muppets.*

"Not much, I'm seeing my parents tomorrow, then probably a relaxed Sunday." I was seeing Kit on Sunday, but it was best not to mention a boyfriend, to avoid being typecast into either (a) tragic-girl-who-is-obsessed-with-her-boyfriend-who-by-the-way-has-not-proposed-yet, or (b) up-herself-she-thinks-I-was-coming-on-to-her-so-she's-dropped-the-boyfriend-card.

"That's wholesome."

"What about you?"

"It's my son's twenty-first. My ex-wife has organized an extravaganza for him."

"What are you getting him for the big two-one?"

"The Notting Hill flat."

"As opposed to your many other London flats?" I teased.

"Yes," David said, deadpan and oblivious to my sarcasm. "It wouldn't make sense for him to have the Liverpool Street place. Obviously, the house on the Heath is out of the question too."

I filled the dead air with more wine. My head was nice and fuzzy, while my stomach grumbled in protest.

"Whereabouts do you live?" David asked, sloshing a little more into my glass. The cream tablecloth bloomed oxblood splotches.

"South London."

"Ooh, trendy South," David sniggered.

"Any digestifs, sir?" asked a waiter.

"I'll have a Scotch. The lady will have a limoncello." He didn't take his eyes off me. The room felt too hot. I looked around for some water.

"Excuse me, Jade, but I have spotted an old client of mine. Do you mind if I pop over and say hello?"

"Sure, go ahead." *It's a two-hundred-person dinner, David, not a first date.* I dug in my purse for my phone.

Adele O'Hara, 3 minutes ago:
Ladies room—as soon as dessert starts!

Eve Slater, now:
Looking cozy with Daddy Reuben . . .

"How is it being teacher's pet?" Josh scooted into David's seat and gently elbowed me in the ribs. I tucked my phone away.

"Why? You upset to be overtaken?" I prodded back.

"Remember me when you're living in his mansion on the Heath. I can see it now: Mrs. Reuben the Sixth."

"Come off it. He has *five* ex-wives?"

"Divorced, beheaded, died, divorced, beh—"

I huffed loudly before giving him a bashful smile.

"To be fair, you'd totally blend into a lineup with them."

"I have no idea what you mean by that."

"I simply mean," Josh said with a big smile, "that Sir Dave cannot resist a woman like you."

"Well . . ." I slurred, slow to rush past his comment, far drunker than I realized. My breathing was labored, like a layer of gauze was covering my nose and mouth. "He's old enough to be my dad."

"Hasn't stopped him before!"

Josh looked like Marlon Brando playing Stanley Kowalski if Marlon changed out of his greasy singlet, wore a tailored suit, and grew curated designer stubble: refined sophistication meets animalistic masculinity. He put his hand on my forearm when asking *another one?* I nodded; he took his hand away and my skin bristled with heat.

A minute later, Josh handed me a fresh glass, looking slowly down the whole length of me. "Jokes aside, you look—"

"Josh—"

"I know," he said.

"I have a—"

"Of course." His eyes, green and flecked with light brown splotches, held mine for another beat. I longed for him to touch me again. "I just wanted you to know."

I blinked and remembered where we were. "Save it for someone else. I'm just here for the vintage wine on the Firm's dime."

"As you wish." He clinked his glass against mine. "Cheers."

After David returned and dessert was served, I excused myself. I fished out my phone and messaged Kit.

Jade Kaya, now:
How is your evening babe? Loooooveee you xxxx
Miss you xxx

"How's it going in here?" Adele said, though it was more like *howzit go-win in he-yah*, given her jangling accent. I was sitting on a tufted rose-colored bench with my head in my hands. The bathroom was encased in teal-framed mirror panels that bounced my reflection infinite times. "Dude, are you okay?"

"Fuck, Del, I'm boozed."

"Good Lord, girl." Adele sat next to me, laughing. "Really dining out on the free wine?"

"Well yes, but also every time I looked away, he was refilling my drink. Feels like he's being a bit of a creep."

"Who?"

"David."

"David who?"

"*The* David, Adele! The guy's name is on our fucking office building! This entire party"—I flailed my arm about—"is to celebrate what he created. Are you with me?"

"Oh."

"Yeah. *Oh*."

"Not someone you can rebuff."

"No."

"Okay. Have a piss, go back inside and just"—*clap*—"drink"—*clap*—"water"—*clap*—"for the next forty-five minutes. I'll keep my eyes on you."

Dessert passed. The lights were dimmed. A live jazz band appeared, the saxophonist crooning as married associates slunk into darkened corners. A senior lawyer clicked at the server for *a round of Negronis!* My feeble attempt to resist was met with *it's the Firm's signature drink, you know that*.

"Miss Jadey, I was beginning to think you might have pulled an Irish exit," David called out at me, his acolytes turning to stare at his target. Nowhere to hide. I smiled weakly and swayed over to him. "If you're getting tired, this should wake you up," David said, replacing my half-drunk Negroni with a fresh cocktail.

Adele followed very closely behind me.

"An espresso martini—I'd love one, David, thanks!" Adele swooped the drink out of my hand and replaced it with water. Being American helped her get away with a brashness that startled the British.

"The more the merrier." David smirked. Now that we were standing, I saw that David was short and beanpole thin. He gestured at the waiter. "Another one." I gulped as much water as possible before the next stem was planted in my hand. Adele had been whisked away. My feet were sore. My cheeks felt hot, and my head was pounding. I'd brushed past Eve maybe half an hour ago, but there was no sign of her now either.

"Jade, you are an exotic creature." David's stubble scuffed my cheek as he whispered his gruff nothings in my ear. The room rippled.

"Sorry, David," I mumbled, "I need to—"

"How are you getting home tonight?" David's fingers clasped my forearm. I looked down in surprise. His fingernails weren't clipped and trapped thin lines of dirt.

"I . . . I don't know. Cab?"

"You can't possibly go back south this late at night. All those stabbings, it's dangerous."

"What?" I said, defensive. I hoped my blinking wasn't as slow as it felt.

"Let me give you a place to stay."

"No. Really, it's fine."

"What's this game you're playing?" David's consonants were sharp.

I stared at him, my face empty and stupid. *Say something.*

"Don't play dumb," his voice said, his face a triple blur.

Say something, for fuck's sake. His hand was clammy against me.

"Jade!" I turned. Josh was walking toward us and I saw him glance at my arm in David's grip. "Sorry to interrupt, David. Do you mind if I steal Jade for a few minutes? I've been meaning to introduce her to a prospective client."

"If you must." David looked like one of those serial killers in Netflix documentaries: high-functioning but a cauldron of simmering rage underneath. "But we have unfinished business."

Josh shepherded me out of the Lincoln Room and down the corridor. All my focus was spent on walking as steadily as possible.

"Who is it you want me to meet?" I asked, looking up at him towering over me.

"No one," Josh chuckled. "I thought you could do with a bit of respite from Dave."

"Oh God, thank you."

"Yeah, fuck, I'm sorry, I should have intervened sooner. Everyone knows he can be a bit full-on."

I felt nauseated, as if the little food I'd had was clambering back up my throat. "Do you mind if I sit for a bit?"

My head slackened against his chest, his arm cradled my shoulders. Our pose was like a couple's engagement photo. He led me to a corner at the back of the cloakroom and, a moment later, held a bottle of water to my lips. "Take a sip," he said, like he was trying to coax a child to eat their vegetables. "Cinderella, I think it's time to get you home." He handed me his phone as he steadied me. "Here, put in your address and I'll order you a pumpkin."

I bundled into the back seat of the taxi and immediately rolled down the windows, planning to hang my head out like a dog in a bid to avoid vomiting over the cabbie's livelihood. Josh closed the door behind me. *You're an embarrassment, Jade*, I thought. *I need to get home.* I felt a twang of mourning for Josh seeing me in this state. Then I clocked that his shape had strode around the car and slid in the other side. I felt my face screw together.

"Don't look so worried!" he laughed. "I live nearby, I'll jump out on the way."

"Mmm."

Josh leaned across me to fasten my seat belt and, abandoning all socially acceptable inhibitions, I inhaled the crook of his neck. It smelled like dry-cleaning.

My neck swung elastically from side to side, no longer supporting my lolling head. The sounds of nocturnal London fleeted past as we swooped through the Strand. Girls screeching about their feet hurting, emulsified with revving motorbikes and distant sirens. My eyelids drooped as we crossed Waterloo Bridge, taking in the glittering black river before I finally surrendered to sleep.

Adele O'Hara, 15 minutes ago:
How are you feeling?

Eve Slater, 5 minutes ago:
Where areeee youuu? We're heading to Dirty Martini for more drinks, meet us there?

Adele O'Hara, 4 minutes ago:
Have you left?

Adele O'Hara, now:
Text me when you're home safe.

"Hey." A firm hand shook my shoulder. "Wake up, Jade."

"What?"

"Wake up—we're here. Is there anyone at home who can take care of you?"

"Nope. I lib alone."

"All right, then. Which one is your place?"

"Flat sixth."

Like a newborn giraffe yet to discover the concept of balance, I teetered and swayed my way out of the car.

"I've got it from here, thanks, man," Josh said to the driver as he shut the car door and the taxi purred along the road.

I blinked at my front door.

Is this flat 6 or flat 9?

"Here, let me help you."

Josh took the keys out of my fumbling hands. Within seconds, he swung open the door to my hallway. It creaked as it moved, the glow of the streetlamps revealing an inky indigo tunnel to nowhere.

"You okay?" Josh leaned against the wall. I swiveled to look back at him, nearly toppling over and having to steady myself against the doorframe. His expression was amused, and I let out a silly giggle.

"D'ya wanna come in for a drink?" I blurted. *Why did I say that?* I felt sick. I needed to be horizontal. Before Josh could answer, I stalked in and slumped on the hallway bench. He shadowed me inside. I stared at the grain in the wood floor, which appeared to be swirling in opposing directions. My phone flopped out of my hand.

Kit Campbell, now:
Haha you sound boozed my love! Make sure you drink lots of water xxx

My love! I wanted Kit here very badly. Instead, I felt Josh sit next to me and lean forward, lifting my left leg up. His hands were tanned and veiny. One hand supported my ankle while he pulled off my heel with the other. I watched, stupefied, as he did the same to my other foot. With minimal effort, he lifted me up off the stool, steadying me as I wobbled.

"I never realized how petite you are without your heels," he murmured. I was at eye level with his chest now. With his left hand propping me up, his right tugged at his tie, pulling one strand out through the other.

2

I'd read Neruda and Yeats poems for school coursework and, lacking any real-world experience of love, expected it to be as they had immortalized it. An intense flash of elation, followed by inevitable pining and romantic torture. So I was surprised by how easy it was to love him. How naturally our togetherness became foundational.

We met on the first night of freshers' week, at the colloquially known "Debutantes' Night." An aggressively heteronormative event where the fresher girls were penned into a room with the third-year boys. In hindsight, it sounded like a smutty soft-core porno: young peasant girls paraded to feudal overlords.

Several of the girls knew each other already, as if cliques had been plucked from school and dropped entirely intact into university. I lacked the effervescence others had, and stood alone with a glass of Lambrini, a tight smile gracing my face. That's when I first saw him. Kit wore a gray T-shirt that hung like a tent from his wide shoulders, and his arms were too long, as if they should have been swinging from trees in the Amazon. He had a slightly darker tan across his forehead that conveyed carefree health. Perhaps brought on by a spot of Sunday-morning tennis. His face was classically angular, his brow bone balconying over his eyes. His stock attractiveness implied an unfairness, another thing bequeathed to him to make his way through life even smoother.

I took a deep breath and looked away from him, introducing myself to a small group of people who didn't look too intimidating. The words and phrases *Westminster*, *summer* (used as a verb—*where do you summer?*), *rollies*, *rugby* (the sport or the school, it was unclear), *by the river*, and *boarding school* were annoying mosquitoes nipping the tops of my arms. As I grew quieter, my cheeks starting to strain, I turned back to Kit and watched him. He stayed in the same spot, as people approached him with exclamations about him being missed at events over the summer. A buzz emanated from every conversation he had. I moved in circles around him, seeing him crumple his can and toss it in the bin from two meters away. I seized the window of opportunity and drifted toward the drinks table, accidentally-on-purpose bumping my elbow with his.

"Hi," I said, flustered, "I don't think we've met?"

"Kit Campbell" were the first words he said to me. He leaned down to give me an introductory kiss on the cheek, but his lips puckered against the curve of my ear instead. "So sorry," he said, jerking away from me.

"It's okay," I said, instantly more at ease than I'd been all evening. "I'm Jade."

"Are you the girl who wrote your personal statement on the right to euthanasia?"

Oh God, I knew that was a pretentious thing to write about.

Be bold, be controversial, write about big topics, the teachers at school had said over and over.

"I thought it was excellent," Kit added, matter-of-fact.

"Really?"

He nodded. "I couldn't have written it better myself."

"How did you get hold of my application?"

"I'm Professor Christou's assistant this year. When I read your comments on the House of Lords' treatment of Tony Nicklinson, I put yours at the top of his pile."

"So I guess I have you to thank?" I probed.

"Not at all." He smiled as he reached for another can of pale ale. "Just saying it was a relief to not read yet another essay on someone's grandma being their role model."

"Hey, my grandma's a legend!" I exclaimed, having never met either of my grandmothers.

Kit laughed into his drink, inhaling then spluttering it out.

We didn't leave each other's side all night. He said my name in conversation repeatedly: "So, Jade, where in London are you from? Jade, has anyone shown you around yet? Jade, have you read *The Children Act* by Ian McEwan? You'd love it, I reckon—I thought about you, I mean I thought about your essay, when I read it."

The room—oak-paneled and overlooking a manicured quadrangle—would swell and dwindle with waves of freshers. The sun cast a dewiness through the windows and backlit his head. I thought him the most delicately beautiful man I'd ever seen. I was so engrossed in him that the Lambrini went down with slightly less of a gag each time. A time lapse would show us rooted in the same spot for hours, as the tinder to other lifelong connections ignited around us. I noticed how empty the room had become.

"Wow, it's late—midnight already!" I squawked, before feeling painfully self-conscious of how childlike I sounded.

Kit took my hand, and I fluttered with the confidence of the move.

"Let's go somewhere else?"

Campus was its own sealed microcosm. We existed inside a terrarium made up of cobbled streets with monastic buildings looming over us on either side. Kit led me through whimsical sandy-stoned courtyards and poky alleyways. The mellow October chill was settling around us, but summer lingered longer here.

"Where are you taking me?" I laughed, still clutching his hand.

"Look," Kit whispered as we emerged and he pushed open a heavy oak door that opened into a cavernous room, with a beamed, convex ceiling. It was dark, but I could see that the windows were all stained glass, dabbling the Virgin Mary's colors over the marble floor.

I turned toward him. "Is this a chapel?"

"Used to be. Now it's closed. Not many people know it's here."

I looked up at the ornate gold carvings in every crevice.

"It really takes your breath away," I murmured.

"You're telling me." He was looking at me as he spoke. I flushed, turned away, tucking then untucking my hair behind my ear. "How are you doing?"

"What do you mean?"

Kit pulled an I-don't-know face before saying, "I realize I've pulled you away into an abandoned creepy chapel in the dead of night on your first day. I want to check you're okay? I can take you back if you'd like?"

"No!" I said, far too quickly. *I want to stay here all night with you.* "I'm good."

He sauntered toward the back pew and sat. He faced forward toward the lectern.

"You know," he said, "I come here alone a lot."

"Mmm?" I manufactured nonchalance despite the thrilling suggestion that I was the exception.

"My dad told me about it. It was his spot too when he was here. We're not religious or anything," he rushed to say.

I came over and sat next to him, feeling bold as our thighs touched. I stole a quick look at him, and again, he was already looking at me.

"I'm glad you were Christou's assistant this year," I eventually said.

"Yeah?"

"I would have got in anyway, to be clear," I teased, "but at least this way you were waiting around for me to arrive."

I expected him to playfully tell me to get fucked. Instead he released a delightful laugh as he looked away.

"I guess you're right." He rubbed his brow. "This is crazy."

"What is?"

Kit motioned toward the air between us. "Meeting you like this."

And then the space between us closed as I slung my arms over his shoulders and kissed him.

3

Morning sunlight pierced through the open curtains. It was November, and the UK was overdue its condemnation to four months of darkness and sleet. Groaning, I rolled over to bury my head in the pillow. Mascara had emulsified in the night and welded my eyes shut with black goo. I pushed myself up in bed to a throbbing head. The room wavered like a canoe on choppy water. I slumped my shoulder blades against the headboard, waiting for the nausea to subside, picking mascara flakes from my eyelashes and running my tongue over fuzzy teeth. The smell was an assault: stale alcohol and the unmistakable stench of bile. I urgently needed a shower.

I padded around the sheets with one hand looking for my phone, the other arm shielding my eyes.

"Hey Siri?" I called out. No response. "Hey *SIRI*," I yelped.

"Good morning. How can I help?" Siri's robotic voice responded.

"Where are you, Siri?"

"I'm over here."

I followed her voice and found my phone under the bed. *How did it get there?* Blood rushed to my skull, and I hung upside down like a bat until the feeling of swelling passed.

Adele O'Hara, 2 hours ago:
Hello? Are you alive?

Kit Campbell, 1 hour ago:
Morning beautiful. How did it go last night? Heading to rugby now but update me when I'm back x

Omma, 25 minutes ago:
Why you no call your mother back? What time are you home today?

I replied first to Adele.

Jade Kaya, now:
Sorry yes, I'm alive and mortally hungover.

Adele O'Hara, now:
Glad to hear it, I'll cancel the helicopter rescue mission now. Where did you go last night?

Jade Kaya, now:
Lord knows. Took myself home and passed out it seems.

Adele O'Hara, now:
You're so premium when you're shit-faced.

Jade Kaya, now:
Don't. IN FRONT OF MY BOSS. Dying. Tell me I didn't do anything career-ending?

Adele O'Hara, now:
Relax, you're good. Rest today.

I scrolled through my messages. Shifting between mental gears felt like wading through tar. I tapped my Barclays app. No transactions. I tapped my Uber app. No receipts.

How did I get home?

My senses woke up one by one. My bare skin registered the clammy dampness of the sheets. I immediately thought about how my pajamas would need a wash. *But my bare skin?* I looked down and confirmed I wasn't wearing any.

Oh.

I glanced at my floordrobe. Last night's green dress, scrunched into a ring with a body-sized circle in the middle.

An upswell of nausea. Globules of sweat formed between my breasts. I wished Kit was here so I could moan about my deadly hangover to him. I signed the lease to this flat in Vauxhall soon after I started at Reuben. I was a grown-up, earning big-girl packet, and I wanted a foyer to show for it. Living alone was a privilege. I always thought that being introverted meant that I was shy, reserved, even antisocial. But it turns out it's all about where you draw your energy from. How you refuel. There was some overcrowding with my parents in childhood, and now, solitude was solace.

I reached around my waist to pull the tangled duvet off me and over-enthusiastically swung my feet across the bed.

Another few minutes with my head in my hands, waiting for the feeling that last night's food was coming up to subside.

I hauled myself to the bathroom and plonked on the toilet. The piss sizzled as it streamed out. *Ow.* The metallic smell of blood made me part my legs and peer into the pan. I wiped and saw shiny red smearing the paper. Better late than never, I guess.

I grabbed a tampon and its dry cotton jarred as it staggered in, making me wince. I fished through the creams section of my medicine cabinet: antiseptic, muscle relief, insect repellent. I found the Vagisil, twisted it open and liberally spread it over my swollen labia.

Still on the loo, I sent a voice message to Kit.

Jade Kaya, now:

Hey babe, sorry, I just woke up. Last night was good, sat next to the Founding Partner who is a massive creep, by the way. But good for exposure at work, you know? He at least knows who I am and what I'm working on. He was annoying so I drank a bit more than I normally would—got wayyyyy too pissed though and now I have mega hangxiety. Finally got my period though, thank God. Was getting nervous. How has your morning been? I miss you! I need nursing back to health. Gonna head to Mum and Dad's once I can muster the energy to get myself into the shower. Can't wait to see you tomorrow. Love you!

I walked nude to the kitchen. It was a cold, cloudless morning. Cool beams of November sun streamed in, filtered by the splayed leaves of a Chinese money plant perched on the windowsill, casting abstract shadows over the dated cabinets. My collection of glass bottles, found in charity shops, and now filled with various oils, refracted emeralds and ambers against the wall. My flat brought me such joy, even in this sorry state.

I drank a glass of water and my dehydrated cells rejoiced. I leaned forward to rest my head on the kitchen counter. Little crescent shadows dabbled over my skin, catching the light. I moved to face the window and peered at the yellowing splotches puckered over my hips and thighs. Some on my forearm too. The drowsy haze I woke in cleared and something unnamed slithered into me. I closed my eyes deliberately, then peeked them open slowly to find the bruises still there, rosebudding on my skin.

Not on my skin.

In my skin, coming from within me.

You've always been a clumsy drunk, I assured myself.

Under me, London was rousing, dewy-eyed for the weekend. Directly under my kitchen window used to be a Morley's. A few years ago, the iconic LED lights flickered off for the last time and the deep fryer stopped sizzling. Renovations labored on. The space was transformed into an open-concept working-space-slash-coffee-shop. It used to be Albanian builders hollering for work at dawn, the smell of grease settling into the furniture, the clanging grind of steel shutters. Now it was the sound of hipsters with ironic mullets and Dickies that were distressed to look vintage, asking the barista what flavor profile the coffee beans had.

I moved toward the fridge and hungrily downed a third of a carton of orange juice. I stood there for a few minutes, enjoying its cool breeze on my clammy body before turning

180 degrees and nudging the fridge door with a flick of my foot. The seal on the door suctioned into place, vacuuming the fridge shut. All senses came into hyper-focus. That sound.

A firm, cushioned thud.

Like a car door closing.

My skin prickled with tiny saucers. *What was that?*

A pocket of fermented air burped out and my stomach began to catapult its contents up. I ran back to the bathroom and emptied myself of the salmon and steak and wine and Campari and coffee.

After forcing down two paracetamol and two ibuprofen tablets, I stared into space for a few minutes, replaying scenes from the night before. Each memory lasted a split second. Flashes of David Reuben's weasel lips curling around his fork. How he ate his food tongue-first. His spindly fingers gripping my forearm. Adele's clean, soft face as she nodded once at me while seizing a glass from my hand. Two pairs of legs in the Savoy's bathroom cubicle as I waited for a moment to sit. A gym membership card left on the cistern. A fiver curling up at the edges on the floor.

I crawled back into bed. The sheets were still damp and made me shudder. I reached across to set my water down when a ringing began in my ears. I blinked a few times to make sure. A wineglass, half-empty. Unapologetically staining a ring into my grandmother's beloved walnut bedside table. *What the fuck?* It was handcrafted in 1911, originally as a dowry chest, with intricate ebony pulls and lacquered carvings on the doors. When my mother moved to London from Korea, she sent for it, and it took two months to arrive by boat. It had seen two world wars and the Korean War. And now, it had surrendered to a wineglass. *My mum is actually going to kill me*, I thought. I stared at the glass, then forensically plucked it up with my thumb and forefinger, retching again as the musk of stale red wine floated to my nostrils.

4

In another life, my parents would have been nomads. This year was their twenty-sixth in the UK, and yet their two-bed-terraced in Morden felt temporary. They had an agility in life, nimbly moving from place to place, business venture to business venture, with an entrepreneurship that seemed to naturally grace immigrants. *Necessity is the mother of invention.*

My father is an Anatolian who came to London in July 1992 from his family's hazelnut farm on the Black Sea coast. A family friend got him a job in a hand car wash in Mitcham. The first month was lonely. With little money, Baba used the network of red buses to learn London. A fluttery skip from the 118 onto the 159 onto the 390. A chain linking him to Brixton to Lambeth North, then Westminster, Trafalgar Square, Piccadilly. What a way to see the city for a pound fifty. Baba climbed on the 390 to see the changing of the guards at Buckingham Palace. And *on that August day, it was all over*.

The only spare seat was next to Omma. She was dressed in a rust-orange linen shirt, denim shorts, and white tennis socks. Her perfect teeth in a smile, marveling at Marble

Arch. Their romance sounded like it belonged on the grainy reel of a film camera. The Polaroids have that soft-focus light, like a layer of gossamer covered them. She was on a three-month trip to Europe before starting a prestigious clerkship at a bank in Seoul. She was supposed to join her friends in Antwerp the following week but never made it, gallivanting across London with my dad instead. Neither spoke much English. When the lack of common language baffled me, to my utmost horror, Baba said with a wink that they both spoke *the international language of love*. The whirlwind halted six weeks later when Omma first made out those two pink lines. *The world's a different place now*, she'd said, but back then, there was incommunicable shame in returning to Seoul, unmarried and pregnant with a foreigner's baby. There was a Korean word for that baby: 혼혈, *mixed blood*. Baba's family also wanted nothing to do with this loose woman who'd led him astray. And someone out of his faith, too, no wonder. *It had to be London, aga*.

Omma and Baba married on New Year's Eve when she was three months pregnant. They celebrated their fledgling family as 1993 was called in, and they were promptly excommunicated from their families. They got to work immediately on their nascent business: brokering the lowest insurance premiums for small local businesses. Omma worked the books, her brain whirring with calculations, her stomach blooming by the day. At four foot nine inches, her compactness conveyed a sense of intimidating efficiency. Late at night, she would flick the switch on her small desk lamp and painstakingly pencil the day's numbers into an old-school exercise book repurposed into a ledger.

Meanwhile, Baba was at the coalface. Fifteen-hour days,

hundred-hour weeks. Every morning he would open his battered London Underground map that was falling apart at the folds and inspect it. I still don't understand why he didn't periodically replace it—they were free in any station. There was an oblique pride in its struggle to keep together at the seams, as if it mapped his struggle to plant roots in this city. He would pick a line and ride it end to end. From Edgware to Morden, Wimbledon to Upminster, West Ruislip to Epping. Some days he wouldn't be able to complete the whole line, alighting so often in Zones 2 to 9. Zone 1 was futile: no florist in Covent Garden or coffee shop in Regent's Park would give their business to the young man with broken English. He wouldn't waste precious time on his Travelcard there. He stuck to areas that had dense immigrant populations and combed their high streets. Walking into every kebab shop, dry cleaner, money-transfer hole in the wall, chippy, Brazilian hairdresser, Nigerian fabric house, and Vietnamese pho shop, he offered their services.

It helped that we didn't comfortably slot into London's patchwork. The Turkish pockets north of the river made Omma's loneliness shine bright like a beacon. The suburbia of Koreatown made Baba itchy with boredom. We moved nearly every year, looking for more fertile pastures for the business. School friends were temporary. Some flats were better, but sometimes Omma and I shared a bed, with Baba on a mattress on the floor. Perhaps that's why they never had more children. It was the three of us knitted together.

Slowly, through word of mouth, their business grew. In 2000, after a particularly good period, Baba took me out and we picked a denim pencil case with a pink sequined heart embroidered on the front, a purple bendy ruler, and a set of gel pens. The same day, Omma splurged on a full-price dress from Monsoon and delightedly twirled for us in it. There are few memories that hold such a nostalgic pull over me as that day.

Everything changed on September 11, 2001. Insurance premiums skyrocketed globally and work dried up. Baba slunk back to the Mitcham car wash after an annus horribilis of business drought. In 2008, six years of loyal service and quiet savings later, Omma and Baba wanted something of their own. They committed to that two-bed-terraced in Morden and bought their own car wash business on the A24 flyover. Three months later, the markets crashed.

I stepped through the front door to see Omma blowing on a spoon of steaming kimchi-chigae.

"Aga," Omma beckoned. My mother still called me *baby*.

"Hey Omma," I said, kissing her on the cheek. She looked smaller every time I came home, her skin more translucent. She wore her uniform of black jersey trousers and a loose linen shirt that was so long it looked like a kaftan. She had an elegant figure. A lifetime of Korean cooking, healthy and high in vital nutrients, made my mother svelte in a relaxed way. No harsh contours, but gentle lines. A man, who we later learned was world-renowned plastic surgeon Terry Shafiq, once stopped Omma in Victoria coach station and informed her that she had a "million-dollar forehead." Since then, I have admired the natural tautness of her brow.

"Eat! Eat!" she exclaimed. My mother's sole mission in life was to feed me until I was bursting, and then send me home laden with Tupperware full of homemade cooking. "How is it?"

"Mmm, tasty." The sour tang of the kimchi soup—the older the kimchi used the better—was refreshing. The traditional pork belly used in the soup was swapped for beef for Baba, such was the fused cuisine in this household.

"Of course it's tasty, I know how you like it." Omma pinched my cheek.

"Babam, come hug your father," my dad said, coming into the kitchen. "Ayy, have you lost weight? Vallahi, you're skin and bones. A fish needs flesh!"

"Possibly," I said, as he pulled me in. I smarted as Baba accidentally prodded my bruises. I'd briefly forgotten about them, but the Turkish were robust huggers. As always, he smelled like the astringent lemon cologne he slapped his face with daily.

"Naber?" I asked. *What's new?*

"You know what they say: the red rose"—Baba gazed out the window to conjure the appropriate sage-like contemplation—"will always be red."

"No one says that, Baba." *Do all brown fathers make up expressions?*

"Here." He thrust a plate of sliced melon in my face, ignoring me. The fruit said, more than words ever could, *I love you, my child.* He looked surprised as I shook my head and pushed the plate away.

"I've got a bit of a headache," I said.

"Aygo, I told you," my mother interjected. "The microwaves from your phone are frying your brain. Tak tak tak tak"—Omma did a schtick of me messaging on my phone—"all day long, tak tak tak on the face book and instant gam. That's why you always have headaches."

"No, Omma," I sighed. "I had too much to drink last night."

"Child! You come to your parents' house drunk?!"

"I'm not drunk, I just have a hangover."

"Children these days," my father tsked, waving his hand toward me, "no respect."

Omma and Baba nodded at each other in agreement. I clocked the number of times they referred to me as a child.

"Sorry." I pouted. "I had a work event."

"Tell me, tell me, how did it go?" my mother said as she set down the ttukbaegi—a clay bowl that went straight from stove to table, soup bubbling within—and clicked her tongue to indicate to my dad that lunch was ready. "My brilliant lawyer," she clucked, holding my face.

"Mashallah!"

I would be lying if I said I've never harbored any resentment toward my parents. In this world nothing can be said to be certain, except death, taxes, and Yumi and Yusuf hoping for a lawyer of a child. An immigrant stereotype that became a self-fulfilling prophecy. A bookworm my whole life, at seventeen I announced to them that I wanted to read English literature at university. It remains the funniest joke they've ever heard.

If I were to dissect this ugly bud of quiet resentment, I'd have to admit that it was rooted in how grossly underprepared I felt arriving at university for the nuances of polite society. I went in trying to summon the chutzpah of my parents. But restraint was a cornerstone of the upper class. Being scrappy was distasteful. Even the concept, the very point, of education in the UK was alien to us. To Omma and Baba, education existed solely to equip someone for a vocation. There was too little time, too much competition, to do anything else. By contrast, at university, it was all about critical thought. Massaging controversial topics for the sake of growth.

Of course, almost everyone liked to think of themselves as ideologically liberal, but their conservative leanings were thinly veiled. Discussions about the welfare state, or the legacy of empire, or equality of opportunity were intellectual Play-Doh, to knead and mold to develop nothing more than one's debating skills. Privilege comes in many forms: having no emotional investment in the political topics you debate is one of them. Peers tussled over the role of devil's advocate because championing for closing borders to refugees can be a gleeful mental exercise when your family have never fled war. There was a flair with which faux liberals discussed politics, as if they were gladiators in the Roman amphitheater. In reality, it looked a lot more like they were standing in a ten-person circle jerk of self-gratification.

Some years later, iterations of these same people suggested at dinner parties that I was a sellout for joining Reuben. They spoke with ennui of needing a job to pay the bills. In their work as a Chelsea gallery curator, money wasn't important. Coincidentally, the only people who think money doesn't matter are those who have always had it.

By the time I went home for Christmas after the first term, I was unable to contain my relief to be with my parents again. By that point, I'd fallen hopelessly for Kit. New to love, I was basking in all its splendor. But also innately understanding that part of loving meant being someone who could be loved in return. Kit unlocked an alternate universe of boat races, lawn croquet, and cream sweaters slung over shoulders. And I played Twister with my personality to see what fit best. It felt like I'd leapt across a crater to come back home to Omma and Baba, to my safe space. Be the three of us again.

The problem, I realized only later, was that I resented needing a safe space.

"I'm not sure, I was sat next to the Founding Partner," I said, tired with my parents' inquisition into last night's blur.

"The Founding Partner?" Omma slapped my dad's arm. "I told you, Yusuf! A dragon rises from the stream! Did you make a good impression?"

"I don't think so. I'm not sure." I struggled to articulate, or remember, last night. I checked my work phone, out of habit.

"Did you speak to him much? Did he like you? What did you talk about? Were you polite?"

"Can we not with all the questions? I feel quite anxious about it, actually."

"It's because you're not eating properly, aga." My mum sprang into action, spooning a portion enough for two grown men onto my plate. Surrounding the soup were dishes of banchan—sides that complemented every meal. Korean food had broken into the mainstream recently. Tiny glass jars of "Kim Kong Kimchi" sold at farmers' markets for extortionate prices. In reality, kimchi was the umbrella term for the hundreds of varieties of salted fermented vegetables. Cabbages, cucumbers, perilla leaves, radishes, turnips, you name it, it was kimchied in our house. Every omma had her own recipe that formed the bedrock of her daily cooking, and her children would spend their lifetimes trying to emulate it.

• • •

On his first visit, a year after we met, Kit had relished the onslaught of flavors that adorned my parents' place. I was a ball of nerves when I answered the door to him. Meshing my Ralph Lauren–shirted boyfriend with my no-frills-attached parents felt as unnatural to me as sprinkling chocolate chips over a pizza. Despite not taking his shoes off as he tracked into our living room—which was definitely registered by Omma—he was the picture of charm.

"Yumi, pleasure to meet you." Kit had to nearly bend in half to give Omma a hug. "A little bird told me that peonies are your favorite—these are for you."

"Aygo, aygo." My mother giggled, accepting the bouquet. Kit looked at me mystified, and I whispered a translation: *oh my, oh my*. "But they're not in season?"

"Ahhh." Kit tapped the end of his nose. "I have my sources!"

Baba was in the hallway, approaching Kit with caution.

"Yusuf!" Kit, overconfident, heartily shook Baba's hand. "How are you, mate?"

"Yani, this morning another man brought my wife her favorite flowers," Baba quipped.

"Well, don't worry, I haven't forgotten about you." Kit pulled a plastic box from his backpack. "I know you have a sweet tooth, so I brought you some baklava."

"Nice doing business with you!" Baba chuckled, already opening the box of syrupy goodies. Warmth glowed in my chest as I watched Omma bustling in the kitchen, trimming her peonies, and Baba's satisfied face as he enjoyed his childhood favorite treat.

"Thank you." I lifted my face toward Kit's like a sunflower searching for the sun.

"The least I could do." He kissed my temple, which I allowed because my parents were preoccupied elsewhere.

For the rest of the afternoon, a shy rapport blossomed between my three loves, and I felt idiotic for ever worrying. Kit was flawlessly polite, inquiring about my mother's traditional cooking methods, asking questions about what was in each jar. She practically expired when he said *no wonder Jade is both smart and a great cook—look at her mother.* When we sat for lunch, Omma, without warning, plopped a pickled garlic clove in Kit's mouth while he was yawning and then nodded enthusiastically as he chewed. He laugh-coughed and his eyes watered. *Too much*, I worried. *We're too much.*

"So, Yumi"—Kit leaned across the table—"what are your thoughts on Kim Jong-Un's nuclear program? Do you think reunification will ever be on the table, or has too much damage been done?" He was oblivious to Omma's startled expression, and carried on. "The *New York Times* did an interesting piece on how the two Koreas are currently the world's most perplexing political problem—have you had a chance to read it?"

Oh dear.

I kicked him under the table. Kit turned to me, genuinely baffled.

"Kit." Baba coughed. Omma stared into her bowl. "What football team do you go for?"

Kit's eyes darted between the three of us, thrown by the sudden stonewalling.

"Erm, I'm more a rugby man myself, to be honest."

"Right."

Thirty gelatinous seconds stretched by, no one knowing what to say.

"Excuse me." Kit got up. "Just going to the loo."

I reached out and grasped Omma's hand.

"What kind of questions were they?" Omma spoke in Korean. Baba's rudimentary grasp couldn't follow us, but he knew what she was saying.

"Kit is trying to find common ground with you. He's trying," I said weakly.

"Common ground?" Omma snapped. "It was a civil war. Remember that." She never could bear to speak about her country halved. Shortly before it was a cacophonous, skyscrapered country bursting with technology and pop culture, Korea was a decimated place. My grandfather was a rice farmer. During the Korean War, his field hands were all conscripted to fight and he had no choice but to employ temporary workers. They were travelers—refugees—fleeing from the North where their homes had been burnt to cinders. After harvest was over, he gave them each a small parcel of rice to aid them on their onward journey. Those grains left a proverbial breadcrumb trail. The next day American soldiers came. Communist sympathizer, they said. Collaborating with the enemy and harboring fugitives. Omma's appa was never seen again.

"I'm sorry," I whispered as Kit returned to the table. "I'm sorry."

We spoke about it that evening. He asked why Omma had clammed up. I felt an unfamiliar flash of annoyance toward her. For making the first meeting—one that I had built up so much in my head—awkward and uncomfortable when Kit didn't mean anything malicious by his questions. I explained why it was *traumatic for her, she finds it hard to talk about.* He apologized, said *God, how could I have been so ignorant*. I soothed him, kissed him, and said *please don't worry about it, you weren't to know.* The following weekend, he took Omma to Columbia Road Flower Market and carried home armfuls of peonies. And for that Christmas, Kit came bearing a bottle of Jo Malone's Peony & Blush Suede.

I spent the afternoon with a hot water bottle tucked into my jeans for my period cramps. I helped my parents with the list of IT tasks they had set out for me. Despite their business acumen, anything remotely technological was a frazzled, flustered affair. Omma swore black and blue that she didn't have a password for her email account. I took a punt on "Jade93" and got in. Meanwhile, Baba was conscientiously objecting to online banking, convinced that the entire concept was a large-scale embezzlement scheme. By the time it was dark out, my hangover had gone from pulsating headaches to intense fatigue. My pores clogged with damp, boozy sweat. I needed to curl up in bed and reassess my life choices.

"Your father will drive you home," Omma said as I pulled on my coat and hugged her goodbye.

"Will I?" my dad piped up. "Stay! There's this new crime show on Netflix. Looks gory!"

We always watched murder documentaries together, but today I couldn't imagine anything worse for my hangxiety.

"No, it's fine, Baba."

"Drive your daughter home, Yusuf," my mother ordered. Baba grumbled as he faffed around, muttering about how there was no rest for the "wicket."

"Haydi, haydi," Baba huffed, "let's go."

• • •

Baba carried two tote bags of Tupperware meals up to my flat and packed them away in the freezer. Then he kissed me on the forehead.

"I'd better get home, babam, it's getting late."

My dad zipped closed his gray-blue fleece, one that he would wear daily from September to March. The buzz of the zipper woke a formless, sinewy vision. Material chafing against itself as a tie was pulled off a collar. Green silk glistening in the dim light, almost like a snake coiled around a neck.

"Okay, hayatim." Baba's voice pierced my thoughts and the image of the snake slithered away, deeper into my memory. The *–m* suffix in Turkish—hayatim, kizim, yavrum—indicated a possessive: *my life*, *my daughter*, *my child*. "Rest tonight. And eat more, please."

"Goodnight, Baba," I mustered, still thinking of that shimmery green.

Baba turned on his heel to walk out of my flat. As his back retreated down the narrow staircase, all four walls around me seemed airless. I felt like a claustrophobe in a lift, watching the doors close. Boxed in, suffocated. His black head of hair was soon out of sight, and a tiny voice inside me felt like gasping *Baba, please don't go.*

5

Kit groaned loudly with his mouth full. "Oh babe! That right there"—he impaled more pasta with his fork—"that ragù will put Padella out of business."

"Do you want to know the secret ingredient?" I smiled. "The baby-making pot."

"Christ." Kit rolled his eyes but sort of laughed. "That Campbell family heirloom."

"I'd be more gracious," I teased, "you have that Le Creuset to thank for your existence."

"Always good to be reminded that my parents shagged in the kitchen over a stroganoff."

"And now, it's on us to *go forth and make more memories!*" I laughed, mimicking Kit's mum when she gifted me the thirty-year-old pot last Christmas.

"That woman needs boundaries." Kit mocked weariness. He reached over and took both my hands. "Thank you, Jadey, dinner's sensational."

"Do you like the wine?" I asked. I was still hanging from Friday but told myself one glass wouldn't hurt. "The guy at Bayley and Sage suggested the pairing."

"Yeah, the tannins are so smooth." Kit held up his wineglass to the candlelight. Sundays together were our ritual. Each winter, we became more committed to our cozy routine. Kit lived in a sharehouse, so we usually stayed at mine. He had floated moving in together a few times, but we ultimately put the discussion on pause as:

1. Doing so would undoubtedly make Omma say *why would he buy the cow now that you've given him the milk for free, eh?* (N.B., during these lectures, one must ignore her and Baba's trajectory);
2. I valued immensely my space and alone time; and
3. Kit wanted to get his living-with-the-lads era out of his system before settling down.

Whenever we spent time with other couples, our pillow talk that night would be discussing the superiority of our relationship to theirs. *We see each other because we want to and we make time for each other, not because we happen to live together.*

Every Sunday, we made messy brunch—today it was cheesy beans on toast. Coffee in bed first, because I had slept fitfully, with nebulous dreams waking me repeatedly. We held hands and walked from my flat in Vauxhall around Elephant and Castle, taking obscure snaps of street art and uploading them to Instagram stories. We commented on how unseasonably mild it was for November, and raised our KeepCups to each other, satisfied that we were doing our bit. We arrived at Borough Market armed with tote bags and flat whites, on the hunt for artisanal cheeses, organic wine, and grass-fed beef. All things Kit had upgraded me to over the course of our relationship. His Midas touch putting my ASDA days behind me. Market-stall hopping was the wholesome day I needed to detox myself after Friday's event at the Savoy. A slow clattering began on the iron roof of the market house. It was soon smudged gray outside. We huddled under cover until Kit gave me his jacket and we ran to the bus stop in the rain. And as his arm cupped my waist, I felt an ambient snatch of unease.

At home, Kit napped on the sofa as a blues record played and raindrops tracked my windows. I started cooking. As weird as it was, I did take pride in Kit's mum gifting me the pot she made all of his childhood meals out of. A seal of approval, perhaps. The flat soon filled with the rich, comforting smell of the ragù sauce on the stovetop. I looked over at Kit, all of him curled under the Soho House blanket he bought me as a housewarming gift. Etta James sang about wanting *A Sunday Kind of Love*, and I took a moment to savor mine.

The morning after the Debutantes' Night—after that kiss—I lay in my student room with a stupid grin on my face. That night switched my sexuality on, and it was flooding into every alcove and recess of my body. All I thought about was Kit's gentle hands, how they turned firm when wrapped around my waist, pulling me toward him. I visualized his face and ran my eyes over it. I revisited our conversations, an internal transcript playing out on loop. *This is crazy. Meeting you like this.*

But then the days lumbered on with no word. Campus was small, but I didn't see him anywhere. Knowing he was in my vicinity, moving in parallel to me but choosing not to seek me out, was so frustrating I cried. Eventually, I committed myself to forgetting about being spurned. My malaise deepened when I realized that Kit was a BNOC (Big Name on Campus—an actual acronym in use). He had multiple exes, each more beautiful, erudite, and impressive than the last. They had names like Lettice and Tilly. The student newspaper was circulated, with a critical opinion piece by Christopher "Kit" Campbell on how David Cameron's leadership of the Tory party exploited the labor of young female employees. One full week after the mixer, my new friend Emma, a girl from Lancashire with strawberry blonde hair and a delightful tooth gap, gushed about how Kit had captained the university rugby team to regional glory. *So that's where he'd been all week.* I didn't want to know, but I also *really* wanted to know.

A few days later, I struggled to find stability in the squashy armchair, pages threatening to spill out of my lap. Professor Kyriakos Christou's study was a racing green, with three battered corduroy armchairs arranged in a triangle. The lights were off, and I tilted my papers toward the pewter light from the rickety sash windows. He was zealously analogue, with stacks upon stacks of bound maroon books containing judgments from Her Majesty's courts. He forbade laptops, hence my harried flipping between sheets of paper.

"Well?" Kyriakos opened our session. "You have something for me?"

"I do?" I said.

Like a male Miranda Priestly, he huffed. "Must I wait forever for your debut essay?"

"Um, sorry, here it is." I held it out for him. He looked blankly at my outstretched hand.

"Read it aloud."

I began reciting, while Kyriakos rested his head against the armchair, eyes closed. I hit my stride in the second paragraph on the practical drawbacks of Parliamentary sovereignty, when a respectful knock sounded out. My breath caught in my stomach. Kyriakos seemed irritated that the flow of argument had been interrupted, and deigned to open his eyes.

"You're late," he grumbled, furry ears twitching. "This is my assistant, Kit Campbell."

"Pleasure." Kit smiled at me as he relaxed into the third armchair, a tiny raise of his right cheek. "Sorry to interrupt."

"Go on." Kyriakos gestured toward me. *Did Kit know I was going to be here?* My palms were sweatier, my breathing was shorter, and any eloquence I had previously possessed was lost. As I read, Kit's eyes burned into me. I crossed and uncrossed my legs and raced to the end of the essay.

"For a first go," Kyriakos steepled his fingers in thought, before finally saying, "not terrible."

"I agree." Kit nodded.

Thanks, I thought.

"I wanted to explore in particular the argument," I started saying, mainly to prove that I wasn't intimidated by Kit's presence, "that the conflict between the supremacy of Parliament and European Union legislation is overstated by some."

"That's interesting," Kit countered, leaning forward, elbows on knees, "because many scholars would say that the practical operation of European law has rendered the concept of Parliamentary supremacy entirely redundant.

Haven't you read the House of Lords' judgment in *Factortame*?" The corner of his mouth raised slightly as he doubled down. "Indeed, some would even say that it goes so far as to damage our country's democracy."

"It's become politically charged," I said. "How is EU membership any different from other international treaties and laws the UK has signed up to and must uphold?"

"You really think that? You think it has just become weaponized by the Eurosceptics? Surely that's a bit reductionist?"

"There are obviously strong arguments for both sides," I backtracked, before deciding to hold my ground, "but yes, I think the specific vilification of EU membership has been engineered by certain parties to further a narrative that benefits them."

"And what, if you are right, is the end goal?"

Damn, I thought, *isn't Kyriakos meant to be the professor?*

"There have been calls to leave the EU for decades, and they are only gaining momentum," I responded.

"Mark my words," Kyriakos boomed, his Greek accent amplified, "we will never leave the European Union."

"Hey!" Kit called after me as I walked back to my room.

"Hello, Mr. Farage," I quipped, "running late to the UKIP conference?"

"Come on," he laughed. "Bit harsh?"

"Ditto." I nodded toward Kyriakos's office. "You could have gone easier on me."

"Where would be the integrity in that?" he laughed. "Kyriakos loves it. He bangs on about it all the time, crushing his students then building them back up. Trust me."

I carried on walking. I was so frustrated. The whole point of those sessions was to argue, so I couldn't exactly be angry about that. He hadn't contacted me after that perfect night. Why hadn't he contacted me? *Had I done something wrong?*

"I was excited to see you again," he said, walking next to me. I kept my head steadfastly forward, even though my heart might have fluttered out of my chest. *So he did know I was going to be there.* "What are you up to tonight?"

"Another derelict place of worship you'd like me to tour?"

"Jade?"

"Sorry," I said, "nothing."

"I'm going to London this afternoon," he said.

"And?"

"Come with?"

After our candlelit ragù, I snuck off to the bathroom to apply more Vagisil. Two paracetamols down, I was still twinging with soreness. I nestled into Kit for a catch-up episode of *Bake Off*. Weeknights were an impossibility for us, given my job and Kit's as a public affairs advisor, reacting with urgency to each day's events as they unfolded. I couldn't stop yawning.

"If you fall asleep before the first ad break, that'll be a record," Kit said. My head was in his lap, and he twirled my hair around his wrist.

"I slept terribly last night," I said, "had some seriously creepy dreams. Obviously, I've completely forgotten what about." I reached for my wineglass, and the ring stain on my grandmother's cabinet flashed in my mind's eye. I quickly brushed past my edginess. Committed it to the archives. "But I know it was creepy."

"You need to stop watching those gory murder documentaries."

Both our heads turned reflexively toward the sound of one of the four phones on the table; we each had a work and a personal. They say women have evolved to wake to the sound of a crying baby. Us overworked millennials were conditioned to come alive at the vibration of an iPhone. I'd changed the notification settings so that work and personal emails had two different alerts: *bell chimes* required urgent attention, *pulse* could wait.

From Genevieve LaGarde to Jade Kaya on November 11, 2018 at 9:35 pm
RE: FIRE DRILL

Jade—call me.

"I'm sorry," I began, "it's wor—"

Kit raised both hands in conciliation. "Duty calls."

Arrow hotspots across London lit up as Will, Genevieve, and I dialed into a conference call at 9:45 on a Sunday night. Arrow's aim was to move wealth away from oil, gas, and arms, and redirect it toward "conscious" companies. Their slogan was: *Money makes the world go round. Arrow points it in the right direction*. An advertising budget well spent, I'd say. After the Claim Form was filed and the allegations hit the papers in a media flurry, another former employee had emerged tonight with further accusations of greased palms.

Kit sat at the other end of the sofa, massaging my feet. He

brought me a stream of black coffee and biscuits. He hung on my door my staple outfit of black trousers and a silk shirt for work tomorrow, knowing I'd be pulling an all-nighter. He eventually retreated to bed with an eye mask and ear-plugs, so that I wouldn't have to fumble in the dark. At five thirty in the morning, I scrambled in behind him to snatch two hours of sleep before a taxi would arrive to take me to Arrow's offices. Kit, half-asleep, rolled over and pulled me in to his chest.

6

2816 was the number Adele and I shared. Floor 28, room 16. A number that was in our email signatures so that other members of the Firm could map us out in this stacked lasagne of lawyers. Offices were set out around the perimeter of the building, with glass walls that hung over the City. No windows that opened. Open-door policy to "promote collaboration," but more so it could be noted if you weren't at your desk. In the center of each floor was a glass-cubed meeting room called the fishbowl. As a student, I'd imagined that working in a law firm would be lots of screaming into headsets, coffee cups hurled across desks before boozed-up lunches. So the biggest surprise was how silent it was. People actually worked. They worked a lot.

The days since the Savoy had been manic. Project Arrow turned on accusations that Arrow's senior manager regularly received bribes to fix corrupt deals. Some of these illegal negotiations lined the pockets of influential people in cabinets and C-suites. The exposure of a criminal underbelly to a supposedly "ethical" firm was a complete PR clusterfuck that needed damage control. Reuben was instructed to defend Arrow, and no stone was to be left unturned. I billed sixteen hours combing through texts that were never meant to see the light of day and emails the senders thought were deleted. *The standard is perfection. Got it?*

I subsisted entirely on Deliveroo for fourteen days in a row. Dining *al desko* was in vogue. Some nights Kit used his set of keys to sleep at my place, and I snuggled up to his back at two a.m., only to leave before he woke. I did revolvers often: a taxi would take me home in the dead of night, park outside for half an hour while I showered and changed, then the same taxi would bring me back to 2816. My work phone was face up at every event I arrived late to and left early from. Corporate jargon bled into my everyday language; I even suggested to Eve that we should "circle back" for a catch-up when we had more "bandwidth." *Who says that?*

The exhaustion seemed to be causing increasingly abstract nightmares that I couldn't piece together in the morning. A nightly rigmarole of silky, noxious darkness. Unable to make out in the morning what lurked beneath. The working hours compounded with the disrupted sleep made me lose snatches of memory: *shit, so sorry, happy belated birthday*; *hello, Ms. Kaya, you missed your appointment today*; *where have I left my gym bag?* I was flustered, zombiefied. I did feel a pathetic gratification when friends cooed about how tired I must be. My base state was one of vibrating tension, of constant anxiety that I might have missed a key email. Work had monopolized my entire life.

"Man, do I need that." Adele reached for me as I arrived in our office with two cappuccinos. "Gimme gimme gimme."

"You all right?" I asked.

projected upward, etching a romantic image of a long summer evening in a Côte d'Azur oasis, laughing with lifelong friends over a bottle of Bandol.

"Jade, come in." Genevieve summoned me into her office, which had mastered the art of minimalism without being clinical. The color palette was three varying shades of beige that somehow managed not to be bland.

"Nice photo. Is that new?" I gestured to the only personal touch in the vast room: a framed picture on her desk of two boys in the bathtub, with toothless grins, covered in soapy bubbles. Genevieve was leaning into the tub, splashed gingham shirt and soft tendrils falling on her face. I speculated that the candid picture was placed there as propaganda. It was positioned facing visitors, not her. She was Arrow's CEO, and that proximity to power had to be offset by showcasing her role as a mother. Suddenly she was nurturing, caring. The tedious, tired narrative of the firesome dragon lady transformed into *how did she do it? With two small boys? She's superwoman!* One wrong step, and that could easily mutate into *she chose work over family, how selfish.*

"Yes, yes, it is," she said absentmindedly. Others at Reuben found her clipped tone rude and dismissive. I thought there was a typical Parisian charm to how little she cared for British platitudes.

"Have you been able to review the documents?"

"We have, we're preparing to give you a full briefing next we—"

"Be honest." She cut across me. "How much are we looking at?"

"Quantum hasn't been decided yet," I said sheepishly. Genevieve raised one fluffy eyebrow. I explained, using all the caveats lawyers were hated for, that she should expect the claim to be for "substantial" damages.

"How much?" She grilled me again, knowing that providing an exact figure was above my pay grade. I think she enjoyed my attempts at diplomacy.

"It's in the nature of these covert dealings that nothing is recorded, so it's hard to tell. But ballpark three hundred." I didn't need to add the "million."

Genevieve exhaled sharply, her expression pendulating between rage and mourning.

"Well, at least we know now we have an idea what we're facing," Genevieve sighed.

I looked down in a show of discretion, and nodded.

"Jade," Genevieve said after a pause, "do you know what the key pattern I've noticed in nearly three decades in this industry is?"

I was used to her abstract, philosophical musings. I now only wore men's cologne because Genevieve told me it was a power move. She also told me exclamation marks were sinful (!!).

"After all the companies I've funded, nurtured. No matter what you give," she said as she stared out of the panoramic window, "they'll try to take more."

It took me a second too long to find the words to respond. Genevieve blinked suddenly, as if she'd been jolted out of a trance. She perked up, signed the documents I'd brought to her, while I took mental snapshots of her environment. She had all the subtle cues of quiet wealth. No ostentatious branding in sight. She opted for the upper echelon of luxury props, the if-you-know-you-know items: Hermès Kelly, Loro Piana blanket on her velvet sofa, Goyard wallet. She would have a drawer full of silk pajamas and cashmere socks. Her seven-bedroom Fitzrovia town house would not have a single particle of dust within it. She would have a kitchen fridge that was always fully stocked, and a separate garage drinks fridge. She wore heavy, thick gold bangles, which clanged together as she signed the final document with a flourish.

"Lunch?"

We went to a tiny, buzzy bistro garden on the King's Road. This part of town had an air of leisure. The landscape was peppered with immaculately dressed women under heaters, mohair blankets across their legs. I had French onion soup and beef carpaccio drizzled in balsamic glaze, and Genevieve ordered rock oysters. She slurped one before tutting that she should have known better than to order seafood in the city.

"You don't mind if I order something else?" she asked me, before saying to the waiter anyway, "The pear salad. And a carafe of your driest white. Two glasses." She spun her arm out, waiting for him to take her menu. I smiled weakly at him in recompense for her lack of niceties.

"We have plenty of time." Genevieve smiled, noticing me glance at my work phone on the table. A symbol of a mind on duty. I'd been away from my desk for nearly two hours. Will had emailed half an hour ago: *Came by, you're not back from Arrow? Update?*

"Jade, you've impressed me," Genevieve said, always forthright. "I've worked with David's place for years, and he knows that's rare."

I started a nod, then promptly stopped myself. When did we internalize that it was arrogant for a woman to openly acknowledge her ability? Genevieve double-tapped a box of cigarettes on the table, never taking her eyes off me as she lit one. The maître d' earned his tip by tactfully placing us around a corner where Genevieve could puff in peace. She propped her elbows on the table, cigarette glowing in her left hand, and rested her chin in her other palm. Her nails were glossy rouge surfboards. "What do you want?" she finally said.

"Sorry?" I laughed as the chilled wine arrived. I poured her a glass.

"You English are so strange. *Sorry?* Why must you apologize always?"

"Sorr—" I stopped myself. "What do you mean?"

She tutted, blowing smoke out. "I mean, what is it that you want? In life!" The creases of her mouth had perfected their fold around her cigarette. "Come on, you must have thought about it. Oh là là, don't tell me you don't know."

I thought about it for a moment, all the while flushing under her scrutiny. My parents wanted me to be a lawyer, and that's what I became. Indeed, I hadn't given it much thought. I didn't yearn for marriage and babies; a homemaker I was not. I didn't write ballads at night. I didn't run marathons on weekends. I didn't hoard knowledge on a niche topic of interest online.

"I want security," I admitted, before immediately feeling twee for giving such a drab answer.

"Aha!" She pointed her scarlet-tipped fingers at me as they still held the blunted ciggy. "And how will you get there?"

"I'm not sure," I said, but Genevieve raised her eyebrows at me. "Paying off my student loan is the first step."

"Yes," she said, "there is nothing elegant about being indebted."

"I eventually want a house," I said finally. I wouldn't dream of being this candid with any other client. But Genevieve and I had a nascent alliance. When she first called David Reuben for assistance on the case, he sent Will and a team of four male associates. By all accounts, Genevieve laughed in Will's face. She propped her Kelly on the table and pulled out a copy of Hesse's *Siddhartha*. Told Will the meeting would not go ahead until a woman was brought onto the team. Nodded at him to *take your time*. Will had sent me a frantic email:

Jade—45 Cadogan Mews. ASAP!

"Good." Genevieve nodded. "You need to know what you want." A cunning side smile before she said, "How else will we get you there?"

I felt a surge of warmth for her.

"Thank you, Gen—" I tried to say, but her hand flew up to stop me.

"I'm not in the business of charity." A woman in total control of herself. "I was like you. Shy. Especially in London, with this accent? Nightmare. Then Catherine Deneuve did *Le Dernier Métro*, and suddenly it was fashionable." She noticed my lost expression. "Anyway, don't thank me. You're the one who will be doing the hard work."

I called a cab to take me back to Reuben, delighted that my path had crossed with Genevieve's. I wondered how I could emulate her airy confidence. In my first week, I spelled "judgment" (in the legal sense) as "judgement" (in the normal English sense), and Will asked me *exactly how many lobotomies have you had?* Genevieve wouldn't take being spoken to like that.

"Hi!" I said, pulling open the passenger door and sliding into the cab. "For Jade?"

The driver nodded in his rearview mirror. "To the City?"

"Yes. Thanks." I looked around the cab. It was stuffy. I pressed the button to open the window. There was the overpowering alpine smell of the car freshener. Suddenly, my brain was scrambled, my sight hypnotized by the freshener as it dangled from the mirror. I got déjà vu. Without particularity or specificity, there was the vague sense that this little green tree was telling me something. I broke my gaze away, exasperated that the window had remained firmly up.

"Excuse me?" I said to the driver. He had an AirPod in and was muttering on the phone.

"What?" He sounded like the Gruffalo.

"Do you mind if I open the window?"

"Child lock," he barked, before returning to his call. The motion of the tree's swing was hypnotizing; it reminded me of my head swaying from side to side that night we drove over Waterloo Bridge.

We.

We?

Was there someone else in the car?

Alarm rose from my stomach, up my throat, pricked my eyeballs, and tingled the roots of my hair.

"Sorry. Excuse me?" My voice was smaller this time. A cyclist whizzed past the window as horns blared.

"What?"

"Sorry, I really need some fresh air, please, could you lower the window?"

"Too cold. It's November, lady."

At school, a teacher once described me as "contained" and "cerebral." I had complained to my parents that it was odd feedback. I didn't know what she meant. Until I was no longer contained nor cerebral.

"Stop the car."

"Relaaax, lady."

A vile panic calcified at the base of my throat.

"Stop the car now."

"Why?"

"Let me out of the car!"

We screeched to a halt just after a bus lane. I pulled ferociously on the door handle, pressing my body weight against the door. I needed to get out of here. *Get me out of here.*

"I told you, lady, it's child lock! What's your problem?"

"You can't lock me in your car. *LET ME OUT!*" The driver's eyes were disbelieving. He sighed and pushed a button on his steering wheel, and I heard the mechanics of the locks click open.

"Crazy lady," he muttered as I lurched my body out, like a drowning person gasping for air.

After an hour's walk, I finally arrived back at the office. With each step, the relaxed affluence of Chelsea morphed into the oppressive glorification of Green Park into the student throngs of the Strand. I halted viciously—like I'd walked into a glass wall—when I passed the Savoy. Its glitz looked ironic in the harsh daylight, the luxurious art deco facade incongruent with the quick-stop coffee franchises a few steps away. I peered at the entrance, willing an explanation to come to me. I continued marching toward the City. Women in Max

Mara cashmere coats were gradually replaced by men who apparently all shared the same barber.

"And then, he has the audacity to ask me for recommendations of books with a *strong female lead*," Eve was ranting to Adele as I walked in. "Imagine that! After squeezing two women out of his team for not being culture fits." She did air quotes around "culture fits." Two senior associates had disappeared from Eve's team, no goodbyes, no leaving drinks. Their profiles were still on the website, so they were technically still with the Firm. Their offices archaeologically preserved: cups of tea with lipstick marks scattered across their desks, their children's crayoned scribbles still push-pinned into corkboards. No explanation was provided. Everyone knew not to ask for one.

I drifted in. Adele was lounging back in her ergonomic chair, legs splayed, eyes sparkling. Eve's butt was perched on the edge of the desk, ankles crossed, gathered. "There you are!" Eve said brightly. "Thought I'd come by and see how you were when you didn't show to the call earlier."

I don't remember leaving the Savoy with anyone?

I don't remember leaving the Savoy at all.

"Earth to Jade!" Adele called, waving her arms at me.

I snapped back into the room. "Hey guys. Sorry, I'm just spaced out."

"Had a cheeky vino at lunch, did we?" Eve teased.

I sank into my chair and turned my monitor on. *I didn't have any Uber receipts, so I must have shared a cab with someone. It would have been a colleague. I hope I didn't say something embarrassing.*

"Looks like you're busy, Jadey. I'll swing by later for dinner?" Eve said. "I have a ten p.m. call, so maybe we can all order from that sushi place and eat in the conference rooms before?"

In my periphery, the two shared glances. Eve shrugged while Adele eyeballed me. They nodded at each other and Eve left, closing the door behind her. A bangled arm reached over my desk, and a finger with chipped polish clicked out of my emails. Adele swung my chair around.

"Hey," she said, with that Boston robustness to the word, "everything kosher with you?"

I think so.

There was nothing actively wrong with me, at least.

"Everything's fine," I said. "I think I'm just really tired."

7

Kit Campbell, 8:05 am:
Morning my love, how are you? Xx

Jade Kaya, 9:30 am:
Crazy busy, running into another meeting. Miss you x

Kit Campbell, 12:36 pm:
I'm passing by your office, do you want to grab lunch?

Kit Campbell, 2:20 pm:
Will you be working this weekend? Em and Ollie have invited us round to meet their new puppy x

Kit Campbell, 5:14 pm:
I've linked you a band on Spotify, so up your alley.

Kit Campbell, 6:40 pm:
I miss you.

Jade Kaya, 7:35 pm:
Hey babe, I'm so sorry been completely slammed.
It's been mental.
Been running around like a headless chicken all day.
Literally so overwhelmed.
I'm crying in the toilets.
I cannot remember the last time I had a proper meal.
Gah.

Jade Kaya, 8:10 pm:
Missing you x

Kit Campbell, 10:20 pm:
Was at the pub with the guys. Sounds rough my love. Please try and take it easier—looking forward to seeing my girl tomorrow x

Jade Kaya, 11:52 pm:
Promise I won't miss it. Love you xx

"I'm here, I'm sorry, so sorry." I bundled toward Kit. "How long have you been waiting?"

"You're all right, not too long," he said. I planted a kiss on him and lingered for a few extra seconds. Since the Savoy weekend, I had missed the following two of our Sundays, spending full weekends on Project Arrow. I expensed pillows and had them delivered to the office, catching naps under my desk. Will gave me work at midnight and asked me to *turn it around by S.O.B.* Emails flooded my inbox at a rate faster than I could read them. I was fully aware that I found self-worth in overwork. A crisp *good job* from a senior was enough validation to keep the engine running. I felt an urgent need to respond to emails at lightning speed. To keep my Skype status green. I once apologized for not replying to an email I got at two a.m. until six a.m. A busy day was referred to in the office as one spent "firefighting," such was the inflated sense of emergency. And of course, self-aggrandization. I relied on Kit to hold the fort. He often said independence and ambition were the most attractive traits in a woman. He understood that sometimes our relationship would have to take the back burner and he would be there to catch me when the thread I was hanging on finally frayed.

Time was a precious scarcity and I'd usually Uber straight from the office to shave ten minutes on the journey. But I hadn't slept well since that cab ride after lunch with Genevieve. It had hatched an ambiguous fear and my senses continued to fire afterward. I couldn't shake that panic of entrapment, so I'd hauled across town on a Boris bike instead, wincing with each pedal as the tough saddle rubbed against my sore spot. We had a table booked at the Coach House. It was freezing, but they'd made it cozy in the beer garden, with couples huddled under patio heaters, sharing tartan blankets. The Coach House was "our place"—every couple has one. Somewhere that your love is indigenous to.

Kit first brought me here seven years ago today. After Kyriakos's class, getting on the train with him felt independent and irresponsible. Tension corkscrewed my insides when we were together. *What was the right way to act around him?* He'd still not acknowledged our kiss in the chapel.

He suggested we go to a place called the Coach House. The first thing I noticed were the dog treats at the entrance under a sign of a Labrador.

"Take a seat, I'll grab us drinks," he had said, his hand grazing the small of my back. I reached for words to explain the effect his touch had on me, but it felt beyond me.

"So, law," Kit stated as I settled into the glass of wine he handed me. I hated wine at the time, but it's not like I could ask him for a Fanta.

"What do you mean?"

"Why did you go for it?"

"I really don't know," I said listlessly. Kit studied me but said nothing. "There were probably other subjects I might have liked more, but uni isn't really about enjoyment, right?"

"It's about intellectual growth, don't you think? Took me a couple of gap years to figure out what subject would keep me ticking over."

I looked at him blankly.

He continued, "What would you have studied if you didn't feel obliged to choose law?"

"I didn't say I felt oblig—"

"I know you didn't," he said softly, "I'm sorry for assuming."

I eyed Kit over my glass, suspicious of how mildly he breached my defenses.

"English, I think."

"I can see that . . ." Kit trailed off. "But I think that would have been a mistake."

I scoffed.

"Laugh all you want," he said, "your essay this morning was really eloquent. I thought the euthanasia piece might have been a fluke, but you proved me wrong."

"Are you trying to be complimentary?" I said. "You're not very good at it."

The corner of his lip lifted. "You might not realize it, but everyone there"—he gestured vaguely around him, I assumed to signify our peers, before leaning forward—"they're all spoon-fed toffs who perform self-hatred about how easy they've had it when actually, deep deep down, they feel entitled to everything they have."

"Odd," I said, my index finger circling the rim of the wineglass, "I don't think there's anything self-hating about you."

"Touché," he wheezed. "You're right. I wish I could be more proud of myself. Like you can be."

"I thought you were done assuming things about me." I feigned prickliness because I guessed it would make me seem aloof and uninterested in his view of me.

"Well, if you're not proud of yourself, you should be."

What did pride have to do with it? I was about to ask what he meant by that, when Kit said, "There's someone I want you to meet."

His face lifted as he looked past me into the middle distance. I turned to see a woman in her fifties swanning in. She was in a crisply ironed pale-blue shirt, oversized blazer, cropped straight-leg jeans and, white plimsoles. She welcomed me with outstretched arms, auburn head tilted and a wonky smile.

"Honey, come here," she exclaimed. I didn't have time to hide my surprise before she enveloped me into a huge hug. "So excited to meet you."

"Jade, this is my mum, Angela."

I was shocked. *His mum? What are the chances of running into her? On our first date? Is this even a date?* I tried to quickly gather my composure.

"Mrs. Campbell! Such a pleasure to meet you." I was keen to come across as the picture of politeness.

"Call me Angie. Mrs. Campbell is my husband's mother as far as I'm concerned!"

"London's such a small world," I exclaimed, "running into you like this."

Kit smiled lovingly. "Jade," he said under his breath, "the Coach House is ours."

"Oh, sorry, I didn't know." I felt a bit provincial for not realizing. So his family owns this place.

Kit reached over and kissed his mum on the cheek. *How civilized was this?* I rarely saw my parents outside their house, whereas Kit and Angie's interaction was so inherently social. So casual. I couldn't imagine updating my parents about a boy I fancied that I'd met only twice before. Angie turned to me while Kit was hanging up her blazer.

"It seems you have quite enraptured my firstborn, he's been texting me about bringing you here tonight," she whispered conspiratorially, nudging me with her elbow. She was so chic, radiating affection. I imagined her as a high-society starlet in her youth, frequenting *Tatler*'s Bystander pages, attending glamorous parties that moonlighted as charity galas. "And I can certainly see why!"

I smiled, not knowing how to act. After a few more minutes of small talk, Angie plucked up her fashionably weathered Mulberry Bayswater bag and kissed us both on the cheeks. "Okay, my loves, I'll get out of your hair. Have a delightful evening!"

"Your mum is gorgeous," I said as we sat back down.

"She's great."

"Will your dad be coming by tonight as well?"

Kit's head turned robotically toward me, as if I had activated a troubleshooting mode.

"No." He cleared his throat. "He'll be in Notting Hill. With Lisa."

There was a new slipperiness in his voice.

"Is she one of your sisters?"

Kit laughed mockingly, though it seemed he was mocking Lisa, not me.

"Absolutely not."

"We can talk about something else," I mumbled.

"No, it's honestly fine." Kit shrugged, with the tense machoism of a man who has learned to not show that anything remotely bothered him. "We can talk about it. We were in Provence, we didn't know it at the time, but it was our last normal family holiday." Kit looked into the fire we were sat opposite of. "My middle sister hit her head doing a cannonball in the pool. There's blood—it always looks worse spreading in water. Dad rushes toward her, screaming, 'Liv, Liv, are you okay?' "

There was a pause. This detail was important.

"My sister's called Elizabeth."

I gasped.

"Mum and Dad are freaking out—my sister was fine in the end, just a concussion. But the bomb had starting ticking. Two days later, over family dinner, it's like a switch flipped. I remember that exact moment." Kit clicked his fingers. "I think that was the moment our family imploded. Mum looks up and goes, 'Ian, who the hell is Liv?' "

"Wow."

"He laughs and insists he said 'Liz,' you know, for 'Lizzie.' Said she must have heard wrong. But the show was already over."

"What happened after that?"

"It came out that Dad had another daughter. The same age as Lizzie—three months apart." Kit almost laughed. "He had an entire double life with his second family. Lisa and Olivia. Liv."

"That's awful," I finally said, slightly shell-shocked. "I'm so sorry. How old were you?"

"Sixteen."

"That's so much for you to cope with at that age." I was eighteen, but I acted like sixteen was distinctly adolescent. I was putting the story together in my head; Angie referred to her "husband" earlier.

"It was fine for me, I had my friends and stuff. My sisters were younger, though. And I know how important having a stable home life is for girls at that age. We flew home and, as soon as we were on British soil, it was like a decision was made: Dad told us we shouldn't upset Mum by bringing it up and, somewhere along the way, that morphed into us all turning a blind eye." Kit sighed. "Dad still spends most weeknights with them; it's so blatant. The nights he's at home with Mum, they stick to their separate quarters of the house. But we never speak about it."

"Never?"

"Never."

I leaned forward and touched his arm. I hadn't had a conversation like this before. That recounted an emotionally fraught experience so openly. To a practical stranger. Omma and Baba had a strict code of silence: family matters stayed within the family. I wanted to show that I could match him on his level, this older guy who had whisked me away from the juvenility of campus to drink wine with grown-ups in leafy pockets of London.

"Life since," Kit continued, "was an eye-opener for me. It's kinda like once it was all out in the open, Dad was free to live this brand-spanking-new life with Lisa and Liv in private, as long as he would go along with Mum's wish for the Happy Campbells in public." He pulled a wry smile. "Being a dad to us since has meant throwing us money. He buys us whatever we ask for on our birthdays, but never spends the day with us. Pays for my sisters' school fees, but hasn't showed up to a single parents' evening. It's one of those things that makes you see, like *seriously*, that money can't replace love. Do you know what I mean?"

I nodded, not knowing what he meant. I was mainly curious about his quartered house.

"God," he suddenly said, "I'm sorry."

"What for? You don't have to be sorry."

There was a pause.

"It's strange," he said, "I've never felt more comfortable saying these things to anyone. I'm lucky to have met you, Jade."

"You don't know me," I murmured, trying to remain nonchalant, while my heart was singing and angels were fanfaring.

"Cheers," Kit said now, holding up his glass. "Happy anniversary!"

"Cheers." I clinked my glass against his, finally relaxing from my nightmarish month.

"Who would have thought, eh? That we'd still be going strong after all these years?"

I put my hand on my heart and mocked concern. "You're not getting the seven-year itch, are you?"

He stood up and walked around the table, as my eyes followed him. He squeezed himself on the bench I was on, lifting the blanket off my lap and swinging both my legs over his. Festoon lights crisscrossed behind him, the heaters crackled and candles flickered in their tumblers. He wrapped his arms around my waist, pulling me closer to him and kissing the tip of my nose.

"Far from it."

"Good, 'cos you're stuck with me."

"Oh"—he pulled back and patted his pockets—"before I forget, I wanted to give this to you."

Kit began digging around and pulled out a small dark-green velvet box. Men in their late twenties loved to engagement fish. But Kit was understandably disillusioned about marriage, and I'd always agreed that it should not be the end goal for us, feeling very nouveau in my rejection of institution. I inhaled deeply and flipped the top open. Inside, a glint of gold. Hanging from the chain was a light-green spherical pendant, nestled on the satin cushion.

"It's a jade stone," Kit explained. "Do you like it?"

I gasped appropriately. The necklace looked antique, with a weathering to the gold that showed it was solid.

"I love it," I said. I pulled his face toward mine and kissed him. "And I love you."

He lifted the necklace out and fumbled to fasten it, before admiring it burrowed in the hollow of my throat. "To many more years with you."

I smiled and my hand went to my neck. Kit got up to go to the bathroom, as one of the Campbells' longest-serving employees came over. He set two wineglasses directly in front of me before opening the Malbec Kit had ordered. With a twist of his wrist, the cork was released with a hollow burp. My gaze blinkered on the deep red welling inside the glass, my body suddenly welded to the bench as the din of the Coach House fell away.

"This Malbec looks . . ." My hearing was muffled, like I had water in my ears. Words apple-bobbed around my head, evading me. My flat was nothing but sensory fuzz around me. My body felt so light it could levitate and, at the same time, sinkingly heavy.

"Yeah." The only word I could bite into.

". . . corkscrew?"

I waved my hand in the general direction of the kitchen. My arm dropped like a dead weight.

My knees wobbled and I dropped onto the sofa. Faint clanging. My eyelids drooped.

The scene was blank for a moment, like a buffering video, before coming back alive. There was a glass in my limp hand, about to tip over.

"I . . . I don't . . ."

It's so late. I need to sleep.

"You're not going to let me drink alone, are you?"

"And here're your starters, enjoy!"

I blinked. *You're okay*, I told myself, *it's okay*. My palms were damp, my eyelids stapled open. *Who was that? When was that?* My pulse rampaged around my skull and sloshed in my eardrums. I jumped as Kit, walking up behind me, clapped his hands together at the food.

"Yum, I'm starving!" We'd ordered a round of shell-on prawns and bruschetta, along with some crispy calamari.

"So," Kit began with trepidation, "when is work going to stop flogging you?"

"Ugh! Can we not?" I whined.

"I'm really worried about you, J." He stroked my arm, a decapitated prawn head in the other hand. Fingers glistening with garlic oil. "I don't want you to fall into the trap of mistaking overwork as an opportunity to prove yourself. Been there, done that."

"I'm not sure what other choice I have."

Kit sighed. "You just seem so stressed. All the time."

"I am stressed all the time." I rubbed my eyes in exasperation.

"I know, but you're going to burn yourself out. And I realize you did the same for me, but it's getting really rubbish not seeing you for a fortnight at a time."

Kit, straight after finishing his law degree, decided that a job in law wasn't for him after all. Three years of tuition fees were incomparable to the moral cost of being in blinkered complicity with us Machiavellian corporates. His calling was shortly discovered at Calthorpe Communications, a public affairs firm specializing in political advisory. It didn't have a website for a reason. Read: spin-doctoring, engineering tactical leaks, image mop-ups, smoothing ethical potholes. All in the name of a utopian end that supposedly justified the means. As I was four years younger than Kit, during my student years I patiently orbited my time around his burgeoning career. Rushed dinners, relentless quoting of *The West Wing*,

BBC Parliament on constantly, canceled holidays following another MP's blunder, describing himself as *apolitical*. Particularly arduous was his phase of listening to podcasts with titles such as *The Five Rules of Persuasion* and reading books solely about power or manipulation. I only lost my temper with him once, after he'd explained the Chatham House Rule to me for the third time during the same dinner.

"I'm sorry it's so tough," he said.

"It's actually better now. You know Genevieve—the client at Arrow?"

"What about her?"

"She likes me."

"Who wouldn't?" Kit said with a grin that mildly irritated me.

"I'm serious. It's a big deal."

"I know it is!"

"Do you? I've never had anyone back me before," I said, unable to stop the bitterness leaking into my voice. Kit's godfather was none other than the eponymous Sebastian Calthorpe, of Calthorpe Communications. Kit stopped chewing for a moment, surprised at my tone. "I love working for her. She's—I don't know—a mentor?"

"I'm so proud of you. You're finally being recognized for your talent."

I was slightly annoyed again at the implication that we were all subject to blind meritocracy. I couldn't stay mad, though, especially when he ordered champagne to celebrate our anniversary. I tried to ignore the pangs of stress at the sudden reminder of the amount of champagne I managed to down at the Savoy. Instead, I let Kit take my hand and forced my mind to go blank.

• • •

"I've missed you so much," Kit murmured, pulling my sweater over my head as we stumbled backward into my bedroom. Somewhere around glass two or three of champagne we'd exchanged looks signaling that it was on tonight. Over the years, sex fell lower and lower on our relationship agenda. I still found Kit hugely attractive. When I saw him across a room, I often noticed other eyes glancing toward him and felt a swell of pride that he was mine. When he was in his navy suit and me in my pencil-skirt set, I was turned on by how we looked commuting to the City together. How young, professional, and successful we must look. We last had sex over a month ago, on his birthday. It could have been years since we'd fucked. But that's fine. Our sex life was replaced by the arousal I felt when someone commented that we made a gorgeous couple.

Kit unhooked my bra. He knelt on the ground and started kissing my stomach.

"Look at how smooth your skin is." His big hands gripped my arse as he suddenly lifted me up and threw me on the bed. After a few minutes between my legs, Kit sprang up and flipped me onto my stomach. He pulled my hips toward the edge of the bed and stood behind me, pushing into me. I flinched. *We haven't had sex in ages, I'll loosen up in a bit.*

He held my wrists behind my back and pushed my head into the pillow. I couldn't see, and with the angle of my body, the booze rushed to my head. My nose was squashed against the pillow and I couldn't breathe. His grip tightened on the back of my head. Panic rose inside me as I gasped for air, feeling only the cotton pillowcase against my tongue. In my head I was thrashing against him, but I felt like I was screaming into a vacuum. My mouth was open, but no sound was coming out. I screwed my eyes shut. I wanted to see a blank black void. Something neutral until this was over. Instead, an image flicked on, like a photographic slide turning in a projector. In it, I was in the same position, face down on the bed, but my cheek was on the pillow, my gaze sideways. My eyelids were the heaviest things I'd ever carried, keeping them open a strain. Just as my eyes shut, an opaque silhouette, flimsy but dangerous like black smoke, came round the side of the bed.

Something within me gave way, and an intense pain ripped through my core. With newfound strength, I pried my head up.

"Ow ow, stop, Kit, stop, stop!" I screeched, back rising like an angry cat and trying to pull my body off his.

"What? What's wrong?" Kit pulled out and half his penis was coated in blood. Not the brown blood from the remnants of my period, but visceral scarlet blood. I coiled myself into a fetal position and tears poured down my face. *Who who who was that? Is my mind playing tricks on me?*

"What is it, Jade?"

In the background, Kit was asking me question after question. *What was that? Are you okay? Talk to me. Jade? Jade? I didn't mean to hurt you. Are you all right?* It was white noise. I remained curled up in the bed, unresponsive. After a while, I can't say how long, Kit lay down next to me.

Some hours later, my eyes flickered open and my heart slammed against my rib cage. Someone was here. A shadow, but definitely a person. A man. At the foot of the bed, approaching me. *What do you want?* I tried to scream, but no sound came out. The room was undulating. He reached an arm out. It felt like hours, his reaching for me. He clamped my ankle and tugged me toward him as I thrashed to free myself.

"Jade! Jade!"

Kit? I thought. *Where are you?*

Help me.

"Jade, wake up!" Kit was shaking me. I kept throwing myself into wilder and wilder shapes. "Please, Jade."

I ripped out of one dimension into another as I bolted awake. Kit was half on top of me, gently holding me down from accidentally hitting him. I turned frantically to take in the surroundings. My IKEA wardrobes with the doors still open, my ugly bra hanging up next to my sexy bra. Last night's outfit thrown on the armchair in the corner that always had a rotating pile of clothes on it. There was no one else here. *I need to work less. The stress is clearly getting to me.* I looked at my grandmother's walnut bedside table, the ring still boldly branded into it, and a chill scurried up my spine.

8

"It'll be okay." Kit placed a hand on my knee to ground my frenetic leg-bouncing. The artificial white light was jarring for my red-rimmed eyes, so they flitted around like trapped flies. I fixated on the collection of pamphlets on display, the wording faded and yellowing. Hot anxiety was brewing in my stomach. I repeatedly massaged a lump of Blu Tack I found in my pocket, and when that didn't provide the relief I needed, my hand drifted to my eye. I held my outer eyelashes between my thumb and forefinger and yanked. Uprooted lashes fluttered to the ground. I wondered if it still counted if I made a wish.

"Jade," Kit spoke, "c'mon, stop." He guided my hand away from my face and held it firmly in his. Not to comfort, more to contain.

"Sorry," I mumbled. "I'm so nervous."

"There's nothing to be nervous about."

Absently, the fingers on my free hand sought out the skin around my thumb. Using the nail of my index finger, I attacked the dry groove on my cuticle. I hooked the skin and tore it away.

"Erm, not sure I'm gonna get this right," the receptionist called out to the waiting room, giggling. "Say-da Kaya-ogg-loo?"

"That's me," I said, getting up.

"The nurse is ready for you—in consultation room five."

"So weird when they call you that." Kit stretched his arm around me and squeezed my shoulder. "I'll be out here, okay?"

"Hello, my love, I'm Andreea," the nurse said as I walked into the consultation room and took a seat. Her face was heart-shaped and plump. A welcome sight. "Full name, please?"

"Ceyda Kayaoğlu."

"What a lovely name!"

"Thanks," I said, self-conscious. "You can call me Jade."

In Turkish, the letter *C* is pronounced like the *J* in jelly. Ceyda was therefore pronounced "Jay-da." Turks only officially adopted surnames in the twentieth century. Prior to that, men distinguished themselves from their fathers with the suffix "oglu": *the son of*. Much like "Johnson." Kayaoğlu means *the son of the rock*, I like to think because my ancestors were tough as boulders. As preteens, us girls squandered our pocket money at the Starbucks kiosk near our school. One day, during Frappuccino season, I gave the name Ceyda when ordering. The barista must have missed the second syllable. He didn't know he was setting off a light bulb of self-actualization when scrawling *Jade* on the coffee cup. *How simple.* Ceyda Kayaoğlu was snuffed out in the years that followed, and Jade Kaya stepped into her shoes.

"Okay, tell me." Andreea swiveled her chair to face me. "You called about bleeding? Occasional spot bleeding is normal with the coil."

"It's not spot bleeding, though. It's much heavier," I said before quickly adding, "I initially thought it was my period?"

"Okay." Andreea flipped through a document as thick as a radio manual. "When did this start?"

I chewed my lip. *When did it start?* I remembered sitting on the loo, rummaging through my cabinets for a tampon. *The morning after the Savoy.* I'd been so frantic. Work was a bucket with holes in the bottom. No matter how much time I poured in, it was never enough. I'd neglected the continuous stream of blood. I remembered tampons beginning to hurt too much so I'd switched to pads. I was so slammed that I often forgot to change them throughout the day. Until they soaked through and stained my underwear.

How many weeks has it been since that night?

"I'm honestly not sure," I said, far from honestly. "I haven't been keeping track."

"You really should have come to me sooner. Let's get this checked out. If I can get you to take your bottom half off and put on the gown with the ties at the back," Andreea said, standing up and pulling the curtain around the patient bed, "and then if you could lie on the bed and put your feet up in the stirrups, that would be great. Do you need a chaperone?"

"No thanks, it's fine."

I lay on the paper-lined bed and stared into the clinically bright light on the gridded ceiling. I fiddled with the new jade pendant around my neck.

"Ceyda, Ceyda, Ceyda." Andreea rolled my first name around her mouth as if it were a Mint Imperial. It was novel to hear someone say it.

"Yes?"

"Sorry, I was thinking aloud what a unique name you have."

"Oh. Thanks." It was strange receiving a compliment when someone was nose deep in my cervix. "I prefer to go by Jade. It's just easier for people to be able to say, I guess."

"I understand that."

"Andreea is a lovely name too."

"In Romania it's very common, like Katie or Jenny."

"You're Romanian?"

"Yes. Surprising, isn't it? A Romanian nurse?"

"No!" I jerked my upper body up, a core feat when my legs were up in the air. "No, that's not what I meant!"

"Relax," Andreea laughed. "I'm joking."

"Phew!" I plodded back on the bed.

"Sadly, my people are better known for being beggars in Knightsbridge. We now have got a worse reputation than the Polish or the Turkish."

"Tell me about it," I sighed. "Turk over here."

"Ay"—Andreea's head popped up in between my legs like she was on *Meerkat Manor*—"I'm sorry."

I shook my head once, to signal no worries.

"Okay." Andreea stood up and faced me. "Can you try to take some deep breaths?" Her eyes flickered to my hands, white-knuckled around the edges of the bed. My abs clenched and my butt rounded in tension. I hadn't showered this morning in the rush to get an appointment at the clinic, and I could faintly smell myself in the new layer of dank sweat I was shrouded in.

"This'll be cold." She positioned the speculum, and the moment it touched me I jerked away. The metal stirrups screeched, and my legs splayed like I was a squashed insect.

"Sorry, sorry." I shook myself. Tears sitting behind my eyes. My muscles anchored in place. After some cajoling, Andreea managed, as gently as she could, to insert the speculum.

"Hmm." She picked up a disposable wooden spatula and met my eyes. "Tell me if you feel any discomfort, okay?"

I nodded. Andreea dived back in. She used the flat side of the spatula to apply the most infinitesimal pressure.

"Ow ow!" I squealed. The pain eclipsed anything I have ever felt before. My back coiled up and my knees snapped shut, nearly trapping Andreea's neck. "Bloody hell, what was that?"

Andreea attempted, and failed, a sleight of hands to wrap the spatula in a paper towel before I noticed that it looked like it had been dipped in red paint.

"Is everything okay?"

"Lovely name Jade, get dressed and let's chat."

"So," Andreea began, "I'm pretty certain you have a vaginal hematoma." I stared back at her. I began imagining my future as a syphilis-ridden wench, lurking through the back streets of Whitechapel. "A hematoma is a collection of blood in the soft tissue of the vagina."

"This is the part where you tell me that I don't have a gory death ahead of me."

"It's not that large. It's essentially a type of bruise, and they usually heal by themselves."

Don't.

Don't ask.

"What caused it?"

"They happen when the blood vessels in your vaginal wall

break or burst. Usually due to childbirth, but your records didn't mention—"

"Yeah, I've never given birth."

"Well, they are caused by some form of injury." Andreea's hands came together. *Why, why did I ask?* "Do you play any high-impact sports?"

"Nope."

"Have you had a fall recently? Any sort of accident?"

I shook my head.

"What about sex recently? Have you had any that is . . . Particularly vigorous?"

Not that I know of.

"No, last night was the first time I've had sex since the bleeding started, and we stopped because it hurt too much."

Andreea's brow furrowed.

"Any other penetration?"

"No."

There was no other penetration, I repeated to myself. I didn't slam that door fast enough to quash the small voice saying *what about what you think you remembered last night?*

"Can't it have, I don't know, grown? Out of the blue."

"That's highly unlikely." Andreea turned to face me straight on. "Jade, you *have* sustained some form of injury, which is when this hematoma started growing. Judging by its size and how much discomfort you've reported . . ." *Oh God, oh God, please, no.* "Is there anything you'd like to tell me?"

I don't know. Dread curdled at the pit of my stomach.

"No." I shrugged.

Andreea looked at me for several seconds. She reached out to touch me, before curling her hand back toward herself, deciding against it.

"All right." She turned back to her screen and began typing up the appointment notes. "Abstain from sex and use a cold compress on it to reduce the swelling, two to three times a day. Like I said, with the compresses it should go away by itself." I nodded furiously. "But if you continue to feel pain, or the bleeding worsens, you have to go to a doctor immediately."

"Yep." My jaw was tightly clenched, my teeth ground together to keep my face from crumpling. *Don't cry, breathe, breathe. Please, Jade. Hold it together.*

"And come back to see me any time, if you ever need to . . . talk . . . okay?"

Andreea's matronly face was so full of worry that I had to look away.

"Okay," I managed to muster.

Kit was watching the rugby highlights on his phone when I came out. I felt like my insides had been violently shaken and my legs were pillars of stone.

"How was it?"

The lie came out so fluently, it startled me.

"Nothing, a bit of irritation." I smiled. "She said it should all clear up by itself."

"See? What did I tell you?" He pulled my coat over my shoulders. "There was nothing to worry about after all."

I set down a towel, then a bag of frozen cauliflower, and sank on top of it. The Leaning Tower of Jade. I flipped open my daybook that was on my person at all working hours. We were expected to take a detailed note of every meeting and call, in the hope that a potentially vindicating or damning morsel of information mentioned in passing was captured in writing. I had been trained to pore over details, comb through seemingly insignificant background information, be familiar with every detail of the story. But when I tried to plunge myself into that night, it was like a glitching disc. No matter how hard I tried to focus, the images scrambled. I hurled my notepad across the room. Its corner collided with the wall and it landed, folded on itself, looking defeated. No Uber receipts. No photos. No texts. Fragments of memory. Momentary flashes of clarity. Like writing in the sand, I could only hold on to them for a few beats until it all washed away with the tide and I was left as blank as ever. Utterly intangible. Like insects crystallized in amber, all the memories I had were preserved in the synthetic smell of car freshener and the sound of glugging wine. *Am I losing my mind? What the fuck is going on?* The voices of catastrophe and denial sat on each shoulder. Denial spoke first:

You don't know for sure what
happened.

Catastrophe replied:

Oh, come on, it's pretty clear
what happened.

Surely no—

You heard what that nurse said.
Why did you get so drunk?
You're a liability.

I didn't mean to.
I'm sure there's an innocent explanation.

What are you going to tell Kit?
Why did you lie to him?

There's nothing to tell him. Yet.

He's going to break up with you when he finds out.

Don't jump to conclusions.

Why are you being SO SLOW?
You need to take ACTION.

Keep it to yourself until you have hard facts.

As I sat there hugging my sofa cushions, brain whirring, partitions being constructed in my mind, so architectural they were worthy of an episode on *Grand Designs*. I stacked the walls high, and atop them rolled out barbed wire to block any attempt to peer into what I might find beyond. My psyche was like a scared dignitary in a conflict zone, cowering within the confines of an embassy. Waiting for the coast to clear.

Adele O'Hara, now:
What you up to? Bored . . .

Jade Kaya, now:
Just chilling at home, come over?

"Dude, she literally made me come, just like that." Adele snapped her fingers. She always dutifully brought me salacious content about her love life. Last week's episode included a disaster date with Mina, whom Adele had invested two weeks of messaging into. Adele said that when they finally met, *she spent an hour explaining in excruciating detail each of her TWENTY tattoos*. Today, however, Adele seemed giddy about her first date with the "dope" Gabby. Adele made everyone around her feel at home. She was the most welcome distraction I could hope for.

"That quick, huh?"

"Seriously, incredible," Adele said, downing a capful of Pepto-Bismol.

"Well, let's hope you don't end up like these poor fuckers getting rinsed for a green card." I gestured to the TV, on episode eight of *90 Day Fiancé*. An ad break came on and I jumped up for a wee. I wiped and sighed as I noticed a menacing streak of red. Pads weren't cutting it anymore, and I'd had to run out earlier to get postpartum monsters, which I quickly changed out. On my way back to the sofa, I grabbed a bag of Doritos and dip. The flat was still for a few minutes, absorbing the sound of our crunching.

"Hey," Adele began.

"Mmm?" I said, balancing as much guacamole as possible on my chip without it breaking.

"Can I talk to you about something?"

"Always," I replied, reaching for a Diet Coke, "but don't tell me you're going on holiday again because I literally don't have the bandwidth to cover your cases as well as my own."

"Is everything good with you?"

I looked away from the screen.

Not really.

"Yeah, why?"

"I'm sure it's just because you've been manic with work, but I dunno, you seem . . . off lately."

"Off how?"

"I don't know. I'm not sure how to put it." She motioned turning a knob. "Like your brightness has been turned down."

Like my light has dimmed?

"No no! Everything's fine!" I squeaked, overcompensating.

"Okay." Adele fiddled with her laces. "That's good, thought I'd check in."

"What is it?"

"Nothing."

"Tell me."

"It's that—" Adele looked down. "I heard about you and Josh."

Adele never joined in with office gossip. Worse still, she was disparaging of anyone who did, shaking her mature, disinterested head at people who were thrilled by lowly peasant squabbles.

"Oh?" If I said anything more, I feared my voice would shake uncontrollably.

"It's probably nothing."

"Del . . ."

"People saw you and Josh leaving the event at the Savoy together."

And then it appeared to me.

In bright Technicolor in my mind's eye. The warm, yellow glow of the car's dome light, reflecting half of Josh's face next to me, the cowlick that fell onto his forehead highlighted. The green silk tied with precision on his collar. He gave me a glinting smile.

Don't look so worried!

I've got it from here, thanks, man.

Here, let me help you.

My heart drummed inside me, and for what felt like hours all I could hear was its beat.

"Ohhhh, that!" I exclaimed, trying my best to appear like it all made sense to me. "We were just sharing a cab. He lives like five minutes away from me!"

"And that's all?"

"Come on! Yes, that's all," I said confidently, but blood was rushing to my eardrums, my saliva clotting in my mouth. *So Josh was the one in the taxi. He took me home. He was the one who opened the wine.*

What was he doing in my bedro—

Was he the one who—

No.

"Okay." Adele's voice sliced through my thoughts. "Damn, that rumor mill is so petty."

I looked at Adele's big gray eyes. She never wore a slip of makeup, which gave her face a permanently earnest expression. And a dart shot through me for lying to her.

I picked up the remote and turned back to the TV. *It's fine, it's fine, it's fine*, I chanted internally. *There'll be an explanation for all this. It's not what you think it is.*

What else could it be, Jade?

9

Adele and I sat facing each other for at least twelve hours a day. Her eyes narrowed when the blood drained from my face as I opened the buttery invitation to the Firm's Christmas party. I wondered if she noticed when Eve leaned against our door and asked *you on some fitness kick, why have you started taking the stairs?* I couldn't risk being in the lift and having its doors open onto Josh's floor. Adele's eyes were on me when at three a.m. I insisted on cycling rather than expense a taxi home. The pain of cycling with the hematoma was the lesser of the two evils. After all, there wasn't a joke, a spilled coffee on the morning commute, a colleague's snarky comment, a stubbed toe, a dead phone, or a tea break that happened in one of our lives that didn't flow through the other's. Words like "trash can," "subway," and "elevator" folded into my language, and into hers were "pavement," "mobile phone," and "sofa."

In the week after my consultation with Andreea, a Particulars of Claim was filed with the Court that detailed the boundaries of, and evidence behind, the claims against Arrow. Will called me at midnight, just to say *let's do it, let's go to fucking war*. As if we were defending the motherland from conquistadors, not office dwellers with vitamin D deficiencies. I was tasked with drafting a report for Genevieve on the allegations. The evidence against Arrow spanned so many years and countries that it formed its own self-sealed, thrilling universe to step into. The perfect distraction. Over the last week, I'd worked myself into the small hours, until the report totaled 105 pages and 30,000 words. The swollen bulge inside my vagina bled slightly less every day. I took fewer painkillers every day. I sent the report to Will for review, then slept for fourteen hours that trapped me in an unending loop of dreams of a shadow lingering in my bedroom. When I woke, Will had sent back his comments in a bombardment of one-line emails:

Pages 25–28: No.

Page 35: Double space in second paragraph? Are we American?

Missing apostrophe in paragraph 87.1.2. Plz fix.

Justify text and send back.

Page 80: undefined term. Sort out.

Jade, have you forgotten about the existence of the Oxford comma?

Pages 95–101: ??????????????????

From Genevieve LaGarde to Jade Kaya on December 9, 2018 at 6:13 am
RE: Report

ETA????

My phone rattled against the table with a new calendar event, pulling my eyes away from Genevieve's email. I stood up.

"Where you heading?" Adele asked.

"Diversity committee. Linda basically tackled me the other day to recruit me—mistook me for Zaynab."

"Ah, classic," Adele said. "Because you guys look so alike."

"Don't," I laughed, "it's too bleak. I don't have time for this. Genevieve has been on my tail all week."

"Should I be offended they didn't invite the queer girl to the committee?" Adele smirked.

"I'll make sure to throw your hat in the ring," I said as I tipped back my third coffee of the morning.

"Godspeed." Adele brought her palms together and did a little bow.

Linda Ellis was one of the few female partners in the Firm. She had unnaturally raven hair in startling contrast to her skin, which was one-dimensional and without texture, like printer paper. She wore a black turtleneck almost every day, usually with some variant of long, beaded necklace. Morticia Addams taking dressing tips from Steve Jobs. Linda perched on the table at the top of the U-shape seating formation, as if she was the CEO of a tech start-up about to deliver a keynote speech.

"So, hi everyone, welcome!" Linda chirped, clasping her hands together. "As you all will know, we are now in the Firm's diversity month." I half expected her to do jazz hands. "First order of business: I'm very pleased to announce that we have two new members, Eve Slater and Jade Kaya. Ladies, if you wouldn't mind briefly introducing yourselves." Linda looked at us expectantly.

"Hi everyone! I'm Eve." She threw a lock of hair over her shoulder and pursed her lips. "I work up in M and A, and recently, I've been so *thankful* for Reuben's efforts to make my workplace more gender inclusive, and it's an initiative I feel really lucky to take part in."

I smiled. She really knew all the right things to say. *Thank you to my amazing employer for letting me (a woman!) be a part of key decisions that impact other women!* As Eve spoke, I heard the door drag against the carpet. I turned and immediately felt winded.

The slope of his shoulders. His neck long like a swan's. The shape of him floating around my bed, looming over my body.

It's him.

My face squashed into my pillows.

His jaw by my ear.

His stubble scraping my temples.

It's definitely him.

I was not expecting Josh here; he's not remotely diverse. I wanted to look away. But he absorbed my attention like a sponge. I watched him, desperate for clues. Perhaps a worried nod, so tiny no one else would notice? A sign that he knew what had been going on? Some reassurance that I've assumed the worst? Instead, he simply pulled up a chair and assumed a relaxed posture, interlacing his hands to signal he was ready for the meeting to resume. I noticed that everyone's eyes had shifted to me and I cleared my throat.

"Hey everyone, I'm Jade." I did a semicircle wave in all my awkward glory. Josh swallowed a smile. "Yeah, Linda asked if I could take part in the diversity committee, and erm, looking forward to it."

"Brilliant. Welcome, ladies. I'm really so proud of the committee we have put together." Linda initiated a round of applause. I tapped my fingers together, knowing they weren't making any noise. A room full of white people, applauding themselves on the formation of a near all-white diversity committee, was painful.

"So, let's begin. Optically, I think it would be great if we could target one diversity event per week." *Optically?* "Black History Month has just passed, and we didn't do an event. We need to be doing *more*"—Linda reached her arms out wide, then swung them into a self-hug—"to invite in certain communities and let them know we are committed to their representation here at Reuben."

I zoned out of the discussion, my senses honed on Josh. I used my willpower to keep myself planted on my seat, breathing carefully. *When is the right time to try and speak to him? He seems totally unfazed to see me? That must be a good sign?* I pulled the skin off my cuticle, and, after a few seconds, blood seeped into the nail bed.

"We also need to plan ahead for recruitment season, and

we're already booking our slots at university careers fairs. I really want this year's intake to show real, visible progress in the range of candidates," Linda was saying in the background. I raised my hand to my mouth and sucked on my thumb, the bitter taste of blood staining my tongue. "Jade, I was wondering if you would be up for taking on the Oxbridge fairs? They are our most important markets, and it's really important the students *see* the steps we are taking toward diversity." I pulled my finger from my mouth, caught off guard. They wanted to cart me around fairs like an exhibit.

"Sure." I smiled. A Pakistani woman at a recruitment dinner was part of the reason I ended up applying to Reuben in the first place. Of the "Big Law Firms," she'd said Reuben's efforts in this space were the most progressive. My time had come to pay the illusion forward.

The session continued for forty minutes. There was a second round of applause when Josh agreed that he would take part in a mentorship competition, where underrepresented candidates could win a Q&A session with him. I'd somehow agreed to have a headshot taken for the Firm's Careers page. A guy they called "Bailey" agreed to ask his QC father—a barrister so distinguished that his office was technically appointed by the Crown—to host an inclusion event in collaboration with Reuben.

"Ultimately," Linda said, "something we're doing at the moment isn't working, right?" She looked around for agreement. Eve was nodding, Josh was looking sincere. "The system is broken, and it takes us as the majority to be part of the conversation to implement change." I caught Josh's eye and his lips raised in a tiny half smile, as if we shared an in-joke. My coffees churned and sloshed inside my stomach.

My scalp felt itchy. "Before we finish, I was wondering if, Jade, you wouldn't mind saying a few words?"

"Sorry?" My fingers were twitching to scratch at my skin, and I couldn't understand why I'd been called upon.

"I'm conscious that I've been talking nonstop all meeting." Linda laughed in a show of self-awareness. "And the first step is for us to listen to people of color and learn from their experiences. I want to make sure you've had your chance to express your thoughts?"

I squirmed internally and was reticent to contribute. When white people interacted with diversity initiatives, they received social kudos. When a minority took part, they were seen as radical warriors, inappropriately politicizing the workplace. Before I had even formulated a thought, my mouth began to speak.

"Thanks for the floor, Linda," I spoke in a flat and colorless tone. "My main thought is that, while representation at recruitment events is important, we need to make sure that translates into tangible changes in the Firm's actual structure." My eyes came into focus to a sea of perplexed faces. "For example, we hire about eighty graduates a year; we could introduce a quota for a specific percentage of this number to be reserved for people from underrepresented communities in the legal industry. So that all of our—erm—efforts result in meaningful change."

Linda nodded but her neck muscles were strained and her eyes slightly bulged. Not the contribution she wanted from me.

"That's such an important point, thank you, Jade," she replied tightly. "Of course, we will recruit from a wide range of the top five universities in the country. We do have to be mindful of maintaining the world-class service Reuben is known for. So we have to balance our efforts to recruit people from different backgrounds against the need to recruit individuals with stellar merit."

"They're not mutually exclusive?" I pushed. There was an uncomfortable bristle that Mexican-waved around the room.

"Oh no, I wasn't suggesting that!" Linda quickly recovered in a chirpy tone. "As always, it's a careful balance that you're so right to draw attention to. I think that's all we have time for today! Thank you, everyone, for your time. Watch this space!"

Eve linked arms with me as we filed out of the room and rounded the corner.

"That was mega awkward," she whispered. "You okay?"

"Meh."

The committee is the last thing I care about.

"Things do seem to be moving in the right direction, though, don't you think?"

I looked at Eve with a raised eyebrow. "Really?"

"I dunno! That Q-and-A thing seems reasonable, no?"

"Sure, make people of color do all the labor of filling out a twelve-page application just to take a half hour out of our day to 'reward' them with advice white people get for free. And after all that, not actually offer them a job, or even an interview. Talk about throwing the dog a bone. And you know Reuben will relentlessly plaster the whole thing on LinkedIn for pats on the back."

"Okay, okay, fair."

"Hashtag diversity! Hashtag mentorship! Hashtag inclusion!" I began calling out, and Eve giggled.

"Make sure you don't die on that hill," she hushed. Always aware, always in control. "Keep coloring inside the lines."

She was right. Any disruption to—or worse, criticism of—the status quo was met with a devaluing of personal currency. The Firm was cultish in its requirement that everyone be a right "fit." You never knew whether you were until you knew you were not.

"See you in a bit?" Eve had arrived at her office and squeezed my arm.

"I'm gonna grab a coffee"—*another coffee!?*—"before hitting the tools again."

The twenty-sixth floor of the Firm's building on first entry appeared like a luxury members' club. There was an in-house dry-cleaner, hairdresser, gym, Olympic-sized swimming pool, an avocado station, smoothie bar, fridges full of aloe vera water, a full-time GP and dentist, and huge private shower rooms. Employees could use any of the amenities free of charge. The floor was packaged, with a huge cherry-red bow on top, as a goodwill gesture. But it didn't take long for realization to dawn that it solely existed to prevent lawyers from leaving the building. Need a triple espresso because you've been awake for forty hours straight? Why go and meet a friend for coffee when you get it for free? If you get free dinner at seven p.m., might as well stay and work until then. Then might as well stay until nine p.m. when you can get the free taxi home, too.

I turned the corner to the coffee station and popped an espresso pod in the machine that, despite my law degree, took me a year to learn how to operate. I stood by as my coffee brewed, attempting to turn swiftly when I heard footsteps right behind me.

"Hey you," Josh said softly, standing directly behind me, hot against my nape. As if we were clandestine lovers, his body leaned against mine, and it expected mine to yield back. I wriggled out of his grasp.

"No one can see us, don't worry," Josh whispered, looking over his shoulder. A sly smile leaked across his face. His teeth glinted against the kitchen light, and I remembered how his canines caught the glow of the streetlamps in my hallway. He looked lupine. Suddenly, it was that night. My head lolled against my sofa cushions, my eyelids collapsing. Meanwhile, he roamed in the dark for a corkscrew, opening my drawers. Invading my spaces.

My teeth clamped to prevent a retch, forcing my vision back.

"Hi," I said curtly.

"How have you been?" His voice was soft, caring. *I must have imagined all this animosity.* "I've been hoping to run into you."

"Good, thanks," I said, spiky. The coffee machine gurgled the end of its task. I picked up my cup and turned to walk out. Josh sidestepped in front of me, blocking my exit. The hairs on my arm stood tall.

"Aren't you going to ask how I am? I've been thinking about you a lot."

"What? We haven't spoken in ages."

"I thought you'd like some space, you know, to get your affairs in order."

"What do you mean?"

Ask him, Jade.

His eyes were boring into mine, and I started to feel damp under the arms. I cleared my throat. Somebody across the canteen caught Josh's eye, and he held back a laugh. I turned to look, and a group of guys I recognized from the tax department were watching us, like we were performing a mating ritual narrated by David Attenborough.

"What's that about?" I asked, tilting my head toward Reuben's frat boys.

"Nothing, ignore them," Josh said, his hand appearing on my waist and leaning me back toward him, "they're being idiots."

Ask him, Jade.

"Listen," I began, tentative, "I don't really listen to firm gossip. And I don't want to jump to conclusions." He was looking at me with an amused expression. "But I've heard a few things that I'd like to talk to you about."

"Jade." He stared me straight in the eyes in a way that made my lungs knot. "You don't need to worry. There's no reason why we can't still be friends." *Did he think he was being gallant?* "Anyway, you have plausible deniability, it never needs to get back to your fella."

"What doesn't?"

"And I'm sorry people have been whispering." Josh had the same smug smile plastered across his face as he spoke. *No no no, why did you say anything?* "I'll nip it in the bud."

"I have no idea what you're talking about," I said, my delivery monotonal. I felt dizzy. *This can't be happening.*

"Right." He winked as if it was all a game. "Neither do I."

"Did something happen?" I spluttered.

"Shall we talk about this outside?" Josh looked over his shoulder, his smile faltering. "I think we'd both like to avoid a scene at work."

No. I don't want to be alone with you.

"Okay."

"Fuck, it's freezing," Josh said, cupping his hands and blowing into them. We huddled outside on a bench until I realized how close we were and shuffled away. He looked up at me, face swarming with sincerity. "Before we start, I want you to know that I think you're great, Jade, I really do. But you should also know that I'm not looking for anything serious at the moment, and I wouldn't want you to get the wrong idea."

"Shut up." I steamrolled past the pitying look on Josh's face that said *of course you want a relationship with me, all women do*. "Can you tell me what's going on?" Josh looked searchingly at my face for a few seconds before shrugging.

"As you wish. We were in an Uber together on the way back from the dinner and you fell asleep." He paused to take a sip of his coffee. *Is he stalling?* "I tried to get out at Vauxhall, but I didn't feel comfortable leaving you in the back of a stranger's car."

"Right . . ."

"So, we got to your flat and I helped you up . . . we had a couple of drinks, and—"

"How did you know which house was mine?"

"You entered it into my Uber app."

"And you went through my bag? For my keys?"

"Jade, I was making sure you got home safe!" His voice was metallic, his consonants harder, his vowels shorter. He tugged on his collar, bristling with defensiveness.

"Okay, go on."

"You really don't remember?"

"No, I bloody don't."

"Look, if this is some ploy to—whatever you're trying to do—it's not funny." Josh's body language had shifted from self-satisfied to cagey.

"What ploy? What are you even saying?"

"When we got up to your flat, we opened some wine, and you went to your bed."

"Okay . . . ? " I kept swallowing the excess saliva in my mouth.

"You sat up and started unzipping your dress."

"Right? And?"

"And what, Jade!" Josh's neck flushed red. "We obviously slept together."

I was at a crossroads. Between the innocence and the awakening. Between the Before and the After. The rise of a hill before it dips clean away.

Then the walls in the rooms in my head began to form cracks. A silent earthquake shaking my foundations, the fractures advancing, deep crevices cleaving against each other. Splintering the careful world I'd constructed. *I worried. But I never truly thought . . . oh my God, what have I done?* The narrative began reeling around in my head, an uncontrollable loop: we had sex after a bit too much to drink. It was stupid, simple, indelicate. A crumb of sordid office gossip at best.

"What the fuck?" I eventually breathed.

"What do you mean?" Josh was gesticulating wildly.

"I didn't realize—"

"Well, we all make mistakes," he said, cavalier. "It's no secret I like you, what am I supposed to do when a girl I've fancied for months starts getting naked in front of me?"

"Don't fucking act like I was the serpent in your Garden of Eden, Josh," I spat.

Josh ran his hand through his hair and looked over his shoulder before turning back to me. "Listen, you propositioned me."

"How the fuck did I do that?"

"You invited me in! You took my hand and led me to your bedroom, Jade! Then you stripped. In front of me!" Josh cited this as if it were the key to da Vinci's code. "What's a man to think?"

I breathed out unsteadily to calm myself. *Is that something I would do? I don't know.*

Does it matter?

"You were supposed to put me to bed and leave me alone. You weren't supposed to take advantage of—"

"No! That's not what happened." Josh's jaw was clenched. "I don't know how many guys you're taking home and showing your pussy to, Jade, but that's a pretty clear sign to me that a girl wants to fuck."

"Don't you dare—" I began faintly.

"You enjoyed it. Trust me." I was so stunned my brain went blank. "Had to cover your mouth at one point, I didn't think you'd be such a moaner."

Oh my God. What have I done? What the fuck have I done?

Josh paused and pinched the bridge of his nose. "Listen, it was inevitable, don't you think? You and me? I'm sorry, I know you have the boyfriend and it shouldn't have happened the way it did. But there's always been this"—he gestured to me—"thing between us."

I couldn't speak.

He continued, "I'm sorry if you feel like you regret what happened between us, but spinning it in this way isn't fair." He leaned one shoulder arrogantly against the back of the bench, taking a moment to sip his coffee. His self-satisfaction was the kerosene on the spark. The velocity of my rage hurtled toward a vortex. It was a swelling wrath, spitting embers and snowballing.

"I'm not spinning anything." I grabbed his coffee cup and smashed it on the ground. Steam rose from the tarmac. Josh looked amused. "This isn't a fucking PR campaign!" I was screaming at the ringing truth flying in my face. The nightmares, the bleeding, the porous memories, the confusion leaking out of me all led me here, to this colorful and definite conclusion.

"Jade, you need to calm down."

"Do not tell me to calm down. If I enjoyed it so much, why have I been bleeding nonstop since that night?"

Josh sprang up and towered over me. I cowered against the bench. Made myself small in the physicality of his presence. For a moment, I thought he was going to spit on my face.

Instead he said, "This conversation is over."

Bank station was a jungle. Lines of bodies ducking and weaving between Underground routes. I was outside myself, watching London pass me by in a blur. People streaming out of exits, asking for directions, saying their Oyster card wasn't working today but please can they be let through. An assembly of school children, holding hands in pairs, were scattering while a flustered teacher tried to contain them. Businessmen clicked their emails out, barely looking up. The gears in my brain were thick like tar. A commute I had made a thousand times seemed unfathomable as I blinked into the crowd.

I wanted to summon Adele and Eve to my flat and have a bitching session, *I thought we were mates but turns out he's a sleaze.* I yearned to reduce this to trivial gossip, with a throwaway *aren't men trash?*

Maybe he's right.

Maybe I did want it.

I remembered the night our project last summer closed. Before I was ever on Project Arrow. Will gave us his company card, saying he would be *rather disappointed if you chaps don't put a severe dent in it.* The team descended into the subterrain of Gordon's Wine Bar, pairs taking free tables in the coveted grottos where available. Josh was too tall for the caves, so he maneuvered through the poky tunnels with his head down and shoulders hunched over. He didn't see me, bending to put my cardigan into my bag. I straightened my back and we collided. His knuckles holding the wineglasses crushing straight into my breasts. My cream dress sullied with splotches of Chianti. *I'm so sorry*, Josh said, *here, have this.* He shrugged his suit jacket off and his chest pressed against his shirt. His arms canopied over me as the jacket was draped around my shoulders. In our nook we were barely two inches apart. Not touching, but my skin singing with the anticipation of being touched. I felt like I might melt if we did. Josh closed the small gap between us, his eyes never leaving mine. There was the frisson of anticipation. But just as he leaned in closer, I broke the moment.

"That's fine, it's not a bother!" I chirped in an unnaturally mumsy voice that snuffed the tension straight out.

Oh shut up, I practically heard Adele's hard twang in my head, *as if an almost-kiss six months ago could justify this.*

On autopilot, without thinking about all the work I was leaving behind at the office, I scanned my Oyster card and went through the ticket barriers, sidestepped into the correct flock. Down, down, down into the ground we sank.

"Baba," I said before my dad had a chance to say hello. I was shivering outside Morden station, and it had taken three attempts for my call to get picked up. My fingers had hovered over Kit's number but never tapped it. What could I say to him? *I slept with someone else and it was a terrible, drunken mistake, I regret it, I'm so sorry.* Or would I say, *this really weird thing happened that I feel sick about and I need you here?* Which one was the truth? Would I feel guilty if he came running and wrapped his arms around me and took care of me?

"Kizim?" Concern seeped into my dad's voice. I had no words. I was gasping into the phone. "What is it, what is wrong?" His bleariness and innocent confusion together were overwhelming.

"I'm at Morden station, Baba, can you come and get me?"

"Is it Jade?" I heard Omma in the background. "What's wrong?"

"Morden station. I can't get into a taxi. The bus is down. Please, I'm sorry, can you come and pick me up from the station?"

"Okay, usual spot. I'm coming, babam. Ten minutes."

10

Last night he pinned me under him, knees prying my legs open. He didn't have a face; it was pixelated like the faces of passersby in news reports. Out of my body, I watched the figure pump into my mannequin. My feet sinking into the ground like quicksand. I was not the only person in the room. Kit was leaning against my washing machine, watching us, his jaw set in a harsh line. And standing next to the out-of-body Jade was David Reuben, laughing like a crazed hyena. I could see through walls, and in the building hallway, Adele was knocking, holding a bag of takeaway.

I sat bolt upright at four in the morning, cold from the damp sweat that soaked through my T-shirt. I didn't go back to sleep for fear of reliving. I put my phone on flight mode and paced. Two hours later, I couldn't bear this gnawing feeling any longer. I woke my parents up by switching the boiler on. The water was hot. Scaldingly hot. I sat under the shower until my skin was red raw. I reached for the pack of Korean washcloths, small squares of abrasive material. And then I scrubbed. Scrubbed as if my skin were a stain I could blot out. Toxins seeped from me. Tears and snot and sweat and blood. The expanse of my skin expelling in unison. Omma tried to enter—the concept of knocking was absurd in this household—but I'd bolted the door.

My parents continued to tiptoe around me this morning. After Baba had picked me up from the station, Omma met us at the door, holding out a blanket that she draped over my shoulders before they silently led me inside. I crawled into bed and lay my head in Omma's lap, while Baba sat on the edge, watching us. Not one word was spoken as I clutched at my mother as if she were sand slipping through my fingers. As I untethered from the world, succumbing to the disbelief and terror pouring out of me. And all she could do was hold me as huge, full-throated sobs heaved from my chest. Because that's what parents do, right? Try to mend a heart they didn't break.

Perhaps they thought the stress of the job had worn me weak, or that Kit and I had had a fight. But no questions were asked. It's strange how parents show their love. With Kit, I was an audience member in a theater production of enviable family interactions. On his twenty-fifth birthday, Angie covered the Campbell house with streamers made of pastel-colored tissue paper, two huge gold helium balloons—a *2* and a *5*—nudged against the ceiling, a lemon meringue pie with twenty-five candles sat on the dining table, and a mound of presents in the fireplace. Whenever Kit was troubled by something, it was all hands on deck: Angie would call, text, email her advice; Ian would put him in touch with an old university friend: *Bertie, he can help you out*.

Omma and Baba were raised in a different world, without the luxury to dissect and analyze their feelings on each and every topic. They kept their emotions compacted deep within themselves, where they hardened. Solidified into granite. In Korean, South Korea is called Han-guk. North Korea is called Buk-han. The Korean language is called Hangeul. Seoul is sliced by the Han River. The concept of "han," the base word that identified something as Korean, was the expression of grief. Of sorrow and injustice and rage and bitterness. My mother would say she felt han when the insurance business went under. Han accumulated, rather than lessened, through generations—a form of collective inheritance. Just like our hair that had the sheen of a fresh brew, or our chestnut eyes, open wounds were passed down too.

Omma taught me a saying: 도를 닦다. It had many loftier interpretations, but as a child, I could only grasp its literal meaning: *to clean a road*. I pictured her on her hands and knees, her weight pressing into sharp gravel, thanklessly washing something that would inevitably remain dirty. The expression was used to convey enduring hardship, to describe situations in which unpleasant circumstances were weathered, in the pursuit of something better. Omma and Baba were both raised in postwar eras in which their infant republics took their first, unstable steps into democracy. Omma was a student when she joined a protest against military-backed dictatorship. She was in the throng of civilians that armed soldiers descended upon, opening fire. With the sole purpose of merciless quashing. Baba was harvesting hazelnuts as soon as he could walk, under the type of sun that smoldered all below it. His living memory was one of constant, relentless labor.

My parents have been cleaning roads all their lives. There

was a responsibility to them to live a happy, fulfilled life. To make their adversity worthwhile. So, when Omma held me while I cried, how could I tell her that this world she had worked so hard to survive in had let me down?

I wrestled with telling them. Of course I did. I hadn't until now because the pieces of the jigsaw were unassembled. I wanted a clear path to a conclusion; I didn't want to have to jump to it. Until now, the gap in memory was twinkling: a pool of hope that maybe *it's not as bad as it seems*. Now it was a dried-up desert. After my shower I got dressed and emerged. My parents didn't notice me watching them from the hallway. Omma was fretting over a lost receipt in the depths of her handbag. She popped a sticky rice cake into her mouth and chewed as she flipped the bag over and shook it out. Baba was on the sofa, his laptop on the coffee table, illegally streaming a Galatasaray game. *GOOOOOOOOL!* The commentator cheered. Baba threw both hands in the air and did a celebratory boogie. He came up behind Omma, wrapping his arms around her chest, and kissed her vigorously on the cheek, buoyantly singing his football team's chant. I observed this oasis they'd created. It scared me to tell them. To fill their sanctuary with such poison. I physically ached at the idea of inflicting that pain on them. The kind of pain that only a parent can feel when someone hurts their child and there's nothing that can undo it.

As soon as Omma noticed me, she whisked into action. Plates of food because *aga, you've lost weight*, layers draped on my shoulders because *aga, you look cold*. They didn't ask what brought me to their door in tears, and I couldn't share. I turned away from the food, instead quietly returned to my room. Omma watched me retreat. I knew her insides hurt with worry. But she didn't have any words.

I need to tell someone. On impulse, I started dialing.

"Sup." The rich timbre of Adele's voice was like a port in a storm.

"Hey," I managed. I didn't know what I'd planned to say. I shared so much with Del. I'd tell her if I had thrush and needed some Canesten. We've sent each other links to the best vibrators on the market. She would drop everything in a moment for me. And yet the words jarred in my throat.

"Bro, where'd you get to yesterday? You never came back to our office." I could hear the jackhammer of construction behind her.

"Had to run to a meeting with Genevieve," I lied. "Was calling to see if you fancied getting some food?" I lied again.

"Can't, sorry, seeing Gabby."

"A second date!"

"I dunno, man, I like this one."

I could hear Del's giddiness and her glee was infectious. We blabbered on the phone while Adele made her way to her date spot. I clung to her voice, to the upward inflections of her accent.

"Okay, I'm here, I gotta go."

"Okay!"

There was a beat, filled with everything I left unsaid.

"I love you, buddy," Adele finally said and hung up, as my tears free-falled down my cheek, sploshing onto my lap.

I sat on my creaky single bed. I've lain here countless times, on this mattress that has molded to the shape of me. I picked up my phone and started to message Kit. I typed and deleted and typed and deleted.

~~Hey, are you free today?~~
~~I really want to talk to you . . .~~
~~Can we hang out tonight?~~
~~Having a rubbish day . . .~~
~~I need to tell you something.~~
~~Can I call?~~
~~I miss you.~~

I threw my phone on the bed in frustration. Words typed in iMessage were too trite to transmit what I needed to say.

Do I know what I need to say?

I kept typing.

I kept deleting.

I tried calling but chickened out before the first ring, jamming the end button with quivering fingers.

Before Kit, I'd never been in a relationship. It was all new to me, but I knew things were going well when, a fortnight after our first date at the Coach House, he invited me to his family cottage in Norfolk with his friends. His crew were there before I arrived. The "cottage" was a five-bedroom, Grade II listed property set on eight acres of prime sea-view land. I spent some of my student loan on two tennis lessons before I came, just in case. The brisk North Sea wind reddened my cheeks and matted my hair with salt. When I arrived, Kit and two of his friends, Leo and Ollie, were sitting around the banquet-style table, drinking wine.

"So glad you could join us, Kit hasn't shut up about you for days," Leo began, as Kit protested. "Where did you say you were from, Jade?"

"London." I said with a nod.

"Whereabouts?"

"South."

"Like Richmond?"

"Near there," I said, "kinda." Omma used to joke that Richmond was a portmanteau of "rich" and "diamond," given its population. Morden was not near there.

"Where did you go to school?" Ollie asked as Kit topped everyone's glasses up.

"London, too," I said. They all laughed. Not unkindly, but as if I had said something completely endearing. I laughed along. Kit walked around the table to take the seat next to mine and held my hand. The dinner strolled on through the evening. Kit kept getting up to make old-fashioneds. I loved watching him. Other boys had ripped cuticles and nails that were bitten raw. His hands were clean, with spirit-level straight fingers. He was manipulating a twist in an orange peel and wiped it around the rim of the whiskey glass before dropping it in. The cocktails got sloppier as the hours turned. We learned that Ollie's family cat was called *Merlot because she whined a lot as a kitten.* Leo told us about a girl he knew who *tipped back so many oysters at the summer ball that she actually cut the corners of her mouth! Yah, like a Glasgow smile only more civilized.* Kit and Ollie fell into each other, laughing, and I laughed too. In the early hours, I took myself off to bed. The windows to the master bedroom were open and I could hear the waves in the distance. I heard the conservatory doors open, the boys' voices mingling underneath.

"Jade . . ." I made out Kit saying. "She's Kyriakos's star pupil."

"More like your star pupil," Ollie snorted. ". . . conflict issues?"

"It's not like I'm her teacher," I heard Kit say, "or breaching . . . power. I wouldn't do that."

"Did you or did you not," I think it was Leo speaking, "pass on your essays, though?"

My ears perked up. Kit had left a binder of his essays outside my room the week earlier, but it had not yet been opened. I hadn't wanted to give him the satisfaction of recycling his work. Not that I needed to. I couldn't make out what Kit said in response.

"So no bloody wonder she's his star pupil!" Leo and Ollie laughed.

"Tell you what, lads," Kit spoke, "there's something about her I love." *Love?! Did he say he loved me?!* My heart could have soared straight out of the window to him. I was drunk and ecstatic and he was in love with me! "She's not like the other . . . not like . . . so stressful . . ."

I strained against the window frame to hear. The water crashed in between his words. The pool glimmered in the moonlight. ". . . refreshing . . . independent."

Why did I think of that weekend in Norfolk now? It was years ago. But there was something in that memory that made me hesitate to call Kit. I thought about the conversations we had in the early days about his exes. The obligatory airing of pasts. Sizing up previous lovers, gauging whether any feelings lingered, the natural questioning of *why me and not her?*

What fell into the unacknowledged abyss was that all of his exes were my physical antithesis. Iterations of rosy-cheeked, blue-eyed, waiflike blondeness. Kit meant it as a compliment when he said that I was *different, unique*. But different from what?

I asked why his past relationships had failed, and Kit had commented that it boiled down to "wanting different things." He said his exes' expectations of a relationship were different from his. His voice was laced with pity because it was clear they wanted more from him than he was willing to give. What immediately followed was the direct comparison to me. *I've never been with someone so independent. We have our own thing going on*, he said. I had glowed with a familiar validation. Omma and Baba also marveled at how lucky they were with their little girl who looked after herself without complaint when they worked long days and nights.

Omma's favorite Korean expression was *collect dust and make a mountain*. Its meaning was close to "little by little" or "day by day." In every relationship, we gather the tiny cues of condition. Morsels of expectation. Until they build mountains between people. I took care of myself. I was the autonomous, self-sufficient, career-driven woman to my boyfriend. That's why he loved me. He broke up with other women for not fulfilling that role. Today wasn't the day to change that.

It occurred to me that there was one person I could speak to. Who I felt an unusual kinship with. Who existed in a vacuum and for whom I didn't need to be anything or anyone. The first few minutes on the phone were filled with mundane questions. *I just need to speak to her.*

"Hello, are you still there?" The voice on the line cut through after a hold tone.

"Hi, yes, I'm still here."

"Brilliant, I've booked you in for tomorrow evening—you'll have Kathy."

"Sorry," I interjected, "but I asked to see Andreea? She knows my history."

"Sweetie, Andreea unfortunately doesn't work with us anymore."

"That's okay." I reached over for a scrap piece of paper and a pen. "Please, could you let me know which clinic she's moved to?"

The receptionist paused.

"Andreea has gone home, love. Back to Romania."

The bright orange lifeline was being pulled back to shore, leaving me stranded in the water. I was kicking, treading water. I needed her.

"What? Why? Why would she do that?"

The voice on the line coughed. "It's just Brexit, isn't it? Taken its toll on all the migrant staff. She weren't happy here—all her friends had left." I barely heard the words this lady was saying, zoning in on the sound of her chewing gum sticking to her teeth as she spoke. "It's been a bloody nightmare round here. The NHS is understaffed as it is, and they only bloody go and make the Europeans feel unwelcome."

"I see."

"I'm part Cypriot myself. Got a British passport, so I'm

not worried, but my husband doesn't—makes you feel stressed, doesn't it?"

I stared at the floor. "Listen, I've got to go now—"

"Well, did you want that appointment with Kathy booked in?"

"No, no, I'll ring back. Bye."

11

Had sex don't remember

457 million results

Drunk sex okay?

168 million results

Flashbacks memories same thing?

13 million results

Panic attacks how to avoid

65 million results

Settings

History

Clear All History

12

The festive period ramped up. Tourists clogged Oxford Street, entranced with childish wonder at the twinkling lights, making lifelong Londoners discombobulated with rage. Christmas parties swamped December, and the space under my desk operated as a mini Amazon warehouse. Genevieve had absconded to Paris for the holidays, for she considered London to be "hellish and gaudy" in its festive merriment. It didn't make her any less demanding.

I stood on the porch and drew out three long breaths. My mind was swirling with snippets of the conversation with Josh, before shutting them down. *What happened between us was a horrible misunderstanding. A terrible mistake. But it's done now.*

"*MERRY CHRISTMAS!*" The door flung open and Kit's mum stood in a high-necked pearl-colored qipao and a bizarre white fur cape draped over one shoulder. My suspicions had been confirmed; she was trying to make it as a Real Housewife. "What are you doing out here in the cold? Come in!"

"Hey Angie," I said, bright and cheery, as if nothing was

wrong. I kissed her on both cheeks, in the demonstratively puckered manner that women develop when neither wants to disrupt the other's makeup.

"Darling, darling, look at you! Pandora, come and look," Angie called over to another woman in her late fifties, also in the traditional Chinese dress, hers in blue. "This is my future daughter-in-law, Jade."

"Mum, don't embarrass her." Kit came round the corner and slotted his arm around my waist and kissed my cheek. This signal of possession soothed me—at least every man at this party would know I'm off-limits.

"You look handsome," I murmured to Kit. He wore a black suit, but with a velvet smoking jacket. "And we match!"

"I knew that dress would look gorgeous on you," he said. The Campbells hosted an annual themed Christmas party. It was a chore to attend, and, in thanks, it had become tradition for Kit to buy me an outfit for it. I wore a fitted black velvet dress that didn't conform to the theme of the party—*The Sun Never Sets: Royal Hong Kong*—because, while Kit was prepared to be tolerant of insensitive themes, he did not wish us to be complicit. I felt vulnerable in a dress, so open and accessible.

"Do you like it?" I did a twirl for him, my waist and butt accentuated by the tight fit. He pulled me in to him at such speed that in a second, I thumped against his chest, my face a centimeter from his.

"Be careful, Miss Kaya, you keep teasing me with that body of yours, I'll have to take you in the bathroom."

I smiled but felt sick inside. *How am I going to get through tonight with this weight on my chest? Should I tell him now? No. Too many people.*

We kissed in the hallway as a bright light flashed from the side. I looked up to see Pandora with a DSLR camera.

"Young love!" she trilled, semi-squatting to take another photo, as if she were Annie Leibovitz shooting for *Vanity Fair*. "I'm taking a photography course and you two can be my muses."

I moved through the house, saying hi to Kit's relatives and family friends I saw once a year at this party. Angie Campbell was definitely inspired by Kris Jenner's annual Christmas party, each more extravagant than the last. I recycled the same conversation fodder: *Oh my God, HI! How ARE you? Haven't seen you in FOREVER, must have been* *looks pensive* *this time last year? Well, let's not leave it that long next time. How is work? How is* *insert partner name**? Yeah yeah, I'm good. Yes,* *nervous laugh* *we have been together for ages. No,* *awkward giggle* *we're not thinking of marriage.*

Baba and Omma never understood Christmas traditions. They made an effort for me, putting up our plastic tree and covering it with homemade decorations: dried orange slices on twine, pine cones, colorful paper chains. But they never attempted to plant Santa's footprints in the living room or stage his cookie crumbs on a plate. My mum saw in American Christmas films that the houses had stockings over their fireplaces. She found some in the Cancer Research one year (none of them matched) and hung them delightedly, never knowing they were meant to be filled. I appreciated that a lot as a child; they poured into me their parental love and attention, without any of the deception.

My parents had never met Angie or Ian Campbell, by my careful design. Angie clucked about how multicultural her son's girlfriend was, but I knew that admiration might not extend to my parents. There was less polish and curation. Baba's English flourished as he traipsed around the far-flung boroughs of London. He started calling white men "boss," brown men "brother." But the thick roundness to his words remained. Omma's fluency never advanced in the same way. She once called Baba from the M40 hard shoulder, hazard lights blinking, to ask where "Bham" was and why every sign led there. I recalled going to a Thai restaurant with Kit's family. Angie spoke slowly and loudly to the staff, haughtily over-enunciating each syllable, exaggerating the vowels. Colliding our parents' worlds would mean sitting through Kit's mother's affected patience and hurried nodding that showed that she was doing her very best to understand my mother. That increased volume just in case Omma might be hard of hearing.

The house was trussed up to look like the Mandarin Oriental meets Park Chinois. The drawing room (which was different from the living room, which was different from the "snug") was furnished like an opulent 1920s Hong Kong club—I half expected to find token Asian dancers lying on curtained daybeds smoking opium. But alas, despite the theme, I was the only Asian guest in attendance.

Jade Kaya, now:
OMG this party is TOO MUCH

Adele O'Hara, now:
Tell me everything.

Jade Kaya, now:
I only needed to travel as far as Richmond to reach the Orient!

Adele O'Hara, now:
Good God, is it THEMED?!

My social batteries were already faltering. I retreated to the kitchen. It looked like a Pottery Barn catalog had vomited over the room. Featuring a long, marbled counter with a boiling water tap and Nespresso machine set against a warm gray shade. Along the kitchen island were two women I didn't recognize, hands fluttering like hummingbird wings as they folded intricate parcels of xiao long bao. They wore logoed aprons and looked about Omma's age. They didn't look up as they placed each dumpling in bamboo steamers, and a third woman materialized, whisking the steamers away.

"Darling." Angie's voice surprised me as her arm came across my back and rested on my opposite shoulder. "Are you having a good evening?"

"You've outdone yourself this year, Angie." I smiled, unable to tear my eyes away from the three women who looked like my mother, their limbs moving in tandem, slick like machinery.

"Gosh, I still remember that first year Kit brought you. You were so shy! So quiet. I wondered if our family madness was scaring you away!"

"Never." I nudged my elbow against Angie's.

"You're part of the furniture now." I must have looked

forlorn, because Angie continued, her ritzy party voice pared back, "You're practically a daughter to me now, Jade. Hell, my girls would have told me to bore off if I tried to give them a decades-old pot as a present. But *you know* how special it was."

I nodded and smiled through the large lump rounding in my throat. *Is it a compliment or an insult that I was gifted a used household item? A battered cooking pot.* Angie always went to extra lengths to prove just how much she accepted me. Comments never made to her other children's partners. Because only people on the outside have to be accepted in.

Angie turned away and addressed one of the industrious ladies in her kitchen. "T minus five minutes until the duck canapés should go out!"

Every year, Angie could be found in the middle of a circle, explaining the brain waves behind her vision.

"It's inspired!" a woman with her face painted to look like a geisha cooed. *Who's going to tell her that geishas are Japanese?* "And you found the time to plan this party all alone with your youngest still at home and Ian away on all his business trips?" The geisha was doing Angie a kindness, adopting the party line explaining Ian's absence.

"I mean, it's hard," Angie said. "I admit I feel like a single mother sometimes!" She laughed harshly, and the three women nodded in synchronized compassion.

"You're so strong," the geisha said.

Kit stepped into the conversation. "It did us kids good to have such a strong female role model."

"Darling." Angie caressed Kit's cheek.

"You've raised a feminist, Angie," the geisha clucked.

"Well," Kit nodded sagely, "the future is female, after all. All the women in my life are strong, fearless, intelligent"—he put his arm around me—"and that's just something I've grown up with."

"You both." Angie smiled on us approvingly. "Cannot wait for you to hurry up and bear me some mixed-race grandbabies."

"Yes," the geisha agreed. "You would have some gorgeous mocha children." *Mocha, that's new! We usually get "caramel" and "cinnamon."* I glanced across the room to Kit's middle sister and her boyfriend, and wondered if their hypothetical future children would be described tonight as "vanilla."

"Did I tell you, Pippa, Jade here is actually part Korean," Angie said to the geisha.

"North or South?" Pippa giggled. Before I had a chance to respond, she doubled down. "You don't look very Asian!"

"No, you're right," I said. "I should have dressed up as Madame Butterfly for tonight!"

"Exactly exactly!" Pippa said. Kit squeezed my hand.

"So tell me, Jade, you're part Korean and part—"

"Turkish," I said, my smile taut.

"Wow, what an exotic mix. And your parents." Pippa paused and I raised my eyebrows. "Do they approve of your relationship with Kit?"

"Why wouldn't they?" I played dumb. *I know you've assumed my parents are restrictive and oppressive. But I want you to say it.*

"I just meant that, you know." Pippa's blushing could just about be seen through her geisha makeup, and her eyes darted around for allies. "Interracial dating can be, you know, taboo sometimes."

"Well, as Angie pointed out earlier, I am mixed race," I

spoke slowly, "so my parents are in an interracial relationship themselves." Pippa looked like she had cacked her pants. It was on me to lighten the mood, to make her feel better about her blunder. I felt a twang of exhaustion at it all. "Besides, there aren't many Turkish Korean fish in the sea!"

A laugh rippled around the circle and the nervous tension dissolved.

"You handled that with grace," Kit said once we were alone in his childhood bedroom. "I'm sorry you have to deal with those kinds of questions."

"It's okay," I sighed.

"It's so backward—no white person would be asked whether their parents approve of their partner. I'll have a word with Mum."

"I see these people once a year, it's really not that big of a deal."

"No, really. I want you to be comfortable. My girlfriend should be able to come into these spaces and not have to swallow stupid comments." Kit was the type of person who saw a mangled squirrel on the motorway as a serious failing by humans, then would rant for the rest of the drive about the need to protect wildlife, before tucking into a juicy steak for dinner.

He kissed my shoulder. "You look spectacular tonight." He planted delicate butterfly kisses over my collarbone. "Your skin is perfect," he breathed on my chest, "smooth and silky."

His hands found the zip of my dress and, with one confident motion, pulled it down. The material slid off me and pooled on the ground. I stood in front of him, naked apart from a pair of glittery platform heels.

He took a step toward me, my feet rooted to the ground. When he knelt in front of me, his face was at my chest. He latched his mouth on my nipple while his hands roamed over my back. *Is this wrong? You shouldn't be into this.* From the top floor, the party's music sounded faint, as if it were happening at a house a few doors down. *No one would be able to hear me if I needed them.*

"I want you," he said.

You want him, too. Yes, you do.

No, I don't.

I don't want this.

I closed my eyes and willed myself to drift away. Exist out of body.

Kit stood and effortlessly picked me up, carrying me to the bed. *I can't stop him now.* He got ready to kneel between my legs. *This isn't fair to him, you need to tell him.* Kit's eyes were shut, focused, which was a relief. The hematoma had stopped bleeding and, when I inserted my fingers every morning, the lump had flattened but remained tender. He didn't see me wince as he pushed inside me. *How would you feel if he slept with someone else and you didn't know?* I threw my head back in a charade of pleasure against the headboard as he picked up momentum. My hips matched the rhythm of his.

Did I do this with Josh?

Every thrust was like a blade cutting into me from the inside out. I moaned at the pain, knowing Kit would misread the sound.

Then I felt disgusted.

Because I enjoyed the pain.

It was raw and searing and white hot. And I felt alive.

"Hold my arms down," I uttered, unable to stop myself. "Hold me down. Don't stop even if I tell you to."

Kit paused for a moment, before grinning. He leaned on his knees and held my arms up, distributing his weight forward. I was pinned under him, helpless. There was another rush. Weeks in a sensory fry-out. Needing scalding water to feel clean. Overwhelmed by the sight of a wineglass. Quivering in my silence. Existing in an exhausted, confused, disbelieving daze. The agony inside me with each stroke showed me I was real. I was still here, capable of feeling something.

"Choke me."

His hand reached up and wrapped around my throat with a gentle, timid pressure that pissed me off. *Punish me like the cheating whore I am.*

"Harder!" I croaked and his grip constricted, even though his brow furrowed. "Fucking choke me."

He looked around the room, and I sensed his discomfort. I didn't care. I grabbed his wrist and forced it harder down on my throat. I needed to hurt. I needed this energy inside me to be released. I needed to know that I had control. His pace picked up. My vagina started spasming. I relished the hot singe inside me. I couldn't breathe for ten, eleven, twelve, thirteen seconds. My face started getting hot, my hands balled into fists. My survival instincts took over and all thoughts evaporated. My chest pushed upward, straining against the weight of Kit. My legs started kicking and I thrashed. *Why isn't he stopping?* Panic raced in my arteries. The choking made me gag for breath. My pain threshold was pushed past its limit and my eyes bulged like a toad's.

Fuck. This is exhilarating.

"I'm going to come," Kit said gruffly, burying his face in my neck and shuddering. His hand went limp around my throat, and I spluttered for air. My esophagus felt crushed. I wiped the tears from my eyes and the room loaded back into focus. I could once again make out the glow-in-the-dark stars Blu-Tacked to the navy ceiling. My abhorrence contrasted against the preserved innocence of a childhood bedroom. As the haze of what felt like a fever dream cleared, I came hurtling from the high to find the pure, complete revulsion that was waiting for me. For what I had done.

"We'd better get back to the party," Kit said, already off me, pulling on his clothes, facing the wall. He held up my dress. I stood and stepped into it. He pulled my hair aside and zipped it up. He coughed awkwardly and couldn't look me in the eye.

"I'll see you down there?" I asked.

"Sure."

Kit walked toward the door and I couldn't contain the guilt. I had used him. Just as Josh had used me. I had to tell him. I couldn't keep this from him, he doesn't deserve this. Not here, not now with all these people here. Tomorrow. When it's the two of us. My voice spoke before I decided it would.

"Hey, in the morning, can we talk?"

"What about?"

"I'll tell you later."

"Is everything okay?"

No.

I nodded. "All good."

"Okay." His face softened. "Let's talk later, then."

"Love you," I called after him.

13

I woke up and felt for him. My eyes bleary and unfocused. I reached for the glass of water on my walnut bedside table and downed the whole pint.

How did we get back to my place? Snippets of Angie's Christmas party floated around my foggy head. Running into Kit's uncle and aunt, who had dressed as pandas. Getting hungry and chomping through five fortune cookies.

"Kit?" I called weakly, my head sore and my throat hoarse.

"Out here."

I found him on the "terrace," a paltry attempt at outdoor space in London, which was actually the roof of the flat underneath, accessed by climbing through my bedroom window. I hugged him from behind.

"Morning, how did you sleep?" I asked.

He pulled my arms off him, his body stiff as a board.

"Everything okay?"

Kit looked at the ground and said nothing.

"What's wrong?" I reached my arm around him. He shrugged me off.

"Jade. Stop."

"Tell me what's wrong."

Kit put his face in his hands and rubbed his eyes. I saw that they were raw and puffy. He took a deep breath. "I'm going to give you one chance to tell me the truth."

"What?"

"There's no point lying."

"I haven't said anything yet, and you're already accusing me of lying."

"That seems to be all you've been doing recently."

"Kit, stop talking in code. What's going on?"

He looked at me searchingly. "There's really nothing you want to tell me?"

Yes. So much I've wanted to tell you.

"No." I shrugged.

Kit's face, which a moment ago was cherubically vulnerable, turned hard. His lips curled in a way that told me I would hate what he was about to say.

"Did you really think I wouldn't find out?"

"Find out what?"

Kit sighed.

"Sam Parsons plays at my rugby club."

"So?"

"Word's spread that you went home with his cousin a few weeks ago. The guys messaged me this morning to give me a heads-up."

My brain was slow to add up the connections. It used to be agile and nimble, forming arguments in seconds, stringing them together with logical propositions. Now, I could hardly parse what I was hearing.

"Listen," I fumbled, "it's not how it looks—"

"Really, Jade? 'Cos it looks really fucking bad for you right now."

"Can we go inside and talk about this?"

"So you're not denying it?"

"What?"

"Look at you, you're not even denying fucking him!"

"Please," I said, "can we go inside and talk?"

"*SEVEN YEARS.*" I jumped as Kit shouted. My body automatically backed itself against the wall. "Seven years I've *wasted* on you. Have you no loyalty?"

"Please, stop, it's not like that," I pleaded. "I can explain—"

"Be my guest!" Kit threw his arms up. "Please, Jade, I'm dying to hear this explanation of yours."

"I don't really know where to start. I'm sorry if this is a bit garbled . . ." I trailed off. I had rehearsed what I was going to say so many times. Had conversations with myself. But Josh got there first. He usurped my experience with his distorted narrative, and now I was on the back foot. The burden now lay with me to disprove his story. "The last few weeks I've been feeling really not myself. I can't sleep, I get nightmares. I'm jumpy and stressed. And obviously, we had that weird night when we tried to have sex . . . and . . . there was all that blood."

"Get to the point," Kit snapped.

"I'm trying." I breathed out. "You know that night with the big Reuben event? Back in November?"

"You're joking," Kit interjected. "This happened a month ago?"

"No! Well, yes. But I'm trying to explain."

"Go ahead."

"Well, I was next to the Founding Partner and the guy was a total creep. He was clearly trying to get me boozed, constantly putting drinks in my hand and telling me to come back to his."

"What has this got to do with anything?"

"Josh pulled me away from him and out of the situation, then put me in a taxi home."

"This isn't where you tell me he's your knight in shining armor, is it?"

"No, no. He's a horrible guy. But that's the last thing I remember. Since then, I've been hearing these whispers around the office, people looking at me funny, so I confronted him—Josh—and . . ."

"And?" Kit prompted.

"And he said we had sex," I said, my voice small and guilty.

Kit put his head in his hands.

"But Kit I literally don't remember anything I don't even remember him being in my flat I was so drunk I swear I had no control over what was happening I don't remember what happened and I know you're going to be like *why has it taken you so long to tell me this?* But it's because I didn't know what happened that night and I didn't know how to process it but you know I would never do anything to hurt you I love you so much and our relationship is so important to me this is all just so fucked I've been so confused and lost but I know I shouldn't have kept it from you I just didn't know what to say but I'm sorry I'm so sorry please can you say something?" My words tumbled over themselves, no space to breathe between sentences.

Kit stared at a leaf on the ground, silent as the seconds passed.

"Kit—" I began again. He held his hand up. "Kit, I don't remember it, I was so drunk." *Is that the truth? He said I wanted it, that I moaned for him. Am I spinning this?* I didn't have time to examine my weak grip on reality as Kit finally looked up.

"Jade . . ." he began. "I don't know what to say—how could yo—" He stopped himself before he finished. *Say it! You want to say how could I have let this happen.* "This is such a mindfuck."

I recoiled at his words.

"The nurse," I added, "she said all my bleeding wasn't a period, it was because of some sort of injury from that night." I thought that having a tangible physical aftermath would back me up. I desperately wanted him to ask if I was okay, how I was feeling, that he was sorry I went through that alone.

"Hang on." Kit's voice was icy. "You told me it was nothing."

"What?"

"When you came out of the appointment, I asked what the nurse said. You told me it was nothing."

"I—I don't know why—I shouldn't have said that—"

"And I asked you about that firm event when I saw you that weekend. You could have told me then."

"I didn't remember anything then!"

"That's just bloody convenient, isn't it."

I took a step back. He looked regretful, but not enough to apologize.

"What are you saying?" I asked. Kit stared out to Vauxhall Bridge, the sky a uniform sheet of slate. The river murky, a few shades darker than the MI6 building that loomed over it, an ominous tank on the bank. Cars were backed up across the bridge, unmoving as the lights cycled twice from green to amber to red.

"You know," Kit began quietly, "before we all found out what Dad was up to, my mum knew something was going on. I remember overhearing her accusing him of having an affair, based only on a hunch. Women's intuition, I guess."

"Kit . . ." I said, unsure of why this trip down memory lane was relevant.

He carried on, "He made us all think she was hysterical. I was sixteen, and he made the mother of his children out to be mentally unwell. She was right all along." He took a deep breath. "My point is that I learned in a pretty traumatizing way the importance of believing women." He looked at me expectantly before saying, "Everything you've said this morning. Do you swear—can you promise me—that's what happened? That I won't be a total mug for trusting you on this?"

"Yes, I promise."

Can I promise him that?

Kit nodded, as if concluding a negotiation with himself. My tongue was taut against the back of my teeth, my shoulders strained, my hands balled, my nails digging into my palms. Then, like an elastic band snapped back, Kit crumpled into me. His body fell limp and his arms swaddled mine.

"I don't know what to say," he whimpered into my hoodie. "This is all such a—it's all such a big shock." I stroked his hair, using my nails to gently massage his scalp in the way I knew soothed him. His distress was the priority now. The shock would wear off, the dust would settle. And then he'd ask me how I was doing. For now, I was so relieved.

"I know, I know it's a lot."

"I just—" Kit pulled away and wiped his eyes. "I don't know why you didn't feel you could tell me. What does our relationship mean if you can't come to me with something so massive? Do you not trust me?"

"It's not a reflection on us!" I exclaimed. "It's me, it's all me. I didn't know how to deal with this properly. It's nothing to do with you." I wasn't sure I believed that, but I would have said anything to erase the furrow in his brow and the heartache in his face. Kit pulled me into his chest and held me tight. The relief was like a tidal wave, sweeping the tension in my body away. "I'm sorry," I gasped into him. "I'm sorry I didn't tell you, I'm sorry I let it spiral so out of control."

"It's okay." Kit cradled my head. "It's okay, I'm not angry with you."

Perhaps we could preserve this position in time; if we were very still, we could maintain this delicate ecosystem. We could reset to factory settings and move on as if this blemish never happened. An arctic gust of wind shot past us and whipped through my thin pajamas, stinging my skin. We hurried inside. I covered Kit's shoulders in a blanket. I went to the kitchen. The walls of my vagina were burning. I was reminded of last night, of my forcing Kit to force me and I cringed. As the kettle boiled, I rested my forehead against the kitchen counter, the same way I did the morning after the Savoy, and took serrated breaths through the pain. I made Kit a tea and went back to the living room with three chocolate cookies. I kissed his forehead and told him I loved him. Kit nestled himself around me, spooning me on the sofa. I cried, he cried. We held each other. The cold outside turned to sleet, and we sat silently huddled under the blanket, harvesting our body heat.

I woke up in a groggy post-nap haze. This morning's conversation felt like it could have happened a week ago. Kit had moved to the other side of the sofa.

"How long was I asleep?" I said. He turned to me, his eyelids swollen and his eyes red-rimmed. He began biting his nails, the clip of his teeth the only sound between us. The atmosphere had transitioned into something much stonier. I wanted to fill the vacuum. Cry out that this wasn't how it was supposed to happen. That this was so bitterly unfair because I was supposed to tell him on my terms, when I was ready. It was meant to be gentle, loving.

"Hey," I said. "How are you feeling?"

Kit exhaled. He moved toward me and kissed me, but in a stiff way. Like he was kissing me to hush me. He didn't speak. Like an inquisitive child told to be seen not heard, I sat, nervous to talk again. The entire setup felt contrived. His arm around me was terse.

"Are you okay?" I turned to face him. Kit looked straight ahead.

"I'm fine."

"You don't seem fine."

"It's a lot for me to think about right now." He used his thumb and forefinger to repeatedly rub his eyes and eventually groaned.

"What—what is it?"

"I'm trying not to. I want to be there for you—this must be so hard for you—but . . ." Kit kept rubbing his eyes as if trying to banish his sight. "The idea of him being . . . intimate with you . . . it makes me . . ." Kit's voice was rising. "It makes me so fucking angry."

I jumped as he rocketed up and punched the sofa cushions.

"What a piece of shit." Kit started pacing. "He knows you're in a relationship, right? You made that clear?"

"Of course I did," I said, taken aback by this surge of outrage. I was still reeling from Kit describing what happened as *intimate*.

"Fuck!" Kit put his head in his hands. "I can't stop imagining you with him, replaying the image of you two together in my head."

The green snake around Josh's neck, the wolf in the streetlight, the wine gurgling into the glass.

I wish I could stop replaying it too.

"It wasn't like that," I managed.

"Right." Kit nodded, coming back over and sitting again. "Right."

"Right?"

"It's just, some things aren't adding up, Jade."

"What things?"

"Well, how well do you even know this guy? Why did he end up in your flat?" Kit waved his hand, gesticulating at my apartment. All I heard in his questions were *what were you doing with him? Why didn't you know better? Why weren't you more vigilant?*

"I've told you already." My voice was so small. *I can't do this. I can't explain myself like this.*

"Can you tell me again?" He held his hand out and squeezed mine gently. "I know it's hard, but I'm here. For my peace of mind, please?"

I stared back at him. *Was he really asking me to relive it?*

"I barely remember, Kit." I stumbled on my words. "I know we took an Uber but that's about it. I don't remember getting into it, or really getting out of it. Trust me, I wish for both of us I had more answers."

"Okay." He leaned into me and rested his head in my lap. "I'm just going to have to put my blind faith in you. This is such a shit situation for everyone."

We shifted, arms and legs wrapped around each other.

"Sorry, a random thought—" Kit's voice was mired in confusion and he rubbed his forehead. "Did you guys—did he use a condom?"

Did he?

"I—I don't know," I said feebly.

"Hang on. You took me to that sexual health clinic." He turned his head like a robot malfunctioning. "Have you been tested?"

I hung my head in shame.

"Jade, I'm trying not to get annoyed with you and be there for you right now. But you might be infected with God knows what and you've been having sex with me without protection."

"Okay." I was rapidly trying to backtrack. "I know that sounds bad, but we can—"

"Stop."

Kit stood up.

"Where are you going?" I shouted.

"I need a minute." He stood up but made no noise. *I can't cry now.* He paced around the kitchen. I couldn't see him, but his steps were a sharp staccato on the wood floor, and they sounded like he might walk away from me.

When he returned, he was taking deep breaths, trying to steady himself.

"Okay." He slumped. "I mean—I'm still in shock, how much you've hidden from me."

"I didn't mean to!"

"I understand why you weren't completely transparent along the way, I really do, but that doesn't stop it being hurtful."

I nodded, silenced.

"What does this mean for us?"

His face was pallid, and I could see him floundering. I stopped breathing as he deliberated. I gasped with relief when Kit eventually picked up my hand and intertwined his fingers with mine. Then he pulled our conjoined hands to his mouth and kissed it.

"We're in this together, J. I'm here for you and we'll get through this."

"We'll get through this," I parroted. Kit's eyes finally conveyed hope, sincerity, support.

And, glimmering under it all, martyrdom.

14

Law firms billed in six-minute increments; every six minutes of the day had to be accounted for. An individual's value measured by one variable: How many hours are you putting in? My Contract of Employment had the clauses *you agree to waive your rights to the limit of 48 hours per week set out in the Working Time Regulations 1998* and *you agree to devote the whole of your time, ability, and attention to your role and duties as an Associate of the Firm*. The past fortnight, I obsessively checked Josh's Skype status. I told myself I did this for my own safety. I started getting in super early when I could see he wasn't online yet; watching until his icon went orange late at night before leaving. I stalked his calendar and only got lunch when I saw he was in a meeting. If I couldn't determine where in the building Josh was, I didn't leave our office. It meant my working hours were expanded even further. I flung myself into Project Arrow with utter devotion, working through the relentless lack of sleep. I steadfastly continued to uphold my duties to the Firm. At the expense of my duties to myself.

Kit and I moved through the fortnight after he'd found out

with timidity. He stayed over at mine more often, woke me up from the nightmares, held me close. In the mornings, he got up, showered, shaved, wore his navy suit, clipped on his Omega, kissed my forehead, and left for work.

Kit held me late one night—the only time of day we came together—and said that he felt like our relationship had taken a hit recently. Desperation leaped across my organs. *What did he mean? I couldn't bear to lose him.*

"I'm sorry I've been so busy," I said quietly.

"It's me too. We're both working too hard." He squeezed me, and I felt halfway to relieved. "But I do think we should prioritize spending more time together."

I nodded against the pillow.

"I've raised this with you before, about the Clapham Flat, what do you think?"

"What do you mean what do I think?"

"For you and me."

"As in . . . ? " I was confused. The Clapham "Flat" was a town house overlooking the Common, where Kit's dad first sequestered his mistress Lisa and their love child, Olivia. Once their affair came to light, he moved them into another home in Notting Hill. There was no mortgage, so the Clapham Flat sat empty. Ian Campbell had suggested it would be a "perfect first home" for us. Kit blanched at the implication that Ian had viewed it as a starter home for his secret family too. It took a few years for me to navigate the grooves of the subject of "Dad" with Kit. *Mutually beneficial* is how he described their relationship. Kit got his foot in the door, when needed, and Ian in return had an only son like Kit to refer to when he spoke of his legacy.

"Don't you think it's time we lived together?" Kit asked. I

said nothing. I didn't have the mental bandwidth to consider such a relationship milestone properly. "It means I can be around more so that . . . nothing can happen . . . again."

I stiffened. *Does he want to move in together to keep an eye on me? I'm being uncharitable.* It grated on me how he alluded to what happened with Josh but had not expressly acknowledged it since it all came to light.

"I'd want to move in together in a shared space so we're on more equal footing," I eventually said. "We can afford to get somewhere nice together."

"I get it," Kit said, with levity. "You're earning a fuckload at the moment."

"No, sorry. That's not what I meant."

"Don't be sorry!" he laughed. "You can be my sugar mama, given I get paid peanuts."

Kit romanticized financial hardship. It was true; I now had some money. I also had a compulsion to save it. Omma and Baba's insurance business went under, then the car wash teetered on the cliff of bankruptcy in 2008. Both due to fates entirely out of their control. So I squirreled my salary away and refused to accept my financial standing as one that now was *comfortable.* Complacency was foolish when you never knew what lay around the corner.

So yes, Kit earned a lot less than me. His choice, allowed by a healthy asset portfolio. When his grandfather died, Kit denounced his inheritance, said he *needed to make it on his own*. Tightrope walking can be exciting when you know there's a net under you. The cash was parked, interest compounding. The Clapham Flat was a cash purchase, relieving Kit from rent, mortgage payments, or the need to save for a deposit. I often wondered what love was, and sometimes I thought it was supporting the person your partner is trying to be. I loved Kit, so I let him believe he was worse off than me.

This time seven years ago, Kit and I had been dating for just over a month. We were back in London for Christmas. We walked hand in hand, crunching on the crisped fallen leaves as we strolled. His hands held my hips to stop me, and he stroked my cheek before kissing me softly.

"Jade," he whispered against my mouth. We could've been there for seconds or minutes, the entire period elided into one memory. Then he turned and pulled me up the mosaiced walkway to a building.

"Where are we going?" I asked.

He unlocked the forest-green door to the flat with one hand and pushed against it with his shoulder. "This is my dad's place."

I wandered in. The place was dimly lit by an overarching lamp in the corner. It was furnished to project masculinity: leather sofas and concrete worktops. He walked up to me and kissed me again, softly, tenderly, before hungrily and passionately. His hands prowled my waist until they moved up to my chest. He cupped my left breast, his hips already pushing against me.

Afterward, we lay in the master bed, sticky and panting.

"Jade?" Kit kissed my shoulder as I lay on my tummy. "Why didn't you tell me you were a virgin?"

"Was it obvious?" My cheeks burned.

"No, it was sensational." That made me beam. "But I wish you had told me—we could have taken it slower."

"Don't worry about me." I laughed his concern off, eager to come across as a woman of experience.

"No, seriously." He held my face. "I want to make sure you were ready."

"Why are you so worried!"

"I can't help it." He smiled at me, as if guarding a secret. "I care about you. I . . . sarang-hae."

My chest trumpeted as my brain caught up with what he'd said.

"What did you—"

Was this a joke? Surely not. That would be cruel.

"Did I not say it right?" he asked. "I looked it up earlier."

"No, you did. But—"

"But nothing." Kit intertwined his fingers with mine and drew our fused hands to his mouth, gently kissing my knuckles. He spoke softly, "I know it's early days, but I know that I do."

He was perfect. Even down to saying it in Korean. It felt like he was saying *I know that you have more sides to you. I'll learn to make space for all of you*. I eventually replied.

"I love you too."

We bunkered down all that weekend. We rolled around in bed in our Clapham haven, tangled in sheets, as it blustered outside. We had that special form of intimacy that could only be created by oversleeping into the late morning together, with no plans for the day. Kit sneaking out on Sunday morning and waking me up to crumbly pastries and coffee. We pulled the mattress into the living room and rotated between sex and naps and movies and sex. We got ingredients and cooked, playing house. We ventured to the pub and asked the deep questions people newly in love asked. Clapham was the land of our future, populated by young professional couples who were looking to get onto the property ladder. It held so much promise then.

• • •

I recounted those gilded memories. The honeyed nostalgia of our early days had immeasurable mileage, especially now that I felt myself corroding inside.

"What about my parents?" I asked. It was a feeble excuse I used to stall. "Living together before marriage, or even an engagement."

"What about them?" Kit shrugged, seeing through me. "Come on, Jade, they were the original mavericks! I doubt they'd even care."

Dammit.

I looked up at the ceiling, and Kit put his head on my chest. I thought of my conversation with Genevieve, where I admitted that it was a goal to own a home. Something so symbolically important. It was always the next big step, one of my "whys" to pushing myself so hard at Reuben. Hard work resulted in security. That was the equation drilled into me. Moving into my boyfriend's gifted flat, not paying rent, was cheating on that dream. Taking a shortcut. Compromising on my integrity, in a way.

"I know what your parents think is important to you, Jadey. I do, that's why we've waited this long, but I need us to take this next step." He paused, thinking about what he should say next. "Surely you know why?"

I knew why. I wanted to cling on to this relationship with both hands. After everything I put Kit through, how could I say no now?

"Let's do it," I whispered, the words spoken before the decision was fully formed in my mind.

• • •

The next morning, Kit showered, shaved, wore his navy suit, clipped on his Omega, kissed my forehead, and left for work. Around noon, he texted me, saying *can't wait for us to live together—bring on the new year!* It was like nothing had happened. And that made me feel an annoying, invisible pain that lingered throughout the day. Like a microscopic but deep paper cut.

It felt like another paper cut when he came over later in the week and put *Game of Thrones* on after dinner. As Sansa's screams reverberated through my living-room speakers while she was attacked by her husband, Kit didn't notice me slip into the bathroom. I stumbled in, the cries of gratuitous violence still bouncing around my flat. It was another paper cut when he told me there was nothing to worry about when I got twitchy that a man was walking close behind us after dark. It was another paper cut that he never once asked what it was I was dreaming of that made me thrash at night.

15

I ignored the shrill doorbell. Voyeuring behind the curtain, I watched the courier give up and push the thin package through. The parcel had landed awkwardly, its edge caught between the letterbox frame and the door. I was jittery. I'd advanced to a single can of Red Bull for lunch. I wanted to get it and head upstairs before anyone saw me. Recently, there had been a scarcity of bodies as the corporate engine slowed for Christmas, so there was plenty of work to pick up. It felt like Kit might be doing the same. On nights when I managed to get home in the evenings, I made myself triple espressos at eleven p.m. and settled in for a night of additional pro bono work. When I did sleep, I was so exhausted that the dreams became increasingly abstract. Last night, I was enwombed in a thick, viscous substance. Sharp fragments were embedded in the fluid and I struggled to breathe. In the morning, I rubbed the sleep from my eyes and a memory came to the forefront.

The first year of senior school, we were eleven years old. A member from a Christian women's charity came to speak to the class. She said *girls, I want to show you something.*

She planted a mason jar on Becky Abraham's desk—we sat alphabetically—and handed her an egg. Becky was asked to put the egg in the jar and shake it twice before handing it to Jenny Ball. The jar made it across twenty-seven girls' desks. By the time it reached Amy Worcester, it was smashed, a mess of yellow and beige and liquid and solid.

"Girls," the lady said, holding up the jar for all to see the mangled mess, "this is what happens when you let yourself be used by man after man. Can this egg ever be repaired? Can it ever go back to its original form?" The silence in the class was her answer. "Remember, you are fragile like this egg, you are soft on the inside. And you must not let yourself become this." She thrust the jar in the air again for good measure.

Upstairs, I laid out all the pieces of the package on the kitchen counter. I scanned the QR code and filled in my details. Full name: Ceyda Kayaoğlu. DOB, address, prior health conditions. I scanned the "Ethnic Group" section. Within "mixed or multiple ethnic groups," the options were "White and Black Caribbean" or "White and Black African" or "White and Asian." And then "Other." Using the alcohol swab, I cleaned and dried the third finger on my left hand. I found the blue stick that looked like the mini highlighters I had as a child, and positioned it against the rounded edge of my finger. I watched the blood drip heavily into the collection tube. Next, I hoisted up my skirt and swiped inside myself with the swab. I sealed everything in the biohazard bag, and packaged it into the free-post envelope, like a Russian doll of STI tests.

I left the house. Everyone was watching me, judging me.

They all knew what I'd done. They were thinking *that slag didn't even check for an STI after cheating on her boyfriend.* My eyes were skittish across South Lambeth Road, flitting over all four corners of my field of vision. I slipped the test into the postbox and itched to return home. Lately, I'd been taking alternate routes back from the station so that no one could memorize my routine. *But Josh already knows where I live.* I couldn't shake that knowledge. *Josh knows where I live. I'm moving soon. Not soon enough.* I paid the emergency fee to have my locks changed. I went to the local Portuguese deli for the most lethal chili peppers money could buy. I boiled and blended them into a homemade pepper-spray concoction that I clutched in my pocket. In the other pocket, I white-knuckled my keys until I got home, before whipping my neck around my periphery to ensure no one saw which building I entered.

A loud, urgent knocking rapped on my door. *Am I dreaming? Is this a nightmare?* I'd fallen asleep on the sofa. I woke fully, blinking. The drumming at my door had become insistent. The winter daylight was fleeting. By four p.m. the flat had darkened, lit only by the TV. I had large sweat circles blossoming at my armpits. I sat staring at the door, frozen.

"Jade?" I heard a woman. "Jade, are you home?"

At the same moment, my phone started ringing. Eve.

The delayed reaction kicked in and I sprang up to the door, letting her in.

"Are you just sitting in the dark?" she asked.

"I fell asleep." I smiled weakly. "Are you okay?"

It was a Saturday afternoon, but she was in a pencil skirt, patent leather pumps, and silk shirt. Odd because if you had to go into the office on a weekend, leggings and a jumper were acceptable. The skirt was creased and she had that distinct overpoweringly fruity smell that could only be created where perfume was liberally sprayed to mask booze and day-old muskiness.

"Can I have some makeup wipes?" She kicked off her shoes and flopped onto the sofa. She smiled cheekily. "Pleeeease!"

You know someone is a best friend when they come over unannounced and treat your house like their own. I retrieved the wipes. I also handed her a spare pair of sweatpants. She stripped in my living room and had no underwear on under her skirt. She scrambled into the trackies and sniffed the hoodie.

"These smell just like you." She smiled, scrubbing at the makeup on her skin. In five minutes, the wily Eve Slater was taken off like a jacket and Evie from Wigan emerged.

I sat next to her, propping my head up with my hand, and raised my eyebrows.

"You gonna explain yourself?" I said.

She dragged her breath in.

"I think I'm in a right bloody mess," Eve groaned, her Mancunian inflections set free.

"How?"

"Julian."

"Shit. Okay. Go on," I urged. Julian Monkford was the Global Head of M&A. The Firm's chief rainmaker. He didn't walk, he peacocked. I was unsure of his age, but he was old enough to refer to *technology these days*. He didn't practice law and hadn't for a decade. His role was solely in business generation. That involved plenty of flights to dubious countries and a company card tab at Annabel's.

And he was also Eve's boss's boss's boss.

"It started at the City v. United game. Julian was trying to hook these clients, got them a box. Huge clients, so I rolled my sleeves up and did my best Northern lass bit to get Julian to take me along." As she spoke, Eve did a cheeky parody of a Rosie the Riveter bicep curl.

"You are the talent, don't let anyone tell you otherwise." I grinned.

"That was—what"—she looked around and paused to guzzle from my water bottle like she was parched—"maybe a month ago?"

"Okay?" I urged.

"Afterward, he invited me out to coffee back in London. That turned into lunch. In fairness, we got on like a house on fire. He's actually very witty. Then the clients at the City–United game ended up instructing us. He gives me a lot of credit for winning the business, far more than was due, fobs Rob off and staffs me as the lead associate on the project instead."

"Wow. He must have really liked you."

The financial press was buzzing with news of a comically large merger between two automotive giants. Rob was Eve's senior and the natural person to lead the matter.

"We go for another lunch, and he says I'm his new 'go-to' associate, even though we've never worked directly together before. But I'm not one to look a gift horse in the mouth. He's a good person to be close with, so it can't hurt, I think."

Without realizing, I was frowning.

"And he's really kind. I didn't mean to, but we'd spent a few hours at lunch and I told him what Mum's been going through." Eve's mum, the light of her life, had been bounced around doctors who had dismissed her symptoms as solely menopausal, without a diagnosis. "And he immediately looked into sorting out private for her. Out of his own pocket? His brother-in-law is an endocrinologist and made space in his diary for her. She came to London last week for blood tests."

"I see." My voice brimmed with more caution than I intended.

"Don't look at me like that," Eve sighed. "I was thinking the same as you. He's obviously not doing it out of the goodness of his heart. I'll need to pay the piper eventually. And honestly, I can live with that. I mean, I sleep with dickheads for free!" She clapped her hands and then melodramatically threw an arm over her eyes while I giggled.

"Then he books our latest lunch at the Dorchester and—"

"Oh."

"Yeah." Eve nodded. "I go with everything below the eyebrows cleaned up."

"God, Evie, you didn't have to do that, he shouldn't—"

"Wait." She held a hand up. "Lunch turned into a hotel room, as expected. By this point I've essentially drunk a full bottle of rosé, to brace myself. He starts off by suggesting I have a shower."

I covered my face with one hand, peeking through my fingers.

"And he just . . . stands there in the bathroom, watching me soap up my tits and shit. Doesn't touch me. Doesn't touch himself. At all."

"Huh?"

"And then, that's it?"

"What do you mean?"

"He doesn't try to kiss me. He basically keeps a six-foot distance from me at all times. He orders room service champagne and I'm thinking this guy is really trying to drag this out, but we talk all night. Until it's so late and I'm so drunk and I'm practically falling asleep."

"Don't."

Fleeting moments of my lolling head, struggling to stay awake, ran through my mind. A feeling I knew all too well.

"He takes me to bed and—this is where it gets really weird. He asks if he can hold me?"

"*Hold* you?"

"Hold me. He doesn't let go of me all night. He's like a child on their mother or something. He was so clammy and gross, smothering me. It was too much. In the morning, it's—" Eve looked out the window, her hand covering her mouth like she was nauseous. I felt sick by extension. I noticed the greasiness of her hair as she ran her fingers through it. "Fuck."

"What? What happened in the morning?"

"He holds my face like we're in some Hallmark movie." She pushed out air slowly, as if she was internally counting to five. "The idiot thinks he's in love with me."

"Shit," I said. "Shit!"

"Said he finds me beautiful and he wouldn't 'feel right' using me for sex when he feels so strongly about me."

"Does he think he's being chivalrous?" I screeched.

"Totally. While he watched me naked and indulged himself in some fantasy that I'll be his girlfriend. Without once asking me what I wanted."

I chewed on my lips as Eve continued to forcefully breathe

out. Her breathing became increasingly feverish. I held her hand.

"Don't panic," I said softly, "we'll work something out."

"Did he think we were going on dates when we were meeting up?" Eve exclaimed. "I was being polite when I first went along! What was I meant to do? Say no when the global head of my department invites me to coffee? And now I'm in this mess. But oh"—Eve held her hands up—"he goes home the good guy because he never banged me."

Eve curled up into a ball on the sofa.

"I can't do *this*? What even is this? What does he want from me? A trophy girlfriend? A secret relationship? A bit of rough to groom? I barely know him."

"Wait, what did you say after he said he loved you?"

"What could I say, Jade? I was naked in bed with him! My mum needs the results of her tests! Project Mercury's only just kicked off." Eve's voice crescendoed.

If Adele's friendship was strengthened by saying "love you" at the end of the day, or by gifts of crumbly almond croissants after a particularly rough all-nighter, Eve's love was shown in the trust she placed in me.

"And the most frustrating part is that he acts like I need him! Mum going private is incredible. Of course it is, but does he expect to claim me as his concubine for that? And Mercury Schmercury. In another year or two I'd be getting staffed on it regardless. He's totally undermined me by handing me something I would have got by myself anyway."

I shuffled closer to her until we were on the same sofa cushion. Eve nuzzled into my chest like a child.

"It just spiraled out of control so quickly," she said, her voice small and muffled.

I opened my mouth to speak, but Eve continued.

"But what can I do? I'm a grown woman, I knew what I was doing. I went there prepared to sleep with him. He hasn't forced me into anything."

"He's the senior person, he knows juniors go along with him—"

"It's too late." Eve's eyes were tremulous. They were blue rhinestones, holding on to glassy tears. "I can tell that everyone on the team has suspicions about us. If I end things now, the reputational damage will be for nothing. He'll obviously be fine. And I'm the trollop who can't be trusted."

I didn't offer any words of comfort because she was right. I knew what would happen if people found out. It was in the things that went unsaid. The glances that would be exchanged if Eve ever received recognition, no matter how deserved.

"I have to keep going with it." Eve was resigned. "Make the best of a bad situation."

"You don't have to!" I said, knowing full well that I had also been steadfastly keeping going. Knowing that this was the advice that she would be giving me if she knew. "He obviously cares about you, wants you to think he's a respectful guy. You could just end it with him?"

Eve laughed. Genuinely laughed with heart. She screwed her eyes shut and threw her head back, the tears finally falling. I felt an overwhelming wave of love for her. People approached Firm politics with effected nonchalance; associates cared about their progression, but visibly caring was embarrassing. Because caring implied trying. And if you were anyone of importance, it would all work out for you without much effort. Eve cared. Eve unabashedly wanted every single arbitrary marker of success. We both carved and chiseled ourselves to the demands of the job in different ways. I gave up every spare hour to prove myself worthy of my place. Eve mobilized her appeal to take advantage of it.

She enjoyed the game of it all. When she was winning.

"I guess these are the things you have to do if you want an SW3 postcode, right?"

It was a rhetorical question. Moments later, Eve was upright, stoic, poised. It was like watching clay dry; she was becoming statuesque. I knew once she'd hardened on a topic, we wouldn't be able to discuss it with that same softness again.

16

"I'm minded to pursue the current approach, given the sensitivities in this area, and reassess once we have greater visibility over how the strategy has been received," Will spoke, baritone and authoritative.

"Urrrrr," Genevieve's voice grumbled, dialed in from the seventh arrondissement, "is your Grand Plan of Action that you will carry on as usual and see what happens?"

Adele and I stifled snorts as Will stammered his way through her dressing down. A UN summit was gathered on this conference call on Christmas Eve while four indistinguishable lawyers bleated at Genevieve for ninety minutes. Adele caught my eye, formed a cylinder with her hand and raised it up and down, mouthing "wankers." Giggling, I reached for my nail scissors and started slicing pieces off my raw cuticles.

"Dude, you can't keep ripping your fingers to shreds like that," Adele said, eyes flicking toward the phone to make sure we were still muted, "get yourself a fidget spinner or some Xanax."

"Ugh, I know, it's become such a gross habit," I said. Adele looked aghast as I maniacally rolled bits of my cuticle skin into a sphere on the desk.

"You look like one of those creepy murderers off *CSI* who have a porcelain-doll collection and collect tendrils of their victims' hair."

"Shut up," I laughed. "Shit, we're on." Adele leaned forward and unmuted the call as Will began talking to us.

"Genevieve, the girls will walk you through the next steps."

Adele and I explained the process: that we would work with the barrister team to prepare the Defense over the coming weeks. Which allegations were flimsy and should be defended, and which were best to admit to so that we appeared reasonable. After hanging up, I swiveled my chair to look at Del.

"You know, it's so messed up he calls us girls," she fumed, unwrapping a cereal bar and taking a big chomp. "I trained for seven fucking years to be here."

"Ah!" I wagged my finger at her. "But Sheryl Sandberg told us to *LEAN IN*! So, I guess we must be the problem?" I joked with a grimace, gesturing to the untouched book on our desks, a gift all the women in the office received. Some not-so-subtle messaging that it wouldn't be the Firm doing any accommodating.

"Merry Christmas, amirite?" Adele drawled. "I cannot believe we're in this godforsaken place. Shall we take off and get drinks?"

"Can't." I rubbed my eyes.

"Why not? I'll still get you home to your parents by midnight, don't worry," Del laughed.

"I'm seeing—I'm meant to be seeing—Kit tonight. We

always spend Christmas Eve together." Adele looked quizzical. "You know, watch *Love Actually*, open gifts? Couple things?"

"Precious as that sounds"—Adele whipped out a bottle of Jägermeister—"come on, just one."

"Absolutely not."

"You're doing shots with me." Adele began pouring the sickly spirit, her tongue poking out in concentration, into a mouthwash cap—we both had full toiletry sets in the office, to equip us for the all-nighters. "Why fight it?"

Del handed me the cap of dark liquid and poured her shot into a used empty coffee cup.

"This is bleak."

"Come onnnn, quit whining." Adele raised her coffee cup in toast. "Merry fuckin' Christmas, because as grim as it is being in this hellhole today, I wouldn't change it for the world. Daddy Reuben brought us together!" Adele kissed my cheek, then sank her shot.

"Cheers, Del." I raised my mouthwash cap to her as she turned to her keyboard and spun her fingers across it.

"Who are you emailing on Christmas Eve?" I asked.

"Pinged the guys on twenty-two to come up and join us."

I wanted to race out as fast as my legs would take me. Josh was on that floor. I'd taken extreme care to avoid him. *I can't do this. I can't see him.* Adele registered my queasy look, for she was fluent in reading my micro-expressions. *I can't tell her, I'm in too deep.* I pretended to type something in a blank email to avoid talking. *Breathe, breathe, breathe, breathe*, I typed over and over. The door swung open. My organs felt as if they were being upended as I braced myself.

"Hey hey hey! Merry Christmas one and all!" Bailey strolled into our office, unironically touting a bottle of Baileys. His office mate, Francisco, followed closely behind him. I messaged Eve to join us.

"Cheer up, Jade," Francisco said, his accent making my name sound like "Jad-eh." "We'll get you out in time to see Father Kriss-mass-eh."

"Is it busy on your floor?" I asked, hoping it was subtle.

"A ghost town," Bailey said. The tense coil inside my stomach unspooled.

"I'd better not miss the last bloody train home," Eve said, scrolling through her phone as she waltzed in. "You're not drinking Jäger are you, Jade?"

"It's not going down a treat," I managed weakly. "It's Adele's."

"Mea culpa." Adele held her hands up.

"Everyone knows Jade hates Jäger," Eve laughed, though her delivery was clunky.

"You guys missed the Christmas party last week." Francisco and Bailey perched on our desks. I had lied and said I had to work late on Arrow, to avoid the party.

Adele said, "Was it good?"

"You bet. Although *some people* had a little too much fun," Francisco said.

"Don't be coy," Eve teased.

"Phil went home with that new trainee, Becca."

Eve and I locked eyes. Everyone caught up on the party, while I felt like I might throw up. *Did people sit around talking about me and Josh like this?*

"He probably took her to the flat."

"To what?" Adele said.

Bailey and Francisco looked at Adele like she was a poor little lamb.

"The Firm owns a flat," I said, unable to look at Eve. "The partners can book it out. Theoretically for overnight stays before a big trial or if a partner has to work really late."

"'Theoretically' being the operative word," Francisco added.

"Camaaan," Adele said, disbelieving.

"What I'd give to be a fly on the wall in there."

I looked at Eve, but she didn't meet my gaze. If she was anxious, she didn't let it show. She laughed, shoving Francisco's shoulder.

"Made the mistake of telling my missus about it." Bailey shook his head. "She obviously doesn't want me to go to any more work events. She just doesn't get that it's half the job."

At a barbecue a few years ago, Kit's father, Ian, said he hoped I had a robust liver when he learned I'd secured a position at Reuben. Networking was important in any industry. But nothing prepared me for the way seniors poured liquor down our throats as if it were a blood sport. It lubed everyone up, lowered inhibitions and quietened protestations. As always, there was a second set of invisible rules for women:

1. Dress nicely, this place has two Michelin stars. Demure but not plain. Tight but not suggestive. Put together but effortless.
2. Not drinking is unacceptable and everyone will think you're a prude. Unless you're pregnant, in which case it's irrelevant because any allure you once possessed is lost anyway.

3. Having two drinks and calling it a night is almost worse because, truly, what was the point? You call time just as the night gets juicy and that naturally translates into the view that you cannot handle pressure.
4. The sweet spot is to be a 6-out-of-10 drunk, where you can be loud and gregarious while still being compos mentis.
5. Ideally, if you find yourself in a large group, say something pithy and cutting so that the boys can act shocked and say *you're actually quite funny!*
6. If a stray hand happens to test the waters by skimming past your arse, don't be pathetic and ignore it. Instead, serve a beaming smile to the intruder. It signals that you've clocked what he did and you are benevolent enough to not cause a scene.
7. Notwithstanding (6) above, don't rebuff anyone. But also don't actively encourage anyone. Be seductive. But don't actually seduce anyone.
8. No canapés if you're talking to someone senior. Greasy napkins and awkward pauses when you have no free hand to shake is sloppy.
9. It is imperative that you (a) have banter; and (b) accept anything that makes you uncomfortable as banter.
10. Even though you will continue to be plied with alcohol past the sweet spot mentioned at (4) above, for the love of God, don't get any drunker. But also don't stop drinking. A sparkling water with a slice of lime will look like a vodka soda, if you get desperate.

• • •

"Hey babe." I clambered up the stairs an hour later to find Kit waiting by my front door, arms crossed and scowling. "Oh shit, sorry—"

"Where on earth have you been?" He sounded like a mum who's stayed up late for her teenage daughter returning from a house party.

"Sorry, train got held at a red light." I checked my watch. "I'm only ten minutes late!"

"Only ten minutes in the freezing cold," Kit hit back, while doing a theatrical shiver. "And why don't my keys fit the lock anymore?"

I completely forgot to tell him.

"I got the locksmith in. I have a spare for you." I fumbled with the keys, my fingers numb from the cold. I held a new set out for him.

"You seem really jolly today." Kit smiled, taking the keys. Not asking why I needed the locks changed.

"I got into the Christmas cheer, had a couple of drinks in the office."

Kit raised his eyebrows, looking taken aback.

"You didn't tell me you had an office party?"

"It wasn't a party!" I said breezily. "Just off-the-cuff drinks."

"Right."

"Is everything okay?" We were still standing in the stair-well, my attention shifting to his tense jaw.

"It's surprising you didn't mention it, that's all."

"Kit, it wasn't a planned thing, there was nothing to tell! What's going on?"

"I just thought we agreed that you would be a bit more

open with me." Kit forced a laugh. "It's fine, I'm not annoyed with you."

"Why would you be annoyed with me? Do I have to update you on my every move now?"

Kit put his arm around my shoulder and squeezed it.

"Relax! Let's drop it. I'm just cranky from the cold."

I nodded. "I'm freezing my tits off, let's get inside."

I tried to regain the dexterity in my fingers. I stared at the lock, feeling like Edward Scissorhands with my keys.

"Here, let me help you." Kit took them out of my hands.

Here, let me help you.

My head reflexively turned, and I saw Josh's Adam's apple reverberating, silhouetted against the hallway light. A fresh image I hadn't seen before, alive and pulsating.

A changeling in my home.

"What did you just say?" I whispered.

Kit swung open the door and gestured for me to go in. They're—Josh and Kit—the same height. How have I not seen it until now? Josh's hair flickered on the doorframe like Kit's now.

I remember.

"I can't."

"What are you talking about?"

"I can't go in there with you." I knew the fear was completely baseless, but still, terror sat at the back of my lungs, clawing its way around my body.

"Jade." Kit's lips thinned into a line. "I don't know what you're playing at, but I'm tired and cold."

My limbs were welded to the stairwell. The same stairwell I walked every morning and night, to and from my daily life. Home—Tube—work—Tube—home. Home—Tube—work—Tube—home. This place of former safety.

"I'm not playing. I know it's stupid, but I cannot go in there with you."

"Why not!"

"I don't know—for a moment, only for a second, you reminded me of Josh, and I can't."

"Him?" Kit puffed his chest forward, and I immediately regretted saying it. "You're likening me to *him*? Why is he even on your mind?"

"He's not on my mind, Kit! I can't control a flashback."

"Flashback?" Kit's lips curled upward. "But I thought you said you don't remember anything?"

"I don't . . ."

"So what's this about flashbacks? Why haven't you mentioned them before?"

"Why are you second-guessing me at every turn?"

"Stop giving me reason to! What else aren't you telling me? Please tell me *he* wasn't there tonight?"

"No. I was with Adele and Eve," I croaked.

"And how many drinks did you have?"

"What does it matter! This guy brought some Baileys round so I—"

"Hang on, what guy? You said it was just Adele and Eve."

"Sorry, it was, these other guys were also there."

"Jade, why do you have to be so slippery with the truth? Who was there?"

"Why are you being like this?" I started crying. "It was me, Adele, Eve, and two guys you don't know." I jangled my way through the list of names while hiccupping.

"And how am I supposed to know you're telling the truth?"

he said, his voice monotone. "Do you even realize that every second you're telling me a different story?" Kit spoke with measured reasonableness, steadily accusatory.

"What? So now you don't trust me, because—"

"It's not that I don't trust you," his voice softened, "but don't you see how this looks? After what happened . . . *that night*, how it might make me feel that you're having secret drinks at work, then aren't forthcoming about the men you're with?"

That's not fair! I wanted to say. *Why are you twisting things?*

But then I saw the little silver gift bag in his hand, and felt in my arms the box of crackers we would split open over our takeaway. I'd ordered a new Christmas candle that I hoped would smell like cinnamon, cloves, and oranges. And I didn't want to ruin this evening that promised security in our traditions. *Bottom line is, I slept with someone else.* I nodded and apologized. He kissed my forehead and the animosity between us dissipated.

He took me inside. Little butterfly kisses landed on my chin, across my cheekbones, my nose. *Jade*, he whispered over my skin. Waves of relief and love washed through and over and under me. *I love this man and he's mine. He could be with someone else. Someone who didn't do what I did. But he's chosen to stay with me. Possibly against his better judgment.* I wanted to grapple on to him with both hands and never let him go. I felt at the center of the earth with him and my hands roamed his back. The smell of him. He lowered himself gently on me, eventually pressing his weight across me. I pulled his jumper off and pressed my palms flat against the expanse of his chest. We made love, slowly and sweetly.

It's okay, it's all going to be okay, I thought. My bedroom glowed as outside was navy. I lay on my back, looking up. In London, you were never alone. Upstairs, downstairs, left and right of us were pensioners, four generations of a family, social media influencers, artists, blue-collar workers, dealers, and white-collar workers (buyers). Through the plaster walls was the faint tinny sound of the bell chimes that opened Mariah Carey's Christmas anthem. Kit was on his side, singing to me that I was all he wanted for Christmas. He wrapped both arms around me, and we bopped to the sparkling tempo. We ordered in a Chinese takeaway and moved the duvet to the living room floor, where we watched *Love Actually* for the seventh Christmas Eve.

He got up and returned a moment later, holding forth the gift bag.

"Your Christmas present." He traced a finger over my bare shoulder. "Open it."

It was much heavier than I'd expected. Inside was a small box wrapped in glittery paper with tiny trees on it. I peeled the wrapping paper off and glimpsed the unmistakable robin's-egg blue of a Tiffany box. I tugged on the white satin bow, feeling a slight twinge at undoing the beauty of the wrapping.

Inside was a silver key, hung on a weighty Tiffany key ring. I held it up and engraved into the tag were the initials *JK*.

My throat choked up and I swallowed hard.

"I got a set to the Clapham Flat cut for you," Kit murmured. "You said you were worried about moving into my dad's place, rather than a place of our own. I wanted you to know that it'll be your home as much as mine."

"Oh." My words caught. "I can't wait, thank you."

Kit was elated and put his arms around me. I gulped against him, still holding the key ring limply in my hand. Look at this day we've had. Our traditions puddling around us. How slow and normal it was. I'll move in in January. Start the year fresh. Clean slate. It was perfect.

But I kept swallowing.

Because all I could think about was how my initials should have been *CK*.

17

"You spent how much on that?" Omma slapped the wrapped fillet of beef I brought home.

"It's Christmas, Mum," I said. "That's how much meat costs!"

"Was it a golden cow?" she retorted. "Did it have champagne coming out of its udders?"

"Very funny," I laughed. "You're the one who is going to be enjoying the delightful meal I cook."

"Ay ay ay, what are you cooking, my daughter?" Baba said as he walked into the kitchen. He picked up the fillet and heartily slapped it as well.

"She says she's going to do a beef Napoleon." Omma shrugged.

"Wellington, Mum."

"Nelson, Churchill, who cares?"

"Noted, Mama," I muttered, before also giving the beef fillet a cursory slap, to see what I was missing.

Christmas was a muted affair for us, an opportunity to spend a few days together, with no competing obligations of work. I pored over the Argos catalog as a child, dog-earing the pages for the toys I wanted from the Boxing Day sales. We would have roast chicken stuffed with ginseng, Chinese dates and rice, basted in a marinade of grated Korean pears and soy sauce. I whined that other kids got a roast gammon, and why did we have to settle for this tiny chicken. Baba swallowed the sting of his daughter whining for pork in his own home.

Three years ago, Kit spent Christmas with us. I took over the cooking that year. I came home a week in advance to make sure the house was decorated like the Harrods' Santa's Grotto. Made it look as far from our home as possible. Wrapped expensive gifts and commanded Omma and Baba to sign cards. Baba hesitated, kept asking questions I didn't have time for. *Write "To Kit, Merry Christmas, Yumi and Yusuf." That's all you need to do!* Baba asked *but why must we do this,* and I snapped *because Angie got me Chanel perfume for Christmas, all right, Dad?* Baba looked at me for a long time before nodding and turning back to the card. I was doing the splits, a foot with Kit and a foot with my parents, the gulf between infinitesimally widening by the moment. I continued with my audit, overhauling our previous traditions and insisting on cooking a turkey with no rice, soy sauce, jujube, or kimchi in sight. Like the fairy godmother's wand metamorphosing the pumpkin, mice, and dress, I bibbidi-bobbidi-booed the baklava, tteokbokki, and galbi-jim into Brussels sprouts, roasted parsnips, and stuffing balls.

He walked through the door saying *thank you for taking in an orphan on Christmas.* Angie, who he normally spent the day with, was on holiday in a resort in Koh Samui. He slept on the living-room sofa bed because, please, some semblance of chastity had to be maintained. Kit had come to a few of our Eid celebrations before. I then overheard him bring it up on the phone to his colleagues with pride the next morning, which, at the time, made me happy. But Christmas felt different, sacred. I had to get it right.

On that Christmas morning three years ago, I was feverish, baking mince pies for breakfast. Baba scrunched his nose up at the concept of *beef mince in a pie?* Kit slapped his shoulder, *Yusuf, you do make me laugh.* I never told Kit what to call my parents. He used their names from day one, and then it felt too late to correct him. I knew they balked every time they were addressed so directly. Respect for elders was built into both their languages. She wasn't his mum, so Omma wasn't right, but perhaps the more respectful Ommonim would work. But Kit would find that weird. Auntie and uncle also jarred. So we carried on.

During lunch, Kit embroiled Baba in a discussion about the Leave campaign's vilification of the Turkish. It was Christmas 2015, six months before the referendum. In a few months, the motorway billboard opposite Omma and Baba's car wash would become twelve square meters of ruby red. It depicted muddy footprints leading into an open doorway, the front of the door being a British passport. From his back office, Baba looked at it every day. Its text looming over his head as he worked twelve hours a day, paid his taxes, and kept a local business running. It stated:

TURKEY
(population 76 million)
IS JOINING THE EU
Vote Leave, take back control

We long knew that the result of the referendum would turn on immigration as a core issue. But it never made it easier for us to hear leading politicians speak of protecting the British public from Turkish criminals. How much it hurt to see Baba never complain. How the flames of racism and xenophobia were stoked at his expense. How embarrassed I was that my boyfriend didn't recognize that, again, it wasn't just about political rhetoric for us. Kit said *but Yusuf, bear with me, I'm just playing devil's advocate, didn't Turkey have quite a serious terrorism problem in the eighties? And the Cyprus ordeal didn't exactly improve its international credibility.* Baba looked at me pointedly and I knew he was thinking *hasn't this boy learned anything since his blunder about the "two Koreas"?* With Kit, I felt pressured to take part in the impartial logical analysis; at home I knew it was more emotional. But I tried to keep the peace, went all fifties housewife and said *now, boys! No politics at the dinner table!*

One of the many times I chose him over them.

We played Monopoly after dinner and Kit wasn't used to the integrity of the game being compromised by Omma and Baba joining forces and combining their properties when it became apparent they were both going bankrupt soon. He joked *my parents barely speak to each other—my father had a child with another woman—so this is nice to see.* The open mention of a love child! I wanted to burrow into a hole. I could practically hear Omma thinking *sons take after their fathers.* I kept my eyes averted as my parents continued to try to make eye contact. Especially when Kit rested his hand on my thigh and I had to bat it away. *Seriously*, I wanted to ask, *did you think I made you sleep on the sofa so you could fondle my thigh in front of my parents?*

We have, without discussion, stuck to our own families for each Christmas since.

Adele O'Hara, 20 minutes ago:
Happy 2018th birthday Jesus.

Eve Slater, 8 minutes ago:
Merry Christmas darling.

Genevieve LaGarde, 4 minutes ago:
Joyeux Noël! I'm back in London in a week—let's regroup then.

Kit Campbell, now:
Merry Christmas my love, I hope you're having a great day. Yesterday and this morning were perfect. I love you xx

I tucked my phone away. I'd reply later. I had the same dream last night, with the figure on me, prying my legs open. The instant before I jolted awake, the man was Kit. His eyes shriveled raisins glaring at my upturned face. I saw him beside me, sleeping, and felt revolted. A cruel trick my mind was playing. I felt trapped in sublimination, between states of reality and illusion. Unsure how to make a move in any direction when I couldn't trust my own mind. I wanted to feel safe again with Kit. But what could I tell him, when he reacted so personally last night?

In the living room, Omma was reading the community Korean newspaper and Baba was on his laptop, looking at WeTransfer. With some encouragement, I got them to open their presents. I got Omma a Fitbit, as she was always complaining that she needed to be more active. I strapped it to her dainty wrist and downloaded the app for her. She began doing strides around the house, watching the step counter tick up.

"Yusuf, Yusuf!" she called to my dad. "Do you want to know my heart rate?"

"I'm dying to know, Yumi," Baba said, laughing.

"Sixty-five! That's good, isn't it? And I've already done two hundred steps! This thing is amazing."

"I'm proud of you, my darling," Baba said, forever the supportive husband.

"And don't you dare snore tonight," Omma called, "my Fitbit will track my sleep and tell you off!"

I picked up the last parcel and handed it to Baba.

"Here you go, Baba, open it."

He handled the present as if it were a newborn kitten, gently peeling off the pieces of tape and unraveling the paper. He lifted his gift with a puzzled expression.

"It's a fleece?"

I prompted, "Because you wear the same one every single day, I wanted to get you a new one."

He held it up and observed it.

"But"—he looked at me—"I already have a fleece?"

"And now you have another."

"Why would I need two?"

"Baba"—I kissed him on the forehead—"just try it on."

He tentatively pulled it over his head.

"Ooh," he said, his voice muffled with his head inside the material, "it's so soft!"

He trotted over to the mirror and began doing catwalk

shapes in front of it, jutting his hip forward and pouting. I made sure to get it in a gray color. Baba always dressed in muted tones, as if to not draw attention to himself.

"I look ten years younger in this!"

"You do, Baba, you do."

My parents watched their "favorite Christmas movie," *Ben-Hur* with Charlton Heston (rogue, I know), Baba cracking sunflower seeds in his mouth, expertly twisting the shell and extracting the meaty inside. Above them both, the father of Turkey, Atatrk, hung on the wall, watching over us. In the kitchen, I methodically built a Wellington. I chopped the mushrooms into earthy crumbs. I sprinkled them in a bowl and added chopped shallots. I slid my mother's slippers on and braved the bracingly cold garden to clip some rosemary stalks from the bush. I fried the mushroom, shallot, and rosemary mixture in the pan until it was reduced to a muddy paste. I looked at my production line: puff pastry and mushroom duxelles. Bland food that wasn't kissed with spices. I was following Gordon Ramsay's recipe. *Why? Why, Jade?* I had in my mind dozens of recipes that were passed from mothers to little daughters standing on stools, peering into pots. We cooked with our "son mat"—literally *hand taste*—adjusting by feel. Recipes never captured in writing but that have fed generations. I knew by eye exactly how much antep biber to scatter into a dish. We had shelves of old jam jars filled with dried spices that aunties packed in suitcases to deliver to us. And here I was, cooking a Waitrose meal.

Who am I doing this for?

In one fell swoop I scrunched up the perfectly rolled dough and tossed it in the bin. Automatically, I began reaching and pouring into a bowl, eyeballing measurements from memory. I sliced the fillet up into thin strips and coated each piece in the marinade. I didn't bother setting the table with shiny decorations, and instead sat in the middle a camping gas stove. Korean barbecue was traditionally over hot coals, but the modern convenient alternative was a portable gas burner to cook meat *on* the dinner table.

Omma squealed with delight as I cracked on the gas and sizzled the meat on the pan. Bulgogi: *fire meat*. Omma expertly used her chopsticks to wrap a strip of bulgogi around a mouthful of rice, adding a layer of kimchi before taking the parcel in one bite, a smile on her face as she kicked her legs adorably. We had ice-cold beer that Omma mixed with shots of soju, before inserting a clean chopstick into her glass and whacking it once to create a tornado in the glass.

"Geum-bae!" Omma held up her glass.

"Şerefe!" Baba laughed, clinking her glass with his lemonade.

"Cheers, you lovely weirdos."

18

"You bitch!" I yelled at Adele as she served a +4 card just before I was about to call Uno.

"Shut up and collect." Adele laughed and took a swig from the gin bottle.

I had come home from my parents' on Boxing Day, the same day Kit flew to the Pyrenees with Leo and Ollie. The Christmas gooch drifted aimlessly, all sense of time and structure lost. Kit said the internet was patchy in the mountains but that he would try to text. I emailed my landlord, giving my month's notice on my tenancy. There was no turning back. *Why would I want to turn back? This is exciting. This is exciting!*

It was surprisingly easy to drive headfirst into self-destruction. Doing so was a means to an end. The end being total numbness. It was reflected everywhere. I let my hair get greasy, wore dirty sweats for days. I checked to see if Kit had texted. I stopped wiping down the counters and let them get covered in crumbs and coffee granules. I starved myself for two days, then gorged myself on a feast. Two burgers that dripped sauce, fries that were still sizzling, nuggets and churros and a milkshake. I saw my bloated stomach after the glut, then calmly took myself to the bathroom and shoved two fingers down my throat.

I caught my reflection in the mirror. I was not a withering romantic beauty in depression, poetically languishing in my misery. White-headed spots sprouted along my cheeks like tiny mountain ranges. My lips flaked. My cheeks sagged into my face. Violet half-moons under my eyes. *How did Josh even want someone as disgusting as me.* I draped sheets over my mirrors after that. I checked to see if Kit had texted. I stopped taking the rubbish out, leaving takeaway boxes strewn over the flat. Spindly spiders scurried out of the hills of dirty clothes. Spongy plasters wrapped around my bloodied thumbs to prevent the pointless ripping at myself. The plants didn't get watered any more or receive any sunlight, for I never opened the curtains. I monitored the locks thirty times a day, so I eventually ordered and drilled a bolt into the door, ensuring no one could come in or out. I checked to see if Kit had texted. I used my body weight to maneuver the sofa against the back wall of my flat, and slept there instead of my bed so that I didn't wake thinking there was a shadow waiting for me at its foot. With the kitchen light on so that I had a full view of the flat all throughout the night. I woke with my joints crunching with stiffness. Eventually I ran out of toilet paper. There I drew the line and left the house for the first time in five days. I walked in the cycle lane, so that I could hurl myself into the road if someone tried to attack me.

I read an article about Richter's rats. The doctor put rats in water to see how long they swam before they drowned. No more than a few minutes before they sank underwater.

The second time round, he rescued his rats just before they started to sink, let them rest, then plunged them back in the water. They carried on swimming for nearly three days straight. I kept swimming, paddling through constant high alert into exhaustion and emotional burnout, hoping hoping hoping that someone would pull me out soon.

I invited Adele over on New Year's Eve, desperately needing to see someone. We FaceTimed countless toothy Yanks, all huddled around an iPhone. We played Uno and worked our way through bottle after bottle.

"What's Kit up to tonight?" Adele asked.

"Skiing!" I said sloppily, rearranging my hand of cards. "Whoosh! Whoosh!" I mimed ski poles in each hand and began to giggle hysterically, throwing my head back on the sofa.

"Everything okay?" Adele's face was humorless.

"Ugh, yes." I waved my finger about Adele's face. "Did you know we're moving in together in January? He says *it's time*."

"Right."

I'd lapped Del on a few drinks, perhaps she was a lot less drunk than I was.

"Anyway, I don't want to talk about my stoopid boyfriend. Tell me about youuu, Del! And drink up!" I held the gin bottle upside down and pulled a maniacal clown smile when nothing came out. "Ooops, all gone!"

"I think you've had enough to drink, Jadey," Del said carefully. The TV in the background showed crowds in Trafalgar Square, huddled penguins in the cold. The camera panned across children in pink puffa jackets holding sparklers, two front teeth missing in their wonderful smiles.

"*NO!* No no no no noooo!" I rolled onto my back like an upturned turtle and kicked my legs in the air. "You know I used to go out boozing *SO* much more than I do now? I miss it." I leaned forward so my head was in Adele's chest. "Do you know what always made the night so special?"

"What's that?"

"*BRIXTON McDONALD'S*! That place is an *INSTITUTION*!"

"Okay, so go out more, Jade—who says you can't?"

"No one does. I just get scared . . ." I trailed off wistfully.

"Scared of what?"

"I think I have wine in the fridge!"

"Right, that's enough." Adele grabbed the drink out of my hand and pulled me up into a sitting position. Adele was a storm of a person. Every choice she made was entirely hers. She had total confidence in herself that wasn't marred by arrogance. She never verbalized a word of opinion about Kit, which was a message itself, because one of Adele's loveliest qualities was her celebration of others.

"Wha— Why dya take ma drink?"

"I'm cutting to the motherfucking chase," she borderline yelled at me. "What the hell is going on with you?"

I hung my head like a dog who has just trailed a roll of toilet paper around the house. I'd normally say everything was fine! I'm all good! Just tired! But the alcohol I'd consumed freed my tongue.

"I slept with Josh Parsons."

"What?" Adele shrieked.

"Well, he told me I slept with him."

The impetuosity of releasing something I had kept within panicked me. I had relinquished control. And now Adele was reacting in what felt like slow motion. Unrestrained passion and visceral protectiveness. It all terrified me. I saw her face make seemingly a thousand expressions at once before she gripped my shoulders and clicked her fingers in my face.

"Rewind. Start from the beginning. I need more context."

"The Savoy."

"I knew something happened that night!"

"You were right to be worried, Del," I mumbled, rapidly sobering up. "You're always bloody right."

"What happened?"

"I don't know."

"What do you mean, you don't know?" Suspicion seeped into Adele's voice.

"I only know what he told me happened, and even then, I can't be sure."

"I remember you disappeared that night; is that why?"

"The details are still so fuzzy. I was—"

"You were smashed," Adele confirmed. It was like she reminded me to breathe.

"Yes." I paused, trying to find the memory amid the booze. I began softly, "Del, do you remember when you came over and told me that my brightness had been turned down?"

She nodded.

"That's exactly how I've felt," I realized now. "Something in me has died."

"Hang on, what did you mean earlier? You said you can't be sure. Sure of what?"

I could see calculations stacking up in Adele's mind, her wariness escalating.

"I remember random flashes, but I can't trust them. I was

so drunk, Del," I cried. "I'm so—so sick and tired of not knowing. There are so many blanks to fill in and all I know is that I can't fucking sleep anymore without thinking someone is going to climb on me in the night." I threw my head in my hands, and realized I was shaking.

"Okay okay okay, Jade." Del pulled me in and cradled the back of my head. "You're okay."

"*DAMMIT*, this is why I *HATE GIN*!"

"Listen, what Josh did to you—I saw you that night, you were hammered. If he had sex with you in that state," Adele spoke slowly and deliberately, holding my face, "you couldn't have consented."

I stared at the dying potted plant behind her head. I knew it was coming, what she was about to say. It was like looking at life in a lake from above the water, two worlds separated by a clear boundary. Adele clapped her hands to jolt my vision back to her. "Do you hear me? Am I getting through to you?" Her lips were blurring and her words reverberated. "What happened to you—that was rape."

Seconds passed. This is why I lied whenever my best friend asked me if I was okay. Why I brushed past all her looks of worry. I knew she would make me face the conclusion that had been loitering behind all my denial, look the truth in the eye.

"Yes," I said, "I suppose it was."

It felt like a head-on truck collision in my chest. There was no delicate way of putting it. Until now, I'd hidden behind euphemisms and allusions. I spoke of "that night," "a weird thing," "a horrible experience," sometimes as cryptically as "November." Dancing around the actual word. Too scared, too ashamed, to say it. Before, I was the unraped. Now, I am the raped. The finality of that change struck complete fear in me. There was no in-between. There was no way to trial it before committing to it.

But even then. A rape was a news headline. A rape was something unspeakable that happened in dark alleyways at knifepoint. Or something that shadowy men in power did to secretaries. A rape happened when the victim fought back. When they said, clearly and unequivocally, *No*. Could I claim that label for myself? Was I an imposter for doing so? Do I deserve to hold a space within those who have had it so much worse?

"Oh my God," I whimpered. "Oh my God, Del."

Adele held me tighter as I clung to her neck.

"All this time," I panted through cries, "I kept telling myself it was a horrific, drunken mistake. That I'd had a stupid one-night stand with a colleague. As if I don't know what rape is! I knew it was wrong, I knew it. But I didn't let myself think—"

"You were trying to cope, Jadey."

"And Kit!" I sobbed. "I convinced myself that I cheated on him."

"Did he say that?" Adele's voice was louder, harsher.

I shook my head.

"No, no. It's my fault. I didn't tell him about Josh for weeks. He was hurt that I didn't tell him." The look on Adele's face made me want to jump to Kit's defense. "Which is fair enough. It was a massive thing to keep from a partner."

"Right, but J"—Adele held my hand and her eyes bore into mine—"based on what you've told me, you don't know for sure what happened. I'm not upset you didn't tell me. I feel honored that you feel safe in sharing this with me, and I'll be here to help you at your pace."

I fell into her lap with relief. It was as if I had been carrying a heavy load and Adele had lifted it off me with ease. There was no affected response I had to curate, no pressure to make her comfortable. I didn't need to ensure her needs were being met over mine.

"Who else knows?" she said softly. "We need to come together to support you."

"No one," I sniffed. "Kit. And now you."

"Your parents? Eve?"

"Just Kit."

Adele's lips thinned.

"And he's gone skiing? Knowing you're here alone and going through this?"

"It's okay—"

"It's not okay!"

"Honestly. I wanted a bit of time to myself," I lied. I wanted to protect Kit from her hard-line condemnation. Everything was so black-and-white for Del.

She narrowed her eyes.

"He shouldn't have left you alone," she finally said.

We could hear neighbors on balconies counting down to the New Year.

Ten! Nine!

"I'm scared about pushing him away," I admitted.

Eight! Seven!

"He loves you, J. There's nothing you could do that would push him away."

I remembered all the times he praised how strong and independent I was, and I knew that wasn't strictly true. But I didn't want to test the limits of his love. The idea of being without him made my stomach churn.

Six! Five!

"We're all here for you, no matter what you need."

Four! Three!

"I think I'm going to be sick." I clasped my palm over my mouth and ran to the bathroom.

Two! One! HAPPY NEW YEAR! Fireworks popped and fizzled through the sky. Sparkles scattered the window outside the bathroom. Gold, silver, pink, orange, blue, and green rained outside as couples kissed across the nation. I raised my head out of the toilet bowl, mid-spew, and faced Adele, who had been steadily holding back my hair.

"Happy New Year, Del."

Adele took me to my bed, which I hadn't slept in for days, and stroked my hair until I fell asleep. With her next to me, I slept vacuously, the night uninterrupted.

On the first morning of the year, Adele brought me breakfast in bed.

"Jade," she began, a little while later, "have you considered making a police report?"

"No, I haven't. I didn't let myself think there was anything to report until now." The thought truly hadn't crossed my mind.

I pulled out my laptop.

"Here, let me help." Adele pulled her chair up next to me. She gripped my hand so tight, as if she thought that if she didn't, I might float away.

report rape how to

441 million results

Metropolitan Police: How to Report Rape and Sexual Assault

Report online

If you'd like to report online, rather than speaking to an officer by telephone in the first instance, you can securely and confidentially report rape or sexual assault to us online.

Call 101

If you'd like to talk to someone, our national non-emergency telephone number is staffed 24/7. Call us on 101 and report what happened or just get some advice.

Visit a police station

If you'd like to speak to an officer in person, we can provide a safe and comfortable environment at any of our police stations.

"It's crazy," I mumbled. I felt sick at the idea of handing over this parcel of shame to the police.

Adele glanced at me.

"I'm a lawyer and I know sweet fuck all about any of this."

"Me neither."

"What happens after I report? What are the chances of prosecution? Who will I have to speak to? What evidence will I have to give?" I was overwhelmed.

police handle rape reports?

13 million results

"They didn't really investigate it at all": Rape Survivors Speak Out in Report

"It felt as if they spent most of their time investigating me," said one. "They didn't actually investigate anything other than constantly bullying me. They had access to information from the beginning and just wasted time getting it, asking the wrong questions, recording things incorrectly."

A survivor from a minority ethnic background whose first language is not English told the report that she struggled to understand the information she was being given.

"I thought it was quite inappropriate because there was information passed on to my mum that I didn't want her to know. It wasn't done very sensitively. I understood everything I was told, but sometimes my mum withheld information from me to try to protect me. I only found out about it afterward, but I wish she'd told me at the time because it would have been really useful."

Explaining why they had decided to withdraw support for a prosecution, some survivors said they were not prepared to wait months or years for their cases to conclude.

"Months? Or years?" Adele breathed. "Surely it should be a priority that these people are off the streets?"

"It took a lot longer than I thought it would," said one. "It impacted me a lot. I started developing post-traumatic stress disorder. I was very anxious and so unsettled. I was very depressed. I felt as if I couldn't live my life while waiting for it all to be over."

Survivors criticized the police for predetermining the outcome of their case from the outset, especially when there was no DNA or physical evidence. Others were disappointed that past allegations against the suspect were not taken into consideration.

"I don't have any evidence."

"You sure?"

"I know I don't."

Adele's face was grim.

"DNA evidence isn't the only thing they'll go off of."

"It'll be pretty important." I grimaced. "Prosecution rates are already so low."

rape charges prosecution percentage?

50 million results

"Fuck." Adele breathed. "These headlines."

BBC: Why do so few rape cases go to court?

***The Guardian*: Rape convictions fall to record low in England and Wales**

***The Independent*: Only 1.7% of reported rapes prosecuted**

***The Telegraph*: Rape victims forced to wait five months for suspects to be charged**

***The Times*: Rape cases dropped due to police stereotyping**

***The New York Times*: UK justice system has failed rape victims, government says**

There are forty-two muscles in the face. Each and every one of them worked in cooperation to stop me from crying.

"That's enough." I snapped the computer shut and pounced up, pacing the length of the living room.

"J—" Adele began. "I know it's a lot."

"I don't think I can do it," I whispered.

"But there's a chance—"

"Did we read the same articles? Not even two percent of rape cases result in prosecution, Del. And at least five months to even get a charge? I can barely find time to do my laundry with any regularity, let alone pause my life for half a year, just for him to be charged."

"I know—"

"And even if he is charged, then what? There's no guarantee of any outcome."

Adele nodded.

"I wouldn't just have to prove that I didn't consent—that isn't enough. We both know that I'd need to prove that he *reasonably believed* that I didn't consent. He'll say he didn't know. That we were both drunk and he thought I was up for it. He'll say *what was I doing in her flat when she had a boyfriend anyway?*"

"Jade, I know, if you—"

"I can barely remember it, there's no evidence. It's pointless!"

"It's not pointless—"

"What if they tear me apart?" I gasped. "They're going to question everything. They'll say I led him on. They'll say *look at her, she was in a long-term relationship and invited him back. What was he supposed to think?*"

"Jade, slow down—"

"And to talk about it all, in front of so many strangers. Who might think God knows what of me, I can't. And fuck's sake, what about Reuben? What's going to happen if I'm the reason police start swarming around another Reuben employee? I'll be the troublemaker, won't I?" I remembered Eve's fear of repercussion if she spoke up about Julian. I practically started hyperventilating. "I can't face derailing my life like that."

"It's completely your decision." Adele pulled me in. "Just please think about it, Jade."

"I don't know."

PART TWO

19

The parties dried up. The effervescence of the festive season fizzled out, leaving Blue January to hobble on. Adele had cautioned Eve that I wasn't doing so well and, like old times, Eve turned up unannounced as I was packing to move house. I told her everything, flitting between bitter diatribe and remorseful guilt. The act of externalization felt like sawing off a limb and handing it over.

"Maybe I gave Josh the wrong message?" I said. "We were always flirty with each other. If I wasn't with Kit, I would have definitely gone there. Ugh, I crossed some lines, I think."

"Please," Eve said, no-nonsense, "Kit is a big boy. You're a young woman in the corporate world; some of these men see the fact of your existence as an offering."

"I know," I said, "but he said I wanted it."

"Fuck what he says." Eve shrugged. "What he did was wrong. He knows it, you know it."

How can it be so simple for her? How are her reactions so lean?

"What do you think I should do?" I asked. Adele was still hopeful I might report.

Eve's lips compressed into a flat, thin line. Her phone lit

up. A message from Julian. Another message from Julian. Then another. A quick succession that told me exactly what she would say next.

"Nothing." She said it with a resignation that left no room for interpretation.

I felt vacuous.

"Listen, it's still in your power," Eve all but whispered. "There's a freedom in that. It's yours and yours alone. Shit, if you wanna go lose your fucking mind for a few months, you do that. I'll be here, Adele will still be here. You'll have Kit, your parents. If you wanna keep going and try to forget about it, good for you too. But don't give your power away." Eve paused, looking guilty for what she was about to say. "Think about it objectively for a moment, Jade. Is what happened, in the grand scheme of things, really worth risking everything you've worked for?"

Eve truly was Adele's counterweight. One curated, the other raw. Cynicism up against hope.

"This flat smells funky." Eve stood up, sniffing. "Is there something dying behind your cabinets?"

The subject was changed. I suspected that Eve considered there was little else to discuss.

"I dunno." I felt embarrassed that I'd become desensitized to the smell. Eve nodded tautly.

"Okay." She ran her finger along my table and examined her blackened finger pad. "I'm sending a cleaner round first thing tomorrow." She gagged as she opened my fridge. "And a food delivery. My shout."

I nearly cried with relief. I'd let my environment decay. There was no escape when I was constantly at home surrounded by the detritus of what Josh did to me. Where Adele was ferociously loving, Eve was practical. With the two of them by my side—and a clean flat—perhaps the mess would be slightly more manageable.

Project Arrow had ramped back up again after the Christmas hiatus. We were due in a matter of weeks to submit Arrow's Defense. Genevieve was back in Chelsea. We went for lunch after a meeting.

"How long have you been with Reuben?" she asked, snapping a breadstick in half.

"Nearly four years."

"So?" she prompted, looking at me with expectant frustration. "What's your next move?"

I had of course already considered leaving Reuben purely to get away from Josh. But most associate positions involved up to six rounds of interviews, an updated CV, and a written test. I didn't have the time or energy.

"Let's talk about you coming on board here," Genevieve said, catching me off guard.

"In-house?"

"There has to be a purge." She rolled the *r* in "purge," making her seem more feline than ever. "This scandal has not been good for us. We need to rebrand, call it a *new phase of transparency* or whatever." Genevieve inflated her cheeks, then blew the air out. "You know, show our commitment to compliance. We can only do that with a fresh team. You could be on it."

"I would love to be considered." I nodded, always remembering to be contained while I was screaming inside *praise be!* "Should I liaise with Rémy about interviewing?" Rémy was Genevieve's equally Parisian assistant.

"Of course not," she tutted. "Why are you British so formal?"

She leaned forward and her breasts pressed against the table. "This case has been your interview. I've been watching you for a while. I know you can be relied on, that you're a hard worker. You clearly care about the company. What is Reuben paying you?"

I told her.

"We can raise by ten percent. Will that help get you across the line?" She lit a cigarette and ran a hand through her silver bob. "I'm a pain in my own behind sometimes—why did I tell you never to move jobs for anything less than ten percent more?"

I laughed. I didn't need to think about it. Genevieve was the fairy godmother that shepherded me onto the case in the first place. Now she was presenting me with the escape from Reuben and from Josh—and with a raise, too. Of course I'd leap at the opportunity.

Genevieve said, "I need you to focus on the Defense first, then let's make it happen, *bien*?"

I wafted back to the office in a dreamlike stupor. We left lunch with two kisses on my cheeks and the promise of greener grass. I thought of the days and nights in our stuffy cuboid. Reuben was the springboard, and Arrow was the opportunity I wanted to propel toward. Working for a woman I admired. No longer having to sit through David Reuben calling me a creature.

Jade Kaya, now:
GENEVIEVE JUST OFFERED ME A JOB AT ARROW!!!!!!!!!

Kit Campbell, now:
I knew you would bloody do it.
I couldn't be prouder of you.

"What's that stupid grin for?" Adele asked, looking amused.

"Just saw Genevieve."

"Yeah?"

I didn't want to say. I wanted to hold the offer close inside myself. It felt like an expensive perfume, clouding the air with its fragrance, but the moment you released it from its ornate bottle, it dissipated away from you, out of your grasp.

"She's offered me a shot at a role at Arrow . . ." I whispered, sheepish. Adele had also sacrificed all her waking hours to Project Arrow. She joined the case a few months after me, and it would be a shame to inject competition into our friendship. Because at some point, we'd been taught that there was only space for one of us to rise. As always, she proved me wrong.

"*YES, THAT'S MY GIRL!*" Adele bellowed. She parkoured toward me and we jumped up and down in our stale office, clutching at each other. Tears welled in our eyes because, at last, the tide was turning.

"It's not set in stone, but she seemed pretty keen. I can't believe it; I actually can't believe it."

"You can!" Adele held me by the shoulders. "You're the hardest-working bitch in this place and you have poured your life into this case. You deserve it. Okay—" Adele magicked the emergency bottle of prosecco we kept in our snack drawer.

"Watch out, world." Adele popped the cork and slurped at the overflowing, warm fizz. "Our Jade Kaya is *ON THE MOTHERFUCKIN' RISE.*"

20

I stood in front of the mirror, assessing myself. My collarbones jutted out of my halter-neck top. New black jeans sucked my waist in. It was Baltic outside, but I wanted to flaunt my new figure. Intense stress and fluctuating periods of starvation had melted away my layer of softness from Deliveroo dinners six nights a week and sedentary desk life. I was pleased with how little space I occupied.

"Wow." Kit poked his head around the door. "You look gorgeous." *See what I mean?* I smiled in the mirror at him as I fastened my necklace. He grazed a finger across my shoulder blades. *Has he noticed I've dropped a dress size? Does he like that?*

"Are you excited for tonight?" he asked.

"I guess."

"What's wrong?"

I spun round.

"Do we have to go? I'd much rather stay in and celebrate Genevieve's offer with you."

"I get that." Kit stroked my hair as he spoke, which made me feel like his doll. "But what better way to celebrate than with all of our friends? Leo will be thrilled for you."

I don't want to get drunk in a room of people I don't know. I also don't want to be the one to say let's not go. I want you to know that it's uncomfortable for me.

"Come on." Kit picked up my bag. "We're going to be late."

We arrived in Islington fashionably late. Leo was standing smoking by the door to the six-bedroom town house. Rumored to have cost in the realm of five million, the house was a classic Victorian building, maintained in its entirety, as opposed to having been carved up to make flats. Leo's brother was gifted the property when their parents "needed to park some cash." Leo was "couch surfing" here while he looked for his own place.

"You made it!" Leo's girlfriend, Suzie, squealed. She swayed as she moved, clearly very pissed.

"Very glad to see you two," Leo joined in, kissing me on both cheeks.

"Ugh, Jade, I love this top," Suzie said, reaching forward and feeling the fabric of my halter-neck, inadvertently massaging my tit. Suzie was short, very busty, and always curled her hair into Hollywood film-star waves. I imagined her having the Andy Warhol pop art prints of Marilyn Monroe and Audrey Hepburn in her bedroom. "You're so lucky you can wear low-cut stuff. I can't with these floaters." She jiggled her chest. I adored Suzie. She'd been dating Leo for two years, and we quickly became allies on group trips or couple dinners. She always said rambunctious things like referring to her breasts as floaters.

I smiled weakly. The street was quiet, but the house was humming. The kitchen—or as Leo called it, the "cellar"—was at full capacity.

"Coming?" Kit said, hand on the small of my waist.

"Right behind you." I smiled.

In no other arena was it clearer that we weren't in the first blush of youth than the House Party. Proper adulthood was singing lullabies as it beckoned us. In one corner a nondescript woman was showing off her nondescript engagement ring, a glassy gumball in a gold claw. I heard her saying that *Charlie saved up three months' salary, before tax, for it.* I ran away before they could tell me that surely I'm next to be taken off the market. They'd look at me with pity, as if I were the last mangy dog in the rescue center, patiently wagging her tail until Kit took me home.

In another part of the room, recent exes Daniella and Otis put in a herculean effort to show how *fine, totally fine* they were seeing each other for the first time since their breakup. Daniella convinced herself an hour ago that she was the bigger person and approached Otis, who acted surprised to see her there, as if he hadn't spent all evening pretending not to notice her. The night would likely end with them locked in the bathroom together. There were people in established careers and people starting out on the bottom rung of their chosen industry. There were people shoehorning their ongoing home renovation into every conversation—*it just made sense to do an attic extension*—and people in sharehouses in Stoke Newington. There were people who didn't know whether to respond with *shit* or *congratulations* to a pregnancy announcement. After an evening in the House Party, I had no idea what direction life was pulling me in, or what direction I should be pushing myself toward. There was one thing that brought this motley crew together: frenetically hovering around a plate of white lines. Because certain behaviors are only glamorous if displayed by the upper-middle class: being multilingual, tax avoidance, secondhand shopping, having financial support from family, and hard drugs.

By midnight, the party was in full swing, the house short of pulsating. I had carefully toed the balance between drinking enough to dull the anxiety, and not drinking too much to induce the panic attack that was squatting under my skin. It occurred to me that Kit hadn't noticed. I hadn't seen him in over an hour. When I felt my blood alcohol level rising a smidgen too high and the subsequent rise of dread, I confidently walked to the bathroom and bolted it shut. I panted against the door.

"You okay, Jade?"

I jolted at the voice and turned to see Suzie with her knickers around her ankles, having a wee in the dark.

"Jesus, Suze! You scared the shit out of me."

She wiped, stood up and flushed.

"It's all a bit much, isn't it?" She grinned at me.

"I have no idea how you do it, Suze."

She laughed as she rinsed her hands in the sink. "I love Leo but . . ." She waved her hand around her head and sighed.

"Yeah," I agreed.

"I still can't wrap my head around the fact that he has"—she picked up the ornate gold Hermès soap tray that sat on the sink, laughing—"all this. It's crazy to have *all this*."

"I feel you. Kit's mum is lovely, but she does think she lives below the breadline because she's had to do her food shopping at Waitrose instead of Fortnum's."

"Stooooop!" Suzie cackled. "Last week, I was round Leo's

grandparents' place. They put out a cheese platter and I ate a chunk of the Stilton. The"—*clap*—"whole"—*clap*—"room"—*clap*—"gasped."

"Why?"

"Got home and Leo starts getting cross with me for eating the nose of the cheese. You know—the pointy end of a wedge of cheese? Apparently, it's an unspeakably rude thing to do."

We drunkenly began podging each other's noses, cackling with the absurdity of draconian traditions that survived solely to demarcate who belonged and who didn't. We fell into a gentle silence, before Suzie whispered as if others could hear us.

"Granny Cannon nearly had a conniption when she heard that her gorgeous grandson was dating an Essex girl."

"Stuffy old bitch," I muttered.

"*STOP, JADE,*" Suze wheezed between her snickers. "You're going to make my mascara run."

"I'm serious! She should cark it already and give the kids the inheritance they're all gagging for."

A rapping started at the bathroom door and we both jumped.

"Let's do this again." Suzie gave me a brief hug. "Next time let's aim to be sober, and preferably not in the bog with no lights on." She flung the door open and melted into the crowd.

"Hey, where have you been?" I purred as I approached Kit from behind. Bodies moved more loosely as the night grew murkier. He turned forty-five degrees to put his arm around me, pulling me in to his chest. The light was dim, but Kit's pupils were giant licorice wheels. "Seriously? You've been getting coked up?"

He laughed with a manic pitch, not realizing that his lips were getting pulled back, his teeth baring like a feral animal.

"Hey there, stranger, where did you get to?" A girl I recognized from around the party, with dyed black hair and a harsh box fringe, approached Kit with an expectant smile. Her eyes darted at me, at Kit. Then at my hand on Kit's chest. Then at Kit's arm around me.

"Errr, hi?" she said, her voice suddenly an octave higher.

"Nell, this is my girlfriend, Jade." If Kit was nervous, he didn't let on at all.

I used to take pride in how much other women were attracted to Kit. We'd go to party after party, each with a different gorgeous woman stealing glances at him, running their manicured fingers innocuously over his forearm. He'd politely excuse himself, then, in their line of vision, ceremoniously kiss me. My coronation as his woman. His Chosen One.

I've known for a long time that Kit made it a routine of getting too close to single, attractive women. It was a key ingredient of his ritual that he appear available and interested, until the precise point he knew that his target was attracted to him. She could signal this by a bite of the lip, a self-conscious hair flick, or a nervous giggle. He'd then pull back, announcing that he had a girlfriend and walking away with the confirmation, the swell of validation, that he's *still got it*. No lines were crossed: he didn't lie about being single, he didn't make any moves, there was no kiss, no actively inappropriate conversation. I partook in this game, this self-serving routine of lassoing women just to reject them, because the common thread through it all was the message that he could have other women if he wanted them. But he chose me. How lucky I was! How jealous these other women must be!

Tonight, my hand was cold and clammy against his chest. I felt sick. I no longer saw it as a dangerous, cool game. It was the most PG, watered-down, fucking narcissistic form of infidelity.

Am I really one to talk? I flirted with Josh because I enjoyed how attractive he found me. Why does it seem different tonight? It all feels like one massive show.

"Your girlfriend!" Nell said, with a sickly sweet smile. "You never mentioned!"

"What is she talking about, Kit?" I said, looking at him.

"Never mind, I was leaving," Nell said, shaking her head and stalking away. Kit and I were still in a mechanical couple's embrace.

"You going to tell me what that was about?"

"She's just this girl who's been hitting on me all night, it's nothing."

"Doesn't sound like nothing."

"Oh, come on, Jade—don't get jealous!" He started laughing like the Joker.

"It's not funny. How do you think it makes me feel when other women come up to you, thinking you're into them?"

"What's gotten into you?" Kit's shoulders squared up and his body came alive. "The Old You used to love it!"

"You're behaving inappropriately."

"Baby, it's a compliment."

"Can we go?"

"Go where?"

"Home."

"I've got a few more hours in me, I reckon."

"You know I don't like traveling alone at night," I said weakly. I hated how needy it made me sound.

"I don't know what to tell you, J." Kit shrugged. "Get a taxi."

At home—alone—I prowled around the house for painkillers for a headache, rifling through my catch-all drawers. I mined through used batteries, random tools, old receipts, until I spied the metallic flash of a blister pack. It was flat against the bottom of the drawer. I used my thumbnail to lift it up. It was a sledgehammer to my chest, the cavity filling with warm, liquid memories. The shiny material wasn't a pack of ibuprofen, but the reflective surface of an old Polaroid. Living inside it were Kit and Jade. He was sitting on a camp chair in front of their tent at Glastonbury, and she was on his lap, her legs swung over the arms of the chair. Her arm was around his shoulder, and she was kissing his cheek. His eyes were closed, his face turned up to the clear skies with a smile across it. His hand around the bottle of Stella was relaxed, and her hair was swept up in a messy bun atop her head. Their Wellies were caked in mud, and they hadn't showered in days, but they radiated bliss.

Who was that girl? The one who pretended she liked British indie rock bands with names like the Living Room Rug or the Rainy Bus Stop? Who played Mis-teeq and the Sugababes only when she was alone. Whose comfort meal was cup ramen with extra shredded cheese, but who says she loves a pub roast. Who heard Leo mention that 2010 was a great year for Bordeaux and has regurgitated it relentlessly since. Who let his friends think she was from an expensive part of London. Who kept her beloved parents away from university events because she worried they might feel out of place. My heart went to her.

I am still her.

21

"Tteokbokki," I concluded. "And yukgaejang."

"그래 우리 아가," Omma laughed. *Okay, my baby.*

We were in New Malden. A seemingly lackluster suburb of cubed semidetached houses, but home to Europe's largest diaspora of Koreans. London's unlikely K-Town. Where it was easier to find kimchi than milk. Where the most common greeting to observe on the high street was a mutual bow, hinging from the hips, head tucked.

Kit had come back to my flat from Leo's in the small hours. The drunken poking at the door pulled me from the light layer of sleep. I'd bolted myself in, so he thumped his shoulder against the door, boisterously calling my name from the hallway. I opened the door and he stumbled in, swaying like a Jenga tower about to topple. I processed that it was Kit. My partner of seven years, the man I love. And yet adrenaline was coursing through my body, searing acid through my arteries. As he plonked himself into bed and started snoring within a minute, I had to take deep, frustrated breaths until dawn to stop from screaming at him. *Did it not occur to you that coming into my flat in the dead of night off your face was going to be scary for me? Do you think about me at all?*

The winter sun streamed in. Kit was tangled around me, the only sound the distant bustle of the coffee shop downstairs. He was still in bed when I got up to meet Omma. *But we always try to spend Sundays together*, Kit said as he rubbed his eyes. I lied and said I needed to help Omma pick out a dress for a wedding. I needed a distraction from my hyper-analysis. It was the small things. When I had a rough day he cuddled me, kissed me, told me *I'm in awe of you. You're the strongest woman I know. You can get through anything.* But he said nothing further. Soothed me with praise of my strength, when I needed him to accept my weakness. Hushed me with a standard I didn't know how to meet anymore. But then I'm the one who wanted things to go back to normal! This was our normal: waking up on a slow Sunday morning together. *What more do you want from him?*

I wanted him to ask me how he could help. I wanted him to acknowledge that he put me in an uncomfortable situation at Leo's. Recognize what happened to me. See me. But I also refused to tell him what I needed. I felt scared asking for help. Of being the needy type he'd broken up with before.

"Go and ask for a table," Omma said as we arrived at the restaurant. "I'm going to go and get some newspapers." The shop next door distributed three of the community newspapers that reported on all things Korean. The restaurant had wooden tables with a hole in the middle with a steel cover. If we ordered meat to grill, a bucket of white-ashed coal would be brought in and dropped in the cavity, for an on-table barbecue.

"안녕하세요!" I said brightly. *Hello!* "두명 이요." *Table for two.*

The owner of the shop, who I saw often as a child, didn't recognize me. She was a homely woman with a red apron and dark green rubber clogs on her feet. In her apron pocket were scissors and tongs so she could lean over tables and quickly flip sizzling pork belly on barbecues.

"You want to eat?" she exclaimed to me in English, motioning a spoon with her hand. Ignoring my Korean. This happened often. In coffee shops, convenience stores, hairdressers. I would enter, speaking Korean, and would repeatedly be responded to in English. Although all other customers were spoken to in their shared language. It stung me deeply every single time. My skin was too dark to seem Korean, my hips too wide, my hair too wavy, and my lips too curved.

The concept of "minjok" was taught in schools. It was the theory that the Korean people formed one unified ethnicity. That there was a single, pure Korean bloodline. So mixed-race Koreans inherently presented a conundrum. *Who are you? You don't seem like one of us.* The "us" confused by the "you." Korean was my first language, the conduit through which I communicated with my mother. Literally, my mother tongue. But without her next to me, I felt unable to lean into her world. Blend into her background. Be cushioned by her community. Feel the camaraderie that existed between people who lived in the same home away from home. I stood awkwardly in the entrance, wanting to walk out.

I rarely had this issue with Turks. All it would take was

booking a table under the name *Ceyda* and the first thing the waitress would ask is *Türk müsün? Are you Turkish?* After that was settled, generous familiarity struck like lightning until hours later when we would leave the venue to calls of *güle güle!* A charming parting expression that translated to *leaving while laughing.* The root of this difference lay, as always, in history. Turkey was once the epicenter of an empire that sprawled continents, merged religions, intertwined languages. By contrast, Korea was once known as the hermit kingdom. Hanging off a continent, flanked on three sides by ocean. Today sharing its only border with a volatile despot. Japanese colonization in its recent memory, during which the idea of minjok flourished. A collective defense mechanism of banding together as one people.

Omma came through the door with a stack of newspapers.

"Unni! Unni!" *Sister! Sister!* The restaurant owner exclaimed, instantly recognizing Omma, ushering us in with both hands flapping. The ajumma pointed at me with big, round eyes, realizing. She clucked, saying how big I was now, how long it had been. There wasn't a hint of malice in her kind face, and my irritation dissolved away. Omma switched into her playful boasting mode, talking about how I studied law, that of course I was a lawyer at a very large firm in the City now. I zoned out and poured two cups of bori cha, soothing barley tea.

The table was soon covered with banchan. Crunchy beansprouts. Fresh kimchi. Marinated anchovies. Spicy cucumber salad. As always, Omma tutted that I shouldn't fill myself up before the main meal. My tteokbokki arrived. Squishy rice cakes cooked in a deep red, tangy, sweet gochujang sauce. Yukgaejang was next, and I slurped the noodles up, relishing the refreshing spice of its soup. Omma and I babbled in Korean about an explosive new K-drama we were both obsessed with.

"Ah, thank you for today," I exhaled, wiping my mouth and leaning back into the chair. "It's been good for me."

"I know you want Omma time when something is wrong," she said. "What is it?"

"I'm struggling a bit, it's nothing."

"Child, what do you have to be struggling with? Life's good for you."

"I don't know." I didn't know how to explain in terms she would understand how morose I was. "I'm not happy with any part of my life right now. Kit and I are about to move in together, but I'm nervous about it." Omma raised her eyebrows but said nothing. "I feel anxious all the time. My job is—"

"At least you have a good job," Omma contributed. "My lawyer."

I sighed. When I was younger, I finished reading *The Boy in the Striped Pajamas* and was a total mess. I sought Omma out for comfort. Climbed behind her and wrapped myself around her torso. She was holding up a compact mirror and gently pulling up her skin at the temples and along her jaw. She looked at me with mild surprise. She gently plucked me off her and said, *aga, you know Koreans don't like hugging*. I went back to my room and squeezed Donkey instead.

I now knew that Omma loved me. But I don't think she wanted to love me as much as she did. She didn't want her entire life devoted to another dependent being. She didn't want her heart to be wandering around outside her body. So she showed her love in muted ways. She couldn't sleep when I had exams in the morning, but never said the words "good luck." When we ate fish, she would give me the juicy, fleshy bits and silently eat the head herself. If she knew I was coming home for the weekend, she slapped my dad's hand away from all the food, saving it for me. Things a child rarely noticed in their myopic vision. In adulthood, I realized how many years were wasted with my inability to read these quiet acts of service. I lost time, frustrated that she didn't overcome all of her traumas, rather than marveling at her strength in overcoming some of them. Now, I appreciated her antiseptic approach; it gave our interactions an organic honesty I valued. Though I can't say it always gave me the unconditional affection I wanted.

"I know. I mean, I feel like nothing is quite going to plan for me. I feel like I'm at a crossroads. With Kit. I don't know. It doesn't feel . . . all relationships go through bad patches, right?"

"Sure, sure. You'll figure it out, aga. You're a smart girl, I never doubt you will make the right choices in life. You never disappoint us."

"Omma!"

Just then, the restaurant ajumma came back over with a plate of candied pumpkin for us.

"근데 언니," the owner began, setting the plate down. She peered at my face with curiosity, her head tilted as she gestured to me.

"정말 외국인 같다."

But sister, she doesn't seem very Korean.

22

A graveyard of possessions piled up by the door. It had taken a week straight to pack my flat up. A by-product of working harsh hours was the habit of repurchasing essential items. Instead of doing a load of laundry, a pack of ten new knickers. Instead of loading and unloading the dishwasher, disposable cutlery and paper plates. I'd generated a shameful amount of waste that I wasn't willing to carry with me into this next chapter. Everything was now out in the open. Moving in with Kit would be a clean start. A hit on the reset button.

I looked around my first adult flat. My shelter, now bastardized. It was bittersweet. I'd thrived here for years, but now I could only see signs of what Josh did everywhere: my stained bedside table, the bolt on the door. In certain moments, after dusk sank and the amber glow of the streetlamps streamed in, I was alone with him again.

I culled ruthlessly. Any item of clothing that I didn't love went to the homeless shelter. Any book that I didn't plan on rereading was donated to the charity shop. I left items of furniture out in the lobby of my building with a sign saying *FREE—please help yourself*. Items of any value, a Vitamix blender and my TV, I gave to my parents. I felt lighter with every item I said goodbye to, each a horcrux of my sadness.

Baba arrived in his trusty gray-blue fleece, his new one nowhere to be seen. The powdery-blue sky did not give away the crisp chill of late January. We worked methodically, carrying boxes downstairs and Tetrising them in the car. Hands rigid but torsos warm.

"Where's the boy?" Baba heaved, as he squatted to pick up another box.

"Kit will meet us at the flat and help us move in," I said, hoping this was true. He hadn't replied to me all morning.

"Interesting," Baba mused. "Only a mile between Clapham and here. This old man will lift all these heavy boxes alone."

I ignored his pointed comments and deflected. "Baba, one of the clients I've been working with has offered me a job at her company."

Baba froze mid-squat.

"When did you apply to her company?" he asked.

"I didn't. She needs a new internal legal team and suggested me for one of the positions."

He let the box thump on the ground. He walk-danced toward me, arms outstretched, hands cupped together until they held my chin.

"Mashallah, hayatim. Your work is paying off." Baba nodded. "Will you take it?"

"Yes," I said, too quickly. "I need to get this filing across the line at the end of the month, then she'll send me all the paperwork. But this client—Genevieve—she is amazing, I've loved working with her." Though that wasn't the whole truth behind why I wanted to leave, nor was it a lie.

Jade Kaya, now:
Babe, we're heading over to Clapham now. ETA—10 mins xxx

The Clapham Flat was undeniably an upgrade. Covetable high ceilings, original wood floors, and deep shelved alcoves which would look glorious filled with books. Every wall was painted a muted gray Farrow & Ball shade that, I'm told, an "expert colorist" chose for Ian Campbell. There were two bedrooms, the master of which had a large bay window with a balconette that you could imagine a rich woman leaning against as she drank her morning espresso. *Am I the rich woman now? I guess so.* The dissonance I felt with the decision to move into this flat crested inside me again. It didn't feel right. I shook past it. I stood by the door and directed Baba to set down each box in a different room.

"Okay, what's left to come up?" I asked.

"That's everything." Baba slapped his hands together. The air clung to the fact that there still hadn't been a sighting of Kit on the plains of Clapham Common.

"Hayatim," Baba began, looking anywhere but at me, "are you sure about this?"

I twinged at his tone.

"Yes, Baba," I said, kissing him on the cheek, "I'm sure."

Am I?

I fished out my double teapot and we brewed tea together in my new kitchen. An elaborate, time-consuming process which was very different from dunking a tea bag in a mug. For Turks, the process of making tea is ritualistic and familial, while the process of drinking tea is communal, essential. It would take under five minutes in any Turkish town to find stools haphazardly scattered along the pavement with uncles chain-smoking and drinking tea. Our teapot was a vertical gadget, with two pots, one on top of the other. Water was boiled on the stove (never in a kettle) in the bottom pot, with the loose tea leaves brewed slowly in the top.

"I must say, I'm very excited." Baba zipped his fleece closed and picked up his toolbox.

"Yeah? What for?"

"I'm excited to find out what excuse that boyfriend of yours has for not being here."

"Baba . . ."

"Listen to me. God gave you two ears and one mouth to listen twice and speak once. He's cutesy and handsome, whatever." I laughed at the word "cutesy" coming from Baba. "That boy has never had to lift a finger in his life, Jade. A girl like you, we have scraped our whole lives to make something out of you. You will clash."

"Where is this coming from?" It was one thing to be annoyed Kit wasn't here today, but Baba hadn't previously expressed any concern about our compatibility. *Has he thought this all along?*

"I see things, babam. You're pretending to be something you're not for him."

"What if I am that person and you're just not happy with that?" I squawked. "Because I'm not where you guys are still?"

Baba, who didn't have a spiteful bone in his body, looked astonished. *God, I didn't mean that.*

He said, very quietly, "You're right, we don't have much." Baba stared through me, before finally saying, "but he's got the best we have to give."

I swallowed hard.

"I'm sorry, that was wrong of m—"

"I'm warning you, Ceyda." I knew he meant business when he drew down his cherished grandmother's name. "I don't want you to wake up one day and realize your train has sailed."

"Train? What train?" I stammered. "It's *SHIP*, Dad! For God's sake, it's that my *SHIP* has sailed."

"Whatever. You're still young." A new pleading crept into his voice. "I don't want you to waste your best years. I didn't raise you to be subservient to some white boy who doesn't understand basic manners."

"Why have you never said any of this before?"

"I know what people think about cultures like ours," he said. "Your father controls you. Tells you what to do, what to wear, who to marry." I felt like my heart might break. "I have always tried to let you make your own mistakes, create your own life."

It was true. As I matured, it became assumed that I could be trusted to make the right choices. It was also gradually inferred that they didn't—or rather, *couldn't*—understand the nuances, the pressures of this career, this lifestyle, this Western relationship. Baba respected this status quo and fettered his observations. This escape of his doubts was momentous.

"And what's changed now?"

"He should be here! Where is he?" Baba started theatrically opening wardrobes and cupboards, looking for Kit. "Hello! Are you in here? Helloooo?"

I tried to keep a straight face, but when Baba moved to the kitchen cupboards, throwing them open with gusto, I spluttered with laughter. He moved toward me, his point made.

"I'm serious, kizim." Baba lifted a finger to my face. "The moment he disrespects you like this again, you come straight home. Do you understand?"

"It won't happen again."

Baba looked at the floor.

"Vallahi, you deserve better."

Kit came home two hours later.

"Hey baby." He kissed me on the forehead.

"Hello," I said coolly.

"How did it go—" he began.

"Where the hell were you today?" I snapped.

"It's been mental. You've seen the news, haven't you? Theresa's been thrashed in Parliament, again. Our clients are all racing to secure their positions in case of a no-deal Brexit—"

"I don't care!" I shouted. "I don't care what *the clients want*," I mimicked him. "I moved in today! You were supposed to be here!"

Kit put his jacket down and placed his hands on his hips.

"What's going on with you, Jade?"

"Excuse me?"

"I don't understand." Kit rubbed his eyes. "We both have demanding jobs. We always have. I thought we both respected that about each other. You've practically been a ghost the past few months with Arrow. You've canceled dates, not replied to me for hours on end. And now I miss one day, and you're going to give me a tough time for it?"

"It's different for me, I *have* to work that hard," I seethed. "You wouldn't understand, you're just—"

"Oh bloody hell, yep yep, I get it. I'm just another straight white guy. How could I possibly understand anything about hard work."

"Did you even tell your boss about today?" I sneered. "Or

are you so far up his arse, eager to please Daddy's best mate, that you said yes to working today?"

"What has gotten into you, Jade! Do you tell Genevieve you can't work a Sunday because you want to go and smell Aesop candles and drink overpriced cocktails with your boyfriend?" Kit stared at me. "Well? Do you? No, you don't. You blow me off to go running to her. Can you appreciate that I might care about my career too? Or is it only you who matters in this relationship anymore?"

"I *beg* your pardon?" I stammered.

Kit threw his hands up and looked at me. He was panting slightly. His brows pulled together, and his face softened. He came to sit next to me.

"I don't know. This is obviously bigger than today," he said. We sat in silence for a while. "A few months ago you never would have picked a fight with me the moment I walked through the door."

"I'm just trying to tell you how I feel!"

"You're always feeling *something*, Jade! You're never—" Kit's hands were turning as if digging for the right word. "I don't know, relaxed! We never have fun anymore!"

There was a lump the size of a golf ball stuck in my throat.

"Sorry my being assaulted has resulted in less fun for you, Kit," I spat.

"Fuck, Jade. You know that's not what I meant. We're both running on fumes." He sounded so defeated. "I want to be there for you, I do."

"You haven't tried to understand what's going on with me, Kit."

"I'm not a mind reader, Jade! I can't miraculously know what you're going through if you don't communicate with me."

"You don't need to be a mind reader to realize that moving out of the place I was raped in was going to be a big deal."

Kit winced. That word hung like a dirty smell in the room. It felt like a rhetorical tool. Like I said it for impact, without sincerity.

"I don't know why you have to be so . . . direct."

"I don't have the luxury of tiptoeing around it," I muttered.

"How are we going to move forward if you keep bringing up what happened in the past?"

"It's not the past for me!" I was exasperated. "It may be long forgotten for you, but I can't just 'move forward.' "

"I can't talk to you when you get like this, J." Kit rubbed his forehead, looking like a new father, weary with his child's wailing. "Everything I say is wrong. I feel like I'm treading on eggshells around you."

"Why am I always the problem!"

"I think we should take a time out," Kit said and stood up. "Cool off, come back to the conversation when we're a little less heated."

What? You can't say all those things about me then walk off! I wanted to scream. But I knew that would get me nowhere. So I just nodded.

Cooking always relaxed me. The boundless possibilities. The method of it. I whipped together a quick fried rice and offered Kit a bowl in silence. A peace offering of sorts. His body language softened.

"Thank you, Jadey."

We put the TV on to avoid speaking, catching a rerun of *Mulan*. We sat in silence. We might not be on the best terms, but relationships go through phases, right? If everyone gave up on a relationship with every rough patch, there would be no couples. Our fuses were short at the moment, but the dust would settle.

"Love you," Kit murmured, calling a ceasefire. "I hate fighting with you."

"Love you too."

I do, I do, I do, I recited inside. He stroked my shin gently. When Donny Osmond's voice hit the screen, we both jauntily jiggled to "I'll Make a Man Out of You"—Kit singing Donny's part with overenthusiastic verve that made him roll straight off the sofa. His head popped up from the floor and he kissed the ball of my foot as I chortled with a mouthful of rice. This is nice. This is us.

"Now that we're living together," he ventured, "maybe we could host something next weekend?"

"So grown-up!"

"Invite Eve. And I've barely met Adele. You spend so much time together, I'd love to get to know her more."

He was trying.

"Okay, I'll organize."

"That was yummy, my Mulan," he said, patting the bun on the top of my head.

Something within me splintered.

He'd called me Mulan before. I guess I thought it was cute. Or had it always jarred and I ignored it?

On the eve of my twenty-first birthday, nearly five years ago, I made my way to see Kit. His place was the penthouse apartment of a converted warehouse off Bermondsey Street, with a wraparound balcony and rooftop. The living room had exposed brickwork that made it seem like an artist's studio. I arrived and let myself in, set the kettle to boil, and began rinsing out some mugs to make tea in. The boys all came in as I was drying a mug and wiping some tea off the counter.

"Hey." Kit saw me at the sink, pulling me in at the waist and making a show of dipping me over and kissing me.

"There she is, our housemaid!" Ollie exclaimed.

"Hey, what the fuck?" Kit's head snapped back to glare at Ollie, and his arm extended in front of me the way a driver does to their passenger when hard braking. "That's not funny, mate."

My cheeks burned with embarrassment.

"It's fine." I tried to laugh it off.

"What was that comment about?" Kit pushed.

"It was a joke, dude." Ollie held his hands up. "Because she was washing up when we came in."

"But would you have said the same thing about a white person?" Kit was animated. I was squirming. "Or are you saying that because she's Asian? Do you think all Asian people are houseworkers?"

Nobody said that.

"Kit, stop . . ." I wheedled. "It was just a misunderstanding."

"No, it wasn't. Ollie, the things you say have *subtext*, you should be mindful of that."

"Yeah, okay." Ollie's bravado melted away, having been scolded by the flat alpha. "I'm sorry, Jade. I never meant to upset you."

I never even said I was upset! Kit was the one who had the issue!

"You don't have to always pull people up on stuff like that," I said later in his bed, facing the window.

"I do." He tapped my shoulder. "Turn over?" I did as he asked, and we were nose to nose. "It's my responsibility to call stuff like that out, the labor shouldn't be yours."

"You making a big deal out of it makes me feel," I whispered, "really awkward and out of place."

"And what would it say about me if I just stood by?"

At the time, I was silent.

I should have told him the truth. It wasn't about him at all.

I went to the kitchen with our empty bowls and took measured breaths with my back against the door. Countless memories came flooding back to me, of all the times Kit had defended my honor. The time when I got kicked out of a club in Shoreditch for being too drunk, despite being on antibiotics and only drinking Pepsi Max all night. Kit ensured the bouncer in question got fired, then tweeted about how he was *saddened to witness the shocking discrimination*. The times we saw other interracial couples—always white men with ethnically ambiguous women—and Kit nodded at the boyfriend. The time we landed in Gatwick and the customs officer questioned the validity of my British passport. Kit hovered nearby, filming us, and told me I should post it to Instagram. The time we went to Tesco's together and he was so thirsty that he opened a bottle of water before paying, and I was the one who got accused of shoplifting. Kit gave a speech in front of a dozen Sunday shoppers. He was prepared to disrupt comfort levels to defend me. *But at the expense of whose comfort?* And if he was so aware in public, why did he call me Mulan in private?

It slipped out, I told myself, *you're so sensitive these days!* Am I the type of woman who picks fights with her man on a Sunday? Or am I the woman who understands he meant no harm and knows not to ruin an evening?

23

I had hoped that the nightmares might stop once I was living in our new home. But my first night in the Clapham Flat was anointed with the faceless figure inside me, hitting against my cervix. My out-of-body self watched, banging on imaginary glass. Kit shook me awake and pulled my head to his chest. *It's okay, it's okay, it's just the two of us here*, he whispered. He stroked my hair, grounding me into the present.

Monday morning. I showered while Kit made breakfast. When I was doing my makeup, my work phone buzzed with an invitation to a Firm social. I remembered what Bailey said about skipping events being career suicide. We'd spent most of January toiling over Arrow's Defense. A single document that represented hundreds of hours of investigation. I needed to just keep pedaling until it was filed and I had proven myself. Law was also a small, incestuous industry. It was in my interests to keep up appearances at Reuben and go to the Firm social. I felt like there was a film of plastic stuck in my throat. Asphyxiated by expectations. I felt dirty again. With my foundation and blusher on, I got back under the shower. Kit walked in, still in his boxers, saying *haven't you just taken a shower?* He saw my mascara disintegrating and, saying nothing, climbed under the water with me. He held me and said *I'm sorry, I should have been there to help you move in this weekend. Don't cry, Jadey.* I wasn't crying about that, but it felt a relief to be held.

"Man, did I tell you," Adele began a few days later, "I saw Gabby last night. The bar played 'On Hold' by The xx and she started crying."

"Oh shit! Why?"

"Said it reminded her of her ex."

"Ooof. Bad news."

"To be fair, she did spend the next thirty minutes apologizing profusely. And she's cute."

"Show me a pic?"

"Ew, stop." Adele frowned. "As if I have a picture of her."

"Mate, that's what social media stalking is for." Adele had zero social media presence. Her virtual identity was a ghost, except for a single sour headshot on Reuben's website.

"Nope." She shook her head as I taunted her with my Instagram search. "Everyone is fake on social media."

"Found her!"

"What? How did you do that so quick?"

"Puhlease, we can look into decade-old frauds, but you think I can't find your girlfriend online?"

"Don't be cute. She's not my girlfriend." Adele gritted her teeth, but curiosity got the better of her. "What did you find?"

"What's your pleasure? We've got her Instagram profile, Facebook, LinkedIn, and what appears to be her Depop page?"

"You're a psycho, you know that?" Adele whipped my phone out of my hand and started scrolling.

"Make sure you don't like something."

"Ugh, her ex is stunning." Adele glowered.

"That's a good thing," I said as I maneuvered to Adele's desk. "It means she has standards." Adele tilted the phone to show me the post: four mini black-and-white images of two women smiling broadly in a photo booth strip. "Which is Gabby?"

"The one on the left." Adele pointed to a svelte woman with long dark hair to her waist, gloriously heavy and full breasts held up by slim shoulders. Her neck was craned as the other woman kissed her cheek, displaying its elegant length and the powerful angle of her jaw.

"Del, that woman is a solid ten."

"I know, right."

"Do you want to bring her to our housewarming?"

"I'll ask if she wants to come along. But I swear to God, if you start playing The xx I'll throttle you."

I fluttered my lashes. "Pinky promise, cross my heart, hope to die."

"Delivery for Jade?" Anton from the post room tapped on our office door. I awkwardly held the door open for him with one hand, while also trying to receive the bouquet in the other.

"Roses? Seriously?" Adele said, thumping her palms on her desk.

I chuckled as I balanced the bunch on my table and fished for the card.

To my new roommate, here's to our next chapter together.

I felt a high rush through my veins. All couples fight, for

God's sake. It's *normal*! We love each other. He wants a future with me. He's smart and good-looking and educated and has a good job and makes me laugh and is caring in his own way. He is everything I have ever wanted. Without realizing, I was nodding at no one, my happy face plastered on. An optimistic, naïve picture.

One hundred hours later, I finally clicked send on the document we'd poured every waking moment into.

"We're over the line," I announced on the call. "The Defense has been filed and served just now."

"Brava." Genevieve was satisfied. "Very good."

"I'll send you hard copies of the final documents on Monday morning, for your records," I said, ever eager to tick box.

"Pft, pft, pft, get some sleep," she said, "you've earned it."

I knew everything about sleep being something to be earned.

"Okay, if that's everything—"

"Jade, before you go," Genevieve began. "Thank you so much for your hard work, but I'm afraid you can't work on Project Arrow anymore."

"What? Why?" I spluttered. "Have I done something wrong?"

"You can't work on the case anymore," her voice gave nothing away, "because shortly, I hope you'll be joining me here as a member of our in-house team. That is, if you still want it."

Relief trampled through my exhausted, delirious body, cantankerous and exuberant.

"Oh my—that is—that is so amazi—thank you, Genevieve," I babbled.

"Are you happy?" Genevieve laughed down the phone.

"I'm so happy, honestly, I can't wait."

"It's well deserved. You've been such a hard worker over these months, and I know I haven't gone easy on you. I have to go, but Rémy will send you the paperwork on Monday with all the boring details on role, pay, benefits, and bonus, etcetera, etcetera."

She hung up.

My heart was battering. I closed my eyes and slumped into my chair.

This is it, I breathed.

You're getting away from this place.

It'll be over soon.

24

From Joshua Parsons to Jade Kaya on January 30, 2019 at 1:10 pm

RE: Hey

Cycled past you this morning but you didn't notice. How have you been?

I blinked at his name, glibly sitting in my inbox. I wanted to reach in, pluck it out, and crush it. I beckoned Adele over and she scanned the email.

"What a fucktard," Adele barked.

"Has he been following me?" My first thought. "Does he know my route into work? How could he? I've moved house! Where exactly did he pass me? Shall I start taking different exits out of the building?"

A protein shake of paranoia and anxiety swirled. Adele rubbed my shoulders.

"If I have to," she growled, "I'll personally escort you out of the building every day."

"I feel so gross," I whispered. We fell into a silence, scrolling over the words repeatedly. *Is this what he wants? Me to writhe over a pithy one-liner.* Fat tears ambled down my face, the saltiness on my lips feeling itchy. "I don't understand how he can be so blasé. The last time we spoke I was yelling at him."

"Jade, you know I love you, right?" Adele said. I sighed, lifting my head up and wiping my tears from my cheeks with my sleeve. "You have to report him."

"We've discussed this."

"I know it's scary, J—"

"You don't get it." My head was back on the desk. "The police don't feel like an option. How can you trust an institution that stops and searches your father for 'suspiciously' wearing long sleeves on a warm day?"

Adele looked helpless as she opened her mouth and closed it again.

We reread the message.

"What about to HR?" she suggested. "You don't have to tell them everything if you don't want to. Say his email made you uncomfortable. They can pull him up on it, give him a spook. That should get him to leave you be?"

It made sense. An interim solution to get him to stop contacting me.

"What do you have to lose, Jade? You're getting out of here."

I sat in the lobby of floor twenty-five, looking out at the panoramic windows that stretched over the City. I told Kit about

Josh's email. After Christmas Eve, I'd promised I'd share important things with him. Kit agreed that HR was absolutely the right port of call. He seemed to think that the biggest transgression was the sheer nonchalance of his email. *If he feels comfortable bandying emails like that to women in relationships, then God knows what else he's willing to do*, he said.

But we all knew what else he was willing to do.

The decision to report to HR fell into place. Rémy had sent across a draft contract of employment. I planned to negotiate on some details, but had a written, confirmed offer from Arrow. Adele was right: I was imminently resigning from Reuben, so why wouldn't I report him internally? Something to make my life easier during my notice period. A black mark lodged on his file. I had my boyfriend and Adele supporting me. Disagreement smudged Eve's face. But she would prop me up regardless.

I dabbed my palms on the end of my skirt, praying that a handshake wouldn't be offered. Feeling compelled to appear poised, I began flicking through a copy of *The Economist*. The words lifted off the page and floated around my eyes, my brain unable to digest the headlines.

"Jade?" a friendly voice called out. I looked up to see a young woman I recognized from around the building. She was very tall and wore a geometric-print wrap dress.

"Hi. Yes, that's me."

"Sarah. Good to properly meet you." I swallowed and nodded, as she led me through to her office. I felt like the subject of a peep show. I could almost hear the salacious whispers about my walk of shame to the HR department spreading like wildfire through the Firm by close of business.

"So, tell me what the issue is." Sarah theatrically closed the door behind us and lowered the blinds. She was as subtle as a dump truck, and she whispered the word "issue" the way old people mouth the word "sex."

I led Sarah through every detail I had rehearsed. Talked about how the email made me feel uncomfortable, ensuring that I paused enough times so she could take notes. Her manicured nails click-clacked as she typed.

"During the Firm's anniversary dinner, in addition to Josh, Mr. Reuben was also quite inappropriate toward me," I said. At that, Sarah became animated, her ears pricked up.

"Mr. Reuben is the most senior member of the Firm; that is a very serious accusation, Jade."

"I haven't told you what he did yet."

Sarah waved her hand to indicate I should go on.

"Well, he made several attempts to get me to go home with him."

"Could you elaborate a bit more?"

"He kept offering me a place to stay."

"Thanks for bringing that to our attention, Ms. Kaya." I sagged into the chair with relief, finally having taken some action. "To clarify, we don't have a written policy against intra-firm dating," she added. "But we will look into it! Is that everything?"

She wasn't taking me seriously.

"No, that's not all!" My relief dissipated. *I didn't want to talk about this*. I wanted to tell HR that Josh was bothering me and freak him out enough to leave me alone. But now, grievances were stacking on top of each other, exasperation rising up my neck, and I divulged more than I ever intended to. "At the end of that evening, I was raped by a member of the Firm."

I wanted to catch the words midair and stuff them back into my mouth.

Odd how three words, strung together in the most basic sentence, could feel so irreversibly monumental.

"Can you wait a moment." It sounded like a question, but Sarah was already out the door. Minutes passed. I plucked until the skin pulled off my cuticles. My leg bounced faster than a polygraph needle. The nape of my neck was slick with sweat, and I spun around, contemplating running out. *Stupid stupid girl. Why did I say anything?* My self-reprimand was cut short as Sarah came back in, with another, much older woman in tow.

"This is Julie. She's here to listen to your account."

"Hi Jade, Sarah has briefly got me up to speed. I'm so very sorry to hear what you have reported. Can you walk me through what happened?" Julie's tone was caring but brusque, like a busy nurse's would be.

"His name is Joshua Parsons. At the end of the Firm's anniversary party last November—"

"November 2018?"

"Erm . . . yes."

Julie scribbled on her notepad.

"Okay, thank you."

"At the end of the party, we shared a taxi home together, as we live quite close. That's what he said, at least. I don't actually know where he lives. I passed out in the cab home, and I don't really remember what happened after that." Julie and Sarah were looking at me with their eyebrows pulled in, eyes consoling. Julie wrote something on her pad, then underlined it with three long scratches. "I don't remember exactly what happened, but since that evening, I've had some very troubling flashbacks and nightmares.

"I spoke to Josh a few weeks after the fact," I continued. I hadn't said all of this out loud so frankly before. It felt like a drink of ice-cold water after a walk in the hot sun. "He doesn't deny sleeping with me. But I was so drunk, there is no way I could have consented." The last syllable of "consented" was a high-pitched squeak as my teeth sank into my shaking bottom lip. Sarah placed a box of Kleenex next to me, while Julie rubbed my shoulder.

"Here, here, it's all right," Julie said, as I hiccupped through my tears and apologized for crying.

"Don't be sorry, get it all out."

There was a long pause. Neither Julie nor Sarah wanted to be the first to speak. Julie, as clearly the more senior member of the team, began.

"Jade, thank you for bringing this to our attention. As you know, we take all allegations of sexual misconduct *very* seriously at the Firm, and I want to assure you that this will be investigated thoroughly." She reached out and touched my knee. "So that I have all the facts, can I ask some quick questions?"

"Sure." I sniffled into my tissue.

"So, where did this happen?"

"My flat. My old flat."

"Ah, and how did Mr. Parsons come to be in your home?"

"I don't remember—to be honest I think he just let himself in."

"Right." Throughout this, Sarah was somewhat inappropriately smiling, an expression I think she intended to be comforting. "And—I'm so sorry to have to ask you this, Jade," Julie said, pulling her lips wide to demonstrate she was cringing, "but it would be helpful for us to know if you and Josh have any sort of romantic history?"

"How is that relevant?"

"It's a silly, minor detail. It's so that we know we have all the context and background information."

"So, any history?" Sarah perked her voice up, in a bid to play good cop.

"No. No history. I actually have a long-term partner."

The moment I said it, I regretted it.

"Okay," Julie said. "I'm so sorry."

It was unclear what specifically Julie was apologizing for. As if my being with Kit made Josh's transgression worse somehow. As if a taken woman was more clearly off-limits to nonconsensual sex than a single woman.

"We will take this away and investigate it. Thank you so much for sharing, Jade. Law firms have sadly got a shocking reputation for dealing with these kinds of things, but rest assured we will take care of this," Julie said, holding my hand. Her palms were cold, but I appreciated the gesture. "I hope you can understand that it is *very, very important* that you keep this confidential while we look into it, if you can do that?"

I nodded.

"Have you reported this to anyone else?"

"No, I didn't feel read—"

"That's good." Julie's eyes screwed small like a mole. "It's best for the integrity of the investigation that we don't involve any outside forces at this stage."

I nodded again.

25

I lay the vinyl on the turntable and lowered the pin on the spinning record. *Rumours* was a familiar, charismatic friend, popular enough to be recognized by guests, but tumultuous enough not to be basic. There was champagne chilling, a stylish Diptyque candle burning on the coffee table next to a bowl of olives. Hosting was one of the conduits through which women measured each other. Do you have everything under control? How aesthetic is your home? Are you and your partner a perfectly symbiotic team? Is he liberated from misogyny enough to cook while you effervescently keep your guests entertained? Do you have one-of-a-kind ceramic serveware by a local artist you support?

Incoming call from Baba

"Hello?" I answered.

"Your mother is very upset" was the first thing he said. No hayatim, no kizim.

"Oh no! What's happened?" *Is she hurt?*

"It was Seollal on Tuesday," Baba said, his voice gritty.

I drew my breath in quickly. God. I was so busy, I'd completely forgotten about the Korean New Year. The biggest celebration on the calendar. Where time was spent with families. I saw Omma text me asking me when I was coming home, but it was one of those texts you mentally noted to reply to, and then never got around to. Along with making the report to HR, getting the Defense in, negotiating my role parameters at Arrow, attempting to preserve my relationship, unpacking into the new flat, and a total lack of sleep, the holiday had flown my mind.

"I feel terrible," I said. Omma didn't make a fuss about much, but Seollal was her time to shine. I would have gone home to a table covered in tteokguk, mandu, japchae, all cooked to perfection, Omma's face accomplished.

"We understand you are a very busy lawyer, kizim, and maybe you couldn't take the day off work. But how could you even forget to call? She was waiting for you all day."

My heart could have wilted on the spot. It was unwritten law that the obligation lay with children to pay their respects to their elders. On Seollal, children bowed to their elders and received money in envelopes. Baba would slip me an extra tenner to distract me from Omma's tears for her own parents. Omma would never have messaged me to follow up.

I called my mum and profusely apologized. Blamed the stress of the job for my forgetfulness, tearing up between words.

"Don't cry. Wrinkles!" Omma laughed softly. That only made me cry more. The soft cushioning of her voice made me want to run home.

"괜찮아." *It's okay*, Omma soothed, half laughing in confusion at how emotional I was at what I claimed was an innocent mistake. I screwed my face tautly to control the tears. Omma told me about the day, how she made her best tteokguk yet, how she ordered her rice cakes weeks in advance. My mouth salivated at the thought of the dishes I'd missed out on. *I should have been there. These are the important things.*

We hung up, and I gathered myself. I feverishly shopped for the ingredients for Kit to cook, tidied, hoovered, wiped mirrors, dusted shelves, and finally managed to have a few minutes to touch up my lipstick and get changed. I wore a black satin blouse, loosely tied at the waist, with buttons undone to reveal a lacey bralette, a long gold lariat chain dangling just above my breasts. I looked like the young trophy wife of a middle-aged CEO, nestling into the family home she's redecorated to remove any trace of his displaced first wife.

Emma and Ollie, our university friends, were the first to arrive. Kit handed Ollie a Birra Moretti, while I poured Emma a glass of champagne. Once we settled into opposite ends of the sofa and our allotted gender roles, Emma asked various interior design questions, while Ollie and Kit initiated an in-depth analysis of the Welsh win at the Six Nations.

"Aw, is that you!" Emma squealed, walking toward the mantelpiece and picking up a framed photo of Omma and me, at around eight months old, having a picnic. "Look at you! Such a chubby bubba!"

I smiled bashfully, as Ollie and Kit sauntered over to peer at the photo.

"Still as cute as a button," Kit said, pulling me in at the waist.

"Your mum is a true nineties fox," Ollie said, whistling.

"A total MILF," Em agreed.

"If you want to know what your girlfriend is going to look like in twenty years' time, just look at her mum, amirite?" Ollie said, tapping his elbow against Kit's.

"You were such an Asian baby!" Emma clucked. My head instinctively turned, my ears turning red.

"Well, makes sense!" I said lightly, trying to keep my tone playful.

"No, but like, you look more . . . ethnic now. You were way more Asian-looking as a kid."

My eyes bulged as I swore internally that I wouldn't derail the night before it had started. I was saved by the bell. I swung the door open to find Leo leaning against the frame.

"Hey." I gave him a lopsided grin and leaned forward for a hug. "Where's Suzie?"

"Total nightmare," he said, walking into the hallway. "She called it quits a couple of days ago."

"What happened?" I was disappointed. I enjoyed Suzie's company more than Leo's most of the time.

"Haven't the foggiest." Leo shrugged. "She said I didn't treat her right, packed her stuff up and left. The removal company I arranged took the last of her things today; the least I could do was make the process easier."

"Legend!" Kit came round the corner, my eyes wide to try to telepathically warn him not to put his foot in it. "Where's the missus?"

"Out the picture, bro. I was telling Jade: she broke it off out of the blue. Totally blindsided me."

"Whoa. Well, she clearly had some issues in that case." Kit slapped Leo on the shoulder. "Let's get you a beer, mate."

While I was closing the door I saw Adele on the other side of the street, looking down at directions on her phone.

"Del!" I waved. "Over here!" As she turned, I spied her date behind her. The two of them, both nearly six feet tall, floated across the street. Now winter was waning, the sun was setting a little later in the day, and together with the marshmallow sky behind them, they were an ethereal image fit for a seventies album cover.

"Jade, this is Gabby," Adele said with a huge Cheshire cat smile of self-satisfaction. "Gabby, this is my best friend, Jade."

"So happy to meet you!" I leaned forward and kissed Gabby on both cheeks. "Glad you could both make it."

"Thank you so much for having me," Gabby said shyly. I noticed an American accent.

"Is Eve here yet?" Adele asked.

"Nah, she couldn't make it—she's moving house today," I said, walking into the living room and introducing Del and Gabby.

As the guests chatted, I sneaked off to the kitchen, where Kit was sticking his tongue out, stirring the ali nazik kebab in the pot I'd prepared for him earlier. It warmed my heart when he asked me for my family's recipe. He wanted to get it exactly right, so he asked questions like *when you say dice the onions, exactly how big should the chunks be? Wait, how do you peel an aubergine, it doesn't have a skin like a banana does? Can I put the rice in now? Or when the water's boiling? What do you mean by "season the water"?*

I had at least managed to convince him to let me prepare the ayran—a salty yoghurt drink—when Leo came in.

"So, who's the other girl?" Leo opened the fridge and pulled out three beers.

"She has a name," I said, rolling my eyes.

"Don't be like that."

"Gabby?"

"Yeah, she's outrageously fit."

"You're a charmer."

"Oh, c'mon, you can't blame me! I'm trying to put my shattered heart back together," he wheedled. "Seriously, though, is she single?"

"She's Adele's date, you blind idiot." I waved my spoon toward the living room.

"Next time do a better job of wingmanning." Leo smirked before kissing me on the cheek and flouncing off in glee. I made a mental note to keep an eye on him.

Two bottles of champagne later and we were finally settling at the dining table for dinner.

"Smells glorious, mate!" Ollie said, as Kit leaned across him to set the platter of kebab—tender lamb over smoky aubergines and garlicky yoghurt—in the middle. "What are we having?"

"Ali nazik kebab," I said, "my grandmother's recipe."

"And you cooked, Kit?" Emma piped up, with her hand over her heart, looking at Ollie with her brows knitted together as if to say *watch this example*. "Aww, so sweet!"

"Oooh," Emma said, peering into the pot, "I think I saw this in Ottolenghi's cookbook, what did you say it was called again?"

"Ali nazik. It originates from Gaziantep, but is pretty common across most of the east coast."

"And that's . . . Israeli?"

"No, Em." I laughed to flood some forced lightness through my gritted teeth. "It's Turkish."

"Ah, I see! All those cuisines blend into each other a bit, don't they?" She continued, "Who *really* invented hummus, for example?"

I smiled warmly, refusing to look up at Adele, whose eyes were boring into me. I was already self-conscious about what Adele would think about this group of university friends. Or rather, what she would think about who I was around them.

"Em," Ollie laughed, "geography has never been your strong suit, has it?" He stood, holding up his glass. "I'd like to raise a toast first, to my dear friends, Jade and Kit, who have always been the mum and dad of our friendship group." Emma, to Ollie's left, nodded sagely. "I am so happy for you both that you have taken this next step in your relationship, and I wish you many happy years in your new home. To Kit and Jade!"

The rest of the guests echoed Ollie's sentiment, and, within a few minutes, multiple side conversations had begun. I had allied myself on the other end of the table with Adele and Gabby.

"So, where are you from, Gabby? I heard an American accent earlier."

"I'm from Chicago originally," she said, nodding, "but I've been in London for six years now." She was pushing her food around her plate, looking queasy.

"Is the food okay?"

"Uh, sorry, I'm a vegan," she said sheepishly.

I slapped Adele's arm. "Why didn't you tell me!"

"Shit, I forgot!" Adele said.

"Let me quickly rustle something up for you." I started to get up.

"No, no, no, it's honestly all right," Gabby said. "I ate loads of the bread and olives earlier, so I'm not even that hungry!"

I was about to insist on cooking something for Gabby when my ears pricked up as I heard across the table, "I put in an offer for the place this morning—a steal, to be honest."

"Are you buying a place, Leo?" *Bit of an odd thing to do when embroiled in a breakup?*

"Hopefully, if the offer is accepted. In Peckham, two bedder for seven two five."

"Good Lord," I breathed.

"Is that normal for London?" Adele asked.

"I went in way over the competition," Leo said, "made an offer they couldn't say no to."

"Were there many others?" Ollie asked.

"A local couple, they tried to low-ball for six thirty. Asking was six seven five."

"You offered fifty grand over asking?" I exclaimed.

"God," Kit coughed. "Not sure how I feel about the increasing gentrification going on there."

Leo shrugged. "I liked the place."

Kit didn't press further. I knew Adele would have clocked Kit's laying down of his markers, only to not interrogate the issue further.

"Is the bank happy to lend you that much?" I asked.

Leo played with his collar. "It's a cash purchase. It's more efficient that way." I balked at the idea of Leo, with his designer trimmed beard and signet ring, walking the streets of Peckham, bulldozing a local couple's offer for a property in their own neighborhood.

But are you going to say anything, Jade? I thought not.

By the time I jolted back into the conversation, it had moved on to the Iraq war.

"Undoubtedly Blair is a war criminal," I heard Leo say. "But I guess I would say that as a bleeding-heart liberal."

The evening rolled into the early hours of the morning. The champagne turned to wine which turned to whiskies. Conversations ducked and weaved: the celebrities our partners fancied (I went for Tommy Shelby from *Peaky Blinders*, Kit went for Zoë Saldaña); whether a second Brexit referendum was in the cards; whether a dog or a cat would win in a fight; the best places to visit in Boston; a group trip itinerary to Ollie's family place in Dorset (early June was penciled in).

As we approached two in the morning, Kit and I were on opposite ends of the sofa, Kit rubbing the soles of my feet. Leo was flicking through a magazine I had left on the coffee table. Em was rummaging through the fridge for late-night snacks. Ollie was leaning against the open bay window, succumbing to his nicotine crutch. Gabby and Adele were entwined together on the armchair, in the unmistakable glow of early lust. The night had taken a lethargic pace, with everyone's movements in slow motion. The record player had been abandoned and songs had been shuffling on Spotify for the past hour.

"Chooooon," Ollie said, as the twang of strummed guitars came on through the speakers.

Kit pointed at the guys. "Another beer?"

Even Del and Gabby were roused from their love nest, swaying to the music, stopping to kiss every few beats.

"Great night, baby, you did an amazing job." Kit leaned over to kiss me.

"Love you." I smiled.

Ollie parked his ciggie in the corner of his lips as he cracked open his beer, then began singing along with Coldplay. As the familiar chords to "Yellow" reverberated around the flat, Ollie stuck his head out of the window, upturned to the sky, mimicking the song's stargazing lyrics.

I lolled my head against the arm of the sofa, body relaxed, barely making out the tuneless crooning.

Ollie pointed at me with an inviting smile.

"Jade, this one's for you!"

Befuddled and drunk, I didn't understand. I looked over at Kit, who laughed in bemusement. Leo had moved toward Ollie, strumming an invisible ukulele. I laughed along confusedly.

"We came along . . . we wrote a song fo-oor Jade!"

Then I realized. I stood up. I didn't want to look, but I couldn't look away either. My feet were welded to the floor. Leo and Ollie put their heads together, using their beer bottles as microphones, eyes shut and shouting, "And she was so yellow!"

It was like a record scratch scraping through my layers of sensibility.

"Whoa," Adele said, mouth agape and looking between me, Kit, and the guys. "Surely they don't mean—"

Kit was looking intensely at his beer bottle, presumably hoping the situation wouldn't escalate.

They hadn't noticed Adele, and were continuing their humiliating serenade, both pointing at me while I willed the ground to swallow me whole. A pounding had begun in my ears, stamping out my hearing.

". . . She was all yellow!"

Gabby sat up and switched the speaker off, her previously soft American twang replaced with hard Chicago dialect. "The hell do you think you're doing?"

"What?" Ollie held up his hands. "It was just a joke, chill. Jade doesn't care!"

"She's obviously not okay!" Gabby shrieked.

"Haven't you just met her tonight? We've known Jade for years."

"Jade, are you okay?" Adele said.

I stared at the floor, squirming to be out of this situation. I may have smiled. I'm not sure. I looked at Kit.

"All right, guys, that was stupid," Kit waded in, the authority figure. "Everyone's drunk, let's not get too heated, shall we?" He nodded at me to play along.

"Kit," I said. The evening was already decomposing at a rapid pace. "Is that all?"

"It's okay, Jadey." His voice was warm in a forced way. "They were just singing along to a song."

I stood still. Emma and Ollie exchanged *uh-oh* glances. Adele and Gabby each took a step to flank me.

Kit quickly glanced at the boys with an embarrassed smile that suggested he was doing his best to manage me. "Jade, it was a joke! A stupid one, but we've had a nice evening. Let's all move on, shall we?"

"Is that the best you can do?" I said.

"I'm not the one who said it, Jade! Why am I in the firing line?"

The memory of Leo and Ollie doing a Borat impression

when Baba came to my graduation burst to the surface. Their laughs as they said *izzz nice* and exclaimed *wa wa wee wa!* I'd smiled then, too. I'd failed to protect the best person in my life. I couldn't fucking take this pretending anymore.

"Why aren't you defending me!" I yelled. *Why, all these years, have you used me as your personal soapbox but won't stand up for me when I actually need you to.*

"Jade," Kit said softly, "our friends have the right to sing along to songs without getting yelled at."

"So I'm the problem now," I said quietly, my insides ballooning with humiliation.

I felt Adele and Gabby watching us.

"I'm just trying to ease the tension, Jadey. No need to take things so personally, okay?"

"Look, I don't want to cause a domestic here." Ollie stood up. He turned to Gabby and Adele, his hand over his heart, and said, "I'm sorry, sincerely, if you both felt like what I said was offensive. It was not my intention at all."

"Oh, fuck off," Adele said, rolling her eyes.

"Don't tell my boyfriend to fuck off!" Emma squealed. "You're so rude!"

"Well, I tried apologizing." Ollie laughed as if to say *hey, I'm the bigger person here*.

There was a stagnant, silent moment that mushroomed, filling the room with awkwardness and sobriety. I wanted to stand with Adele and Gabby and walk out of here. *This* is exactly what I was worried about happening tonight. Adele seeing me fold, to avoid causing a scene. Her seeing me brush past things because the alternative was walking out on the life I'd constructed.

I picked up the salad bowl and threw the wooden servers

inside it. They clattered loudly, which only made me look churlish. Del and Gabby started to fuss around me. *Leave it, we'll clear up*. Seeing my best friend and her date pick up Ollie and Leo's crumpled napkins was too debasing for me to bear.

"Please, Del," I said. "I'm okay. I've got this. Let me order you a cab."

I got their coats together and headed toward the door as they trailed behind me.

"I'm so so so sorry," I pleaded in a whisper.

"I'm not leaving you," Adele concluded. Gabby nodded.

"Del." I held her hands, ashamed at my weakness, mortified by association. I held her gaze, pleading with her. "Please go. Don't worry. I'll be okay."

She understood, and nodded.

"Call me if you need me, okay?"

"Yeah." *Take me with you, please.*

"Love you, Jade."

"Love you." I squeezed Adele's hand. "And really good to meet you," I said to Gabby.

I walked back into the living room to see Kit, Ollie, Emma, and Leo around the coffee table, laughing.

26

I watched the sunrise as I pretended to be asleep. London had never looked prettier. Approaching spring brought earlier mornings; a wash of lavender backdropped the ivory Georgian town houses, lighting up the common. The frost on the grass looked shimmery silver. *I'm lucky, I'm so lucky to have this.* I chose to take the window side of the bed when I moved in because it was further from the door. Kit had joked *so you want me to get murdered first?* But the joke had fallen, leaden and round. Silky streaks fell out of my eyes, over the bridge of my nose and into the pillowcase.

I tried to understand how we got here. I glanced over my shoulder at the man beside me, his splayed lashes gently fluttering with each absorbed, contented breath. There was nothing lonelier than crying in bed, with the person you love fast asleep next to you.

There were some lessons from last night's dinner:

1. I have spent seven years laughing along as I was mocked.

2. Being with me was a mirror for Kit in which he saw the reflection of a savior. I was the tool through which he demonstrated he was a renaissance man prepared to engineer change. But only when he had the floor, could assert his superiority, and it was convenient for him to do so.
3. I am a hypocrite. I wanted to set myself apart from the elitism, but I also was affronted when I wasn't welcomed into the fold. After all, I'd curated a potent mixture of credentials—well-spoken, highly educated, knowledge to remove tacking stitches from new clothes. I wanted my boyfriend to love me for who I was, while I performed something else for him. I wanted to be Jade, but my heart hurt for Ceyda.
4. Notwithstanding all of (3) above, I knew I couldn't stop.
5. You can love someone while detesting them with a viciousness that scares you.

I brought my hand up and clamped my palm over my mouth. To stifle any escaping cries. Absorb them back within myself. My abs were tensed to keep my body rigid. The songbirds of London chorused the dawn. Their melodies helped cover the tiny whimper that I didn't manage to contain.

An hour later, Kit was up and making lattes at our SMEG coffee machine. A chrome behemoth of a thing that sounded like a Boeing 737 taking off. I hated the coffees it made, and much preferred a basic black filter. I threw my head back on the pillow. *Even my coffee preference is a lie?* He brought me a cup full of frothy milk and sat on the bed next to me.

"Last night got pretty hairy, huh?" he said with a smile.

That was my cue to smile too. To laugh about it and de-escalate. Blame it on the alcohol.

I didn't say anything, and after a minute, Kit got up and showered.

He didn't ask how I felt. Whether Adele and Gabby were okay.

The pressure inside me festered.

"Have you seen my cream Zara jumper?" I asked, later in the afternoon.

"Sorry, no," Kit replied.

"I haven't seen it in a few days—weird."

"You've probably left it in the office," he said absentmindedly. "You're always forgetting about things you left there."

"And what exactly do you mean by that?" I shot back, my tone barbed and ready to defend.

Kit looked up, surprised. "Huh? You do always leave stuff in the office?"

"Why don't you just say what you actually mean, that I'm always forgetting things? Is that what you mean? That my memory is fucked?"

Kit looked tired. "J, I didn't mean anything by it. You're reading into it."

The pressure inside me festered. Fermenting and bubbling.

"Look what my dad got us as a housewarming," Kit said when he came home the next Tuesday holding a dark bottle of wine. "It's a Zuccardi Malbec."

This Malbec looks delicious.

You're not going to let me drink alone, are you?

"Get that out of my house," I whispered.

"*Your* house?" Kit raised an eyebrow.

"I'm not playing. Get rid of it."

Kit paused, staring at me. He didn't ask. Didn't react to my fear. Didn't comfort. He simply dipped his head once and said, "Noted."

The pressure inside me festered.

"It's pouring." Kit stood at the doorway of the restaurant on Valentine's Day. You know you're in a long-term relationship when dates have turned into "date night." We'd gone to Dalston, the opposite side of London. We went somewhere actually inconvenient because it was a cool spot! The restaurant was poky and dark, with a logo that could have been drawn by a four-year-old. Kit didn't order a Malbec and I smiled. He told me to choose two dishes off the menu and he'd have the one I liked less. I noted that Dalston was the epicenter of London's Turkish community. He said *next time.* We kissed across the table and held hands.

"Come, I've ordered us a cab."

"What?"

My brain switched into panic mode as I looked up and down the road for signs of danger.

"Jade? The rain?"

"You know . . . taxis are hard."

"It's okay." He smiled and kissed me. "I'll be right next to you the whole way, holding your hand."

He held the door open for me.

The whole car ride I had to remind myself to breathe.

The pressure inside me festered.

• • •

We had sex. He initiated as he normally would. I faked it. He never asked how he could make it more comfortable. He never acknowledged this renaissance of our sex life. Never admitted that we were both using each other to reclaim what was intruded upon. He flipped me onto my stomach like a rag doll. I lay there, seeing Josh come around the corner. Over and over.

The pressure inside me festered.

It was building momentum, compressing my chest. Rising to the tops of my ears and the roots of my hair. Until later in the week when I saw the milk out of the fridge, its blue cap brazenly sitting on the counter, a lukewarm and tangy odor clouding around it.

"Did you leave the milk out this morning?" I asked.

Kit didn't look up from his phone. "Evidently."

There was no going back.

I grabbed the bottle and it crinkled under the force of my grasp, the plastic carton warping between my fingers. With guttural momentum I rotated my shoulder and pelted the whole four pints at him. It narrowly missed Kit's face and hit the wall, and sour liquid dripped down Ian Campbell's limited-edition wallpaper procured from Florence, both of us stunned with the emotional gluttony of what I'd just done. I'd lost control. It only missed him because he had fast reflexes. We both knew that I wanted it to smash him right in the face.

"What the fuck, you psycho!" Kit yelled. "It's just milk, Jade!"

I screamed, unleashing the bedlam inside. "It's not about the milk! Fucking open your eyes, Kit!"

"Then what is it, Jade?"

"It's all these little things you do every day! Every day! But each time it's too small to get angry about so I let them quietly chip away at me. You have no idea . . ." I panted. "You make me . . . you make me feel so . . ."

"I can't *make* you feel anything, Jade," Kit said, in a dead monotone contrasting with my high-pitched wails. "You're the one in control of your emotions."

"*ARRRGHHHH!*" I screamed more. "*WHY CAN'T YOU JUST . . . WHY CAN'T YOU . . .*"

"Just what?" Kit was infuriatingly calm. "Use your words."

"*FUCK YOU! FUCK YOU! YOU'RE A FUCKING CUNT.*"

The silence after that was deafening. But then his expression changed into a look of self-satisfaction. Like he'd won.

"Your behavior is unacceptable, Jade," he said quietly. "You don't get to call me a cunt and expect me to take it."

"You have no idea what's going on with me, and what's worse, you don't even ask."

"I refuse to play your mind games. If there's something you want me to know, you should tell me rather than testing me by waiting to see whether I'll happen to guess what you're going through." He began walking toward the door. "I need to clear my head."

"Don't walk away! I'm talking to you!"

Then he delivered the final blow.

"We can't talk when you're acting so crazy."

And that was his narrative arc: he was the patient, levelheaded man who was driven by reason, in a tough spot navigating this unhinged woman. My mood swings were illogical. He was the bigger person for walking away, letting me cool down. But it was ultimately my fault that the whole day had been derailed.

"Do not call me crazy!"

"I didn't call you crazy. I said you were *acting* crazy. You know the meaning of *acting*, right?"

I cried in frustration. And the worst part was that he looked at me like I was putting on a show. Like he was bored with it all.

The next morning, Kit left in a hurry for a meeting. We hadn't addressed the argument. I'd slept in the spare room. As I packed my bag for work, gathering my wayward essentials from the table, I caught sight of the words "my love" flash on Kit's iPad. *Don't tell me you wouldn't have looked.* I put his iPad on flight mode so the message wouldn't mark as read. My heart was battering my chest as I braced myself to see something that would break me. An untroubled girl at work, perhaps? Someone he would compare to me when complimenting just how chill and relaxed she was?

And then it happened.

And it did break me.

Mum, now:
My love,
How are you doing? When you called me yesterday, I was so worried about you. I know you love Jade, and you both have shared so much. It took a lot of courage for you to tell me what happened between Jade and her colleague. However, your love for Jade might have

clouded your judgment. Darling, it is not normal for your partner to shout at you, to throw things at you. I brought you up right and I can see that in the way you have stayed with her. But she might have surpassed the point of helping. You must see that she has become uncontrollable.

I'm very sorry to say the following, but we must acknowledge the elephant in the room. The only two people who will ever know the full truth are Jade and this man. Are you comfortable with never knowing if she has been honest? There is a risk—however small—that her account of what happened has been invented or embellished in some way to cover her own tracks. Women today have the power to ruin men and, if she is prepared to do that to a colleague, what's to say she won't do the same to you one day?

I will support you, and by extension Jade, in whatever you decide to do. And as you know, I am only a call away if you ever need to talk. But I urge you to consider all possibilities.

With love always,
Mumma

I sank to the ground and tucked my knees to my chest. A hollow feeling seeped around my jaw as my teeth ground together. Angie? Is that really what she thought of me? That

I cheated on Kit and cried rape? That I was trying to wreck Josh in the process? And worse still, that I was a harm to Kit? Could I argue with that accusation? I had become abrasive and confrontational. Violent. I remembered the blinding bright sheet of rage yesterday as I hurled the milk at his head and withered within myself. I felt complete shame at who I had become.

I was so focused on my own pain that I'd become oblivious to what I was inflicting on those around me. But how was I meant to be? What was the right way to feel my way through this? What would make Angie believe me? Should I howl from the rooftops and unleash everything, or would that make me hysterical? Should I call Angie up and ask how she could think so little of me, or would that make me defensive? Should I shut down, or would that make me apathetic? Should I communicate to Kit exactly what I needed from him, or would that be attention-seeking? Should I break up with Kit for his own good, or would that make me look guilty? Should I be a stoic weeping willow, or would that be confirmation that it wasn't that bad after all?

I spent what felt like ages balled on the floor. Coldness bleeding across my insides. How would I ever sanitize myself? Present only the palatable so that people I loved didn't shrivel away from me. So that I could be someone worthy of believing.

I jolted back to reality, realizing I was going to be late for work. I quickly took the iPad off flight mode and went to put it back in its place when the text thread updated itself.

Kit had replied.

Kit Campbell, now:
Mum. She didn't make it up, and I don't want you to make that suggestion again. It's completely inappropriate. I'm going to delete your text now and pretend you never said that. Thanks for your concern, but Jade and I will work our own way through this.

When Kit got home that night, I rugby-tackled him at the front door. I jumped on him and wrapped my legs around him.

"Hey, what's this in aid of?" Kit laughed, somewhat hesitantly.

He was even skeptical of a hug.

"Nothing," I whispered into his neck.

"Seriously, what's up?"

I mewled, still clinging tightly on to him, "I'm sorry. I'm so sorry."

Hot fat tears soaked the shoulder of his shirt.

I love him.

I love him so much. How could I have done what I did to him?

"What are you sorry for, Jadey?" Kit said softly, still carrying me in the doorway.

"For everything. For being such a raging bitch to you," I blubbered and hiccupped. "I don't know who I am anymore. I hate who I see in the mirror."

Kit didn't say anything. But against my shoulder, I felt his head move in what could only have been a nod.

PART THREE

27

It was the famine after the feast. The Defense was filed, Project Arrow was quiet. Everyone tells you to enjoy the downtime while you can. The wheel of fortune would soon turn. I went into full productivity mode for a week: changing up the furniture in the flat, booking holidays for the summer. I started reading again! My food didn't arrive on a motorbike! I addressed the last ten items that had been languishing at the bottom of my to-do list for the past six months. Consolidated my pensions, researched savings accounts with high interest rates, took trousers to the tailor, renewed my passport, framed pictures. I tried to capture the elusive wellness: gratitude journal, ten-step skin care, hot lemon water, wardrobe clear out, overnight chia pudding, habit tracker, podcasts during the commute, dry-brushing, avo toast. All this to chase a tinny sparkle of self-satisfaction that fizzed out moments later to reveal the worming edginess underneath. The immediate, screaming desire to dissolve away from my body, leave it in a puddle on the ground, as soon as I laid eyes on any brown-haired man with Josh's build.

"I'm still getting absolutely ruined by work," Adele barked

as I handed her the coconut latte I'd picked up for her. Our love language of daily caffeinated surprises.

"How come?"

"Arrow, of course." Adele swiveled in her chair to face me. "Gabby is so pissy with me, I spent all night on my laptop shooting off bullshit emails."

"What's been going on?" I tried the most nonchalant tone I could muster. I'd signed and returned the Contract of Employment to join Arrow and was waiting on the final countersigned version before resigning. As blasé as Genevieve was about robust paperwork, the lawyer in me required the comfort of it. I intended to remind Genevieve, but, as soon as the Defense was filed, she'd sent a team-wide email stating that she would be spending time "detoxing" in Cannes and only in an emergency was she to be bothered. I knew better than to annoy my future employer before I even started at her company.

"Just admin bits." She looked up at me coolly. "I assume now that you're the case favorite they're not giving you the grunt work anymore."

"Whoa, Del," I said.

"Sorry," she muttered, "that was the exhaustion talking. I'm just so tired."

"Does the coffee help?"

"Mmm." Adele sipped her coffee and spoke with pensive guruism. "Coconut milk really is better in a cappuccino than a latte."

"Why would you"—I looked up and challenged—"say something so controversial, and yet so brave?"

Adele sprayed her coffee all over her desk, narrowly missing her keyboard, as she snorted with laughter.

"Seriously, thank you for speaking your truth," I carried on with a grin. "You're an everyday hero."

"What can I say—I'm a woman of the people." Adele slowly drank, regaining her energy. "Are you and Kit doing anything fun for the weekend?"

She asked tentatively. We hadn't spoken about him much since the infamous dinner party. The following Monday, after a morning of deafening silence, Adele had said *so, are we gonna address what happened the other night?* I admit my reaction was unwarranted. I snapped back *Del, I am handling it. I'm going through a lot and I don't need you judging me at every turn.* Adele gawped at me before saying *I would never judge you, J.* I apologized.

"Not really. Kit, Ollie, and Leo are going for a boys' trip to Dorset. Leo is still all cut up about his ex, Suzie."

"For fuck's sake!" I jumped as Adele yelled at her screen.

"What's happened?"

"Will's given me more work." She scrolled through his email. "This is seriously going to take me all day and night. Jesus, Will, buy a girl dinner first if you're going to fuck her like this."

I twirled the wooden spatula around my coffee, breathing to pacify my anxiety. Project Arrow owned my life. Why was Adele getting staffed on the project and not me? Why was I being dropped from calls and emails when I hadn't handed in my notice yet? Had she usurped me? Or had Genevieve told Will about my offer to go in-house and he was transitioning me off the case? Or was it because—

"I know what you're thinking." Adele's voice grounded me.

"What?"

"Dude, I can see your cogs turning—and I'm telling you, don't let your mind go there."

"It's just . . . odd."

"Honestly, buddy, you're good. I'm getting staffed on the US side, don't worry."

"You don't think it's—"

"I agree it's odd, but like I said, the New York office is also working on this. Try not to read into it too much."

Adele was my sister. My soul mate. She could see into me, read every thought as it formulated, like the text ticking out of a typewriter. She also knew to pull me back from the edge of a cliff of anxiety.

Unknown number, now:
Hey Jade, how have you been?

Jade Kaya, now:
Who is this?

Unknown number, now:
It's Josh—I thought this was the best way of getting hold of you. Do you want to grab a quick coffee today?

Jade Kaya, now:
Why would I want to meet up with you?

Unknown number, now:
I've heard about some of the things you have reported and I thought we should talk directly. I'd like us to talk face-to-face and find a resolution between us.

Jade Kaya, now:
Stop messaging me.

Unknown number, now:
Please Jade, we can talk about this and sort it all out.

Jade Kaya, now:
Stop messaging me.

Unknown number, now:
Why are you being like this? I don't understand why you're insisting on this witch hunt. Are you trying to ruin my life?

Number blocked.

I rapped on the door. A voice called from inside, ushering me in. I thrust myself into the room with tearstained cheeks, all professional decorum lost.

"Jade!" Sarah said. "Are you all right?"

I didn't say anything. I triumphantly placed the phone in front of her and allowed her to scroll through the brief chain of messages.

"Sorry?" Sarah said. "I don't understand?"

"It's Josh—he's been sending me all these messed-up messages, trying to influence me."

She scrolled through the thread.

"I see." Sarah looked up at me, nonplussed.

"Surely this will help your investigation? Is there any update? It's been three weeks—"

"Yes, I was actually meaning to email you," Sarah began. My breath was bated. "We've come to the decision that Josh will have restricted access to Firm property until the investigation has been concluded. So you won't have to worry about seeing him or having to work with him." She leaned forward. "Ensuring that you feel the office is a safe environment is our utmost priority."

The fear of coming in and seeing him had kept me in a state of constant high alert. But I'd had no alternative. In a culture where face time was paramount, I felt trapped to stay in the office, being constantly visible, despite the acidic disquiet that slowly corroded me.

"His office pass was confiscated this morning, which possibly explains those texts you received," Sarah said. "Thank you for bringing those to me."

"No problem," I whispered.

"Hang in there, Jade." She reached forward and I stepped back. I didn't want to be touched, but she didn't seem to notice. "We will let you know when the investigation has come to a conclusion and we have decided on a course of action, all right?"

"Yeah. All right."

I went to Morden for the weekend. It was a good time to see Omma and Baba, and in truth, I didn't want to be alone in the flat. The nightmares continued. As each night approached and I knew I would spend the hours with images of Josh inside me, I wondered how I would possibly make it through to morning. I felt no safer than I had in my old flat, which made me mourn it often. On evenings when I was alone, I obsessed over the locks, checking checking checking five, ten, fifteen times to make sure I was secure within my walls.

"Hey Baba," I said as I approached my parents' driveway to see my dad muttering to himself.

"Hello, hayatim," Baba said, not looking up from what I now saw was a pile of recycling. He unscrewed the cap off an empty carton of milk and placed it on the ground. With the sprightliness of a springbok, he jumped and crushed the carton under his feet. Without pausing, he reached for a pizza box and began tearing the cardboard into flat sheets.

"How have you been, Baba?"

"Your mother doesn't compress the rubbish. So I have to stand in my pajamas and do it. Vallahi, no matter how many times I tell her!"

I patted him on the back, clearly not able to distract him from his recycling vendetta, and walked past him into the house. A huge pot was simmering on the stove, but I knew better than to lift the lid and investigate—that was a surefire way to get smacked by a wooden spoon on the wrist.

"Aga," my mum called from the bathroom. "Come here."

She was sitting cross-legged inside the tub. There were stains everywhere, and I saw an old takeaway box filled with box dye and immediately understood. We worked methodically as I applied the dye to the underlayers at the back of her head. We were fluent in a plethora of noises, customs, and hand signals. In English, if offered a drink, one would say "No, thanks," or give a shake of the head. In Turkey, you moved your head upward, simultaneously raising your eyebrows and clicking your tongue against the roof of your mouth. Conversations were peppered with these clicks. Similarly, in Korea, when drinking with an elder, you turned away at a ninety-degree angle before taking a sip, to show respect. Home had a constant undercurrent of unspoken signals and cues that filled the gaps between language, forming a binding code of conduct. At Reuben, where each step was strategic, or with Kit, where everything was hyper-intellectualized, it felt relaxing to be able to make a noise and know that the people around me knew exactly what I meant.

After I was done dyeing Omma's hair, I scrubbed the tub clean. I came out into the kitchen to find her draining the pot on the stove. She spun around to reveal a pot of hard-boiled eggs marinated in soy sauce, garnished with sesame seeds and verdant green spring onions. Mayak gyeran—*drug eggs*. My earliest memory of these sweet and salty, jammy-yolked treats was my Year 3 Easter Egg hunt.

"What's this, Omma?" I had asked, seven years old. A gleeful smile spread across her face. I'd had soy-braised eggs a thousand times before, but my mum looked absolutely delighted with herself this time.

"Eggs," she'd said, beaming, "for Easter." There was a pause where I clearly wasn't providing her with the response she'd expected. "You're supposed to give children eggs for Easter, no? I've been marinating these for three days."

I lifted myself onto my tippy-toes in my pink trainers and peered into the pot. There must have been over thirty eggs in there. She looked at her feet with a childlike disappointment that stung me in the chest, even then.

"Thank you so much, Omma," I had said, accepting the pot with two hands, "but I feel really sick today, I don't think I can go to the hunt."

• • •

Over the weekend, we moved in sync around the house, restoring family factory settings. We made bulk batches of kimchi to be fermented in huge tubs in the garden, the smell of garlic wafting from my hands for days after. I helped file tax returns and appeal parking tickets. There was a pride in my doing these things for them, even though they were self-sufficient, because it was a manifestation of my profession. I know Omma had bragging rights about her lawyer daughter who sorted everything out for her parents. I went to the supermarket with Baba to pick up some things on Omma's list. We were parking the car back at home when I spotted the couple next door coming out of their porch.

"Do you need to borrow," Baba called to Iris as she ventured out into the drizzle, ". . . what do you call it? A . . . erm . . . rain-tent?"

"Hello, Yusuf!" Iris cooed, followed by Phil, her husband. "A what-now?"

Baba held his balled hand up to gesture. "A rain-tent!"

Phil leaned forward.

"Ahhh, I've got it!" Phil nudged Iris on the elbow and said something under his breath. "Yusuf, in English," he said slowly, enunciating every syllable, "we call that an *UM-BRELL-AH*. Can you say it with me? It's really easy if you think about it."

"Excuse me?" I called out, my voice edgy. Baba glanced at me and flicked his right hand toward the ground: *stand down*.

"I've got one." Iris tapped her canvas bag. "Thanks, anyway!"

"No problem, no problem," Baba said, holding his palms together. Huge neighborly smile.

Watching a parent—a child's first love and role model—be patronized ignited a protective instinct. One of the countless experiences that trickled and funneled down into the mold of the Dutiful Immigrant Child. A sort of reverse parenting where the child takes on the supervision of their parents, flanking them from an early age if they were being humiliated. And this responsibility to support never leaves.

"I don't know why you're so nice to them, Baba," I muttered as I started lifting the shopping into the house.

"Why wouldn't I be?"

"Dad!" I looked at him. "They had bloody UKIP posters taped to their windows!"

"Jade, you are too headstrong," Baba said sagely, walking behind me with the shopping. "What is the point of not being nice to them?"

Baba opened the fridge and began putting the shopping away.

"Fight fire with kindness," he said, gesticulating with a block of halloumi. "Inshallah, in time, they will see we are good people."

"You shouldn't have to prove yourself to anyone."

Baba looked at me pointedly and I remembered the conversation we had in the Clapham Flat. *You're pretending to be something you're not for him.*

"And yet," Baba said, "we do."

28

From Julian Monkford to All Members on March 8, 2019 at 8:06 am
RE: International Women's Day

Dear all,

To mark International Women's Day today, please join me in #breakingtheglass and celebrating the women of Reuben. As a firm, we place equality at the heart of our culture and are deeply committed to the advancement of our women. I am therefore proud to announce today that 11% of our partnership are now women, a rise from 7% last year.

Today, I urge everyone to challenge their gender biases and take the opportunity to recognize the contributions of women to the firm, past, present, and future.

Julian Monkford
PARTNER

"Hello, hello, hello." Linda swanned in. Zaynab, who Linda first mistook me for, was already sitting. She was beautiful, with soft pillowy lips and honeyed eyes, complemented by her ochre-colored hijab. She infinitesimally lowered her chin in a barely noticeable gesture. I could breathe more freely now that I knew Josh wasn't on-site. I knew he was still working; I checked his Skype status like a nervous tic. The little green sign confirmed that he hadn't actually been suspended. Hadn't stopped putting in those hours for the Firm.

"Q1 has been great, well done, everyone," Linda began. "People ask me *Linda, now that you've got the ball rolling on diversity at Reuben, what next?* And I tell them that it doesn't stop there, we have to keep striving." Linda did a one-eighty-degree look around the room like a cult leader appraising her following.

"In order for us to have a constructive conversation about inequality and the specific disadvantages that some people face," Linda said, pulling her hands toward her chest, before gravely nodding, "we must first acknowledge our own privilege." Bailey looked rather panicky as Linda said, "So I thought we could go around the room and think about how we are personally complicit in upholding oppressive structures."

One by one, the members of the committee timidly offered olive branches.

"Although I am a woman, and therefore diverse to some extent," Linda said, "I am white." People nodded as if this were groundbreaking. "And that gives me certain advantages, which I have to remember to be grateful for."

She looked expectantly at Bailey, who cleared his throat before publicly flogging his entire existence.

"I'm a straight white man," he said, somber enough for a support group for meth addicts. "I went to Eton, and then Oxford. My dad's a Silk." He rubbed his eyes. "When you say it all out loud, I realize just how lucky I have been."

"Thank you," Linda spoke, bringing her palms together in a namaste move, "for being so self-reflective."

I looked up from my lap to see Zaynab. We locked eyes, and she widened hers by only a millimeter and flicked them toward the exit door: *get me out of here*.

Offerings of penance continued. A guy from finance said he wouldn't be able to sleep thinking about his third investment property in Croydon. Eventually, Zaynab and I were the last ones standing.

"Zaynab, as our newest member, do you have anything to add?"

Zaynab said, "I am able-bodied. I can come in and out of work without much difficulty, and I don't need to manage a full-time job with a long-term illness or disability. That is something I am very grateful for."

I added when the eyes shifted to me, "I'm heterosexual. I don't have to come out to each new colleague I work with, or feel isolated by the heteronormative language that pervades our day-to-day vocabulary."

"Yes, thank you both," Linda said. "What a great exercise this has been! Because we've all been so honest with each other, do you see how it acts as an equalizer?" People nodded. "For example, we can see how Zaynab"—Linda smiled in a way it was obvious she thought she was being inclusive of her new recruit when she spoke of equality—"is *just as* privileged as I am."

• • •

I drifted back to my office afterward and checked my emails. Still no countersigned contract from Arrow. "HR are slow everywhere," I grumbled. *I should know.* I was about to complain to Adele when I noticed she was sitting with her head in her hands. Without saying a word, I walked around her desk and hugged her from behind. After a few minutes, she looked up.

"What's up?" I asked.

"Gabby's pulled the plug," she said quietly.

"What happened?"

"She's back in touch with her ex and she said they're going to give it another go."

"I guess we're not listening to The xx for a while, then?"

Del laughed.

"No, I guess not."

We sat in silence, while I carried on hugging Adele's back.

"All right," I said, standing up. I switched off Adele's monitor as her mouth gaped like a fish out of water. "Let's round up Eve and head out tonight."

The Ned was a grandiose building, formerly the Midland Bank, decorated to art deco perfection. Opulence dripped from every orifice of the Banking Hall. It was a millennial members club, with the core clientele being City workers who got a hard-on when they heard that the place was "exclusive." It was populated with wanker bankers who slapped each other on the shoulder and said stuff like, "Boys, the City ain't ready for us!" *You're right, James, London has never seen three white guys with signet rings and mid-2.1s from a Russell Group university, who rent an overpriced flat in Shoreditch and drop their salary on minimum-spend tables.*

"Over here!" Eve waved at us from across the hall, already seated at one of the Ned's restaurants that were open to the general public (the "pleb bits," according to Will). Del and I ducked and weaved through the crowd to reach the pink velvet sofa Eve was perched on.

"So, Eve, talk to us," Adele said. *Twarhk to us.* "What's new?"

"I'm proper falling off the wagon, guys," Eve said, pouring us a glass of wine from the bottle of chardonnay that she had ready and waiting at the table.

"Go on," Adele laughed.

"It's complicated. There's this guy, he's no good," Eve said. She was referring to her embroilment with Julian, but I didn't let on and neither did Eve. "That whole situation is such a complete shit show and I thought to myself—" She put her finger to her lip. "You know what will help me with the crippling state of anxiety I'm in twenty-four-seven now over this man? More toxic men."

"Noooo!" Adele and I both groaned in unison.

"I'm talking the kind of guys who aren't even ashamed of the red flags they are waving around. They're like red rags to a bull."

"Do I even want to know how bad?" I asked, silently grateful for Kit.

"There's like this new trend among twentysomething men who live in the Hams—"

"The where?" I laughed.

"Balham. Clapham. Fulham." Eve drank as if it were her lifeblood, while cymbals clanged in the background. "They all go out of their way to mention several times on the first date that they consider themselves feminists. All right, like, do you want a medal? It's so obvious they want to split the bill at the end of the date."

"This guy I slept with last week"—Eve saw my questioning look—"from Bumble, keep it distant. He's got a few drinks in him, so he's feeling emboldened, saying how he's going to rock my world or whatever."

"Eww."

"He came back to mine, we're having wine and talking. And then obviously we start having sex and it was . . ." She jiggled the tips of her fingers on her lips as she found the right words. "You know when a guy has been watching too much porn?"

"Staaap," Adele spluttered her drink.

"Like, no one wants their legs bent behind their head and their clit to be rubbed like it's a DJ booth. I'm not going to be able to come if you're going to pound-town on me, just stop jackhammering me!"

Adele was banging the table with her palm, her laugh booming.

"Can't say I've ever had that problem," Adele said.

"I couldn't have called him an Uber any faster."

"Although"—she physically shook herself—"I can't complain. Someone always has it worse, right? My new housemate is going through the most horrific breakup."

"How did you meet her?" I said.

"She responded to my SpareRoom listing in three minutes flat. I've been doing my best to nurse her, bless her."

"Do you know what happened?"

"I gather her fella pushed her around."

"God, that's scary," Adele said.

"She told me, the night they broke up, he comes home after a night out and wakes her up, grabs her out of bed, and throws her around while she's shouting for him to get off her. He only jumped off her when neighbors came knocking."

Adele reached under the table and squeezed my knee.

"She told me, the next morning she got a DM. From a friend of a friend."

"What did it say?"

"This girl had seen her boyfriend at Infernos that night."

"Scaliest club in London."

"He had been trying to kiss her. Not just her, lots of women. Just walking up to them and trying to kiss them." I felt sick. Eve caught my look and stopped in her tracks. "I'm sorry, J. I wasn't thinki— Let's talk about something else."

"No," I said stoically, "go on."

I didn't admit that I found comfort in her story. *So I'm not the only person this can happen to.*

"You sure?"

I nodded.

"Well, she told me, this woman told him to fuck off, so he grabbed her and stuck his hand in her knickers."

I felt like my stomach was crushed in Eve's bare hands. *Should I have trusted her with what happened to me? What if she recounts my story over dinner to other people?*

"She was so distraught that the bouncers noticed and kicked him out. So he decided to go home aggro and take it out on his girlfriend. She said that was the final straw, which makes me wonder if it's happened before. She moved out the next morning."

"I really need to wee," I said, immediately getting up. I clambered across the Ned. Is anywhere safe anymore? Jazz music sang around me and suddenly I felt like I was trapped in a hedonistic roaring twenties nightmare.

• • •

By the time I returned to the table, Eve and Del were talking about whether veganism was the only sustainable route for humanity. Adele had been on the road to conversion by Gabby. We ate and drank for hours. No one mentioned work. No one mentioned Josh. No one mentioned Arrow. After three bottles of wine and two rounds of champagne, we shared a chocolate bomb for dessert. I leaned over the plate to spoon myself and I saw Eve's phone light up.

Incoming call from Suzie Carter

Eve clocked the call and chose to ignore it.

"How do you know Suze?" I asked, perplexed.

"Ah, she's my new housemate! Do you know her?" The phone vibrated again. "I bet she's gone and locked herself out."

The phone went dark. Then lit up again.

Incoming call from Suzie Carter

The booze clouded my mind as I slowly put the pieces together.

"Your new housemate?"

"Uh-huh," Eve said, texting her back.

"Oh my God," I gasped, my hand flying over my mouth.

"What?"

"I think I'm going to be sick."

They both looked at me quizzically.

"Leo."

29

"Are you having an aneurysm?" Eve leaned forward, waving her hand in front of my face.

"No, no, sorry, that was a massive shock," I said, reaching for my glass of water.

"I don't understand?" Adele piped up.

"You remember Leo? He was at our dinner party," I explained.

"You mean the one who racially slurred you and acted like he'd never seen a lesbian before? Yeah"—she practically threw the last gulp of wine down her gullet—"let's say I remember him."

I winced at the memory.

"His now-ex, Suzie? That's Eve's new housemate."

"What is London, man?" Adele groaned. "Everyone knows everyone." It was true. Nine million people in this city, but I was forever discovering random overlaps between friendship groups and colleagues. It made me anxious: there were no first impressions with anyone.

I turned to Eve.

"Wha—why—how could thi—" I composed myself. "I mean, how is Suze doing?"

"This is mental," Eve said, setting her glass down. "It's been rough. I don't know her that well, but she doesn't seem to be in a good place."

"I can't believe it."

"Jade, didn't you say that Kit went away with Leo last weekend?" Adele asked.

"Yeah, all this time, he's been sprouting all this wounded-puppy nonsense, about how she broke his heart and blind-sided him with the breakup."

The Ned was swinging with jazz music, glasses clattering. The three of us were speechless. I wanted to rush home and tell Kit as soon as possible.

I rode the line from Bank to Clapham Common, resting my head against the Tube door, my body weary. I started typing a message to Suzie. *I'm so sorry. I'm here if you need anything or want someone to speak to.* And then I paused. Was it intrusive to send a message like that? Would she be suspicious of my proximity to Leo? I wondered how I would feel if I received a message like that. Anxious. Questioning how they found out about what happened to me, who knew, how it got out, how it affected their view of me. I deleted the message and instead asked Eve to, at a suitable moment, pass on my love and support. I wanted Suzie to know I was there for her, that I was her ally, without foisting my presence on her.

"I missed you today," Kit said as I lay along the sofa next to him.

"I missed you too." I sat up, taking a swig of his beer. "Did you get up to anything fun tonight?"

"Nah, watched Netflix and ordered some dinner in, I'm shattered. I was staying up to see my girl."

I stared intently at a crumpled piece of tape that was stuck to the floor.

"Are you okay?" Kit asked.

"Well, no, I heard the weirdest rumor today. Actually, it's not a rumor."

"What is it?"

"I caught up with Eve this evening—"

"How is she?"

"Yeah yeah, good, well, she's just moved in with Suzie."

"Really?" He tensed. "Small world."

"Kit." I held his hand in mine to show my support. "I don't think Leo has been completely honest with you. Or any of us."

"What do you mean?"

"This whole time he's been doing this elaborate victim act, saying that she pulled the rug out from under him, but she had very legitimate reasons for breaking up with him."

Kit shifted on the sofa. "I'm sure there are two sides to every story."

"Kit," I started gently, "I don't think Leo has told you guys the truth."

"Mmm?"

"I don't really know how to say this." My voice was flimsy and limp. "Suzie broke up with Leo for being violent toward her. She then found out that he sexually assaulted another woman."

Kit breathed heavily and stared straight ahead.

He turned to look at me.

"I know."

Time stopped still.

There must be some misunderstanding. Surely, we're talking about two different things.

"You know?" The words dribbled from my mouth as if I didn't have control over my tongue. He nodded. "About everything? About what he did to the woman in Infernos?"

"What he *allegedly* did, yes. I know."

"You know that he put his hands on Suzie?"

"Allegedly. Yes."

"Why do you keep saying 'allegedly'?"

"It's true. It's nothing more than an allegation at this point."

I was in shock. I knew there was an entire spectrum of uncontrolled emotion waiting for me, but right now, it didn't make sense. Kit and I sometimes didn't get each other, but he wasn't a bad person. He was a good person! I wouldn't love him if he wasn't! He condemned assault. For God's sake, of course he did!

"Why didn't you tell me? After all your lectures about how I shouldn't keep things from you?"

"Jade, you were going through so much, I didn't want to upset you." He spoke emphatically, like he wanted to convince me that he'd made the right call. "We've been doing so much better recently, and I didn't want anything to go off between us again."

I pulled my hand out of Kit's and held my fingers to my temples.

"I can't believe it."

"Listen, I know Leo took it too far, but come on, why is this random woman getting involved anyway? Who's to say she's even telling the truth!"

"So you don't believe women now, Kit? Or only when the

perpetrator is one of your boys? What about all that feminism you peddle? What about me?"

"You're a lawyer, Jade." Kit shrugged. "You tell me, should we be blinkered and believe people without any evidence?"

"*YES!*" I screamed. "I cannot believe you're saying this. Who even are you?"

The more worked up I got, the calmer he was. He was perfectly molded into the sofa, the cushions encasing him in his comfort.

"So you're telling me that unless a woman has hard evidence, you don't believe them?" I pushed.

"No, that's not what I'm saying. I'm just saying that we should remain neutral until there is proof either way. If either this woman or Suzie made a formal report and let qualified forces investigate Leo, I would one hundred percent support that. But he shouldn't be condemned by his oldest friends off the back of some airy details."

"Are you joking right now!"

"It's innocent until proven guilty," he said patronizingly.

"Oh my fucki—"

"We spoke about it at length in Dorset." His voice sounded confident, as if he knew everything would be resolved with a simple explanation. This was all a big misunderstanding. "We've gone over what the best thing to do was. I agonized about the right course of action, J." Kit's eyes were round like a kid doing show-and-tell.

I thought of all the times Kit was sure that he knew better than me. How he just told me I'd get through it and left it at that. My anger simmered and overflowed at the idea of those three guys discussing how best to shield Leo.

"Are you patting yourself on the back for discussing *with*

the perpetrator himself what to do? And you seriously concluded that the best thing to do was nothing?" I shrieked. "Are you actually shitting me right now?"

"Look, Jade. I appreciate you bringing this to me, I really do, but, like I said, it's not our place to get involved and meddle."

"You're already involved! You just said what you guys did! You're balls-deep involved!"

"I've known the guy since I was seven years old, Jade!" Kit finally sat up. "What do you want me to do? Never speak to him again?"

"Yes! Yes, I want you to *for once* actually speak with actions, not words."

"What's that supposed to mean?"

"Stop *talking* about how much you care about feminism and blah blah fucking blah. Actually *do* something! When push comes to shove, you're as bad as the bloody rest."

"I didn't realize you thought so little of me. That you thought I was so insubstantial."

I panted. All the hairline fractures from the past seven years were combining. The relationship was cracking before our eyes.

"Baby—"

"Don't call me baby."

"Okay." He raised his eyebrow. "Leo and Suzie are handling it. Besides, he was drunk and it was a packed night out."

"You were there?"

"No."

"So how do you know?"

"Well—"

"And you're saying being drunk is an excuse?"

"I'm not going to be cross-examined. You know what I mean." Kit uncrossed his arms and leaned toward me. "Don't get me wrong, he shouldn't be doing that when he has Suzie. So call him a cheat for all I care. But he shouldn't have to be branded as some sort of sex pest or wife beater."

"Why not?"

"For God's sake, Jade! So he got a bit grabby on a night out. I agree it was wrong. But do I think he deserves to be ostracized by his lifelong friends for it? No, I don't. It's just not that big of a deal."

"*IT IS TO ME!*" I screamed.

I felt the energy drain from me. He didn't understand. He never would.

"Do you have any idea how violating that is? Have you ever felt in genuine fear for your safety?" Kit opened his mouth to speak, but I carried on. "The psychological effect on Suzie and the woman he assaulted—they'll have to live with the damage he's caused."

"Jesus Jade, who made you a therapist suddenly?"

Something—something uncontrolled and compressed—spurred toward a crescendo, jettisoning all resolve.

"Because I know how they feel!" I yelled. "That night, when Josh did what he did to me . . ." I clasped my hands together and focused on calming my ragged breathing. "He climbed on top of me and penetrated me while I was too drunk to tell you my name. So I know how it feels to have someone force themselves on you and take something from you. And I can't believe—I don't know how—just how could you condone that!"

"Please don't get upset," Kit pleaded.

"What do you see when you wake me up every night thrashing and screaming, dripping in sweat? Not once, not fucking once, did you ask me what I was reliving at night. I can't take taxis. I shower *incessantly.* It happened in my own flat where I deserved to feel safe. You see me check the locks fifteen times every night and you've never once asked me why. The day you found out, you banged on about how hurt *you* were, how much I let *you* down. The time I had a flashback on Christmas Eve, you made me feel bad about it! Like it was my fault!"

My face was wet with tears as the dam burst.

"How could you watch this tear me apart and eat me up?" I was gasping for air amid my monologue.

"I didn't think it was helpful to keep bringing it up," Kit offered as his feeble excuse.

"Again. You deciding what's best. You haven't even tried to be there for me."

"Believe me," Kit retorted, "I have tried my bloody best. Sitting through your crazy outbursts. When you yell at me over nothing. When you decide to ruin an evening and lock yourself in the bathroom. Again over nothing." *Nothing. Nothing. Over nothing.* "I have been here throughout, haven't I?"

"Crazy?! You think I'm crazy now?"

He ignored me. "I understand you're going through it. But I'm going through something too. I feel like I've been robbed of my girlfriend. Where did the fun-loving, relaxed girl I fell in love with go? You've changed, Jade! And that's something I've had to process and deal with, and I'm trying!"

I refused to let him turn this on me. "How could you bring Leo into our home? After what he's done? Make me cook for him, console him? How could you protect him? How could you betray me like that?"

I stared at him. The only man I have ever had sex with. *Does that matter? Of course not.*

It mattered that he was the only man I have ever voluntarily had sex with.

"Jade," he said, "this is exactly why I didn't tell you about Leo and Suze. I was trying to protect you from getting so upset."

"I can't stay here." I got up and began walking toward the bedroom.

"For God's sake, why are you being so intense!" I said nothing. He carried on. "You're not even really friends with Suzie. If anything, your loyalty should lie with Leo, you've known him for longer!"

I shoveled my laptop, my passport, wallet, makeup bag, phone, and a handful of underwear into a backpack.

"I'm going home for a few days," I announced.

Kit rolled his eyes and ran his hand through his hair. "Jade, you are home. You've made your point now and I'm sorry that you feel it was the wrong call. Why does Suzie and Leo's breakup have anything to do with us?"

I stopped walking toward the door and turned around.

"You need to have a long, hard think about the choices you make, Kit. I know people like you and Leo think the rules don't apply to you, but you're not above a moral compass."

"People like me and Leo?" He sneered as he stood up. "You know what Jade, you think you're so different from us. That we're some sort of evil breed that you're exempt from. But look around you!" He waved his arms around the flat. "You're living here for free. In the flat that my dad gifted me! Gentrification? Jade Kaya has contributed!"

"That's different!" I began.

"Is it? Is it really, Jade? Because from where I'm standing, you *love* being all sanctimonious, judging us for what we have, but you have had no problem at all benefiting from what I have when it suits you. You're so hung up on what I've had and what you didn't have. But you don't see me getting upset when you go and hang out with your loving family. I didn't have that. What about that privilege, huh? The privilege of having an intact family? Do I make you feel bad for that?"

"Should I feel bad for that?" I yelled back.

"No! You shouldn't! That's my entire bloody point. Stop making me feel bad for who I am, Jade! For being friends with the people I am friends with, or having opportunities you don't have! It's not my fault."

"I'm not angry with what you have!" I exclaimed, although it wasn't strictly true. "I hate the choices you make."

"Oh, choice!" Kit laughed mockingly. "Like how you chose to throw shit at me? One-second delay and I might have had a broken nose. Definitely a black eye. We should condemn people for violence, right? That's what you just said, Jade." Kit squared up. *No.* I wanted to muffle my ears. *I can't listen to this.* "So maybe I go tell everyone what you did, let them shun you too?"

I matched his stance. In his eyes, I swear I saw enjoyment.

"But I wouldn't do that," he said, shoulders slouching in a show of benevolence, "because that wouldn't be fair to you, under the circumstances." He paused to give full weight to his mercy. "So maybe we all shouldn't be so quick to judge."

I tensed my face, gave him nothing. He wanted me to agree with him. Tacitly accept that I'm the same as Leo. I refused to engage, so Kit continued.

"You act like I'm immoral, but at least I'm trying to make a change for the better in the world. Who are the clients you defend, Jade? Same shit, different scale. The sooner you realize you're just the same as the rest of us, the better our future will be."

I wanted to argue with him. Defend myself and say that he was the one who pushed me to move in here. That the milk incident was a moment of blind rage, that it wouldn't happen again. That I needed this career, that nothing else would provide me with the same chance in life. That there was no safety net that allowed me to pursue a more earnest profession based on my *values*. But then Suzie's face and her funny Hollywood curls popped into my head.

"To be absolutely clear," I said quietly, so he had no choice but to listen intently to me, "we can argue back and forth all night. But it's between Leo or me."

I turned around and closed the door behind me.

30

"Morning, sunshine," Adele called from her kitchen like Snow White to her woodland friends. After leaving our home, I had stood on Clapham High Street, paralyzed by indecision. Kit called and called. This morning alone he called eight times. I couldn't bring myself to answer. My body throbbed with the hurt of his betrayal. And a betrayal it was. A total dismissal of me. Confirmation that he never grasped the ache that lived inside. A fault line cracked in the ground separating us. I would always be inside, in the belly of this pain, encased within its walls. And Kit would always be outside it, unable—or unwilling—to comprehend.

I couldn't bear to show up crying on my parents' doorstep again, so I went to Adele's instead. Since she was an international transfer, the Firm had paid for her accommodation in London. She was in a one-bedroom flat in a new-build in Aldgate. It was clean and modern, but soulless, without the constant damp and the creaking that maps every step of your upstairs neighbor. She had Adelified the place as much as possible, with monstera and palm plants dotted around the living space, acquisitions from Columbia Road Flower Market.

Kit Campbell, now:
Jade?
Please pick up.
Where are you?
Pick up now.
Stop mucking around.
Come home.
This isn't fair.
You can't just ignore me.

I flipped my phone over. Fiddled with the leaves of a small succulent sitting on the granite kitchen island and felt Del's hand on my shoulder.

"She's a cute plant, right?" Adele said.

"She is," I mumbled.

"It's a jade plant," Adele said softly, handing me a coffee. My hand reached up to my shoulder and squeezed hers in appreciation.

"How are you feeling?"

My anxiety felt like it was on a spin cycle.

"Kinda like my life is falling apart," I sighed.

"Your life isn't falling apart. You're just dating a cunt."

I winced as she spoke. Adele's words were like a blunt blade carving into my misery. She was a habitual oversimplifier, reducing the most complex mangrove of dilemmas into brief one-liners. Sometimes it was a refreshing perspective, like a cold towel on a fevered, overthinking head. Other times it was plain irritating.

"Look," Adele carried on. "You know I'm all for being judgment free and 'you-do-you' and 'love-is-love.' But seriously,

Jade. You *HAVE* to dump him. The man is an absolute shit-heel!"

"He hasn't always been," I sighed.

"Because you've never been tested before," she concluded. She pulled apart the knobby end of the baguette on her kitchen counter and dragged it through the butter dish, taking a hearty mouthful of warm, salty carbs. "Anyone can love someone when they're perfect."

"Thanks, Del, I know I'm a mess." I smiled wryly.

"That's not what I meant. I meant that you couldn't see his true colors until now because your relationship has never been under pressure like this before."

"So what are you saying? That it's all been a lie?" There was truth to her words: our relationship had been gratifying in its metronomic stability all these years. *When did it all change?* I wanted to hunt Josh down and abuse him for maiming what we had. There was, however, a small voice that asked whether all Josh did was expose the underbelly of who Kit had always been. Or rather, who I never truly was.

"Jade, don't be like that, I'm not the enemy here."

"There is no enemy, Del! No one's the bad guy because that doesn't help me, okay? It doesn't help me to call him a shit-heel. Demonizing him doesn't suddenly make me feel better. And infantilizing me doesn't make me feel any less shit about how this has played out."

I lifted my head to see Adele, mouth full of baguette and butter, bewildered by my gust of frustration.

"I've never been without him," I whispered. "I don't know who I am without him."

"What do you mean?"

"I didn't know who I was when I met him. Who knows who they are when they're eighteen?"

"I still thought I was straight at eighteen," Adele chortled.

"Precisely."

"You're not who you are because of him, J." Adele's body language softened, her tone compassionate.

"No, I am." I fiddled with the strings on my pajama bottoms, wrapping them around my index finger. "My personality feels dependent on his."

That was an understatement. My existence had turned on his axis, shape-shifting constantly, as I'd tried to make myself palatable to him. Adele's face had contorted into the unmistakable picture of pity, which made me tingle with irritation.

Guilt's sickly tentacles reached into my gut. Pins and needles flashed across my arms, thinking about how self-conscious I'd been of my parents' house. The home that anchored them to this country, bartered for with cash squirreled under mattresses. So much bounty squashed into fifty square meters. Our appliances sang with Samsung's jingle, an Ottoman tapestry hung on the wall, and a panel adorned in ancient Korean calligraphy divided the living room. Every summer, Baba would procure apricots, aubergines, chili peppers, and figs, string them up using a needle and thick thread, and hang them around the house like bunting. Kit had said it *looked like a market* and that it was *small but mighty in culture*. At the time, I took it as a compliment. But now I wondered if it was just a way to belittle us. I cringed at how much I let him define my attributes. In our early days, he read my essays and told me they were eloquent and original, that he was impressed. He'd say it with a secretive smile and the task of deciphering his posturing used to be fun. It made me feel like he saw potential in me where no one else had. From the moment he made sure Kyriakos read my essay, the undertone to our interactions was that he saw the person I could be. That he could take credit for my place in the world. When I got my degree, he made a comment about the binder of essays he'd left on my doorstep. He insinuated that he had made me smarter, had polished my rough edges. Plucked me out and raised me up. In exchange, being with me made him interesting, nodded to his liberalism and alluded to his generosity. He used me to bolster his identity politics. The feather in his cap of virtuousness.

"I've spent so much of my adult life trying to be the type of girl he would be with. I don't know who I really am, Del."

"Yes, you do." Adele straightened her back and smacked her hand on the counter. "Bitch, I love you! You're so fucking great. You were not put on this world to be Kit's girlfriend." Adele was shaking me now, I felt like a bobblehead on a dashboard.

I smiled weakly.

"Okay, we need a game plan," Adele said. "I've never been in a hetero relationship but I'm pretty sure this is how it goes." She held up her hand and began ticking off the steps: "Boy is a dick, girl gets angry and leaves, boy leaves girl to stew for a little while, boy realizes girl isn't going to cave, boy activates his groveling and begging tactic, girl forgives boy."

I laughed.

"Sounds about right," I said, "although I doubt Kit will grovel or beg."

"You're right." She shrugged. "Instead, he'll twist a situation to make you think you're in the wrong." Adele spotted my expression and continued before I had a chance to defend him. "Sorry, J, I saw him do it to you at that god-awful dinner party and I can't hold my tongue anymore."

My work phone pinged.

From Will Janson to Jade Kaya on March 9, 2019 at 10:05 am
RE: Project Arrow

Are you free for a quick buzz now?
Tks,
Will

"What do they want now?" Adele called.

"Will wants a call, about Arrow."

"Obviously put him on speaker when you do speak to him."

"I wouldn't deprive you of a front seat to the global premiere of *What Fresh Hell Jade Is In*."

As Will's dial tone tolled, I felt a clammy chill cover my palms.

"William Janson." His name was a statement in and of itself.

"Hi Will, it's Jade, you asked me to call?"

"Ah yes. Hi Jade, sorry to bother you on a Saturday, but I thought it better to discuss these things over the phone."

What things? Why don't you want to put them in writing?

"Sure."

"So, Jade, let me get straight into it. I really do appreciate your proactivity on this case, and it's clear you've put a lot of hard work into it."

"Thank you."

The corners of Adele's mouth turned south as she cocked her head back in confusion.

"The thing is, the management team has discussed, and we're going to cycle you off Project Arrow, though we thank you for your commitment to the case thus far."

I haven't gone through my emails since last night. The final contract from Arrow must have come through.

"I understand, Will. I guess you've heard from Genevieve. It was an opportunity that was too good to pass up, I hope you understan—"

"I have," Will interrupted me. "Heard from Genevieve, that is."

There was dead air between us. I heard papers being moved in the background; he wasn't even paying attention. Adele rolled her hand at me, indicating that I should prompt him.

"Sorry, I'm not sure I understand. I was offered an in-house role at Arrow, so I can't work on the project with Reuben anymore . . ."

"I unfortunately can't speak to that, Jade. This is a purely internal staffing decision, I have a responsibility to ensure my associates are getting diverse case experience, so we want to rotate the team."

Adele shook her head no.

"The rotations happened three months ago, Will," I pushed. "It was decided that I should be kept on the case."

"Errr," Will grumbled, irritation escalating. I was meant

to say I understood and accepted it. "We've decided that you're no longer . . . a right fit for the project."

"Excuse me? Apart from you, I'm the only person who has been on the case consistently throughout. How could I not be a right fit for it?"

He paused. "This will be good for you, Jade, you can start to work on other matters now."

"I've said no to all other work for nearly a year for Project Arrow. I've put ninety hours a week into this case for months. Please, could you provide a bit more explanation as to why I, as the only person with the relevant case experience to work on this matter, am being removed from it?"

There was a sharp intake of breath down the line. Adele and I were staring at the phone, willing him to say something soon.

"Jade, I'm going to level with you. I have every faith that you'll land on your feet. But look, this, er, staffing decision has come from up top. Even I answer to the higher powers that be."

"Sorry, Will," I said, my voice wiry, "I'm still not sure I follow."

Adele's head was in her hands.

"Listen . . ." Will hesitated. "It's an uncomfortable situation for everyone. This isn't a call I would like to be making."

"What do you mean by 'everyone'?" I hated how shriveling—how rattled—I sounded. And I hated how Will was talking in code, scared to say the wrong thing.

"Whatever the *goings-on* were, on which I don't wish to pass comment, it's a tough spot. Josh is David's nephew, after all."

Adele, slowly, like a huge crane on London's skyline, lifted her head. She closed her eyes, as if she wanted to shut this scene out, like one of the three wise monkeys: *see no evil*.

"Can I confirm," I quietly said, "Josh Parsons is the Founding Partner's nephew?"

"Ex-nephew, if that's even a term, through David's second wife. Or maybe his third? You know how it is," Will said, his voice in a talk-whisper. "How hush-hush these things are kept."

Of course. Of course. Of course. His brazen nonchalance. Him messaging me despite an ongoing HR investigation into him. The most token attempt at an investigation that allowed him to work from the comfort of his Suffolk home. That fucking hug at the Savoy. He'd always been confident that he was a protected species. But how was I supposed to know that? Would it have changed anything?

Yes. It would have changed everything.

I stared into Adele's eyes, my edifice of strength.

"It's a shame, truly," Will continued. "I understand that Genevieve was a big fan of yours, though I didn't know she was trying to poach you over to Arrow. She and David are close friends, after all. My advice to you, Jade, is to keep your head down. This will blow over. Soon all will be forgiven and you can start your second act." *What do I need to be forgiven for?* "Sorry, I have to run. I've got to drive my five-year-old to ballet—my wife's put me on babysitting duties this weekend. All the best."

31

From Jade Kaya to Genevieve LaGarde on March 11, 2019 at 9:00 am
RE: Offer of Employment—Jade Kaya

Dear Genevieve,

I hope you are well. I have received an unexpected update on Project Arrow that does not align with our prior conversations. I'm sure it is a misunderstanding, but I would be grateful if we could please have a call to discuss?

All my best,
Jade

From Jade Kaya to Genevieve LaGarde on March 14, 2019 at 3:45 pm
RE: Offer of Employment—Jade Kaya

Dear Genevieve,

With apologies to chase, grateful if you could please get back to me on Monday's email.

Thank you,
Jade

From Jade Kaya to Julie Nicholls on March 15, 2019 at 8:30 am
RE: Update

Dear Julie,

Grateful for an update on the findings of HR's investigation? Please do let me know if a meeting or call would be helpful.

Best,
Jade

From Jade Kaya to Rémy Portier on March 18, 2019 at 11:00 am
RE: Offer of Employment—Jade Kaya

Dear Rémy,

I hope this email finds you well! I was wondering if you could please let me know the status of the countersigned contract? Additionally, please would you be able to find some time in Genevieve's diary this week for a quick meeting?

Many thanks in advance,
Jade

From Jade Kaya to Genevieve LaGarde on March 20, 2019 at 2:17 pm
RE: Offer of Employment—Jade Kaya

Dear Genevieve,

Further to my last few emails, would you have any time this week to speak?

Thanks,
Jade

From Microsoft Outlook to Jade Kaya on March 20, 2019 at 2:18 pm

Your message to Genevieve LaGarde could not be delivered.

32

From Rémy Portier to Jade Kaya on March 25, 2019 at 11:00 am
RE: Offer of Employment—Jade Kaya

Dear Jade,

Thank you for your email. It is with regret that I inform you that, after careful consideration, Arrow has decided to go in another direction for this role. At this stage, we are unable to provide specific feedback. We wish you the best in all your future endeavors and are grateful for your time.

Kind regards,
Rémy

When I realized Genevieve had blocked me, I knew it was all over. But the callousness, the cowardice to not tell me to my face—to not tell me at all—rocked me. Genevieve had nurtured me. Had positioned herself as my mentor. Only to cast me aside as soon as association with me jeopardized a business relationship of hers. I was a virus.

I wasn't angry, exactly. After all, her ruthless business mind was what I had admired about her for so long. Was numbness a feeling, or an absence of feelings? Even if I did feel angry, what could I do about it? Show up at Arrow's offices in a fit of histrionics, demanding they deliver on an offer of a job? Confirm everyone's suspicions that I was unhinged? No. It was clear that if I wanted to progress the career I had invested almost a third of my life into, a show of tacit acceptance of my treatment was required.

In the fortnight after my call with Will, there was a watchful pressure to react accordingly. Receive the humiliation graciously and, for the love of God, quietly. Perish the thought of causing a scene. It was imperative that I evoke a nonchalant lightness, betraying no trace of bitterness. A scorned woman was an unattractive woman. At work, I had to keep a low profile—show penance for seeking to leave—but not so low that I was pushed into obscurity. I had to attend every event, display myself as Still Standing. If I wasn't furious before, I certainly was after two weeks of this charade. The seeping wound I had carried for the last four months had overnight been trivialized to a cliché of the young woman burned by the wolf in sheepskin, man in power. A woman's indignity is simply so mass market, it's irrelevant what part the man played in her downfall. I had become ornamental, twinkling a warning. *Poor Jade, it's really such a shame. All that hard work circling the drain.*

I managed to shoehorn myself into another, much more

dormant, case. Tuning out on a conference call, I picked up my phone, automatically tapped the Instagram icon and began scrolling. A puppy, new homeowners, Donald Trump satire memes, targeted ads for self-help books. Like a magpie, the colorful infographic drew my attention. To use the parlance of Instagram, a paltry *TW* was insufficient warning for the juicy bubble letters: *RAPE 101*. Social media was a minefield. A constant barrage of forced empowerment. Healing narratives about *overcoming*. Neat arcs tied up with eureka moments. Butterflies not caterpillars. But I had a barren resignation that this aching was forever. There was no guaranteed happy ending at the end of this shitty pilgrimage. Far from a straightforward road ahead, it would be more like a circuit. I would have to learn how to orbit around my new sun.

I kept scrolling until I saw it. @leo_cannon had posted two hours ago. Against my better judgment, I clicked on Leo's profile. His life appeared to have carried on with barely an interruption. I looked through the photos posted by Emma and Ollie in Leo's chalet in the Alps, their cheeks burned from the spring sun that bounced off the fresh snow. They would know too; Ollie was on the trip to Dorset. And they still chose to go on holiday with him.

View all 3 comments:
@charlotte_cannon, 2 hours ago: a well-deserved break bro, come home soon!
@mich.morgan, 1 hour ago: beautiful shot xx
@kit.campbell, 3 minutes ago: looks great mate!

I had replied to Kit once in the past fortnight. A brief text saying *please stop calling. I need space.* I missed him. My body twitched at night because it missed being held by him. But then, three minutes ago, a mile away in his office, Kit had commented on Leo's post, and my chest simply ached at the idea of looking at him. It hurt so much I wondered if I would shortly crumble to dust.

Suddenly, I was furious. Furious that Leo appeared to be coasting through life with as little resistance as the room-temperature butter spreading over his morning crumpet. Before I could stop myself, I started typing a cathartic flurry to Kit.

~~*You're a coward.*~~
~~*I feel so utterly let down.*~~
~~*How could you?*~~
~~*Fuck you.*~~

I scrolled through my vitriol and deleted it all. I saw the last message he sent me.

I love you, Jade. Please come home. I was exhausted. I was so sad, so mad, but so tired.

I clicked on his message and called him.

"Jade." Kit picked up on the first ring.

I was lost for words. That voice of his. So familiar, so warm.

"Hey," I managed.

"Hey," he said, "it's a relief to hear your voice."

"How have you been?"

He said softly, "I can't do this on the phone, I have to see you."

London weather laughed in the face of the changing seasons, with blustering wind nearly blowing me over on the walk from Clapham Common to the flat. All my efforts to look immaculate on arrival were futile. Kit stood in the hallway, hands pocketed, head to one side. I halted. We gazed at each other. Wordlessly, he took tentative steps toward me and gave me a hug that filled me with nostalgia. The smell of him: clean linen and coffee. My cheek against his chest, my arms around his waist. Maybe this was, we were, salvageable. We could reset, recharge. Pretend the last few months never happened.

"How've you been?" Kit murmured.

"Pretty rubbish, to be honest." I looked up at him. Kit was over a foot taller than me and nearly double my weight. I felt safe in the shadow of his size. His arms wrapped around my shoulders and his chin rested atop my head.

"I know, me too," he muffled into my hair. "This time without you has been awful. Who knew I'd miss you waking up every day and saying 'it's morning everyone, today's the day! The sun is shining, the tank is clean!' "

I gasped. "*THA TANK IS CLEAN!*"

We both chuckled into each other.

I whispered, "I was so embarrassed the first time I said that, I felt like such a kid."

Kit lifted my chin up. His eyes had clouded over, lacked the clarity I was used to.

"Shall we talk?" I asked, walking toward the sofa.

Kit was like a recalcitrant dog being persuaded to leave the park.

"I know we need to," he said, "but I don't want to. I want to move on with you."

I wondered if this is how cows feel before going to the slaughterhouse. Do they know what's coming? I got the hollow sense that we both did.

"Things haven't been good between us for a long time," I started.

He puffed out his cheeks.

"Are you okay?" I asked.

"Yes."

"Have you had a chance to think about our last conversation?"

"Yes."

"Will all your responses be monosyllabic going forward?"

"No."

"What are your thoughts on our argument?"

Kit stared into the middle distance, his body perpendicular to mine. He sighed and put his head in his hands.

"Kit, I need you to communicate with me. You're not saying anything."

"Listen, this is a waste of time. We've both had a horrendous time without each other, haven't we learned we should be together?"

"Kit," I said quietly, "if you think it's a waste of time, then it will be. You need to be willing to have difficult conversations with me."

I tried again.

"This is something that's really important to me." I injected as much softness into my tone as possible, to clear the hostility in the air. I didn't really know what I came here thinking would happen. I thought it was clear there was no way back. Not after everything. But now that I was here, in our home, I still wanted to say it was all okay. Let's forget about that horrible conversation. Let's live in amazing ignorant bliss together, overlooking our differences. But everything we had was marred by what we both now saw in each other. Luxurious warm memories trimmed down by cynicism. "But Kit, ultimately it's so important to me that it's not something I can move past. I hope you'll tell me that you've had a chance to reflect and reconsider. But, if not, I'm sorry—"

"I won't respond to an ultimatum, Jade." Kit was firm.

"It's not an ultimatum. It's my position."

"Who are you?" Kit was staring at me with incredulity. "I'm not in some boardroom negotiation with you! We're not in *The Apprentice*, all right?"

"You know what I mean."

"So what are you saying? I have to choose between you or one of my oldest friends?"

When he put it that way, it did seem unreasonable. I nearly dissolved, said *no of course that's not what I'm saying*. But then I thought about Leo pushing that woman—I wish I knew her name—his grubby fingers reaching inside her. Suzie's bleary-eyed fear and confusion.

"Yes. That's what I'm saying."

"Fuck, J."

"What do you mean! Don't you think there is anything questionable about remaining friends with him?"

"Who am I to judge? He's been a good friend to me. Yes, he made a mistake. Everyone makes mistakes"—he looked at me pointedly—"people can change. They deserve second chances."

Kit continued, "I mean, for God's sake, he was drunk! People do dumb shit when they're drunk! Plus, it's all just hearsay. It's his word against hers."

I held Kit's eyes square on as I played my last card.

"So you think it's Josh's word against mine?"

"Stop it, Jade," Kit snapped. "This isn't some fucking thought experiment. Why can't we agree to disagree? Why do you need me to see things the same way you do? I want to be his friend. End of story."

Kit's legs were spread over two seats on the sofa, his arms out like an albatross, motioning ferociously as if he were a Tory MP in Parliament opposing a bill to give schoolchildren free meals. My cup was empty. I had nothing more to give to him. He carried on ranting about how it wasn't my place to judge his and Leo's friendship, how what he'd done wasn't *that* bad, how the woman who tipped Suzie off was clearly a liar, a vindictive shrew going after Leo. He said all this with eloquence, clear articulation. His oratorial skills alone almost made me give in. So much of what is perceived to be "intelligence" was Kit talking in a deep, male voice, being white and educated, and packaging up abhorrent views in grandiloquent, pretentious language. Men like Kit had been groomed from birth to speak the vernacular of success. An extremely precise monotone that conveyed to the listener *hey, I'm posh and civilized and I know you will equate that with intellect and skill*. I hated myself for falling for this cycle of arrogance for so long.

"I don't think there's anything more to say," I said quietly.

"What do you mean?"

"It's a red line for me." I was on the edge of a moment. The second before a waterfall reaches a river. "We can't move past this."

Kit looked dazed. My intestines felt like they were being used as a skipping rope.

"So . . . this is it?"

"It is." I knew, with intense conviction, that we were no

longer. Kit bit his lip to stop it from trembling, and innately I moved to comfort him, before stopping myself.

Actually, no.

He called Leo's victim a liar. Deep down, he must think I'm a liar too.

"This can't be it, J." Kit clasped both my hands. "It's always been us. How can we not be us?"

I was crying. Tears of mourning. Not for our relationship. For myself. For trying so hard to make this work. For wasting all this time. For losing myself in Kit.

"I love you." He tried to hold me close. "And you love me too. I know we've hit a rough patch, but it's you and me, J. Please remember that. Remember all our good times?"

"We've moved so far from the people we fell in love with," I cried. It was all too much. "What is the point of remembering them? They're gone. What are we even holding on to, Kit?" My hands were in his and we leaned into each other, our foreheads touching. Kit sniffled and squeezed his eyes shut. I pulled away, looked around the house we shared, where I never truly felt at home. They puddled around me, our years together. Our relationship the linchpin of our lives. *I have to do this. I have to.* But if I stay here, if I hear him tell me he loves me again, I won't have the strength to leave.

"I should—" I tried to shift and stand up.

"Don't go." Kit held me tighter. "Please."

I gently pulled his arms off me.

"I'm sorry."

I held my chin up, and for the first time in months, felt in control of my grief.

33

I felt electric with independence. I recited the clichéd motivational post-breakup lines about other fish in the sea, the world being my oyster, dodging bullets and so on. But the flipside of thinking someone completes you, that they're your other half, is the implication that I was incomplete—merely half a person—without Kit.

"Hello?" Adele's twang echoed over the intercom.

"It's me!" I smiled like a crazed clown at the tiny dot camera and manically held up a bottle of gin.

The door buzzed and swung open. I ran up the stairs to the fourth floor, to find Adele biting her thumbnail in the corridor.

"Is it true?"

"Yep."

"You're not going to get back together in a few weeks after I've called him a fuckwit a thousand times?"

"Nope. I'm basically homeless now." I grinned. Adele pulled me into a hug at breakneck speed before dragging me by the arm into her flat.

"I'm so proud of you, I knew you could do it." She pushed

me onto the kitchen stool. "Real talk though, what happened? How are you? Are you okay? Do you want a cup of tea?"

"Whoa, so many questions. I'm knackered, but I'm fine. And yes, please to the tea, but only if it's a G and T."

"As you wish!" She cracked open the gin and sloshed it into two pint glasses. "I don't have any tonic, so it'll have to be a gin and juice." She held up both glasses and inspected her fruity concoction like a scientist in the lab before handing me one. Within the hour the bottle was decimated, and I was feebly protesting as Adele bundled me onto a Soho-bound bus.

"Hey, sorry, do either one of yous have a lighter?" Adele and I blearily turned around in the queue to get into the bar to find a tattooed woman with Boudicca curls wearing ripped denim shorts, fishnet tights, and wearing cherry-red Dr. Martens.

"No, sorry, buddy." Adele turned back to face me before something caught her eye and she did a double take. "You go for the Red Sox?"

She laughed, "Not really," and rubbed the sticker on her phone. "I just stuck this on here to remind me of my year abroad."

"No shit?" Adele pointed to herself. "I'm from Boston."

The two of them engaged in a slurred babble that I'd need subtitles for if I had any hopes of following. I gingerly sat on a stoop on Wardour Street, head against the doorframe, my four gin cocktails slushing around my stomach. Tonight was meant to mark my liberation. But it didn't feel like a celebration. Boston Girl's friends, all Scousers, materialized. After accidentally relinquishing our place in the line for the bar, the six of us stumbled down the street arm-in-arm, passing around a bottle of Bacardi. Several blisters later, we teetered up to the rooftop on Adele's building. Boston Girl, who was actually Linnie from Liverpool, and her friends were actors who had recently moved to London. I sidled up to Adele, who was sat in a bizarre rattan swinging egg-chair that her landlord seemingly thought was an essential piece. I curled up with her.

I wanted this night to be over.

I wanted to sleep and never wake up.

I wanted to disappear. Not die, even that would be too much fanfare. I wanted to dissolve into nothingness.

"I think I'm in love with the redhead," Adele said in a volume that she clearly thought was a whisper, before giggling incessantly. "Her accent makes me wet."

I snorted and we began swinging in the chair, both in hysterics. We sat on the rooftop until the sky lightened and the sun's pink and peach shades inked the horizon.

"All right, we're gonna clear out." Linnie stood up. "I have an audition in four hours and like a dickhead I've been out all night."

Inside Adele's flat, the girls faffed about, gathering their bags and jackets. As they finally filed out, Adele, like a rowdy heckler at a stand-up comedy show, ran down the stairs after them, bellowing, "*I LOVE YOU, LINNIE!*"

Adele's minimalist new-build space, after a night of sensory overload, felt empty. The silence so loud. Questions I'd tried to ignore came roaring up at me. How am I going to be alone? Do I even know how to be single? I've never been with another man, am I going to be able to have sex again? What if I'm shockingly awful in bed, and I've never known? Was our entire relationship a complete waste of time? Did he ever love me? Did he ever respect me? What if I never find anyone again? Should I go to the police? Would they take me seriously after all this time? Do I want to put myself through that? What if they don't believe me? Is my career over? Am I a pariah at work? What options do I have now? Do I have enough savings to quit? Do I need to tell my parents? How can I do that to them?

There was a lingering, frustrating, infuriating numbness. An inability to access the chasm. Like losing your sense of smell when you have a cold.

And then, on the cold granite floor of Adele's flat, Pandora's box unlatched.

"Guess who's a good kisser?" Adele waltzed through the door, Linnie's magenta lipstick smudged against her chin. "Where are you? Jade?"

I was kneeling in the land between her sofa and marble coffee table, heaving with sobs. My arms wrapped around my chest, trying to contain the grief spilling out of me. My entire body quaked with the flash flood of my tears, my lungs gasping for air.

After trying, and failing, to calm me, Del stood up.

"Let's get you home, Jadey."

Baba had never met Adele, but he'd heard plenty about her. That didn't help his shock when she brought his daughter to Morden and told him, to his relief, that Kit Campbell was no longer at risk of being his future son-in-law. They guided me to bed and Adele fished through my handbag for my work phone. I had worked myself into the ground on Project Arrow for months, and most of my annual leave was outstanding.

"What're you doing?" I groaned from bed, watching Del tap with her brow furrowed.

"Requesting holiday for you."

"No, don't, not so soon after everything." My voice was hoarse. "They'll think I'm having a breakdown or something."

"Jade, I hate to say it, but you *are* having a breakdown."

"Is this an intervention?" Salty water seeped from my eyes, oozing like an infected wound.

"Pretty much." I heard the whoosh sound of an email being sent.

"What did you do?"

"Requested all your holiday. You need time. And I'll be watching your Skype status, so don't you dare try and come online."

"Don't worry, I can't, I've been dropped from my case, remember?"

"I love you. I'll be in touch to check how you're doing. Call me whenever you need, okay?"

"Okay." My lip trembled. "I love you too."

34

I hardly left bed for seven days, despite my mother's tactics to smoke me out. She tried suggesting we make sujebi, a comforting soup where small clumps of dough were plopped in to make little noodle balls. One of Omma's other strategies was entering my bedroom at six in the morning to vacuum. When I groggily groaned from bed, she put her hand to her chest and feigned surprise to see me in there. In the passing days, I heard her and Baba's footsteps padding outside my door, patrolling for clues as to what was wrong with me.

On day five of my bed rest, Baba peeked his head around the door after Friday prayer. I was scrolling through my emails, desperate for someone to tell me there was a work emergency and I was needed in the office right away. That I was as essential as I thought I was. That I wasn't so replaceable. Disposable. I was going crazy, alone with my thoughts. Missing Kit, then questioning whether it was him I missed, or the space he took up in my life, or the person I was trying to be for him. Or if I just needed time to mourn the life we could have had together. Wondering whether Genevieve thought of me. How she could sleep at night. Convincing myself that she felt bad when I knew she didn't. Baba gently pried the phone out of my hand, switching it off.

"So," he prompted. "Talk."

"What do you mean, Baba?"

He held up a plate of baklava. I picked one piece up.

"You know."

"Huh?" I said, lips curling to catch all the syrup oozing out.

"I know we're not a talky, emotional family, but you can talk to me."

"I know, Baba."

I said nothing more.

On day eight, even I knew I couldn't stay in bed much longer. I pulled myself up, scrubbed myself clean. Rolls of dirt lifted from my skin. My ribs hung off me like a ladder. My cheeks had sunk into my skull, and my hair was falling out in large clumps.

"Happy birthday, Omma." I smiled, emerging from my bedroom slowly, like a turtle out of hibernation. I kissed my mother on both cheeks. Her mouth was agape in a surprise that quickly transformed into an appreciative smile as I motioned her into the kitchen. Korean women are encouraged to eat seaweed soup for a month after giving birth, to nourish their bodies. In honor of your mother's pain, and in gratitude for the life she gave you, it was eaten on birthdays for a lifetime.

"So, aga," Omma said, as I prepared the soup. Baba was inspecting his garden, and I knew Omma had waited until he wouldn't hear us to question me. "What is your plan?" The notions of flying by the seat of your pants, doing what makes you happy, going with the wind were unfamiliar in this household. I was surprised it had taken this long for the sermon on how much I've ruined my own life to begin.

"What do you mean?"

"Kit, he was your security. What will you do now?"

"Omma—"

"Be realistic," Omma said, holding up her hand to stop me. "When your father and I die, you will have no one. You will be alone in this world."

"Jeez," I sighed. "Way to be morbid."

"Mo-bid? What mo-bid?"

"It means gloomy, like, what you're saying is depressing."

"It's true. You have no family, Jade, no one to help you if you need anything."

"Yep. I heard you the first time."

"I don't understand," she muttered, taking the knife out of my hand and chopping the garlic with such speed I thought it might claim one of her fingers. "You went to live with that boy, the next step was marriage, not breaking up."

"Breakups are normal in your twenties, Omma! I don't even know why you care."

"He was a safe option."

"We weren't happy in the end."

"Happiness!" She thwacked my arm.

"*OW!*" I rubbed the red patch forming on my skin.

"You think you need a man for happiness?"

"I don't need a man for anything. You taught me that. You went for Baba. The least safe option imaginable!"

"We didn't have a choice. Things were different back then, and we suffered for a long time because of that choice. I want an easier path for you." Omma's tone softened.

"Omma, please, can we drop it?"

"Drop it where? On the floor? Your life is already on the floor!"

I groaned.

"I need to know you have a plan."

"Well, I don't." I avoided her searching eyes and instead fixated on stirring my soup base.

"Ay, my blood pressure! What are you doing to me? You had your whole life ready. University, boy, so many years together. What for? All that time. Your best years! Wasted! Bye-bye!"

"Mum!"

"It's not so terrible," Omma said, reassuring herself. "You're a lawyer. Your career and education won't wake up one day and decide to leave you."

"Kit didn't leave me," I retorted petulantly, before adding, "I'm thinking about leaving Reuben." It wasn't until I'd said it out loud that I realized it was true. Arrow or no Arrow.

"Your father mentioned your job offer. When are you starting at the new place?"

"I'm not." I grimaced as I spoke. *Your message to Genevieve LaGarde could not be delivered.*

"What? What else will you do?"

"Nothing. I'm thinking of taking some time off." It felt good to test the idea out, even just by saying it.

"My Gad, oh my Gad, oh my Gaaaaad." Omma clutched her chest.

"It's really not a big deal." I waited for Omma to explode.

"Nat a big deal?! *NAT* a big deal?" Omma switched to Korean. "You think we worked so hard, days and nights to provide for you, for you to do this? Do you think I imagined I'd spend my life in a car wash shack on the side of the motorway? Do you know what kind of future I had in Korea? But I kept going to give you"—she jabbed my arm—"what you have now. And now you have a stable job that pays you good money, and you want to just quit?"

"I never asked you to sacrifice so much. You chose to do that! Stop putting that on to me!"

I didn't see it coming until Omma's hand collided with my cheek. A warmth rushed to the side of my face, as it sang with the stinging pain. I froze on impact. I stared at the floor, unsure how to react.

"You ungrateful child, you bring your parents shame," Omma spat. *I bring everything I touch shame, I know.*

"Vay, vay, vay, what is happening here?" Baba intervened. He had a knack for timing his entry in a particularly tense moment between the two women in his life.

"Yusuf," she huffed, blowing a strand of hair away from her face, "talk to your daughter."

"What's this, Jade?" Baba looked at me.

Not now. I can't tell them now. It's all wrong. I wanted to run back into my bedroom and hide.

"Nothing, Dad." My cheek was hot and tingling.

"This girl of ours, stubborn like her father," Omma began.

"How is this somehow my fault?" Baba laughed.

"She has no man, no plan. And now she wants to quit work. Quit, Yusuf. *QUIT!*" Omma might as well have had steam coming out of her ears. Baba looked at me, but before he could react, Omma carried on as if she were a woeful war widow in a Greek tragedy. "I raised you wrong, it's all my fault!" she decried. "Tell me, what did we deny you? You had a roof over your head. You went to a good school. Did we ever let you go to bed hungry? When we lost the business"—she pointed at herself—"I'm the one who went hungry. How dare you. How dare you disrespect us like this."

Guilt washed through me.

"Yumi, stop," Baba said to his wife wearily before turning to me. "What is this about, child?"

"It's nothing. I need some time off and maybe I'd like to travel," I said as casually as possible.

"*LIES!*" Omma shrieked. Baba pursed his lips toward his wife, shushing her.

"Kizim," Baba said, "remember when you fractured your collarbone? Yani, your mother and I were away working. You never called us. You put yourself in a sling and waited for us to come home. We taught you to be strong by yourself, but"—he turned to Omma—"we also taught her to hide from us." He looked at me. "You can trust us with anything, hayatim."

I wanted to point out that Omma had just backhanded me when I tried to tell her my plans, but I knew better than to point out the wrongs of my mother.

"I'm not trying to hide things from you guys, I just don't want to worry or burden you."

"Why not?"

"Because you've both been through so much!" I said, exasperated. "And you keep telling me how much you've given up. I don't want to fail you by saying I'm not happy in the life you've always wanted for me!"

"I gave you life. I *AM YOUR MOTHER*!" Omma all but screamed. "You must consider what I want for you too."

Baba said to Omma, "You shouldn't make her feel bad. Especially not about Kit." She looked shocked that Baba was questioning her in front of me. "Vallahi, that boy was a waste of space. She wouldn't be crying in bed nonstop for a week over Kit. There's something else going on here." Baba turned back to me. "What is it?"

Baba's eyes were searching, urging, comforting. Omma looked genuinely worried.

"I didn't want to tell you. I don't know how to—" I whispered.

Omma's hand was on my arm across the table.

"Are you in some kind of trouble, Jade? We can help you if you are."

I took a deep breath and looked up, straight ahead and out the window behind my parents.

"In November, there was a big work event. There was lots of pressure to impress. I was next to the Founding Partner; he was being really pushy with me."

"Did this man hurt you?" Baba's voice turned hard.

"No, he didn't. He was being very predatory, though. I'm sure he would have taken advantage of me if he'd had the chance. This other man, a friend, I thought, made sure I got home." I breathed. The worry etched across my parents' faces was too much to look directly at. I squeezed my eyes shut and let the words tumble out. "This 'friend,' he raped me. Kit found out and . . . it didn't work, we couldn't recover from it. I've been a different person since that night. I don't know what's wrong with me." I looked up. Omma's lips had thinned into a stiff line as if I had said something impolite. Baba looked shell-shocked. No one spoke for a period as thick and gelatinous as caramel.

"Well," Omma began. I swear I saw her face visibly harden. Her hand was no longer on my arm. "You're very lucky to be alive. What if this man had hurt you?"

"He did hurt me."

"Why didn't you tell us?" she said. "I remember, you were here the day after the party, you could have told us then. What is the point of telling us now, months later? You insult us!"

"It's not about you, Mum!" I exploded, months of repressing the truth bubbling over. "It's not about you or my duties to you. I didn't tell you this one thing because I couldn't. I wasn't ready to! I'm telling you now."

"A lady," Omma spoke, "doesn't drink in front of her boss. Of course a man will use you when you're drunk."

"Stop, Yumi," Baba said. His voice was metallic.

"That's what men do," Omma carried on, "they're animals. All they think about is sex."

"It's not 'sex'! If someone pushed your head underwater, you wouldn't call it 'swimming,' would you?" I said.

"You should have been more careful. We've taught you this again and again. Don't leave your drink unattended, be careful. You should not have been so drunk—what were you thinking?"

"I need a time out," I said, standing up. "I can't do this." I walked into my bedroom, stripped, and pulled my smelly unwashed pajamas back on.

35

"Aga? Are you asleep?"

I faced the wall, my laptop in bed with me. Omma perched on the side of my bed. She shook my shoulder gently.

"Mmmhmm."

"Aga."

I flipped myself over in bed. Omma looked smaller than ever, and it seemed as if she had sprouted tens of gray hairs in the past few hours. She couldn't look me in the eye and stared at the sheets as she spoke.

"I'm sorry to hear about the pain you carry," Omma finally said. "It hurts to hear someone has damaged my child like this."

Damaged? Why would you say that?

I ignored her, looking up at the yellowing magnolia paint on the ceiling. I remembered the day Omma learned the word "magnolia." When they laid down roots in this Morden house, she began asking Baba to plant her the tree with the lotus-like pink flowers. Omma didn't know the name of the plant in English, and Baba was stumped. So he drove her to five different Homebases and let her roam until she found the tree that reminded her of home. They brought it back and planted it outside their bedroom window. *My magnolia, my magnolia* she would say every morning, before WhatsApping me close-up shots of its new buds.

"But," Omma spoke, "we all carry pain, my girl."

"For once can we stop with the musings?" I snapped. I then noticed the melancholic look on my mum's face. She was glazed over. "Omma?"

"Your father and I think," she eventually spoke, "that it's best if we don't speak of this again."

I waited a beat to see if there was anything further.

"That's it?" I exploded. "You came in here to tell me you never want to hear about it again?"

"Talking won't help you."

"Just because you're emotionally repressed doesn't mean it's the right way to do things," I shot back.

Omma looked as though a bucket of ice-cold water had been dumped on her head. I thought she would humble me again. But her lips pressed together. She brought her hands to cover her face. They had a patina of age spots splattered over the papery skin. I heard Omma suck in air and then slowly push it out. In and out, in and out, all the while unwilling to let me see her face. In this position, I could clearly see the raised squishy skin of the scar on her forearm. It was half a foot long and jagged, with haphazard lines across it that made clear the stitches were the work of no surgeon. I used to trace it as a child and ask her how she got it. And each time she would tell fantastical, mythical stories about mermaids on Jeju Island. Her revisionist history. I never learned what caused the injury that left this brutish gash. That was Omma: always holding herself back, keeping her secrets lingering within. Never sharing her scars, even with us.

"Omma?" I gently tapped at her forearm, nudging her to stop covering her face. "Please stop. Look at me."

"I can't."

"Why not?"

"Trust me, a widow knows another widow's sorrow."

"So why can't we talk about it?" I asked. Omma said nothing and I said, "It'll eat you up inside if you don't speak about it." *I should know.* "What is it?"

"There is no one thing." She switched to Korean. "I know your pain because I know it is not one thing. It is layers and layers and layers. You wouldn't leave your relationship, want to leave your job, if it was one thing. What happened to you, aga, it kills me to hear. I knew there was something wrong with you since you came here crying that night in December." She eyeballed me with laser vision and I felt as though she opened me up completely. A wry smile spilled across her face. "But in my mind, in some ways," she raised her shoulders and eyebrows, "it was a good thing."

I nearly popped out of myself. *How could she say it was a good thing?*

"It opened your eyes," she said, her body leaning forward, her eyes grave like an oracle. "You see now, eh? What I was telling you all these years? The world will not bend for you. When you were born, we had no one. We couldn't speak the language here. We were turned away from job after job. No matter how desperate we got, no one helped us. And no one will help you either. We learned how to press it down"—she held her hand flat horizontally and mimed pushing down her torso—"push push push. That's what han is."

I finally understood. It's not that Omma thought it was best for me to never speak of what had happened. She snuffed out her pain because she never had an alternative. She experienced tragedies in her motherland. But it was being here, in this country, that caused the death of her inner self by a thousand cuts. When we spoke in Korean, she was articulate and erudite. She had panache and wit. That part of her—her sparkling intelligence—had been hidden behind a lexicon inaccessible to her. She was rageful, but forced to be silent. And that was now her only mode of operating. Encouraging me to continue in that cycle of repression was the only advice she knew to give. It had become almost a source of pride; Omma considered herself the Knower of All Hard Things, things I could only experience diluted.

"I don't tell you not to speak about it because I don't want to hear it," Omma said. "I say it because you must learn." Her back straightened; her face hardened. "You need to learn to hold yourself back. You *must* control yourself."

I felt numb. I wanted softness. I wanted tenderness from my mother. I wanted her to sit with me into the night because she knew I was scared to sleep. Scared to remember it all again in the morning. I wanted heart emojis on my phone to remind me I was loved. I wanted to be told it would all be okay, even if she didn't know it would be. But as I looked at my mother, I realized I have always craved something from her that she was unable to give me.

I could see now. How similar we really were. How much silence had robbed the both of us.

"I'm sure you will overcome this. My brave girl." She kissed me on the forehead. "Now rest. I'll see you in the morning."

36

The time off work rattled by. I kept myself distracted, but my head felt like it lived outside an ambulance station. Sirens wailing at the sight of basic items—Omma's wineglass, Baba's tie slung over a chair—relentlessly piercing any moment of still. My brittle senses skittering as they tried to regulate.

Omma and I hadn't spoken since those brief five minutes in my bedroom. We edged around each other, both harboring our own resentment for pushing one another's limits. I suppose she wasn't used to me being in the house because I made her jump when she was dusting my grandfather's vase. We both watched it cut a streak through the air, hitting the kitchen tiles, its neck snapping with pathetic fragility. When the only item of my beloved grandad's smashed before my mum's eyes, I expected a piece of her to break with it. Instead, she beckoned me to sit on the floor with her. She fished out a shoebox of art supplies and mixed in a takeaway lid clear glue with gold paint. In silence, I held the base steady as she aligned and pressed the neck onto it. Then she got up and walked away, taking the vase with her. Now, the art of kintsugi has become a kitsch, insta-metaphor for embracing one's setbacks or flaws. A cute afternoon activity for millennials as they talked about how it was beautiful to be broken. Korea was annexed and colonized by Japan. Identities and women were stolen. But as with all occupations, there was also an osmosis-like transmission of culture between the countries. So for us, kintsugi was reluctantly functional: the vase had to live on, albeit damaged. It appeared on our dining table a day later, a gold streak twinkling along its body, highlighting the crack. The breakage now a part of its story. She saw me staring at it, biting my lip as the tears fell anyway. She held my forearm for three long seconds, and the way she looked at me added one extra suture to the wound inside.

Certain other things helped:

1. Time in nature helped because it reminded me that there existed something far greater than me, and more powerful than Josh Parsons. Nature didn't care about anything besides survival and regeneration. And that encouraged me to do the same.
2 I read the news incessantly. Reading about catastrophes elsewhere was a sadomasochistic exercise. A way to stop feeling sorry for myself.
3. Music helped. I compiled a playlist of songs to listen to when the panic threatened to take over. I never hit "shuffle play;" the playlist had to start with Nina Nesbitt. I'd go on long walks by the river, repeating her assurances like a mantra.
4 I walked and walked and walked. All over London. At least ten miles a day. Sometimes I thought that precious time off work could be better spent by going on holiday somewhere sunny or catching up with friends I've had to repeatedly cancel on for work, such that they no

> longer reached out to make plans. I struggled with time off because I didn't know what to do with the militating urge to be constantly productive. I needed to feel like I was achieving something. I tried reading, but it quickly became an exercise in *how fast can I rate this book on Goodreads?* But walking endlessly felt like I was propelling myself forward in some way. I'd still compete with the prior day's step count, trying to outdo myself. Adele's ode to London, *Hometown Glory*, was also on my playlist (*the* Adele, obviously, not my Adele). I retraced Baba's steps in the early years of the insurance business. I clasped his battered Underground map in my pocket, my evil eye to keep me safe.

The last Sunday before I returned to work, Easter Sunday, I went to the park. I spread out a blanket on the ground and had a date with myself. I'd bought strawberries, blueberries, and olives and peeled them open on my rug, lazily wafting away curious bees. I read all day, basking in the sunshine. I was only able to read nonfiction; the shape-shifting parameters of fiction were too anxiety-inducing. I struggled too much to stay rooted in my own reality that I didn't need to be immersed in someone else's creation.

Adele O'Hara, 5 minutes ago:
How's life as a lady of leisure?

Jade Kaya, now:
I'd better start thinking about my Real Housewives tagline quick.

Adele O'Hara, now:
Yours would def be "life's not easy, but I love a challenge," followed by a minxy wink.

Jade Kaya, now:
Have you considered a career in screenwriting?

I picked up a tired bumble bee and carefully placed him on the bitten end of a strawberry, watching him regain his strength and eventually flutter away. Before dusk, a group of women my age settled about ten meters away from me. I fished out my sunglasses and put them on, watching these friends undetected. They sucked on lime and orange Calippos. One of them, a petite blonde with freckles sprayed over her nose and cheeks and a red polka-dot headband, had a thermos and she poured what looked like sangria out for the others. They chattered without pausing. I missed that. Trying to tell a story but taking so many tangents that you ended up talking about something else, not knowing how you got there. I watched this group, each person with their own problems and dramas, their own loved ones, their own hopes and disappointments.

Statistically, one of them will have been raped or sexually abused.

Each of their universes overlayed today, on a gloriously balmy April evening. They looked so carefree and breezy, the exact image Tampax would want on their next campaign.

They looked so happy. I wondered if they were pretending.

37

From Reception to All Members on April 23, 2019 at 8:03 am
RE: Lost Property

Dear all—thank you for joining us with your families for the annual Reuben Easter Egg Hunt! The children had a delightful time. A Barbie and her outfit were left behind—if it is your little one's, please collect it from reception.

From Jeremy Benson to All Members on April 23, 2019 at 8:06 am
RE: RE: Lost Property

Who undressed Barbie?! #MeToo

Jeremy Benson
PARTNER

"I'm proud of you, dude," Adele said, nudging my shoulder with hers. We sat on a bench outside Reuben's offices, with flat whites I'd picked up, both staring into the trickling water feature. I didn't tell Adele that my hand was throbbing; I'd thought I saw Josh in the coffee shop. I flinched with such a start that the stupid coffee spurted out of the stupid hole, sizzling my hand.

"It's not like I have a choice to be back here," I said. "My mum will likely disown me if I quit."

I felt a sharp twist of sorrow.

"Maybe she's right—it would be such a sad waste for you to leave law over this."

I threw back the last of my coffee and stood up. "C'mon, let's do this."

Outside our office were the secretary bays. Something was off. Sitting at my secretary's desk was an unfamiliar figure, though I didn't see their face.

"Where's Claire?" I asked Adele.

"Shhhh," she scolded before closing the door.

"What?"

"The other secretaries don't know yet."

"Know what?"

"Claire was let go last week." Adele pulled her lips back to show her gritted teeth.

"Why?"

"She was adding her own food when sorting out Will's dinner deliveries, and then expensing the whole order to the client. She's been doing it for years. They said it amounts to fraud and fired her on the spot."

I stared at my desk. "That's a shame. I hope she's okay."

Like a rusty bicycle, I slowly pedaled into my usual routine. By noon, it felt like I had never been away. I was back operating at peak efficiency, juggling five action points, preparing for meetings, replying to emails, and reading into new cases. On Mondays there was a taco truck outside our office. We loaded up with two Styrofoam boxes each, one full of birria beef tacos, and the other with crispy fries. Despite my parents' coaxing, I'd barely eaten more than an apple and a yoghurt pot a day over the past weeks. My appetite came hurtling back with a vengeance as I picked up a taco and dipped it in sour cream. I had stuffed three cheesy loaded fries in my mouth when my computer pinged.

From Julie Nicholls to Jade Kaya on April 23, 2019 at 1:06 pm
RE: Case #1201

Jade,

I hope you have been keeping well and that you enjoyed your period of leave. We did not want to disturb your time off, but I am writing to let you know that we have an update for you. Are you available today to meet to discuss?

Kind regards,
Julie

"Jade, hello! How are you?" Julie singsonged as she bustled in. She was in a bland beige pantsuit with a giant amber pendant swinging from her neck that had the potential to knock me out.

"Been better," I said, my stomach turning like a cement mixer.

"So." She slid in her ergonomic chair as if it were lined with jelly. "How've you been getting on?"

"You said you had updates on the investigation?" I was over the pleasantries. My expectations for this meeting were on the floor, jaded as I was. "I'd rather discuss that first."

"As you wish." She ruffled sheets of paper on her desk and lowered her glasses from her head. "Reuben takes sexual assault very seriously, and"—she looked down again—"we maintain a zero-tolerance policy on any behavior that is sexually inappropriate." *Jesus. Is she reading a script?* "We will continue to take actionable steps to ensure that our workplace is one in which women feel comfortable and safe." Julie looked up at me, and I wondered if I should give her a gold star for her recital.

"Okay . . . ? " I prompted.

"I, on behalf of Reuben, would like to apologize to you for the experiences you've reported. The Firm is very sorry that you feel it was not a protective environment." Julie nodded in a confirmatory way.

"Is that it?"

"Like I said, we strive to take steps every day to combat the issue of sexual assault and that's why Reuben would like to offer our support to you."

She slid a greige paper file across the table, as if we were in an espionage film.

"What's this?"

"The Firm is extremely grateful for your continued hard

work in the face of such challenging times. As such, we would like to show our appreciation."

She nodded her head toward the file, which I flipped open.

AS BETWEEN:
1. JADE KAYA
2. REUBEN, FLEISHER & WISHALL LLP (THE "FIRM")

SETTLEMENT AGREEMENT

I closed the file.

Of course.

These past months, they were never investigating. They were stalling while building a steel cage to lead me into.

I never even made a claim. How can you settle a claim that was never made?

"How much?" I asked, my voice low with shame.

"Page six." Julie nodded.

I opened the file again. A slim sheath to the eye, but a muzzle in practice. My breath caught in my chest when I saw the figure. Or figures, rather.

"It will be taxed, as all bonuses are," Julie added. *What did this mean? Were they gearing up to fire me and this is meant to cover lost earnings?*

"Of course," I murmured. I flicked through the pages. The words drifted and hovered in my short distance.

Without admission of liability by any Party, the Parties have agreed the below terms for the full and final settlement of any current, pending, or future claims against the Firm.

Ms. Kaya, with effect from the date of this Agreement, hereby definitively and irrevocably waives the right to bring proceedings, actions, claims, or allegations of any nature against the Firm, whether directly or through a third party.

Ms. Kaya hereby withdraws any complaint as against the Firm.

The terms of this Agreement, its existence and its content, as well as the discussions and meetings that led to the conclusion of the Agreement and any documents related to it, are confidential and shall not be disclosed to any third party.

It is agreed that this Agreement is not an admission whatsoever of any fault by the Firm.

"Brilliant! If I could get you to sign below—"

I performatively "read" the contract to buy myself time with Julie. To consider what this meant. Case number 1201. Were there really one thousand two hundred other people, living double lives, smothering their truth? If I assumed the same amount was paid out to some, if not all, of my predecessors, that would be millions spent. With that money, they could have hired a designated women's representative for every office worldwide. They could have hired ten for every office. Someone whose role it was to solely provide support and counseling to the workforce Reuben relied on daily. With that money, they could have invested in a third-party consultant to carry out an overhaul of Reuben's policies and practices. They could have rolled out training for every employee on acceptable behavior in the office. They could have promulgated a plethora of mental health resources designed to prioritize the welfare of employees, not just their capacity to churn out hours. They could have set up a complete network of CCTV and surveillance for every corner of the office. They could have brought in experts designed to find solutions for this viral epidemic of men thinking women existed for their taking.

They could have.

They could have.

They could have.

But they hadn't.

"Julie?" I cleared my throat. "This isn't what I envisaged when meeting with you today."

"Jade, I can assure you that we have taken every possible route into consideration." Julie became animated again. "We will also be rolling out new policies on Firm-sponsored events."

"Right?" I was a little lost.

"It'll be a clampdown on the culture of drinking at Firm events, as alcohol clearly comes with its"—Julie raised her hand toward me—"specific dangers."

I laughed callously. *The specific dangers of alcohol.* Correlation mistaken for causation. As inevitable as damaged lungs are to a chain-smoker. Josh simply couldn't help himself, it was the alcohol!

"What's happened to Josh?" I abruptly asked.

"Ah, yes." Julie brought both hands together and intertwined her fingers. She looked like an evil villain watching her plan for world domination unfold. "We've thought long and hard about the appropriate sanction for Mr. Parsons, while also considering that we have no evidence to verify or corroborate the allegations against him." She was back to looking at her crib sheet. "So, Mr. Parsons will be removed, with immediate effect—" *finally*, I held my breath, *some vindication* "—from the London office."

"What does that mean?"

"He will be transferred to the New York office."

I scoffed. "What, where the salary is significantly higher than ours in the UK?"

"I'm afraid I can't discuss remuneration with you. But additionally, he is required to attend a minimum of five counseling sessions."

Julie was self-congratulatory as she leaned back in her chair. *Is that all my pain amounted to?* A token action that would barely inconvenience him. No, *benefit* him. He would continue earning an eye-watering amount and have transatlantic experience to bolster his CV.

"Is that all?" My voice fractured as I spoke. "A slap on the wrist? And a nice serviced apartment on West 57th?"

"I think you're forgetting the reputational hit Mr. Parsons has also suffered, Ms. Kaya."

"So? Why are you acting like I've inflicted that on him?"

"Jade, please, we really don't want to get into the blame game."

"Why not? He *is* to blame!"

Julie all but rolled her eyes. As if I were a stupid little girl.

"I'm afraid that's not necessarily the conclusion we have come to, but that's not relevant now."

"I don't care what conclusion you have come to—" My voice sounded whiny. "This isn't right!"

Julie pulled an it-is-what-it-is face.

"Claire!" I exclaimed.

"Sorry?" Julie said. "I don't understand."

"Claire Tooley was fired last week."

"I'm sorry, I really can't go into details—"

"She was fired for fixing expense reports." I held my palms up. "Don't get me wrong, she shouldn't have done that, and I understand why she was let go. But are you seriously telling me that sneaking a meal deal onto an expense sheet is a greater offense than raping someone?"

"I'm sorry, Jade, I really don't understand how the two situations are comparable." Julie furrowed her brow.

"Well, Claire doesn't work here anymore, and Josh still has his job. That's how they're comparable."

Julie was silent. I'd hit a brick wall.

"I came to you for help," I pleaded. "I was abused by someone senior in the company and I didn't know who to turn to. You"—I jabbed my finger toward her—"you told me not to take it to the police! I thought you would help me!"

Julie took a deep breath, and, for a moment, I thought she might have something insightful to say.

"We'd love to help you, but you have to let us. The offer's on the table, Jade. Please do think about it carefully."

38

"I'll have a banana bread, please," Eve said, sweet as a sugar cube, "and I love your dress!"

"Thank you so much!" The waitress was in her early twenties, in an A-line swing dress with a safari print. "I worried that I would look too old in such a vintage style. Be honest"—she leaned in to Eve—"do I look fifty years old in this?"

"Not at all!" Eve did a theatrical show of appraising the dress. "Honey, you don't look a day over forty!" They laughed heartily, while I sat redundant. I itched to get out of the office, feeling eyes on me like fleas. The investigation was confidential in name, but not in nature. The lawyers of Reuben rarely actually left Reuben. As gossip inflated, it had nowhere to go, so it expanded within the walls of the Firm, snowballing.

"I'll go and get you guys your drinks now," the waitress said with a huge smile. Eve's ability to endear people to her never ceased to amaze me. She was the type of person to make a lifelong friend out of someone she once asked for directions.

"How do you feel?" Eve said. There was a pause before she said, "Will you take it?"

The fact that Eve had even asked that made me feel an immense wave of sadness. So I really was the naïve one.

"They offered you a 'discretionary bonus,' right?" She tried to laugh, but it was hollow. An empty barrel. I twirled my teaspoon in my coffee.

"What should I do?" I asked.

"Well, you either take it and carry on—" She paused to take another sip. "Or they suffocate you."

My expression was vacant. *Why are those the only two options?*

"But you know what'll happen if you don't take it," Eve carried on. "They'll slowly but surely stop giving you any work, until you have no choice but to leave."

"Surely that's constructive dismissal?"

Eve snorted.

"Right, and who's gonna make an employment law claim against this place? And get completely buried in legal fees? Not to mention scuppering their chances of getting hired by any other decent firm in the City."

"So why do we work here, then? Why are you doing what you're doing with Julian, why did I push myself so hard on Arrow when I was breaking down, what's the point of it all?"

She blinked at me as if I had asked the most stupid question imaginable. Eve had been giving Julian the girlfriend experience. Going to bed next to a man she didn't love, big-spooning him, playing a role purely for his titillation.

"It's the price you pay to work at a big-brand firm. You know that. It's the same everywhere, could even be worse." She shrugged.

"What are you talking about?"

Eve held her hands up, *don't shoot the messenger*.

"I told you it would be a dead end. And didn't want to be right. Really, I'm so sorry." She reached across and held both my hands, like she was desperately urging me to see something I couldn't yet. "But at least now it hasn't completely amounted to nothing. That sort of money could set you up, J. You'd be silly not to take it."

"What, and let my silence be bought? People already think victims report for personal gain. What kind of bullshit suppression program would I be complicit in?"

"Oh, don't be so bloody pious," Eve snapped. "Get real. You and I aren't going to reform the corporate landscape. Moralizing all day long won't change the fact that you could pay off your parents' mortgage and the money is *right there.*"

I sank further into the leather armchair.

"Being puritanical isn't going to give you the career, the life you've worked so hard for," Eve said, softer this time. Her face was somber, but her voice was silky, like a voice-over narrator of a film. A neutral observer of the follies and vices of the characters she overlooked.

"I'm sorry you're going through what you are, I really am. If I were you, I'd take the money and keep your head down. You wouldn't be the first." There was a beat. "And you're definitely not going to be the last."

The knowledge of the one thousand two hundred people before me flashed across my mind. How many will come after? How many more stories will go unheard?

I managed a weak smile.

"We'll get through it," Eve said. She was talking to herself as much as me. Just then, the waitress approached with her banana bread. Eve's earnest sincerity was quickly replaced by the brilliant smile she flashed.

Eve had to hurry off to make another meeting, but I stayed a while longer before taking the most circuitous route imaginable back to the office. An ambulance screeched by, and I turned to see where it was hurtling off to. That's when I saw her. She was a pillar of neutral elegance, standing on the curb on the other side of the street, encased in a knitted beige dress and knee-high tan boots. Her long, slender arm was stretched out into the road, hailing a black cab.

"Genevieve!" I called over the street. I would have run across the road to greet her but for two lanes of nonstop traffic. "Genevieve! Genevieve! Stop, wait!" Her silver bob remained sleek—the work of a professional blow-dry—as her head jerked up. She looked directly at me. I was panting, springing on my heel, ready to leap the moment the traffic provided a split-second opportunity. For a second, I was driven by a deluded fantasy that this serendipitous moment would reunite us. We held eye contact for several seconds, as if we were communicating via an invisible string along a tin-can telephone. She turned away for a second, then lifted her head to match my gaze again, her brow slackened. She raised, then lowered, one shoulder toward me: a resigned *c'est la vie*. In a fluid motion, she slid into the seat of the black cab. I watched the back of her head as it drove away.

39

The page loaded for the thousandth time today. I'd been hitting refresh every ten seconds, scratching my skin with urgency. Until I finally understood the saying about money *hitting* an account. It felt boorish.

After meeting with Julie, I'd invited Eve to Adele's flat, where I was still staying, and told them both about the draft Settlement Agreement. I recited the clauses from memory because Julie wouldn't let a copy out of her sight. Asked for their professional opinions. All verbally, to avoid a paper trail of my breaching the confidentiality clause. In those bleak hours, we pored over a template agreement with the same boilerplate clauses we found on the file system, with Post-it Notes in hand (that I later personally shredded). I found it all suddenly hilarious. Remembering the fresh versions of us, the optimistic recruits who would never have guessed this use of our legal education. The agreement stipulated that I had to hand over for HR's review any evidence that was "property of the Firm": emails, notebooks, work phone, work laptop, Skype chat history, all hard-copy documents that sat in 2816. I would not be able to speak of the investigation, either the fact of it or its outcome. The money was listed on my pay slip as a "midyear bonus." After I'd signed the agreement, I was not permitted to have the original or a copy. I could request to see it, supervised in Reuben's offices.

The three of us had agreed that there was a loophole in the agreement, though: it was silent on the possibility of one day reporting Josh to the police. It only prevented me from implicating the Firm or mentioning its investigation. *Well, well, well*, I thought. It was deliciously *Lion King*–esque to watch an uncle cast his nephew aside.

That was for my meager personal enjoyment only. We researched the latest criminal case law. We set up a call with a criminal barrister to discuss the merits of "the case"—being my case—on a no-names basis. He didn't sugarcoat it: based on precedent, criminal proceedings were not a realistic avenue. To start with, I didn't have a shred of physical evidence. Certainly no DNA evidence—I'd scrubbed my skin until it began to crisp off. The bruises had melted back into me. I hadn't taken any photos of them. I never told anyone right after it happened—let alone the police—so there was no statement on record. I'd moved out of the flat it happened in. I knew from an old bike theft that my building in Vauxhall didn't have CCTV, and the front door was in a surveillance blind spot. The only tangible record I had were the notes from my appointment with Andreea. *Symptoms consistent with vaginal injury*. But that appointment took place nearly three weeks after the Savoy party. That period disconnected Josh from said injury.

I didn't have the Uber receipts, Josh did. There were witnesses who saw us leave the Savoy in a cab together, but there was a vastly long chain of events after that which couldn't be accounted for. Plus they were all Reuben lawyers, likely unwilling to join my cause. My conversation with Josh was verbal. I didn't have the foresight to record it. That wine-glass was thrown out because I couldn't bear to return it to the cupboard.

Eve and Adele couldn't meet my eye when I asked the barrister how likely it was that the CPS would decide to prosecute. *I'm sorry to say this, but there's a chance it might not make it out of a police station.*

The question of evidence was a neutral, clinical matter. It was a clean, salient answer if anyone asked, with accusing eyes, *but why didn't she report?*

It didn't account for the silent political power of Reuben. The business relationships barristers would undoubtedly have with the Reuben family—of which Josh was a part. I didn't have deep pockets and wasn't high-profile enough to be prioritized.

It didn't account for the fact that, if the case was taken up, I would struggle to continue to work effectively as a lawyer while being simultaneously embroiled in a trial. The stop-start nature of it, the numerous procedural events: CPS decisions; plea hearings; the preparation of evidence through indictments, exhibits, witness statements, expert evidence; disclosure and fights about admissibility. My digital and medical records requested and combed over. The dragging months of purgatory followed by intense interruptions to daily life. That my mother's sacrifices and hopes and dreams and social standing rested on my continuing this career. That I had my family on my back when trying to climb upward.

It didn't account for how, if the case then made it into a courtroom, a legal armada would be hired to discredit me. How they would read my evidence, spill coffee and eat doughnuts over my words. How a Silk would command the room with serene poise. How I would wear a dowdy polka-dot blouse to ensure I looked as demure and respectable as possible. How my lack of memory would innocuously be turned against me. My relationship used to suggest this was a simple case of regretted infidelity. My drunkenness used to imply that I was a liability. How there were restrictions on asking me about my prior sexual history, but inventive methods could suggest I was loose; establish that I invited him in, allude that I was the initiator. That minuscule discrepancies in my account would be latched upon: *you previously said you left the Savoy at one a.m., now you say it was around midnight—which account is inaccurate?* Like a master painter, the Silk would work on the undertones and shading, establishing the premise that I was an unreliable narrator. How I'd be asked why I hadn't reported it to the police the morning after. Why I hadn't fought back. Why, if he was so dangerous, I had gotten into a taxi with him. Why I continued to show up to Reuben every day.

It didn't account for the fact that white women lost to white men in sexual assault cases. They say justice is blind, but why did a brown woman's chances against a white man feel insurmountable?

It didn't account for my unwillingness to retraumatize myself, over and over. Slice myself open and let strangers rummage into me. Be cooperative, likeable, and transparent, lay my innards bare. While Josh was cotton-wooled in a system skewed to protect his kind. Admit to strangers what happened to me and watch them decide whether I deserved to be believed. Watch them fight the default assumption that I am lying.

It didn't account for the fact that reporting would require me to silently unshackle myself from the role of the model minority who was grateful, industrious, accepting, and quiet. Omma and Baba's life had consisted of weathering, enduring. It didn't account for the fireworks I'd be setting off within my family.

In the end, Eve was right. There was no point in clinging to sanctimony. My lack of proof didn't make it any less real for me. I had spent months trying to outrun my own body, while it rebelled. Worming the truth into my head through blood and nightmares and sweat and panic and terror. I had a life to live, a future to move on to, privacy to protect. Eve reminded me of Omma. So rooted in harsh reality that she seemed disconnected from natural emotion. I did feel a modicum of guilt, a quiet twang that *I've allowed myself to be bought. I should have taken more of an ethical stand. This will validate others. Angie, who questioned whether I made it all up. Kit, who treated me like I was dramatic. Leo, who got away with it.*

But why shouldn't I be entitled to reparations? I knew now that I couldn't realistically continue working at Reuben. But without a salary, how was I going to pay rent? Let alone for years of therapy at hundreds of pounds an hour? Who else would pay for moving costs? Why shouldn't Reuben compensate me for the time off work needed to recover and the subsequent lost earnings? The cost of a car because traveling alone after dark is still terrifying? The cost of a home security system?

Recovery was not only emotionally arduous, mentally grueling, and physically exhausting. It was also expensive.

I knocked on Will's door.

"Come in."

"Hi Will."

He looked up. "Jade, you're back! You exist in the real world!"

"Yes, I do."

"To what do I owe this pleasure?" He motioned toward the plush bourbon leather sofa, surrounded by cricket paraphernalia.

"Well," I said as I sat down, carefully crossing my ankles, "I'm not sure it's going to be a pleasure, but I wanted to come by and tell you in person that I intend to hand in my resignation." I pulled out the letter I had carefully folded into its thick, buttery envelope. "I've put it in writing, too, for your records."

Looking troubled, he took the letter and read it. I felt as awkward as I do when I give someone a Christmas present and they open it in front of me.

"Jade, I don't know what to say." He folded the letter back up, wearily leaning forward to look me straight in the eyes. "I'm so sorry it has come to this."

"I am too."

"And there's nothing I can say to convince you to stay?"

"Unfortunately not. I've given this a lot of thought, and it's been a hard decision, but it's the right one."

"Possibly now isn't the right time to say this to you," Will said, staring at the carpet, "but you really are a brilliant team member. I'd be willing to tell anyone that, should you ever need a reference."

"Thanks, Will."

Kind words now weren't enough. Where was all this faith in me when I was being dropped from the case I had poured all my time and energy into? Will was in a position to have my back when it could have made a difference, and he chose not to rock the boat. I didn't doubt that Will thought this outcome was a shame. But I also didn't doubt that he was saying these things so that when he got home tonight and his head hit the pillow, he could feel like a good guy. He wasn't a bad person. But men like him—in positions of power, who watched the wheels of suppression turn from a distance, standing by and doing nothing—were the protectors of the broken system. They're the fuel that made the fire burn.

"Once you've had a bit of a break," Will said, "get in touch and I'll call around to a few friends in other firms, see what I can do to get you back on your feet again."

40

"I lied, I'm not out of this relationship," she said, earnestly. *"I'm in. I'm so in, it's humiliating, because here I am, begging."*

"Meredith," he said.

"Shut up. You say 'Meredith' and I yell, remember? Okay, here it is: your choice? It's simple: her or me. And I'm sure she's really great. But Derek, I love you. In a really really big, pretend-to-like-your-taste-in-music, let-you-eat-the-last-piece-of-cheesecake, hold-a-radio-over-my-head-outside-your-window, unfortunate-way-that-makes-me-hate-you, love you. So pick me. Choose me. Love me."

"Oh Lord." Adele's voice jerked me out of my *Grey's Anatomy* reverie. "Have you moved since I left?"

I shook my head. Although I contractually had a three-month notice period, Reuben wanted me, a liability on legs, gone. The same day I resigned, I was placed on immediate gardening leave. Escorted out of the building by security. Adele had had to meet me outside with my coat and bag. In the last two weeks, I had watched seven hours of *Grey's Anatomy* a day. It took me half a day to recover from Lexie and Mark's final moments. Having exhausted all available seasons, I started revisiting favorite episodes. Watching the same scenes swirl round and round, unchanged by time, knowing that I couldn't be blindsided by any twist the writers threw at me, was a huge solace. Safe in the comfort of knowing that Ross and Rachel, or Meredith and Derek, finally ended up together, I could enjoy all the dramatic turns that predated the happy ending. I had control.

"Have you eaten?" Adele asked.

"I have."

"A mini Babybel doesn't count as a meal, Jade."

"You've got me there."

"When did Eve leave?" Adele sauntered over and plonked on the sofa next to me.

"About two hours ago."

Adele and Eve had worked shifts, rallying to keep me company round the clock. A crèche for a brokenhearted woman. Baba had tried to convince me to come home. As the sun set over Adele's building, I thought of him preparing for iftar. People acted as if Ramadan was so restrictive, a month of starvation and deprivation. But it was a time of joy. I envied Baba's annual month of faithfulness, and the peace it brought him. The solitary nights in prayer and reflection, the introspective discipline of his days, the smile of camaraderie he returned from the mosque with, the submission to the rising and setting of the sun, the spirit of charity and community.

Baba didn't break his fast by chugging a bottle of water or cramming food in as fast as possible. Instead, I pictured him in my mind's eye, calmly going to the cupboard as he always did, reaching for the jar of Medjool dates and forking out three little brown beads. He would go outside after saying his duas and eat each date one by one, watching the last of the sunset behind the oblong gardens and fading fences of South London. He did this because the Prophet broke his fast with three dates and water. Omma was not a Muslim, but she and Baba came to an agreement when they married that they would both celebrate each other's festivals. So, our blended family lived by the moon: our two biggest celebrations, Eid and Lunar New Year, decided by the celestial calendar.

I welled up, watching the same sky as Baba. Viewing its transition through coats of coral and peach. I missed him. Omma too. How can there be a world in which the three of us no longer knew how to exist in our unit?

We had spoken once since I left Reuben. Baba had called me a few days ago.

Baba opened with, "Hayatim." He was in proactive mode. He hired a van and drove over to the Clapham Flat with my set of keys. Packed up my old life and brought it all home where it belonged.

"Baba?"

"Of course it's your baba. Who else is calling you 'hayatim'? You have a Turkish boyfriend now?"

"No, Baba," I laughed. "No boyfriend on the scene."

There was a semibreve rest, the four beats passing on the phone before he spoke.

"I wanted to check, you know, how you are."

"I'm good, Baba." I knew why he was calling. My mum had sent him in as a spy—too bad he was the least subtle person imaginable.

"Is it done?"

"Is what done?"

"Child, tell me."

"Yes, Baba." I paused. "I've handed in my resignation." The period of silence seemed to stretch out as long as the telephone wires in the ground that connected us. "Are you still on the line?"

"I'm here, kizim."

"Are you going to say anything?"

He let out a long sigh.

"Your mother," he eventually said, "she will be very disappointed."

"Funnily enough, Dad, I'm pretty disappointed in her too."

"It is not your place to be disappointed in your parents." Baba sounded resigned. "It's not that she doesn't care about you. Yani, you don't know yet, but it's hard for a parent to see their child in so much pain. And she especially doesn't understand why leaving your job is the solution to all of this. Why must you burn the whole blanket to kill a flea?"

"Well, I don't understand her, either. Not talking to me also isn't the solution," I retorted.

"Give her time. She's broken too."

I suddenly realized my cheeks were wet. A small whimper broke free.

"Geçmiş olsun, yavrum," Baba said finally, his voice cracking. "Geçmiş olsun."

May it pass, my darling. May it pass.

41

"Hello? Hi."

There was a beat of silence.

Hang up. Hang up now.

"My name's Emily," I gurgled. "Emily Johnson." After a moment, I added, "Sorry—that was a lie, God, sorry."

The voice was gentle.

Don't worry, you don't have to say if you'd feel uncomfortable, she said.

"Thank you."

More silence. Anticipatory and hopeful.

My throat held a round lump.

"I was calling—" I stopped again. I started crying. "I don't know. I don't know why I called."

Take your time, she said.

"I was just hoping to . . . I had a look at your website and it said I could call this number?

"I don't really know where to begin. Everything's fallen apart and I don't know how to fix it.

"It happened six months ago. I still find it hard to physically say the words. I didn't tell anyone straight after. Even now, I don't really remember it. But I do remember bits—" I trailed off again.

"I mean, how can something I don't properly remember hurt this much?"

Our bodies remember, she said, *even if our minds don't.*

"Yeah." I nodded to no one. "Yeah."

You said everything's fallen apart. What does everything falling apart look like for you?

Her voice was so tender.

"My boyfriend and I. He found out and we tried. But we're not together anymore. I told work and, well, I don't work there anymore. I told my parents, and . . ." I pictured Omma's tiny feet in her slippers, inspecting her magnolia tree. My lips clamped shut. "I'm sorry, I don't know why I'm crying, sorry—hold on a minute—sorry." I looked around for some tissues, then used my sleeve instead.

"I feel very alone.

"Yeah, it was someone I know. Or knew, I should say.

"I'm struggling. I get flashbacks and nightmares. I had a panic attack yesterday. In the middle of the street. Because some guy that looked like him glanced at me. I couldn't breathe. I felt like I might die on the spot. And . . . and the problem is, I don't know how to be around normal people anymore.

"But mainly I'm so angry all the time. So bitter. I could be doing nothing and suddenly I want to destroy my flat because I'm just so furious."

I had screamed and howled and raged and cried and shook and kicked and pounded and sung and danced and clawed my fury out. To no avail. Anger was a waterfall, a never-ending gush that swept me off my feet.

"Just how is it that no one faced any consequences? I know that's not how life works. But there was no comeuppance for what was taken from me. Something *was* stolen from me! How can I live with that? How am I meant to go on and not be angry?

"I'm crying because sometimes it feels like the only way to release the pressure and get some relief.

"And I don't miss my ex. I don't miss my job." I hiccupped and didn't try to apologize for my gasping tears. "I miss not being this way. I don't want to be like this. I didn't choose this."

Finally I was silent, feeling my nervous system fizzle and crack.

"I was wondering," I began, timidly, because asking for anything felt like vulnerability, "if you might be able to steer me in the right direction."

Because I knew what I yearned for. It just took me a long time to admit it. After so long wandering lost, what I needed seemed painfully, stupidly clear.

"I want help."

Epilogue

If I could fold time, I would hold my younger self on that morning after the Savoy party. Gently, I'd tell her that life from this point on will be difficult, harder than she'd ever imagine. That just when she's catching her breath at rock bottom, she'll find there's another hatch to fall through.

I'd warn her that in the days and weeks and months to come, she would tell herself anything to minimize her reality. She'd scold herself for hurting so much because at least she wasn't permanently physically injured. At least she wasn't killed. At least she wasn't underage. At least it wasn't a family member. At least she had supportive friends. At least she had money so she could leave her job, allow herself the luxury of time to recover that so few could afford. At least she wasn't trapped in a relationship with her rapist. At least she didn't get pregnant. At least she didn't catch any infections. At least she was in the UK and wasn't expected to pay for medical care. It would be years before she realized that, each time she concluded that it wasn't *that* bad, she was only robbing herself.

I'd warn her that she would spend years cringing at how

she set herself on fire to keep Kit Campbell warm. And although she wouldn't wish what happened on anyone, it felled the first domino in a chain that would set her free. Otherwise, she'd have peered ahead into the life that was almost hers—the house, the kitchen remodel, the oval-cut engagement ring, the wedding in Norfolk, the children that were paler than her—and free-fallen into it.

I'd warn her that confiding in people about what happened to her would never stop feeling like the utmost form of misery. That every time she did speak of it, to a friend, a new partner, a medical professional, the relinquishing of control would never cease to be unbearable.

Night and day each had the companionship of Temazepam and Modafinil. I'd warn her that she'd spend the next half decade reliant on both, slipping one to send her to sleep, and the other in the morning to help her perform daily tasks through the grogginess.

And finally, I'd tell her of the trip to Korea with her mother. I'd tell her that it would take a few years, but that one day she and her mother will be in a place where they can try to understand each other better. That she'd use the last dregs of the settlement money to take Omma home. They'd go to the temple in her village, built atop a steep mountain as is the Buddhist way, to represent the struggle to reach enlightenment. Their legs would be weary after the climb. I'd tell her recovery would be like the temple: built between an enormous boulder and a cliff's edge. The construction would be perilous, with the laying of every stone risking a drop into an abyss. Her trauma would be the boulder, an unforgiving hard ball within her. It can never be removed. It would never yield, erode, or soften. It would take time, and respect for the delicate ecosystem, but she would slowly build something intricate around this boulder. The architecture she assembled encased the boulder, protected it from rolling over the cliff's edge. Every time she needed more building materials, she would have to descend the mountain and carry each brick up. It would break her back, turn her hands and feet hard with callouses, crush her spirit. But when the final tile slotted into place, the painstaking years on the brutal mountainside would be worthwhile in the way the far-reaching views of the landscape from the temple made her catch her breath. She would finally take in the sky and the sea, the colorful boats docked at the harbor below, the verdant rice paddies, and the tiny villages dotted in between the valleys.

The boulder and the cliff won't be all she sees anymore.

Sources

Chapter 18

- Metropolitan Police: How to Report Rape and Sexual Assault. https://www.met.police.uk/advice/advice-and-information/rsa/rape-and-sexual-assault/how-to-report-rape-and-sexual-assault/.
- Topping, Alexandra. "'They didn't really investigate it at all': Rape Survivors Speak Out in Report." *The Guardian*. https://www.theguardian.com/society/2021/jul/16/they-didnt-really-investigate-it-at-all-survivors-speak-out-in-report.
- Reality Check Team. "Why Do So Few Rape Cases Go to Court?" BBC News. https://www.bbc.co.uk/news/uk-48095118.
- Topping, Alexandra, and Caelainn Barr. "Rape Convictions Fall to Record Low in England and Wales." *The Guardian*. https://www.theguardian.com/society/2020/jul/30/convictions-fall-record-low-england-wales-prosecutions.
- Dearden, Lizzie. "Only 1.7% of Reported Rapes Prosecuted in England and Wales, New Figures Show." *The Independent*. https://www.independent.co.uk/news/uk/crime

/rape-prosecution-england-wales-victims-court-cps-police-a8885961.html.

- Hymas, Charles. "Rape Victims Forced to Wait Five Months for Suspects to Be Charged." *The Telegraph*. https://www.telegraph.co.uk/news/2021//04/ 26/rape-victims-forced-wait-five-months-suspects-charged/.
- Karim, Fariha. "Rape Cases Dropped 'Due to Police Stereotyping.'" *The Times*. https://www.thetimes.co.uk/article/rape-cases-dropped-due-topolice-stereotyping-dmppl2799.
- Khan, Aina J. "UK Justice System Has Failed Rape Victims, Government Says." *New York Times*. https://www.nytimes.com/2021/06/18/world/europe/britain-rape-apology-prosecutions.html.

Chapter 25

- Coldplay. "Yellow." *Parachutes*. Parlophone Records Ltd. 2000.

Chapter 40

- Shonda Rhimes. *Grey's Anatomy*. Season 2, episode 5, "Bring the Pain." Aired October 23, 2005, on ABC.

Acknowledgments

I would not have been able to write this book without the compassion and knowingness of other survivors. To those I have the privilege of knowing, and those I do not know but who understand, thank you. I have followed, and will continue to follow, your lead.

Thank you:

To Hellie Ogden, for changing my life.

To Ma'suma Amiri, who plucked my manuscript out of a generic submission inbox in the very first place.

To Katie Ellis-Brown, for your unflappable passion, expertise, and kindness. You have vehemently championed Jade's story, and I couldn't have hoped for a better person to have shaped it with.

To Carina Guiterman, for your wisdom and thoughtfulness.

To Kate Fogg, for your pure generosity and guidance.

To Liz Foley, Dredhëza Maloku, Sania Riaz, Sophie Painter, Mia Quibell-Smith, Hannah Shorten, Maya Koffi, Emily Randle, Yeti Lambregts, Petra Eriksson, and everyone at Harvill Secker, Vintage, Simon & Schuster,

Janklow & Nesbit UK, and WME. Thank you for bringing Jade to readers.

To readers, librarians, and booksellers. From one bookworm to another, thank you for all that you do.

To Anna Barrett, without whom this book might not have seen the light of day.

To Carolyn, for pushing me.

To those who sat with me in the heaviness and showed me patience, grace, and love. I am forever grateful.

To my cherished close friends, for your early readings, your infectious excitement for this book, and the endless support. I'm so happy to know you.

To my in-laws, a bonus family which I feel lucky to be a part of.

To Bo, for the unconditional love.

To Pete, for being the best thing that has ever happened to me. Thank you for the happiest, most peaceful life with, and because of, you.

And finally, to my parents, who are the beginning and end of all that I do, all that I have, and all that I am.

About the Author

Ela Lee was raised in London by her parents, who emigrated from South Korea and Turkey. She attended the University of Oxford and previously practiced as a litigation lawyer.